“You’ ... ffee?”

“Is the ... an makin ...

Ouch. ... ed her on it. Fairly. “I guess not.”

D1376300

“Don’t make assumptions,” he said softly. “Especially if you’re basing them on what the press says about me.”

Was he telling her that he wasn’t the playboy the press suggested he was? Or was he playing games? Brandon Stone flustered her. Big-time. And she couldn’t quite work out why. Was it just because he was so good-looking? Or did she see a tiny hint of vulnerability in his gray eyes, showing that there was more to him than just the cocky, confident racing champion? Or was that all just wishful thinking and he really was a shallow playboy?

What she did know was that he was her business rival. One who wanted to buy her out. Part of her thought she shouldn’t even be talking to him.

HIS SHY CINDERELLA

BY

KATE HARDY

MILLS & BOON

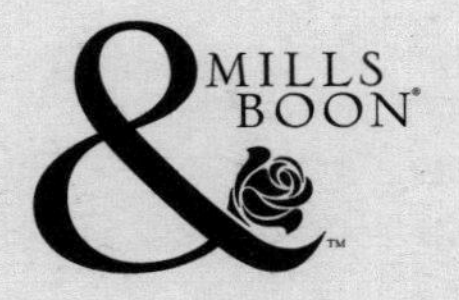

All rights reserved including the right of reproduction in whole or in part in any form. This edition is published by arrangement with Harlequin Books S.A.

This is a work of fiction. Names, characters, places, locations and incidents are purely fictional and bear no relationship to any real life individuals, living or dead, or to any actual places, business establishments, locations, events or incidents. Any resemblance is entirely coincidental.

This book is sold subject to the condition that it shall not, by way of trade or otherwise, be lent, resold, hired out or otherwise circulated without the prior consent of the publisher in any form of binding or cover other than that in which it is published and without a similar condition including this condition being imposed on the subsequent purchaser.

® and ™ are trademarks owned and used by the trademark owner and/or its licensee. Trademarks marked with ® are registered with the United Kingdom Patent Office and/or the Office for Harmonisation in the Internal Market and in other countries.

First Published in Great Britain 2017
By Mills & Boon, an imprint of HarperCollins*Publishers*
1 London Bridge Street, London, SE1 9GF

© 2017 Pamela Brooks

ISBN: 978-0-263-92295-0

23-0517

Our policy is to use papers that are natural, renewable and recyclable products and made from wood grown in sustainable forests. The logging and manufacturing processes conform to the legal environmental regulations of the country of origin.

Printed and bound in Spain
by CPI, Barcelona

Kate Hardy has always loved books and could read before she went to school. She discovered Mills & Boon books when she was twelve and decided this was what she wanted to do. When she isn't writing Kate enjoys reading, cinema, ballroom dancing and the gym. You can contact her via her website: www.katehardy.com.

SCOTTISH BORDERS
LIBRARY SERVICES
009894516
Bertrams 13/04/2017
£5.99

For Gerard, who answered a lot of very weird
questions about motor racing with a great
deal of patience (but I am still not going
to a Grand Prix with you!) xxx

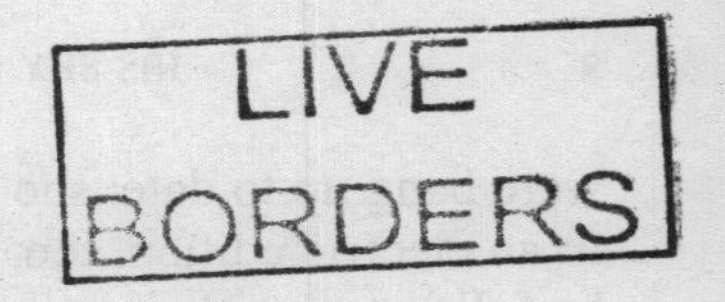
LIVE
BORDERS

CHAPTER ONE

ANGEL FLICKED THROUGH the pile of mail on her desk.

Bills, bills, circulars and—just for a change—bills. Bills she really hoped she could pay without temporarily borrowing from the account she'd earmarked for paying the company's half-yearly tax liability.

And there was still no sign of the large envelope with an American postmark she'd been waiting for, containing the contract for supplying the new McKenzie Frost to feature in the next instalment of *Spyline*, a high-profile action movie series. Triffid Studios hadn't emailed to her it instead, either, because Angel had already checked her inbox and the spam box. Twice.

Maybe she'd send a polite enquiring email to their legal department tomorrow. There was a fine line between being enthusiastic about the project and coming across as desperate and needy.

Even though right now Angel felt desperate and needy. She couldn't let McKenzie's go under. Not on her watch. How could she live with herself if she lost the company her grandfather had started seventy years ago? The contract with Triffid would make all the difference. Seeing the McKenzie Frost in the film would remind people of just how wonderful McKenzie's cars were: hand-made, stylish, classic, and with full attention to every detail. And they were bang up to date: she intended to produce the Frost in an electric edition, too. Then their waiting list would be full again, with everyone wanting their own specially customised Frost, and she wouldn't have to lay anyone off at the factory.

Though she couldn't even talk about the deal yet. Not until she'd actually signed the contract—which she couldn't do until her lawyer had checked it over, and her lawyer couldn't do that until the contract actually arrived…

But there was no point in brooding over something she couldn't change. She'd just have to get on with things as best as she could, and hope that she didn't have to come up with plan B. And she didn't want to burden her parents with her worries. She knew they were enjoying their retirement, and the last thing she wanted was to drag them back from the extended vacation they'd been planning for years.

She'd grin and bear it, and if necessary she'd tell a white lie or two.

She went through the post, dealing with each piece as she opened it, and paused at the last envelope: cream vellum, with a handwritten address. Most people nowadays used computer-printed address labels, or if they did have to write something they'd simply grab the nearest ballpoint pen. This bold, flamboyant script looked as if it had been written with a proper fountain pen. Disappointingly, the letter itself was typewritten, but the signature at the bottom was in the same flamboyant handwriting as the envelope.

And her jaw dropped as she read the letter.

It was an offer to buy the company.

Selling up would be one way to solve McKenzie's financial problems. But selling McKenzie's to Brandon Stone? He seriously thought she would even consider it?

She knew the family history well enough. Her grandfather had set up in business with his best friend just after the Second World War, building quality cars that everyone could afford. Except then they'd both fallen in love with the same woman. Esther had chosen Jimmy McKenzie; in response, Barnaby Stone had dissolved their business partnership and left with all the equipment to go and start up another business, this time based on making factory-built cars. Jimmy McKenzie had started over, too, making his hand-built cars customisable—just as McKenzie's still built their cars today.

On the eve of the wedding, Barnaby Stone had come back and asked Esther to run away with him. She'd said no.

Since then, the two families had never spoken again.

Until now.

If you could call a letter speaking.

Angel could see it from Brandon's point of view. Buying McKenzie's would salve his sense of family honour because then, although the grandfather had lost the girl, the grandson had won the business. It would also be the end of everything McKenzie's did, because Stone's would definitely get rid of their hand-made and customised process. She knew that Stone's racing cars were all factory built, using robots and the newest technology; it was the total opposite of the hand-craftsmanship and personal experience at McKenzie's.

She'd heard on the grapevine that Stone's wanted to branch out into making roadsters, which would put them in direct competition with McKenzie's: and what better way to get rid of your competitor than to buy them out? No doubt he'd keep the name—McKenzie's was known for high quality, so the brand was definitely worth something. She'd overheard her parents discussing it during the last recession, when Larry Stone had offered to buy McKenzie's. According to her father, Barnaby Stone had been a ruthless businessman, and his sons and grandsons came from the same mould. She knew Max McKenzie was a good judge of character, so it was obvious that Brandon would asset-strip the business and make all her staff redundant.

No way.

She wouldn't sell her family business to Brandon Stone, not even if she was utterly desperate and he was the last person on earth.

And what did he really know about business, anyway? Driving race cars, yes: he'd won a few championships in his career, and had narrowly missed becoming the world champion a couple of times. But being good at driving a racing car wasn't the same as being good at running a business that made racing cars. As far as she knew, dating supermodels and quaffing magnums of champagne weren't requirements for running a successful business either. She was pretty sure that he was just the figurehead and someone else did the actual running of Stone's.

Regardless, she wasn't selling. Not to him.

She flicked into her email program. In his letter, Brandon Stone had said he looked forward to hearing from her at her earliest convenience. So she'd give him his answer right now.

Dear Mr Stone

No way is the McKenzie's logo going on the front of your factory-made identikit cars. I wouldn't sell my family business to you if you were the last person on earth. My grandfather would be turning in his grave even at the thought of it.

Then she took a deep breath and deleted the paragraph. Much as she'd like to send the email as it was, it sounded like a challenge. She wasn't looking for a fight; she was simply looking to shut down his attempts at buying her out.

What was it that all the experts said about saying no? Keep it short. No apologies, no explanations—just no.

Dear Mr Stone
Thank you for your letter. My company is not for sale.
Yours sincerely
Angel McKenzie

She couldn't make it much clearer than that.

When his computer pinged, Brandon flicked into his email program. Angel McKenzie was giving him an answer already? Good.

Then he read the email.

It was short, polite and definite.

And she was living in cloud cuckoo land.

She might not want to sell the business, but McKenzie's was definitely going under. He'd seen their published accounts for the last four years, and the balance sheet looked grimmer every year. The recession had bitten hard in their corner of the market. The way things were going, she couldn't afford not to sell the company.

Maybe he'd taken the wrong approach, writing to her. Maybe he should try shock tactics instead and be the first Stone to speak to a McKenzie for almost seven decades.

And, if he could talk her into selling the company to him, then finally he'd prove he was worthy of heading up Stone's. To his father, to his uncle, and to everyone else who thought that Brandon Stone was just an empty-headed playboy who was only bothered about driving fast cars. To those who were just waiting for the golden boy to fail.

He glanced at the photograph of his older brother on his desk. And maybe, if he could pull off the deal, it would be the one thing to help assuage the guilt he'd spent three years failing to get rid of. The knowledge that it should've been him in that car, the day of the race, not Sam. That if he hadn't gone skiing the week before the race and recklessly taken a diamond run, falling and breaking a rib in the process, he would've been fit to drive. Meaning that Sam wouldn't have been his backup driver, so he wouldn't have been in the crash; and Sam's baby daughter would've grown up knowing her father as more than just a photograph.

Brandon wasn't sure he'd ever be able to forgive himself for that.

But doing well by Stone's was one way to atone for what he'd done. He'd worked hard and learned fast, and the company was going from strength to strength. But it still wasn't enough to assuage the guilt.

'I'm sorry, Sammy,' he said quietly. 'I'm sorry I was such an immature, selfish brat. And I really wish you were still here.' For so many reasons. Sure, Brandon would still have been working in the family business by this point in his career—but Sam would've been at the helm of the company, where he belonged. Nobody would've doubted Sam's managerial abilities. And their uncle Eric wouldn't have been scrutinising Sam's every move, waiting for an opportunity to criticise.

He shook himself. Eric was just disappointed because he thought that he should be heading up the business. Brandon needed to find him a different role, one that would make him happy and feel that he had a say in things. If Brandon could bring McKenzie's into the fold, then maybe Eric could take charge there.

Getting Angel McKenzie to sell to him was definitely his priority now. Whatever the personal cost.

He rang her office to set up a meeting.

'I'm afraid Ms McKenzie's diary is full for the next

month,' the voice on the other end of the line informed him, with the clear implication that it would be 'full' for the month after, too, and the month after that.

Like hell it was.

Clearly Angel had anticipated his next move, and had briefed her PA to refuse to book any meetings with him.

'Maybe you could email her instead,' the PA suggested sweetly.

Any email would no doubt find its way straight into her trash box. 'I'll do that. Thank you,' Brandon said. Though he had no intention of sending an email. He'd try something else entirely. When he'd replaced the receiver, he went to talk to his own PA. 'Gina, I need everything you can find about Angel McKenzie, please,' he said. 'Her CV, what she likes doing, who she dates.'

'If you're interested in her, sweetie, shouldn't you be looking up that sort of thing for yourself?' Gina asked.

Oh, the joys of inheriting a PA who'd known you since you were a baby and was best friends with your mum, Brandon thought. 'I'm not interested in dating her,' he said. 'This is work. Angel McKenzie.' He emphasised the surname, in case she'd just blocked it out.

Gina winced. 'Ah. *Those* McKenzies.'

'I already know the business data,' he said. 'Now I need to know the personal stuff.'

'This sounds as if it's going to end in tears,' Gina warned.

'It's not. It's about knowing who you're doing business with and being prepared. And I'd prefer you not to mention any of this to Mum, Dad or Eric, please. OK?'

'Yes, Mr Bond. I'll keep it top secret,' Gina drawled.

Brandon groaned. 'Bond's PAs used to sigh with longing, flutter their eyelashes and do exactly what he asked.'

'Bond didn't have a PA. He flirted with everyone else's

PAs. And you can't flirt with someone who changed your nappy,' Gina retorted.

Brandon knew when he was beaten. 'I'll make the coffee. Skinny latte with half a spoonful of sweetener, right?'

She grinned. 'That's my boy.'

'You're supposed to respect your boss,' he grumbled, only half teasing.

'I do respect you, sweetie. But I also think you're about to do something stupid. And your mum—'

'Would never forgive you for letting me go right ahead,' Brandon finished. He'd heard that line from her quite a few times over the years. The worst thing was that she was usually right.

He made the coffee, then buried himself in paperwork.

Gina came in an hour later. 'One dossier, as requested,' she said, and put the buff-coloured folder on his desk.

She'd also printed a label for the folder, with the words *Top Sekrit!* typed in red ink and in a font that resembled a toddler's scrawled handwriting.

'You've made your point,' he said. She thought he was behaving like a three-year-old.

'Good. I hope you're listening.'

Given that Gina was one of the few people in the company who'd actually batted his corner when he'd first taken over from his father, he couldn't be angry with her. He knew she had his best interests at heart.

'There aren't going to be any tears at the end of this,' he said gently. 'I promise.'

'Good. Because I worry about you almost as much as your mum does.'

'I know. And I appreciate it.' He reached over to squeeze her hand, hoping he wasn't about to get the lecture regarding it being time he stopped playing the field and settled down. Because that didn't figure in his plans, either. How could he ever settle down and have a family, knowing he'd taken that opportunity away from his brother? He didn't deserve that kind of future. Which meant his focus was strictly on the business. 'Thanks, Gina.'

'I've emailed it to you as well,' she said. 'Don't do anything stupid.'

'I won't.'

The top of the file contained a photograph. Angel McKenzie looked like every other generic businesswoman, dressed in a well-cut dark suit teamed with a plain white shirt buttoned up to the neck, and her dark hair cut in a neat bob.

But her eyes were arresting.

Violet blue.

Brandon shook himself. An irrelevant detail. He wasn't intending to date her.

Her CV was impressive. A first-class degree in engineering from a top university, followed by an MA in automotive design from another top institution. And she hadn't gone in straight at the top of her family business, unlike himself: it looked as if she'd done a stint in every single department before becoming her father's second-in-command, and then Max McKenzie had stepped aside two years ago to let her take charge. Again, impressive: it meant she knew her business inside out.

But there was nothing in the dossier about her personal life. He had the distinct impression that she put the business first and spent all her time on it. Given the state of those balance sheets, he would've done the same.

But there was one small thing that he could use. Angel McKenzie went to the gym every morning before work. Even more helpfully, the gym she used belonged to the leisure club of a hotel near to her factory. All he had to do was book a room at the hotel, and he could use the leisure club and then accidentally-on-purpose bump into her.

Once they were face to face, she'd have to talk to him.

And it would all be done and dusted within a week.

At seven the next morning, Brandon walked into the leisure club's reception area and paused at the window. The badge on the woman's neat black polo shirt identified her as *Lorraine, Senior Trainer.*

'Good morning,' he said with a smile. 'I wonder if you can help me.'

She smiled back. 'Of course, sir. Are you a guest at the hotel?'

'I am.' He showed her his room key.

'And you'd like to use the facilities?'

'Sort of,' he said. 'I'm meeting Angel McKenzie here.'

'It's Thursday, so she'll be in the pool,' Lorraine told him. 'Would you like a towel?'

'Yes, please.' And he was glad he'd thought to bring swimming trunks as well as a T-shirt and sweatpants.

She handed him a thick cream-coloured towel. 'I just need you to sign in here, please.' She gestured to the book on the windowsill with its neatly ruled columns: name, room number, time in, time out. 'The changing rooms are through there on the left,' she said, indicating the door. 'The lockers take a pound coin, which will be returned to you when you open the locker. As a guest, you also have use of the sauna, steam room and spa pool. Just let us know if you need anything.' She gave him another smile.

'Thanks.' He signed in, went to change into his swimming gear, and followed the instructions on the wall to shower before using the pool.

The pool room itself was a little warm for his liking. Nobody was sitting in the spa pool, but there were three people using the small swimming pool: a middle-aged man and woman who were clearly there together, and a woman who was swimming length after length in a neat front crawl.

Angel McKenzie.

Brandon slid into the water in the lane next to hers and swam half a dozen lengths, enjoying the feel of slicing through the water.

Then he changed his course just enough that he accidentally bumped into her, knocking her very slightly off balance so she was forced to stand up in the pool.

He, too, halted and stood up. 'I'm so sorry.'

She looked at him. The first thing he noticed was how vivid her eyes were; the photograph had barely done her justice.

The second thing he noticed was that she was wearing earplugs, so she wouldn't have heard his apology.

'Sorry,' he said again, exaggerating the movement of his mouth.

She shrugged. 'It's OK.'

Clearly she planned to go straight back to swimming. Which wasn't what he wanted. 'No, it's not. Can I buy you a coffee?'

She took out one of the earplugs. 'I'm afraid I missed what you said.'

'Can I buy you a coffee to apologise?'

'There's no need.' She was starting to smile, but Brandon saw the exact moment that she recognised him, when her smile disappeared and those amazing violet eyes narrowed. 'Did you bump into me on purpose?'

He might as well be honest with her. 'Yes.'

'Why? And what are you doing here anyway?'

'I wanted to talk to you.'

'There's nothing to say.'

He rather thought there was. 'Hear me out?'

'We really have nothing to talk about, Mr Stone,' she repeated.

'I think we do, and your PA won't book a meeting with me.'

'So you stalked me?'

Put like that, it sounded bad. He spread his hands. 'Short of pitching up on your doorstep and refusing to budge, how else was I going to get you to speak to me other than by interrupting your morning workout?'

'My company isn't for sale. That isn't going to change.'

'That's not what I want to talk about.'

She frowned. 'Then why do you want to talk to me?'

'Have breakfast with me, and I'll tell you.'

She shook her head. 'I don't have time.'

'Lunch, then. Or dinner. Or breakfast tomorrow morning.' Brandon didn't usually have to work this hard with women, and it unsettled him slightly.

She folded her arms. 'You're persistent.'

'Persistence is a business asset,' he said. 'Have breakfast with me, Ms McKenzie. You have to eat before work, surely?'

'I...'

'Let's just have breakfast and a chat.' He summoned up his most charming smile. 'No strings.'

She said nothing while she thought about it; Brandon, sure that she was going to refuse, was planning his next argument to convince her when she said, 'All right. Breakfast and a chat. No strings.'

That was the first hurdle over. Good. He could work with this. 'Thank you. See you in the restaurant in—what, half an hour?'

'Fifteen minutes,' she corrected, and hauled herself out of the pool.

Brandon did the same, then showered and changed into his business suit and was sitting at a table in the hotel restaurant exactly fourteen minutes later.

One minute after that, Angel walked in, wearing a business suit, and he was glad that he'd second-guessed her and worn formal clothing rather than jeans. Though he also noticed that her hair was still wet and pulled back in a ponytail, her shoes were flat and she wasn't wearing any make-up. The women in his life would never have shown up for anything without perfect hair, high heels and full make-up; then again, they would also have made him wait for two hours while they finished getting ready. Angel McKenzie clearly valued time over her personal appearance, and he found that refreshing.

The other thing he noticed was that she was wearing a hearing aid in her left ear.

That hadn't been in his dossier. He was surprised that Gina had missed it, but it felt too awkward and intrusive to ask Angel about it.

Then she knocked him the tiniest bit off kilter by being the one to bring it up.

'Do you mind if we swap places? It's a bit noisy in here and it's easier for me to lip-read you if your face is in the light.'

'No problem,' he said, standing up immediately. 'And I'll ask if we can move tables to a quieter one.'

She gestured to the floor. 'It's wooden floor, so it's going to be noisy wherever we sit. Carpet dampens speech as well as footsteps.'

And there was a group of businessmen nearby; they were laughing heartily enough to drown out a conversation on the other side of the room. 'Or we could change the venue to my room, which really will be quieter,' Brandon said, 'but I don't want you to think I'm hitting on you.'

Though in other circumstances, he thought, I probably would, because she has the most amazing eyes.

He was shocked to realise how much he was attracted to Angel McKenzie. She was meant to be his business rival, from a family that was his own family's sworn enemy. He wasn't supposed to be attracted to her. Particularly as she was about six inches shorter and way less glamorous than the women he usually dated. She really wasn't his type.

'The restaurant's fine,' she said, and changed places with him. 'So what did you want to talk about? If it's your offer to buy McKenzie's, then it's going to be rather a short and pointless conversation, because the company isn't for sale.'

Before he could answer, the waitress came over. 'May I take your order?'

'Thank you.' Angel smiled at the waitress and ordered coffee, granola, fruit and yoghurt.

Brandon hadn't been expecting that smile, either.

It lit up her face, turning her from average to pretty; in all the photographs he'd seen, Angel had been serious and unsmiling.

And how weird was it that he wanted to be the one to make her smile like that?

Worse than that, focusing on her mouth had made him wonder what it would be like to kiss her. How crazy was that? He was supposed to be talking to her about business, not fantasising about her. She wasn't even his type.

He shook himself and glanced quickly through the menu.

'Sir?' the waitress asked.

'Coffee, please, and eggs Florentine on wholemeal toast—but without the hollandaise sauce, please.'

'Of course, sir.'

'I would've had you pegged as a full English man,' Angel said when the waitress had gone.

'Load up on fatty food and junk, and you're going to feel like a dog's breakfast by the end of a race,' he said with a grimace. 'Food's fuel. If you want to work effectively, you eat effectively. Lean protein, complex carbs, plenty of fruit and veg, and no added sugar.'

She inclined her head. 'Fair point.'

He needed to get this back on the rails. 'So. As I was saying, this discussion isn't about buying the company.'

She waited to let him explain more.

So that was her tactic in business. Say little and let the other party talk themselves into a hole. OK. He'd draw her out. 'I wanted to talk about research and development.'

She frowned. 'What about it?'

'I'm looking for someone to head up my R and D department.' He paused. 'I was considering headhunting you.'

She blinked. 'Yesterday you wanted to buy my company.'

He still did.

'And today you're offering me a job?'

'Yes.'

She looked wary. 'Why?'

'I heard you're a good designer. A first-class degree in engineering, followed by an MA in automotive design.'

'So you *have* been stalking me.'

'Doing research prior to headhunting you,' he corrected. 'You're a difficult woman to pin down, Ms McKenzie.' And he noticed that she still hadn't suggested that he used her first name. She was clearly keeping as many barriers between them as possible.

'Thank you for the job offer, Mr Stone,' she said. 'I'm flattered. But I rather like my current job.' She waited a beat to ram the point home. 'Running the company my grandfather started.'

'Together with my grandfather,' he pointed out.

'Who then dissolved the partnership and took all the equipment with him. McKenzie's has absolutely nothing to do with Barnaby Stone.'

'Not right now.' He held her gaze. 'But it could do.'

'I'm not selling to you, Mr Stone,' she said wearily. 'And I'm not working for you, either. So can you please just give up and stop wasting your time and mine?'

He applauded her loyalty to her family, but this was business and it was time for a reality check. 'I've seen your accounts for the last four years.'

She shrugged, seeming unbothered. 'They're on public record. As are yours.'

'And every year you're struggling more. You need an investor,' Brandon said.

Angel had been here before. The last man who'd wanted to invest in McKenzie's had assumed that it would give him rights over her as well. She'd put him very straight about that, and in response he'd withdrawn the offer.

No way would she let herself get in that situation again. She wasn't for sale, and neither was her business. 'I don't think so.'

'Hand-built cars are a luxury item. Yours are underpriced.'

'The idea was, and still is, to make hand-built customisable cars that anyone can afford,' she said. 'We have a waiting list.'

'Not a very long one.'

That was true; and it was worrying that he knew that. Did that mean she had a mole in the company—someone who might even scupper the deal with Triffid by talking about the McKenzie Frost too soon? No. Of course not. That was sheer paranoia. She'd known most of the staff since she was a small child, and had interviewed the newer members of staff herself. People didn't tend to leave McKenzie's unless they retired. And she trusted everyone on her team. 'Have you been spying on me?'

The waitress, who'd just arrived with their food and coffee, clearly overheard Angel's comment, because she looked a bit nervous and disappeared quickly.

'I think we just made our waitress feel a bit awkward,' Brandon said.

'You mean *you* did,' she said. 'Because you're the one who's been spying.'

'Making a very common-sense deduction, actually,' he countered. 'If you had a long waiting list, your balance sheet would look a lot healthier than it does.'

She knew that was true. 'So if we don't have a great balance sheet, why do you want to buy…?' She broke off. 'Hold on. You said you want a designer to head up your research and development team. Which means the rumours are true—Stone's really is looking at moving into the production of road cars.'

He said nothing and his expression was completely inscrutable, but she knew she was right.

So his plan was obvious: to buy McKenzie's, knocking out his closest competitor, and then use her to make his family's name in a different area.

No way.

She stared at him. His dark blond hair was just a little too long, making him look more like a rock star than a businessman; clearly it was a hangover from his days as the racing world's equivalent of a rock star. And he was obviously used to charming his way through life; he knew just how good-looking he was, and used that full-wattage smile and sensual grey eyes to make every female within a radius of a hundred metres feel as if her heart had just done a somersault. He was clearly well aware that men wanted to be him—a former star racing driver—and women wanted to be with him.

Well, he'd find out that she was immune to his charm. Yes, Brandon Stone was very easy on the eye; but she wasn't going to let any ridiculous attraction she felt towards him get in the way of her business. His family had been her family's rivals for seventy years. That wasn't about to change.

'So basically you want to buy McKenzie's so you can put our badge on the front of your roadsters?' She grimaced. 'That's tantamount to misleading the public—using a brand known for its handmade production and attention to detail to sell cars made in a factory.'

'Cars made using the latest technology to streamline the process,' he corrected. 'We still pay very close attention to detail.'

'It's not the same as a customer being able to meet and shake the hands of the actual people who built their car. McKenzie's has a unique selling point.'

'McKenzie's is in danger of going under.'

'That's not happening on my watch,' she said. 'And I'm not selling to you. To anyone,' she corrected herself swiftly.

But he picked up on her mistake. 'You're not selling to me because I'm a Stone.'

'Would you sell your company to me?' she countered.

'If my balance sheet was as bad as yours, you were going to keep on all my staff, and my family name was still going to be in the market place, then yes, I'd consider it—depending on the deal you were offering.'

'But that's the point. You won't keep my staff,' she said. 'You'll move production to your factory to take advantage of economies of scale. My staff might not want to move, for all kinds of reasons—their children might be in the middle of a crucial year at school, or they might have elderly parents they want to keep an eye on.' Her own parents were still both middle-aged and healthy, but she wouldn't want to move miles away from them in case that changed. If they needed her, she'd want to be there.

'Your staff would still have a job. I can guarantee that all their jobs will be safe when you sell to me.'

'Firstly, I'm not selling, however often you ask me. Secondly, they already have a job. With me.' She folded her arms. 'Whatever you think, McKenzie's isn't going under.'

'We could work together,' he said. 'It would be a win for both companies. Between us we could negotiate better discounts from our suppliers. You'd still be in charge of research and development.'

The thing she loved most. Instead of worrying about balance sheets and sales and PR, she could spend her days working on designing cars.

It was tempting.

But, even if they ignored the bad blood between their families, it couldn't work. Their management styles were too far apart. McKenzie's had always considered their teams to be part of the family, whereas Stone's was ruthless. Between them they had two completely opposing cultures—and there was no middle ground.

'I don't think so. And there's nothing more to say,' she said. 'Thank you for breakfast.' Even though she hadn't eaten her granola and had only drunk a couple of sips of coffee, she couldn't face any more. 'Goodbye, Mr Stone.' She gave him a tight smile, pushed her chair back and left.

CHAPTER TWO

'MISS MCKENZIE? THANK YOU for coming in.'

James Saunders gave her a very professional smile which did nothing to ease Angel's fears. When your bank asked you to come in to the branch for a meeting, it didn't usually mean good news. She'd been hoping all the way here that it was just a courtesy meeting for him to introduce himself as their new account manager, but she had a nasty feeling that it was nothing of the kind.

'My pleasure, Mr Saunders.' She gave him an equally professional smile. 'I'm assuming that today is simply to touch base, as you've just taken over from Miss Lennox?'

'I'm afraid it's a little more than that. May I offer you some coffee?'

Funny how that sounded more like, 'You're going to need a stiff gin.'

'Thanks, but I'm fine,' she said. 'So how can I help?'

'I've been going through your published accounts,' James said.

Uh-oh. She'd heard that from someone else, very recently. And that hadn't been a good meeting, either.

'I need to be frank with you, Miss McKenzie. We're really not happy with the way things are going. We're not sure you're going to be able to pay back your overdraft.'

'I can reassure you that I have a deal in the pipeline,'

she said. 'Obviously I'm telling you this in strictest business confidence, because you're my bank manager, but Triffid Studios is sending me a contract because they want to use our new design in their next *Spyline* film. Once the film comes out and people see the car, our waiting list will be full for at least the next year. We'll have to expand to meet demand.'

'And you've signed this contract?'

'I'm still waiting for them to send it. The film industry seems to drag its heels a bit where paperwork's concerned,' she admitted. 'But we've built the prototype, tweaked it and they're happy with it, so it's really just a formality.' She just wished they'd hurry up with the paperwork.

'I'd be much happier if I could see that signed contract,' James said.

So would she.

'Because,' he continued, 'I'm afraid I can't extend your overdraft any more.'

'You're calling it all back in? Right now?' Angel went cold. She had no idea where she'd get the money to pay back the overdraft. Even if she could negotiate a breathing space before it had to be paid back, and put her house on the market so it was priced to sell, she still wouldn't make that much money once she'd cleared the mortgage. Nowhere near enough to prop up McKenzie's. And, unlike her father in the last recession, she didn't have a valuable private car collection to sell.

So how else could she raise the money?

'I'll give you a month to get that contract signed,' James said. 'And then I'm afraid I'll have to call the majority of the overdraft in. In these times, banks have to be seen to lend responsibly.'

And businesses like hers that were going through temporary difficulties—despite being good clients for decades—ended up as the scapegoats. 'I see. Well, thank you for your frankness, Mr Saunders.'

'I'm sorry I can't give you better news.'

To his credit, he did look a little bit sorry. Or maybe that was how bank managers were trained nowadays, Angel thought. Though he didn't look quite old enough to manage a bank.

'I'll keep you posted on the contract development,' she said.

Her next stop was at her lawyer's, to see if they could get in contact with Triffid's lawyers and persuade them to firm up a date by when they'd have the contract.

She brooded all the way back to the factory. There had to be a way out of this. The last thing she wanted to do was worry her father or burden him with her problems. He'd trusted her to run the company, and she wasn't going to let him down.

If her parents rang in the next couple of days she'd either miss the call deliberately and blame it on her deafness—she'd been in the shower and hadn't heard the phone ring—or she'd distract her father by talking car design. It was the way she dealt with the shyness that had dogged her since childhood: switching the conversation to cars, engines or business, where she was confident in her abilities, meant she didn't have to worry about the personal stuff.

But she was really worried about this.

If the bank called in their loan before the contract was signed…

She'd just have to be more persuasive. She could put a presentation together quickly enough, with sales projections, based on the new Frost. Though she had a nasty feeling that only the signed contract would be enough to satisfy James Saunders.

The more she thought about it, the more she wondered

if she should've taken up Brandon Stone's offer after all. He'd said that every job at McKenzie's would be safe. He'd implied that they'd keep the McKenzie name on the road cars. He'd even offered her a job, heading up his research and development team, though it wasn't a part of the offer she could bring herself accept. Selling to him was probably the best thing she could do for everyone else.

But how could she live with herself if she threw away seventy years of her family's history and sold out to the company started by her grandfather's ex-best friend?

There had to be another way, beyond selling the company to Brandon Stone.

Plus there was something else she needed to address. Cambridge was a reasonably small city; if anyone had seen her with Brandon the other day and realised who he was, rumours could start circulating. The last thing she wanted was for her team to be unsettled. She needed everyone to pull together.

When she got back to the office, she called a team meeting on the factory floor. Everyone looked anxious, and she knew why. 'First of all,' she said, 'I want to reassure everyone that it's business as usual. Things are a bit slow, right now, but once that new contract's signed and the PR starts, it's going to pick up and the bank will be happy again.'

'Do you want us to go on short time?' Ravi, one of the engineers, asked.

It would be another solution, but Angel didn't think it was fair for her staff to bear the brunt of the company's problems. 'No. We'll manage,' she said firmly. 'The other thing is that Stone's has offered to buy us out.'

There was a general gasp. Ernie, the oldest member of her team, stood up. 'It might not be my place to say this, but I hope you said no. I worked for your grandfather. No way could I work for a Stone. They don't do things like we do.'

'I heard their staff's all on zero-hours contracts,' someone else said. 'I can't take that risk. I've got a mortgage and kids.'

'I can't comment on how they run their business,' Angel said, 'but I'm not selling. McKenzie's will continue to do things the way we always do things. The only change is that we'll be producing a new model, and I know I can trust you to keep everything under wraps.'

'What can we do to help?' Jane, one of the leather cutters, asked.

She smiled. 'Just keep doing what you do. Make our cars the best they can be—and leave the worrying to me. I just wanted you all to know what was going on and hear the truth from me. If anyone hears any rumours to the contrary, they're probably not true, so come and talk to me rather than panic, OK?'

'If things are tight,' Ernie said, 'you could always use our pension fund to plug the gap.'

'That's a nice offer,' she said, 'but using that money for anything except your pensions would get me slung straight into jail. And I'm not asking any of you to take any kind of risk.'

'I've got savings,' Jane said.

'Me, too,' Ravi said. 'We could invest in the company.'

It warmed Angel that her team trusted her that much. 'It's not going to come to that, but thank you for offering. It's good to know that my team believes in me. Well, you're not just my team. You're *family*.'

'Your grandad would be proud of you, lass,' Ernie said. 'Your dad, too. You're a McKenzie through and through.'

Tears pricked her eyelids. 'Thank you. All of you.' She

swallowed hard. 'So is anyone worried about anything else?'

Everyone shook their heads.

'OK, You know where I am if you think of anything later. And thank you all for being so supportive.'

Though after she'd left the team she found it hard to concentrate on her work. She just kept coming back to Brandon Stone and his offer to buy her out.

What really bothered her was that she couldn't get the man himself out of her head. The way he'd looked standing up in the swimming pool, with the water barely reaching his ribs: his shoulders had been broad and his chest and biceps firm. He'd looked just as good in the restaurant, clothed in a formal suit, shirt and tie. Those grey eyes had seemed to see everything. And that beautiful mouth…

Oh, for pity's sake.

She didn't do relationships. Her parents had pretty much wrapped her up in cotton wool after her deafness had been diagnosed, and as a result she'd been too shy to join in with parties when she'd gone to university. Once she'd finished her studies, her focus had been on working in the family business.

But when Brandon Stone had accidentally-on-purpose bumped into her in the pool, her skin had actually tingled where his touched hers. And, even though she was pretty sure that he turned that megawatt smile on anyone with an X chromosome, she had to admit that she was attracted to him—to the last man she should date.

Was he really the playboy she suspected he was?

She knew he had a dossier on her, so she had no compunction about looking up details about him.

He'd started heading up the family firm three years ago. Something about the date jogged a memory; she checked on a news archive site, and there it was. *Sam Stone killed in championship race.*

Brandon hadn't raced professionally since the crash. There had been no announcements about his retirement in the press; then again, there probably hadn't needed to be. Sam's death had clearly affected his younger brother badly. And the rest of his family, too, because Brandon's father had had a heart attack a couple of weeks after Sam's death—no doubt brought on by the stress of losing his oldest child. Poor man.

Angel continued to flick through the articles brought up by the search engine. Eric Stone—Brandon's uncle—had sideswiped him a few times in the press. Then again, Brandon had walked into the top job with no real experience; Eric probably thought he was the one who should be running Stone's and was making the point to anyone who'd listen.

Angel felt a twinge of sympathy for Brandon. Everyone at McKenzie's had supported her when she'd taken over from her father. Brandon had barely had time to settle in before his father had been taken ill and he'd taken over the reins, and it wouldn't be surprising if a few people resented him for it. She'd had the chance to get to know the business thoroughly before she'd taken over, whereas he'd had to hit the ground running. Despite what she'd thought earlier about his background not really qualifying him for the job, he'd done well in running the company, using the same concentration and focus on the business that he'd used to win races in his professional driving days. From the look of their published accounts, Stone's was going from strength to strength. They certainly had enough money to buy her out.

The rest of the newspaper stories she found made her wince. Even allowing for press exaggeration, Brandon

Stone seemed to be pictured with a different girl every couple of weeks. Most of them were supermodels and high-profile actresses, and none of the relationships seemed to last for more than three or four dates. His personal life was a complete disaster zone. He really wasn't the kind of guy she should even consider dating. She should be sensible about this and stop thinking about him as anything else other than a business rival.

Brandon scrubbed his hair in the shower on Sunday morning after his run, hoping to scrub some common sense back into his head.

This was ridiculous.

Why couldn't he stop thinking about Angel McKenzie and her violet eyes—and the smile that had made him practically want to sit up and beg? It had been three days since he'd met her, and he still kept wondering about her.

It threw him, because he'd never reacted to anyone like this before. Angel was nothing like the kind of women he normally dated: she was quiet and serious, and she probably didn't even own a pair of high heels. He wasn't even sure if she owned lipstick. Though he also had the feeling that, if they could put aside the family rivalry, he'd have a better conversation with her than he usually had with his girlfriends. She wouldn't glaze over if he talked about cars and engineering.

Oh, for pity's sake. Why was he even thinking like this? He didn't want to date anyone seriously. He really wasn't looking to settle down. Seeing the way that Maria, his sister-in-law, had fallen apart after Sam's death had cured him of ever wanting to get involved seriously with anyone; even though he didn't race now, he still didn't want to put anyone in Maria's position.

But he just couldn't get Angel McKenzie out of his head.

Or the crazy idea of dating her…

And then he smiled as he dried himself. Maybe that was the answer. If he dated her, it would get her out of his system; plus he'd be able to charm her into doing what he wanted and she'd sell the business to him. It was a win-win scenario.

So how was he going to ask her out?

Sending her a bouquet of red roses would be way too obvious. Too flashy. Too corny. Besides, did she even like flowers? Some women hated cut flowers, preferring to see them grow rather than withering in a vase. None of that information was in his dossier.

He could ring her PA and talk her into setting up a meeting, though he was pretty sure that Angel had given her strict instructions to do nothing of the kind.

Or he could try a slightly riskier option. He was pretty sure that Angel McKenzie spent all her energies on her business; so there was a very good chance that she'd work through her lunch break and eat a sandwich at her desk.

If he supplied the sandwich, she couldn't really refuse a lunch meeting with him on Monday, could she?

The more he thought about it all day, the more he liked the idea.

Gina's dossier didn't tell him whether Angel was vegetarian, hated fish or had any kind of food allergies. So at the supermarket on Monday morning he erred on the side of caution and bought good bread, good cheese, heritage tomatoes, a couple of deli salads and olives.

Though he had to be realistic: Angel could still say no and close the door in his face, so he needed a plan B to make sure she said yes. And there was one obvious thing. Something that, in her shoes, he wouldn't be able to resist.

He flicked the switch to trigger his car's voice-control audio system, connected it to his phone and called Gina as he drove home. 'I'm not going to be in the office today,' he said, 'and I won't be able to answer my phone, so can you text me if there's anything I need to deal with?'

'You're taking a day's holiday?' She sounded surprised: fair enough. He didn't take many days off, and he normally gave her a reasonable amount of notice.

'This is work,' he said. Of sorts.

'And it involves a girl,' Gina said dryly.

Yes, but not quite how she thought. And he could do without the lecture. 'I'll check in with you later,' he said.

Back at his house, he collected a couple of sharp knives, cutlery, glasses and plates from the kitchen, dug out a bottle of sparkling water, put the lot into a picnic basket and then headed out to his garage. He backed one of his cars into the driveway and took a photograph of it, then put the picnic basket in the back. If Angel refused to have lunch with him or even talk to him, he was pretty sure that the photograph would change her mind.

Angel's PA gave Brandon a rueful smile. 'I'm afraid you don't have an appointment, Mr Stone, and Ms McKenzie's diary is fully booked.'

Brandon glanced at the nameplate on her desk. 'If I didn't already have a fabulous PA who also happens to be my mother's best friend,' he said, 'I'd definitely think about poaching you, Stephanie, because I really admire your loyalty to Ms McKenzie.'

Stephanie went pink. 'Oh.'

'And, because I think you keep an eye on her,' he said, 'I'm pretty sure you're the one who actually makes her take a break at lunchtime, even if it's just five minutes for a sandwich at her desk.'

'Well—yes,' Stephanie admitted.

'So today I brought the sandwich instead of you having to do it,' he said, gesturing to the picnic basket he was carrying.

'I really can't—' she began.

'Stephie, is there a prob—?' Angel asked, walking out of her office. Then she stopped as she saw Brandon. 'Oh. You.'

'Yes. Me,' he agreed with a broad smile.

'What do you want?'

'I brought us some lunch.' He focused on charming her PA. 'Stephanie, if you'd like to join us, you're very welcome.'

'I, um…' Stephanie went even pinker.

'Don't try to use my PA as a pawn,' Angel said grimly. 'And I don't have time for lunch.'

'The same as your diary's allegedly fully booked, but there's nobody actually sitting in your office right now having a meeting with you?'

She frowned. 'You really are persistent, aren't you?'

'We've already discussed that. Persistence is a business asset.'

'Wasn't it Einstein who said the definition of insanity was doing the same thing over and over again and expecting different results?' she asked coolly.

'That's been attributed to quite a few other people, from ancient Chinese proverbs to Rita Mae Brown,' he said, enjoying himself. Sparring with someone with a mind like Angel McKenzie's was fun. 'Actually, I'm not doing the same thing over and over again. This is lunch, not breakfast.'

If Brandon had driven to Cambridgeshire from his family's factory near Oxford, that would've taken him at least a couple of hours if the traffic was good, Angel thought. He'd made an effort. Maybe she should make a little effort back. If she talked to him, maybe she might get him to understand that she was serious about not selling her company. 'Do you want some coffee?'

'Thank you. That would be lovely.'

And his smile wasn't in the least bit smug or triumphant. It was just…nice. And it made her spine tingle.

'I'll make it, if you like.'

Had her hearing system just gone wrong? The man was used to women hanging on his every word. He hadn't even been invited here and yet he'd walked in. And now… She blinked. 'You're offering to make coffee?'

'Is there something wrong with the idea of a man making coffee?'

Ouch. She'd just been sexist and he'd called her on it. Fairly. 'I guess not.'

'Don't make assumptions,' he said softly. 'Especially if you're basing them on what the press says about me.'

Was he telling her that he wasn't the playboy the press suggested he was? Or was he playing games? Brandon Stone flustered her. Big time. And she couldn't quite work out why. Was it just because he was so good-looking? Or did she see a tiny hint of vulnerability in his grey eyes, showing that there was more to him than just the cocky, confident racing champion? Or was that all just wishful thinking and he really was a shallow playboy?

What she did know was that he was her business rival. One who wanted to buy her out. She probably shouldn't even be talking to him.

On the other hand, if Triffid didn't get that contract to her and the bank carried out its threat of calling in her overdraft, she might be forced to eat humble pie and sell McKenzie's to him, no matter how much she'd hate it. Short of winning the lottery, right now she was all out of ideas.

'So where's the coffee machine?' he asked.

'The staff kitchen's next down the corridor on the left as you go out of the door,' Stephanie said. 'The mugs are in the cupboard and so are the coffee pods.'

'Thank you.' He smiled at her, and turned to Angel. 'Cappuccino, no sugar, right?'

She nodded. 'Thank you.'

'How do you like your coffee, Stephanie?' he asked.

His courtesy made Angel feel a little bit better about Plan C. If he treated junior staff well rather than ignoring them or being dismissive, that was a good sign for the future if he did end up taking over McKenzie's. Maybe he wasn't as ruthless as she feared, despite his family background. Or maybe he just wanted her to think that.

'I'm not drinking coffee at the moment,' Stephanie said, and rested her hand briefly on her stomach.

Angel could see from the change in Brandon's expression that he'd noticed the tiny gesture, too, and realised what it meant. Stephanie was pregnant. Was it her imagination, or did she see pain and regret flicker briefly over his expression? But why would a pregnancy make him react like that?

None of her business, she reminded herself.

'What can I get you, Stephanie?' Brandon asked.

'Fruit tea, please. There's some strawberry tea in the cupboard.'

He smiled. 'Got you. Is it OK to leave my basket here on your desk for a second?'

'Sure,' she said.

As he walked out, Stephanie mouthed to Angel, 'He's *nice*.'

Yeah. That was the problem. He wasn't just an arrogant playboy. There was another side to Brandon Stone—a side she could let herself like very, very much. Which made him dangerous to her peace of mind.

* * *

Brandon returned to Angel's office, carrying three mugs. He put Stephanie's strawberry tea on her desk, then picked up the picnic basket. 'Are you sure you don't want to join us, Stephanie?'

She went very pink again. 'No, but thank you for asking.'

'Is it OK to put the coffee on your desk?' he asked when he followed Angel through to her office.

'Sure.' She looked surprised that he'd asked. Did she have a downer on all men? That would explain why Gina hadn't been able to find any information about Angel dating anyone. But she was reportedly close to her father, so maybe it wasn't *all* men. Maybe someone had hurt her badly and she hadn't trusted anyone since.

And how weird was it that the thought made him want to bunch his fists and dispense a little rough justice to the guy who'd hurt her? Angel McKenzie seemed quite capable of looking after herself. She didn't need a tame thug. Besides, Brandon didn't settle arguments with fists: there were much better ways to sort out problems.

Angel made him feel slightly off balance, and he couldn't work out why.

He scanned the room. Her office was super-neat and tidy. There were photographs on the walls; some were of cars he recognised as being iconic McKenzie designs, but there was also a picture on her desk of a couple who were clearly her parents, and one more on the wall of someone he didn't recognise but he guessed had something to do with the business—maybe her grandfather?

He unpacked the picnic basket, put the bread on a plate and cut a few slices, then handed her a plate and his other sharp knife. 'Help yourself to cheese.'

'Thank you.'

'It's not much of a choice, but I wasn't sure if you were a vegetarian,' he said.

'No, though I do try to do meat-free Mondays.' She paused. 'It's nice of you to have brought lunch.'

There was definitely a hint of suspicion in those beautiful violet eyes. She was clearly wondering what he wanted, because there was no such thing as a free lunch.

He wasn't quite sure he could answer her unasked question. He wanted McKenzie's. That was the main reason he was here. But he also wanted her, and that threw him. 'Think of it as a sandwich at your desk,' he said.

She took a nibble of the cheese and then the bread. 'A very nice sandwich, too.'

'So who are the people in the photographs?' he asked.

'The one on the wall over there is my grandfather Jimmy, back in the early days of McKenzie's.' She gestured to her desk. 'My mum and dad, Sadie and Max.'

Just as he'd guessed; but there were no pictures of Esther, who'd been at the centre of the rift between Barnaby Stone and Jimmy McKenzie. He wondered if Angel looked anything like her. Not that he was going to ask. He kept the conversation light and anodyne, then cleared away when they'd both finished.

'So,' he said. 'We managed to have a civilised meal together.'

'I guess.'

'We've done breakfast and lunch.' But the next words out of his mouth weren't quite the ones he'd intended to say. 'Would you like to come to a gala dinner with me?'

CHAPTER THREE

ANGEL REALLY HADN'T expected that, and it flustered her. 'You're asking me on a date?' she queried, hoping she looked and sounded a lot calmer than she felt.

'I guess so,' he drawled.

'No.'

'Why?'

Because gala dinners tended to be noisy and she found it wearing, having to make small talk and being forced to concentrate really hard to hear what people said.

Plus Brandon Stone dated a lot and he wasn't the serious type. She didn't want to get involved with him, professionally or personally. 'You're a Stone and I'm a McKenzie,' she said finally.

'"A rose by any other name would smell as sweet."'

'Don't quote Shakespeare at me.'

He raised his eyebrows. 'I thought you were an engineer?'

'I did *Romeo and Juliet* for GCSE. Besides, doesn't everyone know that line?'

'Maybe. So are we Montagues and Capulets?'

She scoffed. 'I have no intention of swooning over you on a balcony. Or drinking poison. And,' she pointed out, 'at thirty, I'm also more than twice Juliet's age.'

'Ouch. Thus speaks the engineer.'

'And that's why I don't want to date you. You'd spend all evening either flirting with me or making smart, annoying remarks.'

'Firstly,' he said, 'you're meant to flirt with your date.'

'Flirting's superficial and overrated.'

'Clearly nobody's flirted properly with you.'

That was a little too near the mark. 'I don't need to be flirted with.'

He held her gaze. 'No?'

'No.' She looked away.

'When was the last time you dated?' he asked.

Too long ago. 'Wasn't that in your dossier?' she retorted.

'Now who's making the smart remarks?'

At her silence, he continued, 'The gala evening is a charity dinner. The proceeds go to help the families of drivers who've been hurt or killed on the track.'

Was he trying to guilt her into agreeing? It was for a cause she knew was close to his heart, given that his brother had been killed; and it was a cause she'd be happy to support. But going to a posh dinner with Brandon, where she'd have to dress up and she'd feel totally out of place among all the glamorous socialites…

He sighed. 'At least think about it.'

She made a noncommittal noise, which she hoped he'd take as meaning 'maybe' and would back off.

Brandon was furious with himself. There were plenty of women who'd love to go to the gala dinner with him, so why was he spending this much effort on someone who'd made it quite clear that she didn't want to go anywhere with him?

He should never have mentioned the gala dinner.

He should've stuck to business.

At least if they'd been talking about cars, they would've

had something in common. Maybe that was the way to get this conversation back on track. 'Would you show me round the factory?'

Those beautiful violet eyes widened in surprise. 'That's direct. Don't you prefer other people to look things up for you and report back?'

Maybe he deserved that one. 'I'm not spying on you, if that's your implication. Anyone who works in our industry would be itching to look round, and sit in one of your cars and pretend to be its owner.'

She scoffed. 'My cars are very affordable. If you wanted one, you could buy one. In fact, you could buy a whole fleet for the price of just one of yours.'

'If that's your best patter,' he said, 'you should sack yourself as head of sales.'

She narrowed her eyes at him. 'What do you want from me, Mr Stone?'

A lot of things. Some of which he hadn't quite worked out. 'First-name terms, for a start.' He paused. 'Angel.'

She looked as if she was warring with herself, but then finally nodded. 'Brandon. OK. I'll show you round the factory.'

Walking through the factory with Brandon felt weird. Tantamount to parading her flock of lambs in front of a wolf. Though at least she'd already warned her staff that he'd made an offer and she'd refused. She'd reinforce that later

Please let that contract come through today.

She knew that the Frost prototype was in a partitioned-off part of the factory, safely away from his gaze. But he could see the areas where the body parts were sprayed, the leather seats were hand-cut and hand-sewn, the engines were built and the final cars were assembled. If he saw the process for himself he'd understand what was so special about McKenzie's, and why she was so adamant about keeping things as they were.

'This is the Luna,' she said. 'This one's being built by Ernie and Ravi. Ernie, Ravi, this is Brandon Stone.'

Ernie gave him a curt nod, but Ravi shook his hand enthusiastically and smiled. 'I've seen you race. I was there when you won the that championship, six years ago.'

'A lifetime ago,' Brandon said softly. 'I'm on the other side of the business now.'

Ravi looked awkward. 'Sorry. I didn't...'

'It's fine.' Brandon clearly knew what the other man wasn't saying. He hadn't meant to trample over a sore spot and bring up Sam's death. He patted Ravi's shoulder briefly. 'I really like the lines of this car. Is it OK for me to have a look at the engine?'

'Sure.' Ravi popped the catch on the bonnet.

Ernie gestured to Angel to step to the side while Ravi was showing Brandon the engine. 'What are you doing, Angel?' he asked in an angry whisper. 'I thought you said you weren't selling?'

'I'm not. He turned up today. I'm showing him round the factory so he can see our processes for himself,' Angel said, 'and to prove we're not compatible with Stone's.'

'You're a good boss, lass, but you're no match for a company that ruthless.' He shook his head. 'You be careful.'

'I will.' Even though Ernie should've retired a couple of years back, Angel appreciated the fact he'd decided to stay on, training their younger staff and making sure the quality control lived up to their brand's promise. And she knew he had the company's interests at heart; he'd accepted her as his boss because he knew she paid the same attention to detail that he did, and she wasn't afraid to get her hands dirty and work on the factory floor if she was needed.

As they walked through the different stations, she could see Brandon looking intrigued. 'This is very different from the way we do things at Stone's,' he said.

'Exactly. I'm glad you see your business is completely incompatible with mine.'

He raised an eyebrow. 'I didn't say that.'

'I'm saying it for you.'

He just looked at her as if to say he knew something she didn't. She brushed off her worries by switching the conversation back to technical issues. 'I guess you need more tech in a race car than in a roadster. Doesn't its steering wheel alone cost as much as we charge for a basic Luna?'

'There are a lot more electronics in one of our steering wheels than in a Luna's,' he said, and she noticed that he avoided the question. 'Maybe you should come and take a look at our place in Oxford and see how we do things.'

See where he planned to change her beloved hand-built into mass-produced monsters? She fell back on a noncommittal, 'Mmm.'

'Thanks for showing me round,' he said as she walked him back to the reception area. 'But, before I go, I thought you might like to see my favourite car ever.' He took his phone from his pocket and showed her a photograph of a gorgeous iridescent turquoise car with outrageous tail fins.

She recognised it instantly as her own favourite car. Did he know that from his dossier? Was he playing her? 'That's a McKenzie Mermaid. My grandfather designed it in the early sixties.'

'I know.'

She narrowed her eyes at him. 'I would've expected you to prefer one of your own family's cars, or one of the classic 1960s sports cars.'

'I like the classics,' he said, 'but I fell in love with the Mermaid when I saw a picture of it as a kid.'

It had been the same for her. If only there had been more than a hundred of them ever produced. The only one she'd ever seen had been in a museum, years ago, and even the fact that she was a McKenzie hadn't been enough for the curators to allow her to touch it, let alone sit in it. And because Mermaids were so rare they almost never came up for sale.

His next comment floored her completely. 'Which is why I bought one, six years ago. After I won the championship race.'

She stared at him, not quite believing what she was hearing. 'That picture… Are you telling me that's actually *yours*?'

'Uh-huh. It was a bit of a mess when I first saw it. It'd been left in a barn for years. There was more rust than anything else, and mice had eaten their way through the leather.'

'So you picked it up for a song.' That figured.

'Actually, I paid a fair price,' he said.

Why did she suddenly feel so guilty? She pushed the thought away. All her life, she'd been told that Stones were ruthless asset-strippers, and what she'd read in the business press had only confirmed that. Hadn't Barnaby walked away from the original company with way more than his fair share?

'I thought about having it restored here,' Brandon continued, 'but then I decided it'd be too much like rubbing your dad's nose in it, a Stone asking a McKenzie to restore one of their most iconic cars.'

Which was a fair point: but, actually, her father wouldn't have minded. He would've loved the chance to get his hands on a Mermaid.

So would she.

And then she thought about what he was telling her. 'So you're saying the factory at Stone's restored it?'

'No. I did it myself at home. Little by little, over a few months.'

If he'd restored it himself, by hand, that mean he had to understand craftsmanship. Everything from the precision of the angles in the spokes of the chrome wheels through to the cut of the leather in the seats and the walnut of the dash.

'Do you want to see it?'

Absolutely. Though she knew better than to appear too eager. 'And the price of seeing it is going to this gala thing with you?' She still couldn't work out why he even wanted her to go with him to a gala dinner. He had a string of super-glamorous women queuing up to date him. Why would he want to date a nerdy engineer?

Though she already knew the reason for that: one particular nerdy engineer who happened to head up his rival company, and whom he was trying to charm into selling to him.

He didn't answer her question. 'I drove over here in it today.' He shrugged. 'It's sunny. The perfect day to drive a Mermaid.'

Along a coast road, with the roof down and the radio playing upbeat early sixties' pop tunes, and he'd be wearing the coolest pair of sunglasses in the world, looking sexy as hell. Like a young Paul Newman, albeit with longer hair and grey eyes instead of blue. She could imagine it all too easily.

To stop herself thinking about that, she asked, 'You *really* own a Mermaid?'

'Don't you?' he parried.

'Unfortunately not,' she said dryly. 'Are you going to tell me that you have every single model that Stone's ever produced?'

'We have all bar one of them, actually,' he said, making her wonder which one he was missing. 'We have a museum at the factory. They're all on display.'

Something she would've loved to do here, too. But they couldn't afford the building for a museum, let alone the cars to go inside. Her dad had sold off most of his personal collection to prop up the business during the last recession, and she knew how much it had hurt him.

'Come and see the Mermaid,' Brandon said, giving her the most sensual smile she'd ever seen. Her knees almost buckled. That smile; and her grandfather's iconic design. How could she resist such a combination?

The paint sparkled underneath the sun, looking even more gorgeous than the car she'd seen all those years ago in the museum. 'It's so pretty.' Her hand went out instinctively to touch the paintwork; then she stopped herself.

'I don't mind touching,' he said.

For a second, she thought he meant touching *him*, and she went hot all over at the thought.

But of course he meant the car.

'It's the iridescent paint,' she said. 'It actually shimmers in the light.'

'That's what I loved about it, too. When I was little, I thought it ought to be an undersea car.'

So had she.

Unable to resist the lure, she ran her fingers over the bodywork. 'It's a lovely finish.' Given what he'd said about the rust, he would've had to respray it, but she could barely tell what was original and what was new. She bent down to inspect the wheels. 'And the chrome's perfect.' She ought to give credit where it was due. 'You did a good job.'

'Thank you.' He popped the catch on the bonnet. 'I guess you'd like to see the engine?'

'Yes. Please.' This time, she couldn't quite contain her eagerness.

And it was everything she'd hoped it would be. She skimmed the lines of it, memorising every detail. When she'd looked her fill, she put the bonnet back down again. 'Thank you,' she said. 'That was a really kind thing to do.'

'I'm not your enemy, Angel.'

His voice was low and husky, and his eyes had grown so dark they were almost black. For a moment, she thought he was going to kiss her. Worse still, she actually wanted it to happen. Her mouth tingled, and she felt her lips parting ever so slightly.

How ridiculous was she to feel disappointed when, instead, he took a step back?

Then he handed her the keys. 'Want to take it for a spin?'

She couldn't quite believe this. 'Seriously?'

'Your grandfather designed this car. In your shoes, I'd be pretty desperate to drive it.'

She was. And she didn't need a second invitation. She slid into the driver's seat. 'It's perfect. 'Though I could do with being a few inches taller,' she added ruefully.

'That's the thing about vintage cars. Fixed seats.' He gestured to the passenger seat. 'May I?'

'It's your car,' she said. 'Is it OK to take it round the test track?'

'The place where it was driven for the very first time? I like that idea.'

She drove the Mermaid very, very carefully over to the test track, a long thin right angle around two sides of the factory land. And then very, very carefully she drove it along one of the straights.

He smiled. 'It's a Mermaid, not a snail. You can put your foot down a bit if you want.'

Suppressing the urge to yell, 'Whoo-hoo,' she grinned and did so.

Driving this car was just like she'd always imagined it would be, with the wind whipping through her hair and the sun warming her skin. The wooden steering wheel felt almost alive under her fingers, and driving round the racetrack made her feel full of the joys of summer. The speed, the sound of the engine, the scent of the pine woods around the edge of the track… This was perfection in a single heartbeat.

Brandon had been pretty sure Angel would like the car and it would make her talk to him—but he was gratified that she liked it this much. Her hair was streaming behind her as she put her foot down along the straight, and she was laughing as she hurtled the car round a hairpin bend. She clearly loved this as much as he'd once loved racing cars. He'd forgotten that feeling. He'd barely been out in his garage, tinkering with his private collection of classic cars, since Sam died; he certainly hadn't added to the collection. But being in the passenger seat beside her reminded him of the sheer joy he'd once found in driving.

He was still catching his breath when she'd done a second lap and brought the car gently to a halt, not sure whether it was the thrill of the speed or the thrill of seeing quiet, serious Angel McKenzie all laughing and lit up and knowing that he was the cause of that smile.

And then he knew exactly what to do.

'This gala dinner,' he said.

The look on her face told him she thought he'd only let her drive the Mermaid to soften her up.

'Here's the deal. You and me—we race for it. If you win, I shut up about it. If I win, you go to the gala with me.'

CHAPTER FOUR

IF ANGEL WON the race, Brandon would leave her alone. If he won, she'd have to go to the gala dinner with him.

It was tempting. She knew the track like the back of her hand, and she knew her car even better. On paper, she should win the bet pretty easily. Yet, on the other hand, Brandon had won several championship races and he'd almost been the world champion. Twice. Even though he didn't know the track at McKenzie's, there was a risk that she was underestimating him very badly. He'd be able to drive pretty much any car, on any track, and he'd acquit himself well even if it was the first time he'd got behind the wheel of that particular model.

'Are you talking about driving side by side, or a time trial?' she asked.

'Your choice.'

'Time trial,' she said, 'and we use the same car. My Luna.'

'Nought to sixty in six seconds and a top speed of one hundred and seventy miles an hour,' he said.

She could just imagine him as a little boy, earnestly learning all the stats of his favourite cars. Funny how endearing she found it. Though she wasn't going to underestimate him—or play unfairly. This was going to be done strictly by the book.

'But I know the track and the car really well,' she said. 'Which gives me an unfair advantage. I should give you a ten-second lead.'

'And I spent years working as a racing driver,' he said, 'which gives me an unfair advantage. Especially as you've just driven me round the track, so I already know where the hairpins are and where the sharp turns are.'

She noticed that he didn't talk about how good he'd been during his career, how many races he'd won and his two world championship bids. He'd stuck to the facts rather than taking the opportunity to boast, and she rather liked that. 'I guess the advantages cancel each other out,' she said.

'We'll do three laps,' he said. 'Do you want to count just the time of the fastest lap, or average the times out over the three laps?'

Go for broke, she thought. 'The fastest. And we'll toss a coin for who goes first.'

He pulled a coin out of his pocket. 'Heads or tails?'

'Heads.'

He spun the coin, then caught it mid-air and slapped it down on the back of his hand. 'Heads,' he said, showing her.

His hands were beautiful.

Which was ridiculous. She was supposed to be thinking about the race, not about Brandon Stone's hands and what they might feel like against her skin. And since when did she fantasise about men anyway? There wasn't time to think about anything else except her work. Especially now, when she was trying her hardest to save her family business. She needed to concentrate. 'OK. The track's one and three-quarter miles long. We'll do three laps in the Luna, timing each one, and whoever does the fastest lap wins.'

'Agreed,' he said.

'Do you need to borrow a helmet, overalls or gloves?'

He smiled. 'This is a road car, so no. But if you're happier in a helmet, overalls and gloves, that's fine by me and I'm happy to wait while you get ready.'

'No.' She wrinkled her nose. 'Sorry. That was a stupid thing to ask. This isn't like professional driving. Of course you don't need racing driver stuff.'

'So do you have a transponder on the front of your car for timing the laps?' he asked.

She shook her head. 'Our test track isn't an officially accredited racing track. Yes, it's smooth enough for us to test that the car performs at high speed, and the bends are sharp enough for us to test the steering, but we tend to do lap timing here the same as we do everything else: the old-fashioned way. With a stopwatch.'

He took his phone from his pocket. 'OK. Are you happy to use my phone as the stopwatch, or would you rather use yours?'

'Yours is fine. Let's do this.'

It didn't really matter whether she won or lost. The important thing was that McKenzie's carried on. And, if the worst happened and she ended up having to sell the business to Brandon Stone, she wanted to convince him that he didn't need to change the way McKenzie's built their cars. If that meant meeting him on his own terms and acquitting herself well enough in the race to make him respect her opinion, so be it.

She ignored the other thing riding on their bet, because he couldn't possibly be serious about wanting to date her.

Butterflies did a stampede in her stomach as she led him over to her car. And again that was weird, because this was work—kind of—and she was always confident about her work. Maybe it was just adrenaline because of the race. She didn't want to think of any other reason why her heart was beating faster.

'I thought you'd pick grey,' he said, gesturing to the car's paintwork.

'Because it's mousy and boring?' The words were out before she could stop them.

'No. Because it's classic, understated—and usually underestimated.'

Was he saying that he thought she underestimated herself, or that she was trying to make him underestimate her? She didn't want to ask for clarification, because she wasn't sure she wanted to know the answer.

She unlocked the car and he climbed into the passenger seat. She could feel him assessing the car as she drove them back to the test track.

'If you want to know which options I chose,' she said, 'it was to have the wing mirrors and vents body-coloured, graphite spoke wheels, heated seats, air conditioning, and the touchscreen GPS.'

'So you're all about comfort and efficiency, then.' He touched the walnut dash, then grimaced. 'Sorry. I should've asked first, and I've probably put fingerprints on it now.'

What was it he'd said to her when she'd been itching to get up close to the Mermaid and touch the iridescent paint? 'It's OK. I don't mind touching.'

She gave him a sidelong glance and was gratified to see a slash of colour across his cheeks.

So did he, too, feel this weird pull between them? she wondered. Had he asked her to go to the gala dinner with him because he actually wanted to spend time with her, rather than it being some kind of tactic to charm her, soften her up and persuade her to sell McKenzie's to him?

The possibilities made her tingle.

But she rarely dated. The last thing she wanted to do

was start discussing the subject, only to find that he wasn't interested in her at all.

Better to stick to a safe subject. Cars and driving. The stuff she knew about. The stuff they had in common. There was more to this than met the eye, and she was going to be careful what she said to him.

'So you've never driven a Luna before?' she asked when she brought the car to a halt.

'No,' he admitted.

'I know you've probably driven many more different cars than I have, but I still don't think it's fair to race you without you taking the Luna round the track a couple of times first.'

'In business,' he said, 'you take your advantages where you find them.'

'In business,' she countered, 'McKenzie's has always believed in fairness.'

He gave her an assessing look. 'I'm going to assume that was a straightforward comment on your family's way of doing things and not an aspersion on mine.'

'It was,' she said. There had been enough bitterness between the two families. She wasn't planning to add to it. 'Just humour me and take the Luna round the track a few times.' She climbed out of the car.

He did the same, and moved the seat back before sliding in behind the steering wheel. He ran his fingers lightly round the polished wood of the steering wheel. 'I think,' he said softly, 'I'm going to enjoy this.'

Oh, help. Was he flirting with her again? What did he expect her to say?

She fell back on, 'Have fun,' and walked to the side of the track.

She watched him drive and noticed that he took the first lap very slowly; he was clearly thinking about the circuit and the angles he'd need to take the turns as fast as possible. The second time, he drove faster, handling the car perfectly.

Yup. It was pretty clear that she was going to lose this race.

But she was going to give it her best shot. This was her car, her track.

He did one more lap, then pulled up next to her and climbed out of the car. 'OK. Let's do this.'

Angel had always enjoyed driving, but she was surprised by the adrenaline surge as she took Brandon's place in the driver's seat. This wasn't just driving. And there was more than just their bet about the gala dinner resting on this.

She did the first lap and knew it wasn't fast enough. The second lap was worse, because she made a stupid error and had to overcompensate with the steering. The third lap, she knew she had to really give it her all—to get her angles right as she drove round the sharper turns, to ease off the throttle enough to let her make the turn smoothly, and to accelerate at the right time so she could make the most of the straights.

If she won, he'd leave her alone.

But did that mean he'd leave McKenzie's alone?

'Shut up and do it,' she told herself, and drove the very best she could on the last lap.

It definitely felt better than the previous two, but was it good enough?

She took a deep breath and went to face him.

'Your best lap was the last one,' he confirmed. 'One minute, fifteen point six seconds.' He showed her the stopwatch on his phone, so she knew he was telling the absolute truth. And it was a respectable time. Though she had a nasty feeling that it wouldn't be good enough.

'Your turn. May the best driver win,' she said.

His eyes crinkled at the corners. 'It's not just about driving.'

And why did that comment make her pulse speed up?

She concentrated hard as he drove off. His first lap was a careful one minute and eighteen seconds. Two seconds slower than her best. The next lap surprised her because it was even slower: one minute twenty.

Was he deliberately trying to lose?

If so, why? Had he changed his mind about going to the gala dinner with her? Or was he softening her up?

But then, on his final lap, his driving seemed different: much more focused, and very smooth.

The stopwatch confirmed what she already knew.

He'd won.

When he pulled to a halt beside her, she climbed into the passenger seat. 'I'm not sure I even need to show you this, but…' She handed his phone back.

'One minute, fourteen point nine seconds. So it was close. Closer than a breath,' he said.

Almost as close as a kiss....

She pushed the thought away and narrowed her eyes at him. 'Are you telling me you could've driven it faster than you did? That you were planning to let me win?'

'No. I'm saying the result was close. I don't know many people who could have driven it in your time.'

She scoffed. 'On my home track, in my own car?'

'Or on their home track of a similar length, in their own car.' He rolled his eyes. 'It was a good time and I'm trying to pay you a genuine compliment here, Angel. Why do you have to be so difficult about it?'

'Oh.' She felt a mixture of shame and embarrassment heating her face. She'd assumed he'd had all kinds of motives that he didn't actually have. 'Sorry.'

'You drove well. It's good to race against an opponent who's worth it.'

She felt herself flush even more because his grey eyes were serious. He really meant it. 'Thank you.'

Somehow they'd both twisted their upper bodies so they were facing each other, and he seemed to have moved closer.

The air suddenly felt too thick to breathe. What would it be like if Brandon Stone kissed her? Her heartbeat spiked at the thought.

He reached across and tucked a strand of hair behind her ear, and the touch of his skin against hers made every nerve-end tingle.

'Angel,' he said, his voice soft and husky and incredibly sexy.

And then he leaned forward and brushed his mouth against hers.

Soft. Sweet. Asking, rather than demanding.

Then he pulled back and looked at her.

She was unable to resist resting her palm against his face; she liked the fact that he was clean-shaven rather than sporting designer stubble to go with the rock-star effect of his hair. His skin was soft and smooth under her hand, and somehow the pad of her thumb seemed to be tracing his lower lip.

His lips parted and his pupils dilated.

Could she do this?

Should she do this?

But her body wasn't listening to her head. She closed the distance between them and kissed him back. This time, her arms ended up wound round his neck and his were wrapped round her waist.

She couldn't remember the last time she'd been kissed,

but she knew she'd never felt like this before. This hot, drugging need for more.

Time seemed to stop, and there was nothing in the world except Brandon Stone and the warmth of his body and the way his mouth teased hers: but then he broke the kiss. 'Sorry. That wasn't supposed to happen.'

So he regretted it already? It had been a stupid mistake. And she'd been the more stupid of them for letting it happen. Disappointment sagged through her, and she pulled away. 'It wasn't just you. I'm sorry, too.'

'Put it down to the adrenaline of the race.'

'Yeah.' Though she'd never actually wanted to kiss anyone senseless after driving a car round a track. Not until today.

'Thank you. It was good to drive round a track again.'

'Do you miss racing? Because you haven't raced since—' The words were out before she could stop them, and she grimaced. It wasn't fair to stomp all over past hurt. 'I'm sorry about your brother. That must've been rough.'

The worst feeling in the whole world. And nothing had been the same ever since. 'It was.' Brandon paused. She'd asked him a straight question. He'd give her a straight answer. 'And yes, I do miss racing. I occasionally take a rally car round the track in Oxford for a test drive, but it's not the same thing.'

'Why don't you go back to it?'

He shrugged. 'I'm getting on a bit, in terms of driver age.'

'You're only thirty-two.'

'Which is getting on a bit,' he said.

But the way she looked at him told him that she could see right through him. She knew as well as he did that it was a feeble excuse. Plenty of professional racing drivers carried on until at least their forties. True, you needed to be at the peak of your fitness to drive a car well, but age wasn't a real barrier.

Of course he missed racing.

But he'd seen the way his mother and his sister-in-law had fallen apart when Sam was killed. And there was always that risk, no matter how good a driver you were. Your car might malfunction and there would be nothing you could do about it. Someone else's car could malfunction and you might not have time to avoid the fallout from it.

He couldn't put his family through that again.

So, the day after Sam's funeral, Brandon had talked to his family and agreed to give it up.

It wasn't as if he was totally cut off from the world of racing. Stone's made excellent racing cars. Just Brandon happened to be making them for their own drivers and other teams rather than driving them himself.

He liked running the business, but it didn't give him the same adrenaline rush as driving. Which was one of the reasons why he wanted to develop a road car: to help himself push some boundaries and remind him that he was still alive, but without taking all the risks that came with professional racing.

He could change the subject.

Or he could give in to this weird impulse and tell her something he'd never told anyone else.

It was a risk. She could go to the press with what he told her. But he somehow didn't think she would.

'All right. If you want the truth…' For a moment, the words stuck in his throat. But then she squeezed his hand. Just once. Not in pity: he could see that in her expression. She was just letting him know without words that it was OK to talk—and that it was also OK not to talk. She wasn't going to push him.

And that made it easier to speak. 'When Sam died, I saw my sister-in-law Maria fall apart. I saw my mum fall apart,' he said. 'And I saw the fear in their eyes every time they looked at me. Sam was always the careful one out of the two of us, and he died.' And it had been his fault, though he didn't want to tell Angel that. He didn't want her to think less of him.

'I was the fearless one, so it was more likely that I'd be the one to take a stupid risk and have an accident.'

'Maybe,' she said, her voice gentle, 'but, by not driving any more, you're denying part of yourself.'

Was that the reason he always felt so restless? But he'd been restless before Sam's death, too, never finding the real contentment that Sam had found with Maria. He'd been ruthless about ending things with his dates. Three dates, and if he still felt restless he'd leave.

It had been so much worse since Sam's death, because he felt he didn't deserve the future he'd taken from his brother—love and a family. He just hadn't been able to let himself connect emotionally with anyone, so it had been easier to focus on the business and keep his relationships short.

'Surely there's some way you can compromise?'

He shook his head. 'If I drive again, my family's going to be sick with fear for the entire race. Watching it through their fingers, willing nothing bad to happen, flinching every time they hear a report of someone coming off the track. I can't do it to them.'

'So instead you're suppressing yourself?'

'Plenty of people would love my life.'

'But if *you* don't love it,' she said, 'there's a problem.'

Those violet eyes were deceptive, pretty enough to lull you into a false sense of security and letting you forget how sharp the brain was behind them, he thought ruefully.

Angel McKenzie could be seriously dangerous to his peace of mind. 'I find other ways to challenge myself.'

'Like trying to buy me out?'

'Or talk you into working for me.'

'And then buying McKenzie's.'

'Would it be such a bad thing?'

'My grandfather built up this business from scratch. If I sell, I'm letting him down, and I'm letting Dad down,' she said. 'If it was the other way round, wouldn't you feel the same?'

'I guess.' And wasn't that most of the reason why he was so insistent on buying McKenzie's? To make his family feel that he'd pulled out all the stops and restored their family honour? That in some way he'd made up for causing his brother's death? 'So what's your plan B?'

'Confidential,' she said.

He wasn't entirely sure that she had a plan B. 'You can't carry on as you are.'

'I know. I'm stubborn,' she said, 'but I'm not daft.'

He smiled. 'Your education is quite a few rungs above mine. I don't have a first degree, let alone an MA. You're the last person I'd dare to call daft.'

'You're not exactly an airhead yourself,' she said. 'You understand velocity, angles and wind speed. And you know your way round an engine.'

He'd had all kinds of compliments showered on him in the past. But this one was the most genuine—and it was odd how much it affected him. 'I guess,' he said gruffly, hoping she hadn't worked out how much she unsettled him.

And now was definitely time to change the subject. 'Have you always worn this?' He traced the edge of her ear with the tip of his finger. Mistake, because touching her made him want to kiss her again.

'No.'

'So what happened?'

She winced. 'It's a terrible story.'

'Tell me anyway,' he coaxed.

'OK. You know when you're five years old, you do some really stupid things because you're too young to think about the risks?'

He nodded. At thirty-two, he still did stupid things without considering the risks. Kissing her being his most recent one.

'Well, I was playing ghosts with my oldest cousins on Mum's side of the family—which basically meant walking around with a tablecloth over your head, waving your hands and saying, "Whoo, whoo, I'm a ghost," and pretending to be scary.'

He could just imagine young Angel throwing herself earnestly into the game and trying to be just as good at it as her older cousins, and grinned. 'It's the sort of thing Sammy and I would've done, too.'

'Because obviously I couldn't see where I was going with a cloth over my head, I walked into a table,' she said, 'and the corner hit me just behind my ear. Obviously I cried a lot, but everyone thought I'd simply bumped myself a bit hard, and we were banned from playing ghosts for the rest of the day.' She took a deep breath. 'But apparently that night a lump the size of an egg developed behind my ear and I became delirious, so my parents took me to hospital.'

Brandon frowned. 'That doesn't sound good.'

'They gave me some medicine and I was kept in overnight for observation, but I was fine. We didn't really think more of it. But after then, if I was drawing or had my nose in a book, I wouldn't hear my parents calling me. They thought I was just really focused on what I was doing and tuning them out, but a couple of years later I was getting really low marks on my spelling tests, even though I never spelled things wrong outside tests, and my teacher noticed that the words I was writing down weren't actually the ones she was reading out. They sounded like the words she was saying, so she thought I might have a problem with my hearing. She got my parents to take me for a hearing test.'

'And then they discovered you can't hear in that ear?'

She nodded. 'The audiologist said it was caused by impact damage, and my parents were horrified. They said there was no way they'd ever hit me, so they had no idea how it could've happened. Then they remembered the table incident, and the audiologist said that was the most likely cause.' She grimaced. 'My parents felt so guilty about it—even though it wasn't their fault, it was mine.'

'You were five, Angel. It wasn't anybody's fault, just an accident.' But he could guess the rest. Angel was only child and she'd still been quite young when her hearing problem had been diagnosed; no doubt her parents had overprotected her and sheltered her too much, just as his own mother had been overprotective with him ever since Sam's death.

And it also made him wonder something else. He looked at her. 'So it wasn't just because I'm a Stone that you didn't want to go to the gala with me?'

She looked puzzled. 'I'm not with you.'

'I remember what you said in the hotel restaurant about wooden floors making it hard for you to hear properly. It must be much worse at a party, where there's a constant background drone of noise from people talking.'

Her expression told him that he'd hit the nail on the head. That was precisely why Angel didn't enjoy parties.

She lifted her chin. 'You won the bet and I said I'd go with you if you won. I won't go back on my word.'

'If you're going to hate every minute of it, I'd rather not make you go,' he said.

She blinked. 'I didn't expect that.'

'What?'

'You. Being sensitive. Given how many girlfriends you go through.'

'Don't judge me by what the press says about me,' he said with a sigh. 'They like a good story, and half the time they make up quotes.'

'Uh-huh.' Though she didn't look quite convinced.

'And don't judge me by our family history, either,' he said.

'Didn't you judge me that way?' she asked.

'Fair point.' He reached over and took her hand. 'Let's agree to be nice to each other.'

'I'm not selling McKenzie's,' she warned. 'Or coming to work for you.'

He was pretty sure she'd do both. Because, from the look of her balance sheet, she didn't really have any other option. But he'd try to make it as easy as he could for her. 'That wasn't under discussion. This is about…' What the hell was it about? He'd never met a woman who flummoxed him like this enough to lose his train of thought totally. 'Getting to know each other, I guess,' he finished.

'Do we even want to do that?'

It probably wouldn't be tactful to point out that, just a few minutes ago, she'd been kissing him back, so it was pretty obvious that they were both interested.

'I want to get to know you,' he said. 'Imagine if you weren't a McKenzie and I wasn't a Stone. Look at what we have in common. We like cars. We like engines.' 'And my guess is that if we'd met without actually knowing who each other was, we might've liked each other.'

'You,' she said, 'have had more girlfriends than I've had hot dinners, so you'd get bored and dump me within a week. And I'm not interested in a relationship in any case. Right now, my focus is on my business.'

That stung. She made him sound like a tomcat. And he wasn't. He never led his girlfriends on or pretended he was going to offer them more than just fun for now. 'I don't sleep with everyone I date.'

'Even so, I'm not your type. You go for leggy models and actresses. And they're just the ones you're photographed with.' She shook her head. 'Maybe you're right. Maybe if our grandparents didn't have a history, we'd like each other. But we do have that history. Plus I'm not your type and you're not mine.'

'So what is your type?' he asked.

'That's for me to know and you to wonder.'

In other words, she didn't date. If he goaded her, she might eventually slip up and tell him what her type was. On the other hand, there had to be a reason why she didn't date. Maybe she'd had a really bad breakup, and her ex had crushed her ability to trust. He didn't want her to tar him with the same brush as whoever had hurt her.

'So currently we're at stalemate,' he said.

'You won the race. I agreed to your terms. So just let me know when and where I have to show up, and the dress code, and we'll leave it at that,' she said.

He had no intention of leaving it at that, but now was a good time to regroup. 'OK. Thank you for the hospitality.'

'You provided most of it,' she said. 'Thank you for lunch. And for letting me drive the Mermaid.'

'Pleasure.' He itched to kiss her again, but he knew it wouldn't be appropriate. He didn't want to give her an excuse to back away. Instead, he drove them back to the staff car park and parked the Luna next to his Mermaid. 'I'll be in touch, then.' His hand brushed against hers when he gave her car keys back to her, and every nerve-end tingled.

Her beautiful violet eyes had grown darker, he noticed; so did she feel it, too? Not that he was going to ask her. Right now he needed to tread carefully.

'OK. I, um… Drive safely.'

For a moment, he thought she was going to kiss him on the cheek. He even felt himself swaying slightly towards her. Ridiculous.

'Laters,' he drawled, and climbed into the Mermaid.

Though he was gratified to note that she stayed to see him drive off and she even gave him the tiniest wave as he reached the end of the driveway.

Angel McKenzie was a puzzle.

As she'd said very openly, she wasn't his type. She was very, very different from the women he usually dated. She wasn't fussed about appearances, and he'd just bet she was happiest wearing a boiler suit with her sleeves rolled up, getting to grips with an engine, or sketching out a design at a draughtsman's board.

His tour of the factory had left him in no doubt that she really loved McKenzie's, and her staff felt the same way about her. Ernie, the older guy who'd obviously worked out who Brandon was and didn't approve of her fraternising with the enemy, had looked concerned about her when he'd talked to her while Ravi showed Brandon the Luna. Almost like a grandfather keeping an eye out for a favourite grandchild: and there really had been a kind of family feel about the place. Nothing like the way his own factory was.

He didn't think Angel's team would respond to his uncle Eric in quite the same way as they did to her. Eric would throw his weight about and make it clear that he expected everyone to toe the line he drew, whereas Brandon had the strongest impression that Angel talked to her team and gave their ideas full consideration, and explained exactly why she did or didn't run with them.

She'd sell the company to him. Her balance sheet didn't offer any other option.

But he'd need to think hard about the best way forward and how to keep her team firmly on board—and then hopefully Angel would stay, too. Because that was the one thing he was very clear on, now: he didn't just want McKenzie's. He wanted Angel as well.

CHAPTER FIVE

'YOU HAVE TO speculate to accumulate, Miss McKenzie,' the lawyer drawled.

Which was a bit tricky when you didn't have anything to speculate with. 'Of course,' Angel agreed mildly. 'But would Triffid shoot a film on spec without a distribution deal? Because then you'd have to pay the actors and the crew up front, along with location fees and costumes and props, and you'd be spending all that money without even knowing if you'd see a return on your investment. You have to speculate to accumulate, yes—but you have to speculate *sensibly*.'

'I guess,' the lawyer said.

'So you understand that I can't just take one of my teams off their production rota for cars that have customers actually waiting for them, to make more Frosts for you that you might not use at all because you might want to make further changes to the spec. It'd be a waste of time and resources for both of us.' Resources she didn't have, and she was pretty sure Triffid wouldn't pay her for anything they didn't use, even if she pointed out that they were development costs specifically incurred for them.

'Noted,' the lawyer said. 'So are you saying you want to pull out of the deal?'

'No. I'm saying that I need to work out my factory production schedules for the Frost and my other models—just as Triffid has to work out how much time they need to film at each location, and how long they need for editing, and how long they need to get the films distributed to the various screens for the launch date,' Angel said. 'So I'd like to firm up numbers and dates, and I really think we should have everything signed off by the end of the week.'

'I'll talk to my people.'

Meaning more delay? Angel forced herself to smile and hoped that the lawyer couldn't see the anxiety in her eyes. Video conference calls could be tricky, but at least then she could be sure she was picking up every single word. Phone calls, where she had to concentrate super-hard because she had no visuals to work with, left her tired and cranky.

'I'd like to firm up the PR plans, too. To agree when we do the photoshoot of the car, when we draft the press release, and if you want to give anyone an exclusive interview. Perhaps we can have that signed off by the end of the week, too? I know the Internet makes things almost instant nowadays, but the car magazines still have lead times, and it'd be great to capitalise on this over the summer.'

'I'll talk to my people,' the lawyer said again.

'Great. I'll speak to you tomorrow, then. Same time?' Angel suggested brightly. 'Because then we can all get our ducks in a row and it'll be great for everyone.' And a signed contract would keep her bank manager happy and give her what she needed to refuse Brandon Stone's offer.

'Same time tomorrow,' the lawyer agreed. 'First thing.'

Ten a.m. in LA might be first thing, Angel thought, but it was six p.m. in England and she'd already been at her desk for ten hours. 'Lovely,' she said, and ended the call.

And please let the talking go quickly, this time. No more delays. She was running everything way too close to the wire.

Stephanie came in with a skinny cappuccino and a plate of chocolate biscuits. 'Given who you've just been talking to, I'm guessing you need this.'

'Thank you,' Angel said gratefully. 'Though you should've left an hour ago.'

'I knew you were calling Triffid—that's why I stayed behind,' Stephanie explained. 'I thought you could do with this when you were finished.'

'I could. Thank you.'

'Oh, and Brandon rang while you were on the phone to LA.'

Not 'Mr Stone', Angel noticed. So he'd clearly charmed her PA.

'Can you give him a call on his mobile?' Stephanie gave her a sticky note with the number written down.

'I will. Thanks, Stephie. Go home. And come in an hour later tomorrow morning to make up for this.'

'Yes, boss.' Stephanie smiled at her.

Angel was really too tired right now to concentrate on a phone call. Instead, she texted Brandon.

Stephie said you rang.

His reply came back immediately.

Busy or can you talk?

There was her ready-made excuse. All she had to do was say she was busy. But she surprised herself by actually wanting to talk to him.

Skype? she suggested, and typed in her profile ID.

A couple of minutes later, he called her on Skype.

'You OK?'

'Just a bit tired,' she admitted. 'It's been a long day.'

'And having to concentrate on listening to someone on the phone is hard work when you're tired.'

Again she was surprised by how perceptive he was. Since when did a Stone have a soft centre like this? 'A bit.'

'OK, then I'll keep this brief. Are you busy tomorrow night?'

'Why?' she asked carefully.

'Because I have a suggestion for you. I thought we could maybe meet halfway.'

'Halfway?' she repeated, feeling a bit stupid. What was he talking about? Selling the company to him? Because there was no halfway where McKenzie's and Stone's were concerned.

'St Albans is roughly halfway between Oxford and Cambridge.'

'St Albans?' So he'd been talking about geography after all.

'There's an outdoor performance of *Romeo and Juliet* tomorrow night in the Roman Theatre of Verulamium.' He gave her the sweetest, cheekiest smile. 'I thought it might be appropriate for us.'

The two warring houses he'd once compared them to: Montagues and Capulets. He had a point. They probably ought to keep well away from each other. But that smile was irresistible. 'Can you even get tickets for the performance, this late?' she asked.

'I can get tickets. And it'll be fun.'

'Fun.' There hadn't been a lot of that in her life, lately, with all her worries about the business. She'd almost forgotten how to have fun. It was tempting: but she simply didn't have the time.

As if he guessed at the excuse she was about to give, he said, 'You work hard. An evening off will do you good—refresh you, so you can work harder the next day.' The way he looked at her made her knees go weak. 'Are you up for it?'

She ought to say no.

She wasn't meant to be fraternising with the enemy. Or letting herself think about what it might be like to date Brandon Stone properly.

But completely the wrong word came out of her mouth. 'OK.'

'Great. Apparently they have food stalls, so we can grab dinner there. I'll bring a couple of foldaway chairs for us.'

'What time?'

'It starts at seven, so I'll meet you outside the gates at half-past six?'

Which would mean leaving work early to get there on time. As she was expecting a call from the lawyers in LA at six, it just wasn't doable. 'Sorry. I can't get there by then,' she said. But it felt mean to just knock him back. He'd been thoughtful. And she did actually want to go to the play with him. 'Can you make it another night?'

'How about Friday?' he suggested.

'Our factory finishes at half-past three on Fridays.'

'So does ours,' he said. 'Then Friday would work for both of us. Excellent. Friday it is. *Ciao*.' And then he hung up.

Ciao? *Ciao?*

She should've had him pegged as corny and ridiculous. Nobody English said *ciao* nowadays. It wasn't quite old enough to be retro, and it was cheesy and… And… That smile made it so charming.

That was the problem.

With Brandon, she still couldn't be sure what was charm and what was substance. She hated herself for being so suspicious but, given their family history and his offer to buy out her company, was he schmoozing her or did he really like her? If she'd dated more, maybe she would've had more of a clue. As it was, Brandon left her in a spin.

On Wednesday night, Angel's call to LA went much better. 'I'll email the contract over now,' the lawyer said. 'We have a digital signing system. I'll send you a link, and you can sign it once you've read it through.'

Once her own legal team had read it through, to make sure there weren't any last-minute changes, she thought. 'Thank you. I will.'

'Pleasure doing business with you, ma'am.'

'And you,' she said, lying through her teeth. The delays had driven her crazy. She definitely wouldn't have been able to cope with a career in law, where the wheels ground so very slowly. Give her the straightforwardness of engineering any day: either it worked, or it didn't—in which case you could work out how to fix it.

It was nearly two hours before the contract arrived in her inbox. But she was able to open the document without a problem, and she scanned it through quickly to make sure that everything she'd agreed was roughly there.

And then she sagged in relief.

She wasn't going to have to sell the company to Brandon after all. As long as her legal team was happy with the terms, she could sign the contract, and then she'd be able to start talking about the Frost. She could work with Triffid's PR team on a teaser campaign that would have people flocking to their dealers and asking to be put on the waiting list for a McKenzie Frost, or maybe a Luna if they couldn't wait for a Frost to be built. She'd be able to offer her staff overtime if they wanted it. Expand the business, maybe. And hopefully the Frost would become the iconic design of her generation, just as the Luna was her father's and the Mermaid was her grandfather's. She'd do McKenzie's proud.

Nobody would be at the bank at this time on a Wednesday night, she knew, but she dropped an email to James Saunders saying that the contract was now in her hands and her lawyers were looking through it.

By the time she got home, she was too tired to bother cooking dinner, opting for a bowl of cereal instead. Once she'd changed into her pyjamas, she thought about her date with Brandon on Friday night. And again the ugliest question raised its head: was this a real date, or was he simply softening her up to persuade him to sell to her?

Except she didn't have to sell the company any more.

She didn't want to make a fool of herself. Even allowing for press exaggeration, Brandon had dated a lot of women. On average, she was pretty sure he had more dates in a month than she'd had in her entire life so far. He was so far out of her league, it was untrue.

Maybe she should call it off.

Or maybe she was just tired and overthinking it. Maybe she should just go and have some fun.

The next day at work, Angel was mulling about what to wear on her date. She didn't often go to the theatre. Were you supposed to dress up? Or, given that it was an outdoor production and it might get cold as the evening went on, should you dress for comfort?

A call from the bank distracted her for a little while. This time James Saunders seemed prepared to discuss her business plan, and to her relief there was no more talk about calling in her overdraft. But then her lawyer called, wanting to make a change in one of the clauses.

'I know it means you'll have to stay after normal office hours here to talk to LA, because of the time difference,' she said, 'but you're the expert on contracts. Maybe it'd be best if you liaised with LA directly, rather than me acting as a kind of postman between you and getting it wrong?' She really couldn't face any more delays and excuses to drag things out.

Finally, on Friday lunchtime, she was able to call into her lawyer's office to sign the contract and it was sent electronically to LA.

And all the worry was over at last. She didn't have to let her family down and sell the company. Triffid's PR team would talk to her next week about the shoot and interviews, and then things would start to look up in the sales department.

She finished locking up the factory at four, and then headed for St Albans.

There were a thousand butterflies doing a stampede in her stomach as she drove to meet Brandon. Was she doing the right thing, or making a fool of herself? Though it was too late to change her mind, now.

She parked the car and texted Brandon to let him know she'd arrived.

He replied instantly.

Am in the queue by the gates. Will look out for you.

As she reached the group of people by the gates, she scanned the queue for him. He clearly spotted her first because he raised his hand to her and gave her that rock star smile.

'Hi.' She could see that he had a couple of fold-up chairs in bags slung over his shoulder; and he was dressed much more casually than she was. So she'd got the dress code well and truly wrong. 'Sorry. I came straight from work.'

He kissed her cheek. 'You look lovely.'

Was that gallantry, she wondered, or did he mean it? 'Thank you. How much do I owe you for my ticket?'

'Nothing. My treat. And no strings,' he added swiftly.

'Then I'll buy the pizza,' she said firmly, not wanting to be beholden to him. 'Especially as you've already bought me breakfast and lunch.'

'I'm not totting it all up, you know,' he said.

It made her feel even more awkward. And it must have shown in her expression, because he smiled and touched her cheek briefly with the back of his hand. 'Relax, Angel. We're just going to see a play together. Have you decided which of us is the Montague and which the Capulet, by the way?'

Strange how suddenly she felt so much more at ease. 'A rose by any other name, hmm?'

'Indeed. I brought a blanket as well as the chairs, because I thought the temperature might drop a bit once the sun sets.'

Was he suggesting that they'd share the blanket? It sounded cosy. *Intimate*. And it made her feel hot all over. She just about managed to cover her confusion.

Finally they were through the gates and Brandon set up their chairs with the minimum of fuss.

'What would you like to eat?' she asked.

'The pizza smells good,' he suggested.

'Pizza it is.'

His hand brushed against hers as they walked over to the stripy tent, sending a spike of adrenaline through her. His fingers caught hers and then curled round hers. This was definitely starting to feel like a date, she thought. A real one.

They chose from the menu chalked on a sandwich board, but when they reached the front of the queue Angel didn't quite catch what the pizza guy said to her through all the chatter round her; his face was in the shadows, and his beard meant that she couldn't lip-read what he was saying.

Without making a fuss, Brandon took over the conversation and ordered their pizzas. Angel was grateful and frustrated at the same time; most of the time, she could work round her hearing loss, but sometimes it made her feel just as she had as a child: stupid and useless.

Back at their seats, he asked gently, 'Are you OK?'

'Sure.' Though he knew he'd rescued her from a struggle, so she could hardly pretend that everything had been totally fine. She looked away. 'Thanks for helping me out. Occasionally my hearing lets me down. I could probably do with a reassessment and maybe a tweak to my hearing aid program, but I haven't had the time.'

'Make the time,' he said, 'because you're important.'

Part of her felt nettled that he was bossing her about; but she could see that his motivation was concern for her. She was used to her parents wrapping her in cotton wool, and some of the team at McKenzie's—particularly the older ones—were a bit overprotective of her, but she'd put that down to them having known her since she was a toddler.

But Brandon showing that same consideration... It actually felt good that he seemed protective of her. It made her feel cherished. Which she knew was ridiculous, because she didn't need anyone looking after her: she was doing perfectly well on her own.

Angel thoroughly enjoyed the play; and it was particularly lovely to see it in the old Roman amphitheatre with minimum props, just as plays had been produced here nearly two thousand years ago.

It started to get chilly after the sun set and, although Angel tried really hard not to shiver, Brandon noticed that she was cold. He tucked his blanket round them both and slid his arm around her.

'Do you want me to get you some hot chocolate?' he asked.

'No, I'm fine, thanks. Don't miss any of the play for me.' A cup of hot chocolate would've been nice, but she had to admit to herself that she much preferred sitting there with his arm round her.

She knew he'd chosen *Romeo and Juliet* as a nod to the rivalry between their own families; but there was a serious side to the issue, too. She had no idea how her parents would react to the idea of her dating him, or how his family would react to him dating her. On balance, as long as he treated her well, she was pretty sure that her parents wouldn't mind that he was a Stone. The rift between their families had happened seventy years ago, so it was way past time that the breach was healed.

But would his family mind that she was a McKenzie? Would they welcome her, or would they mistrust her? Especially as Brandon was now their only child?

She pushed the thought away and concentrated on the performance.

Sitting here with his arm round Angel, snuggled together under a blanket, felt oddly domestic. Brandon knew he ought to be running a mile. Domestic wasn't in his vocabulary.

But this was actually *nice*. He liked being with her. And that really surprised him.

This whole thing had been supposed to be a way of getting under her skin and talking her into doing what he wanted. But Brandon had a nasty feeling that he'd miscalculated this badly; if he wasn't careful, he could actually lose his heart to Angel McKenzie. There was so much more to her than the focused businesswoman, the engineer who did everything by the book. She was shy and sweet, and he really liked the woman he was getting to know behind her shell.

Was it possible that he was looking at this completely the wrong way round—that maybe he should be dating her properly and just forget about the business? The whole idea of dating someone seriously scared him: he'd backed away from it for so long, and a large part of him thought he didn't deserve to be loved. But for the life of him he couldn't think of an excuse to pull away; if he was honest with himself, he didn't want an excuse. And at the end of the play, when he had to pack away the blanket and the chairs, it felt a real wrench to move away from her.

He covered his confusion by playing the clown, just as he'd always covered his nerves when racing by making everyone else laugh. '"A rose by any other name would smell as sweet."' He looked at her. 'A Stone by any other name would…' He wrinkled his nose. 'The only thing I can think of would sound wrong if I said it. I'm not meaning to be smutty.'

She grinned, picking up what he hadn't said. 'Sandstone's soft.'

He gave her a pained look. 'Please.'

'Best leave it to Shakespeare,' she advised, laughing.

Like this, she was irresistible. Those eyes. If they were anything like her grandmother's eyes, he could quite understand now why his grandfather had totally lost his head over his best friend's girl.

Worse still, he found himself holding her hand when he walked her back to her car. Just as if this was a real date.

'Thank you for this evening,' she said. 'I really enjoyed it.'

'Me, too.' And to his horror he realised that he meant it. It freaked him slightly when he realised that he couldn't take his eyes off her mouth. A perfect rosebud.

For pity's sake, what was wrong with him? He didn't do soppy, and he always kept that little bit of distance between himself and his girlfriends.

The last thing he should do right now was kiss her.

Yet it was inevitable. With her looking up at him like that, all cute and soft and sweet, he simply couldn't resist dipping his head to brush his mouth against hers. Or to hold her: she was so soft and warm in his arms. The perfect fit.

One kiss wasn't enough, and he knew this shouldn't be happening, especially when she kissed him back. He never, but never, let himself get deeply involved.

Angel was the one who broke the kiss, and Brandon was actually shaking. What on earth was wrong with him? Had he gone insane? He needed to keep control of the situation. Not seeing her wasn't an option, at least not until she'd agreed to sell the business. But maybe he'd be able to be more in control of himself on his home territory.

'Can I see you again?' he asked.

She actually blushed, and Brandon wanted to pick her up, carry her off somewhere very private and make her blush even more. This really, really wasn't good.

'When were you thinking?' she asked.

My house. Now. And breakfast tomorrow morning.

He stopped himself saying it. Just. 'Next week. You showed me round McKenzie's, so I thought maybe you'd like to come to Oxford to see how we do things.'

'So I get a private tour of this famous museum of yours? I'd like that.'

His mouth was really on a roll. 'And maybe you'd like to take one of our cars round a track.'

She blinked. 'I'd be driving an actual racing car? The one whose steering wheel costs more than a whole one of my cars?'

'It'd be a rally car, if you want to drive,' he said. 'Or we have a two-seater racing car we use for "experience" days. I could drive you.'

And why on earth had he said that? He didn't drive racing cars any more.

'I'd like that,' she said.

Too late. He couldn't back out of it now. Not without explaining—and all of a sudden it was important to him that she didn't think he was a lowlife. If he told her he was responsible for his brother's death, she'd think a lot less of him. Just as he thought a lot less of himself for it.

'When's your diary free?' he asked. If those violet eyes were focused on her phone screen rather than his face, he might have a chance of getting his common sense back for long enough to deal with this properly.

To his relief, she took her phone from her bag and checked her diary. 'I've got a couple of meetings I can move on Wednesday.'

'That works for me,' he said, knowing he could ask Gina to move things around in his diary. 'Wednesday it is.'

'OK.' She looked awkward, as if wondering what they did now.

He knew what he wanted to do. He also knew it wouldn't be sensible. 'I'd better let you go. The traffic could be bad,' he said.

'Yes.'

'Text me to let me know you got home safely?' And again, where had that come from? It was more than just polite concern. He really wanted to know she was home safely.

'I will. You, too.'

And that was weird, too. He wasn't used to his girlfriends being concerned about him. It should make him want to run a mile, especially as he'd given up driving racing cars to stop his family worrying about it. He'd told himself for years that he didn't want to feel trapped by other people's emotions. But it actually felt nice that someone else cared what happened to him.

He waited for her to get into her car and drive off before he went to find his own car, but it made him antsy. Why on earth did waving goodbye to her make him feel as if he ached physically? Was he actually *missing* her? And all this after a first official date that he'd organised so casually that it wasn't supposed to be a *date* date.

And yet he'd held her hand. Snuggled with her under a blanket. Kissed her goodnight.

Somehow he was going to have to get himself under control. This was all about getting her out of his system and talking her into selling to him. Nothing more than that.

Nothing at all.

CHAPTER SIX

THE FOLLOWING WEDNESDAY morning, Angel drove to Oxford. The rush-hour traffic on the M25 kept her too busy to think about the stupidity of what she was actually doing—practically going into the lion's den.

She was still trying to work out whether she and Brandon were actually dating or not. She didn't have a clue about the etiquette of dating; as a teen, she'd been so shy that nobody had ever asked her out. She'd developed an unfair reputation as an ice maiden at university, so she knew that the men who'd asked her out had seen her as a challenge rather than actually wanting to date her, and were probably boasting about it to their friends; she'd turned them down.

After her Master's degree, she'd concentrated on work; dating Brandon was out of her comfort zone. She was surprised to realise that actually she was a little bit nervous about today. How ridiculous. Brandon had invited her here to see round the factory. She needed to think about this as business.

When she arrived at Stone's, the first thing she noticed was that the site was much larger than her own. But then again Brandon's business was more diverse than hers; as well as making the cars here, there was an accredited race track which she knew was used by other local manufacturers, and he'd talked about the museum next to the factory.

Though it set her to thinking that this was how McKenzie's could be. And maybe diversifying the business a little might help with cash flow. She definitely needed to think about how they could make the most of the Frost—an exhibition, maybe an experience day where people could drive a Frost…

But first she needed the money from the contract to come through from Triffid. And if that took as long as the paperwork had, her bank manager would be nagging her again.

She parked her car where the man on the security gate had directed her, but before she had the chance to call Brandon to let him know that she'd arrived, he came walking over to her.

In a dark grey suit and with his hair brushed back from his face, he looked every inch the businessman.

So would today be all about business?

Or would he kiss her again? Because he didn't just look like a businessman. He looked sexy as hell, with that perfectly cut suit and crisp shirt and understated tie.

She pushed the thought away. She wasn't even sure what she was really doing here anyway. He was out of her league and she'd better remember that.

'Thanks for coming,' Brandon said as she climbed out of her car.

He smiled at her, and she was cross with her knees for going slightly weak on her. Yes, he was gorgeous, but she shouldn't let herself get distracted. 'Well, who's going to turn down a personal tour of the factory of someone who's planning to be their business rival?' she asked brightly.

He coughed. 'Not necessarily rival. Where would you like to start? The museum? Coffee in my office?' Then he smiled again. 'Scratch that. You've just driven two hours to get here. Let me show you to the restroom first and sort out some coffee for you.'

When he was thoughtful like this, he was utterly irresistible. But did he know that? Was he really pleased to see her—or was he schmoozing her?

Brandon was surprised to discover how relieved he was to see Angel. He'd half expected her to call off today at the last minute, pleading pressure of work. He resisted the urge to curl his fingers round hers—after all, this was supposed to be a kind of business meeting—and led her to his office. Gina was sitting at the desk in the anteroom.

'Angel, this is my PA, Gina,' he said. 'Gina, this is Angel McKenzie.'

Gina stood up and shook Angel's hand. 'It's lovely to meet you. And you've had to drive such a long way this morning. Can I get you tea, coffee, or a fruit infusion?'

Angel gave one of those shy smiles that set all Brandon's nerve-ends tingling. 'Coffee would be lovely, thanks—milk and no sugar, please.'

'Coffee. Would that be cappuccino, latte or Americano?'

Oh, help. Gina was definitely overdoing the hospitality thing.

But Angel didn't seem in the least bit fazed. 'Cappuccino, please.'

'I'll be right in.' Gina gave Brandon her sweetest smile. 'I know how you like your coffee, sir.'

Sir? *Sir?* Oh, no. The last thing he wanted was to give Angel the impression that he was one of those bosses who insisted on being called 'sir', especially after he'd seen the way she was with her own staff.

'She never calls me that usually,' he muttered as Gina left the room. 'Do you need the restroom?'

'I'm fine,' Angel said with a smile.

Was she amused by all this? Had she worked out that his PA was teasing?

And, more to the point, how come he felt so flustered when he was on his home territory and should be feeling totally at ease and confident?

'Come through,' he said, and ushered her into his office.

The room was very neat and tidy, Angel noticed, and Brandon's desk was immaculate. Was he a figurehead, or did he just have a tidy mind?

And then she noticed the blueprint on the wall. Unable to resist, she went over to it for a closer look. 'That's a beautiful car.'

'I can show you the car itself in the museum,' he said. 'It's my favourite of all the ones we've produced. But I'm probably biased because I drove it for a couple of years.'

She looked at the date on the blueprint and realised what it was. 'The one you drove for your first world championship.'

'I didn't actually win,' he reminded her. 'I came second.'

'Which still makes you in the top two drivers of the world, that year.'

'There's an element of luck as well,' he said, 'and it depends on how the others drive on the day.'

She liked the fact that he wasn't arrogant about his success. Funny, she hadn't expected him to be humble.

Like her, he had photographs on his desk. One was clearly of his parents. The second showed a young man with a shy smile—a kind of toned-down version of Brandon, so she had a pretty good idea who he was. 'That's your brother?' she asked.

'Sammy. Yes.'

'He looks like you.' She wanted to give him a hug, but

it felt like the wrong place and the wrong time. Instead, she said, 'I'm an only child, so I can't even imagine what it must be like. But you must miss him horribly.'

'Every day.' His words were heartfelt. Then he looked shocked, as if he hadn't meant to say that out loud.

Before he could backtrack, Gina brought in coffee and a plate of posh chocolate biscuits.

'Since when have we had these in the office?' Brandon asked, gesturing to the biscuits.

'They're strictly for visitors. Mind your manners and don't have more than your fair share,' Gina said crisply.

Brandon groaned. 'Gina, can't we have *one* meeting where you're just my PA?'

'No.' Gina added to Angel in a stage whisper, 'I've known him since he was a baby. And I've changed his nappy on more than one occasion.'

Brandon put his head in his hands and groaned even more. 'I can't even sack you for being over-familiar, because my mum's your best friend and she'd kill me.'

'Exactly,' Gina said with a grin.

Angel thoroughly enjoyed the teasing; here she was seeing another side to Brandon, one with a soft centre and one she liked very much. If he'd been simply an arrogant, cocky playboy, he wouldn't have such a good relationship with his PA. Gina clearly adored him and was perfectly comfortable teasing him. And she liked the fact that at least one corner of Stone's had the family feel of McKenzie's rather than being a ruthless money-making machine.

She grinned. 'I'm glad to see I'm not the only one bossed around by my PA. Stephie's having a baby in five months and she's practising her parenting skills on me.'

Gina grinned back. 'Good for her.'

'I really like your PA,' she said when Gina had closed the door.

'Don't get any ideas of poaching her for Stephie's maternity cover,' Brandon warned.

'Because she adores you so much that she'd never leave you?'

'More like she really enjoys being my mum's spy,' he said ruefully. 'You can expect to be reported on later.'

'Is that a good thing, or a bad?' The words were out before she could stop them.

'You got the approving look—and she brought in the special biscuits I didn't even know she kept. So on balance I'd say that's a good thing.' He sighed. 'Though my mother's going to be asking a lot of questions about my intentions.'

'Parents,' she said lightly. Her own were careful not to pressure her, but she knew her mother in particular was hoping for future grandchildren.

The trouble was, Angel hadn't even met anyone she wanted to date over the last few years, since she'd taken over from her dad, let alone settle down with. Apart from going out with Brandon Stone: who was just about the worst person she could date in the first place.

To distract herself, she said, 'So tell me about your roadsters.'

'You're asking me to talk to you about confidential business stuff?'

'If someone asks me to head up their R&D department and suggests developing a new car for them, I'd kind of want to know what sort of thing they have in mind.'

'You turned the job down,' he reminded her. His eyes glittered. 'Or have you changed your mind and you're thinking seriously about it?'

She took a sip of coffee. 'That would be confidential business stuff,' she retorted.

He laughed. 'I deserved that. OK. I want a new range.

Everything from the affordable sports car—' *her* market '—through to the top end.'

'Super-expensive?'

'Luxury and super-technical,' he said.

Which is the same thing,' she said dryly.

He gave her another of those knee-melting smiles. 'I guess. Basically I'm looking at working with the newest materials, and at a range of fuel options. But what I most want is to give my clients the experience of driving a racing car. Except *safely*.'

The ends of Angel's fingers tingled at the possibilities and she itched to start sketching.

It must have shown in her face, because he took a pad and pencil from his desk and handed it to her. 'Feel free.'

'You,' she said, 'are not playing fair.'

'I'm not talking to Angel McKenzie, the CEO of a very old manufacturing company who's sort of our rival. I'm talking to Angel McKenzie, the designer. The one who loves the Mermaid.' He paused. 'Imagine bringing the Mermaid up to date. New aerodynamics, new materials. Carbon fibre and titanium.'

'That's going to be seriously expensive.'

He nodded. 'And I'm looking at a good ride quality. Maybe a different kind of suspension system.'

'So not really the Mermaid at all.'

'The feel of it,' he said. 'But brought right up to date.'

'With materials like you're suggesting, that's the opposite of what I do: making beautiful cars that ordinary people can afford. And I can tell you now, I am *not* going to design an affordable car for a rival company.'

'Think about the super-techy one instead, then,' he said. 'And, when you've finished your coffee, I'll show you round the museum.'

'Deal.' She didn't touch the pencil and paper, but pictures were forming in her head as he took her over to the museum. A joint design. The first McKenzie-Stone car in years.

It was oh, so tempting.

But it would be the start of a slippery slope. One where she couldn't predict the final destination. Way, way out of her comfort zone.

The museum was a gorgeous building, light and airy. The cars were displayed well, too; even though it was clear that you couldn't touch the exhibits, you could still see everything.

'So which is the model you're missing?' she asked.

'A very early one,' he said. 'I might have sourced one. But I need to be a little more persuasive.'

'You mean, you need to offer more money,' she said dryly.

'The seller isn't bothered about money.'

'So the seller's just bothered about selling it to you? Tsk. And who was it who told me my sales patter was rubbish?' she teased.

'Yeah.' He gave her a considering look. 'Maybe we'll talk about that later. Come and see the factory.'

When he showed her round Stone's, she could see just how far apart their production techniques were. 'So your bodies are all pre-cut.'

'Precision cut,' he said.

'And put together by robots.'

'So we can pinpoint any problem immediately on the computer instead of having to wait until we do a test drive and then narrow it down—which you know can take days.'

'Uh-huh.' It wasn't the way she would want to produce a car. She liked the way they did things at McKenzie's. But she did enjoy poking around the engines in the factory and seeing just how they did things here.

'That's what I'd plan to use for the new car. Precision cutting,' he said.

'My team does precision cutting,' she pointed out. 'By hand.'

'But they haven't worked with the materials I want to work with. Not the new top-end stuff.'

The pictures flickered in her head again, and she could clearly see the new car being produced at her factory, side by side with the Frost. 'Supposing,' she said, 'you mix the old and the new. Old-fashioned craftsmanship and new materials.'

He regarded her with interest. 'Are you suggesting a joint venture?'

Was this what he'd been after all along? she wondered. And was it something that could work? Then again, now the Triffid contract was signed, McKenzie's were going to be at full capacity. She didn't have the space to produce a new car for Brandon—even though she was seriously tempted. She loved the idea he'd come up with: a cross between the Mermaid and a racing car, with aerodynamic lines.

Before she could reply, a voice boomed behind them. 'So Golden Boy's showing you round, is he?'

Angel straightened up and faced the man who'd just addressed her. 'I—er—yes.'

'Angel, this is my Uncle Eric,' Brandon said. 'Eric, this is Angel McKenzie.'

'I know who she is.' Eric's voice was full of contempt. For her, Angel wondered, or for Brandon? Or both?

She flinched on Brandon's behalf. None of her aunts and uncles on her mum's side would ever be rude to her like this, in public or in private.

'She looks like her grandmother,' Eric continued.

Ah. Was that the problem? If so, no wonder he was talking about her rather than to her.

But then he looked straight at her. 'So you've finally decided to see sense and sell to us, have you?'

Clearly he'd been discussing it with Brandon. And maybe that was why Brandon had invited her over today: for a charm offensive to persuade her round to his way of thinking. His uncle was completely the opposite of charming; hostility radiated out of him.

'McKenzie's isn't for sale,' she said quietly. She knew she really ought to be diplomatic, but that remark about seeing sense rankled so much that she couldn't just be polite and keep her mouth shut. 'But thank you for your concern about my mental state,' she added. 'I can assure that you I'm just fine.'

His eyes narrowed as he registered that she wasn't cowed by him. 'So why are you here?'

'I'm discussing possible business with Brandon,' she said. Which was true to a point. Poor Brandon, having to deal with so much resentfulness and rudeness every day.

'It looks more like he's giving you a factory tour,' Eric said. 'Golden Boy here's not bad as a factory tour guide.' He gave a nasty little laugh. 'We should probably put him in charge of the factory tours.'

And let Eric be the CEO of Stone's instead? Hardly. And if Angel had been forced to sell McKenzie's to Brandon, her staff would all have resigned rather than work for someone like Eric Stone, who blundered about totally uncaring of how the people around him felt. She smiled sweetly at him. 'A good manager understands how every job in a place fits in—so he understands the problems his staff face and the potential solutions. Plus there's a little thing called empathy. I've found it quite useful.'

'Humph,' Eric said, giving her an assessing look. 'Carry

on with the tour, Brandon.' And then, to Angel's relief, he stomped off.

'I'm sorry about that,' Brandon said, looking as if he wanted to punch the nearest wall.

And she couldn't blame him. In his shoes, she'd feel the same. His uncle had just been totally unprofessional, and it hadn't shown Stone's in a good light at all. 'It's not your fault.' She grimaced. 'I can't believe he was so rude to you.'

Brandon shrugged. 'I guess he thought he'd take over, after Dad's heart attack. He hasn't quite forgiven me for getting the top job.'

'But you've been here for three years or so. That's more than long enough for you to prove yourself. Especially as your balance sheets have improved every year since you took over.'

He raised an eyebrow. 'Been checking me out, Ms McKenzie?'

And now she was on surer ground. She'd keep this light and teasing, just as it had been before Eric's interruption. 'Pots and kettles, Mr Stone,' she parried. 'Your balance sheets are in the public domain, too.'

He smiled. 'I guess. OK. So what would you like to see now?'

'What would you like to show me?'

She regretted the question the instant she asked it, because then he looked at her mouth and she remembered how he'd kissed her in St Albans. It made her want him to do it again, and she really, really hoped he couldn't guess what she was thinking right now. 'You said something about showing me the track?' she mumbled.

'I probably should've told you to wear jeans today,' he said. 'But we can do something about that. Come with me.'

He took her over to an area with cupboards that contained bright blue overalls with the words 'Stone Racing' in white on the back, and a rack of helmets. He glanced at her shoes. 'Obviously you can drive in those?'

'Not all women wear high heels all the time, you know.'

'I'm not judging you,' he said, holding both hands up.

She grimaced. 'Sorry. I was being over-defensive.'

'That's OK—and I didn't mean to make you feel awkward,' he said. 'Find something that fits and is comfortable, so you don't get oil on your business clothes. Meet me outside through that door there—' he indicated the door at the other end of the room—'and then I'll take you round the track in the racing car.'

As soon as Brandon climbed into the driving seat, he wished he hadn't suggested this. Maybe he should've just stuck to driving her in the rally car. But she'd stood up to Eric and it had been nice to have someone bat his corner, for once. He'd wanted to show her the joy of racing round a track.

Even though it wasn't really a joy for him any more. Driving and racing was spiked with guilt.

Grimly, he brought the two-seater racing car round by the door to the changing rooms, then switched off the engine, climbed out and leaned against the car until she was ready.

She emerged a couple of minutes later in overalls and helmet. The outfit should've made her look totally unsexy, but for a moment she distracted him from his misery because the whole thing made her look so hot.

Then he remembered where they were—pretty much the last place where he could kiss her until they were both dizzy. Not unless he wanted his uncle slinging his weight around, and his mother calling him to ask him why he was kissing that nice young lady Gina had just told him about, right in the middle of the test track.

'Hey. Ready?' he asked.

'I think so.' She smiled at him. 'Would you believe I've never done anything like this?'

'Not even when someone else brought their car to your track?'

'Not even then,' she said.

'OK. You're going to be sitting very low down and the adrenaline level's going to be high, but I'm not going to show off or drive stupidly,' he reassured her. 'You'll be perfectly safe with me.'

She regarded the tyres, looking suddenly nervous. 'Slicks.'

'It's what we use in dry weather. It's the best tyre for the car. And the track's bone dry.'

'All right.' She took a deep breath. 'Let's do this.'

He helped her in and made sure her seat belt was fastened properly, then climbed into his seat. He took the first lap slowly, knowing that the seating position was very different from a road car's and could feel intimidating if you weren't used to it, and then he sped up.

Funny. He'd driven round this track so many times over the years. But it had lost its magic for him, and it felt plain *wrong* to be whizzing her round in the racing car. He'd just have to ignore it, because he'd promised to drive her in the car and it wasn't fair that she should have it spoiled by the misery that ate at him. 'Suck it up, buttercup,' he mouthed.

And he forced himself to get out of the car and smile at her when he helped her out of the back. 'So what did you think?'

'Um—adrenaline, as you said.'

'Too much?'

'Being hemmed in like this is a bit claustrophobic,' she said, 'and being this low down takes a bit of getting used to. But you're right—it was fun. Thank you.'

Fun? No. Not any more. He dredged up his best smile. 'Want to take the rally car round? You'll probably enjoy that a bit more. And this time you can drive.'

'Great. That sounds good.'

'OK. I'll take this car out of your way, first.'

Was it her imagination, Angel wondered, or had Brandon's mood changed since he'd taken her round the factory? She was pretty sure she hadn't put her foot in it, but something definitely felt wrong.

When he parked the rally car next to her, she climbed into the passenger seat before he had a chance to get out and asked, 'Are you OK?'

'Sure.' He gave her the full megawatt smile, but it didn't reach his eyes.

'Engineers are pretty good at noticing big fat lies, you know,' she said softly. 'What's wrong?'

He was silent for so long that she thought he was going to stonewall her. But then he sighed. 'I guess I owe you the truth. I've hardly sat in a racing car since Sam died. I've done the odd test drive round this track, but my heart just hasn't been in it any more.'

And yet he'd admitted to her back at McKenzie's track that he missed racing. If she asked him whether he wanted to talk about it, he might clam up—but at the same time she couldn't just sit there and watch him suffer and say nothing at all. She wanted to help him.

She reached over and squeezed his hand. 'Damned if you do, damned if you don't?'

'Something like that.' He looked anguished.

'Talk to me, Brandon,' she said softly. 'Whatever you say isn't going anywhere but me.

He paused for so long, she thought he was going to refuse. But then he swallowed hard. 'It's the guilt. It chokes me every time I get in a racing car.'

'Guilt?' she prompted, not understanding what he was talking about.

He dragged in a breath. 'Because it's my fault that my brother died.'

CHAPTER SEVEN

IT WAS BRANDON'S fault that Sam had died? Angel stared at him, not understanding.

'And that my little niece is growing up knowing her dad as just a photograph,' he continued miserably, 'instead of as the man who taught her to swim and ride a bike and made sandcastles with her and took her to the park.'

'How was it your fault?' she asked. 'You weren't driving.'

'But I should've been driving,' he said. 'The week before the race, I'd gone skiing. I'd gone on a black diamond run, showing off—and I came a bit of a cropper. I broke a rib, and that meant the officials said I wasn't fit to drive in the race, so Sam had to be my substitute.' He shook his head in apparent self-disgust. 'If I hadn't been so bratty and selfish and stupid, Sam wouldn't have been anywhere near that car—he wouldn't have been on the track at all, and he wouldn't have been killed.'

'OK, maybe I can see at a stretch that it's your fault that Sam was behind the wheel—but it's *not* your fault that the accident happened,' she said. 'What about the driver who caused the crash in the first place?'

'Micky?' Brandon wrinkled his nose. 'It wasn't really his fault. The car steering malfunctioned and there was nothing he could do about it. And he didn't exactly get off lightly. He was in plaster for months and the poor guy hasn't been able to drive professionally since.' He sighed. 'No matter how good a driver you are, you can't always get out of trouble if a car goes wrong.'

'Exactly. So the accident was just that, Brandon—a freak event that nobody could've foreseen. It *wasn't* your fault. If you'd been driving in the race, you might not even have been involved in the crash anyway, because you might not have been in exactly the same position on the track that Sam was, plus Micky's car might not have gone wrong at all. There are so many variables, Brandon. You can't blame yourself.'

He said nothing, merely grimacing.

She took his hand. 'It really wasn't your fault.'

'In my head, I can see that. But my heart's saying something different,' he said. 'I can't forgive myself. I miss him every day. I see him in the way my niece smiles, and I hate myself for what I took from her.'

And the despair in his grey eyes went deep.

Angel had no idea what to say or how to make him feel better. Wanting to convey at least some kind of sympathy—fellow-feeling rather than pity—she placed her palm gently against his cheek.

He twisted slightly so he could press his lips into her palm, and her skin tingled where his mouth touched her.

Helplessly, she slid her other arm round his neck and reached up to kiss him.

And he kissed her back as if he were drowning and she was the only thing keeping him afloat. Her heart broke for him. He'd spent the last three years convinced that he was at fault for his brother's death; how did you live with a feeling like that?

'I'm sorry,' he said when he broke the kiss. 'I'm supposed to be driving you round the circuit in the rally car.'

'It's OK. You don't have to if you don't want to.' She bit her lip. 'If I'd had any idea how painful it would be for you to get behind the wheel of that racing car this morning, I would've suggested we skip it.'

He leaned forward and kissed the corner of her mouth. 'Because you're a much nicer woman than I deserve.'

Was that why Brandon seemed to date his way through such a long line of women? Because he didn't think he deserved love, so he never stayed with anyone long enough to let them love him? Her heart broke for him just a little bit more.

'No. Because I think you're hurting enough without me adding to it,' she said softly. And she wasn't that nice. She was a coward who'd buried herself in work rather than dealing with her shyness in her personal life.

'You're nice,' he said softly.

'And you're nicer than you give yourself credit for,' she said. OK, so maybe bringing the Mermaid to show her had originally been part of a plan to talk her into selling her the company, but he'd still let her sit in it and actually drive it. He hadn't had to go that far.

'I'm not as nice as you deserve.'

She went still. Was this his way of ending their fledgling relationship? Was she about to get the 'it's not you, it's me' speech?

Then she shook herself. This wasn't about her. This was about him feeling horrible and not being able to deal with it. And she really wanted to make him feel better. 'You know what?'

'What?'

'You're a Stone and I'm a McKenzie. We're not supposed to think each other is nice.'

That earned her a wry smile. 'Maybe.'

'Sam was your older brother, right?'

He nodded.

'So I'm guessing he bossed you around?'

Brandon smiled then. 'When I was little. Before I was old enough to be stroppy and do things my way.'

'But he loved you as much as you loved him?'

'He worried about me. Nagged me about burning the candle both ends and taking risks,' Brandon admitted.

Just as she'd thought. 'I didn't know him, but from what you'd told me I'd guess that he would've been livid with you for blaming yourself for his death.'

'Maybe.'

'Definitely,' she corrected. 'And I also think he might've been sad that you'd lost the joy you once had in driving.'

'Probably.' Brandon's face was tight.

'Hating yourself isn't going to bring him back. And in the end that hatred is going to tarnish your memory of him,' she said softly. 'My dad's sister died when he was little. He always says she would want us all to remember her with smiles and focus on the good stuff.'

'But how do you do that?' Brandon asked.

'Be kind to yourself, for a start. Block out how bad you feel and think of something that makes your heart feel light.'

'That sounds,' he said, 'like personal experience.'

'It is,' she said. 'When I was a teen, I was crippled by shyness. I hated people treating me as if I was stupid and useless just because I was deaf. I didn't know how to talk to people and I clammed up. I saw a counsellor about it, and she suggested that when I felt bad, I should focus instead on something I loved talking about—engines, cars, that sort of thing.'

'And it worked?'

She nodded. 'It's as if this lump in my throat just dissolves and I can talk easily again.'

'So you had to make a real effort.'

'I didn't say it was easy,' she said. 'Just it's a method that works for me. So maybe look at what you're good at. What you love. Focus on that and distract yourself.'

He stole a kiss. 'Angel McKenzie, you're amazing.'

'I'm very ordinary,' she said. And, because the look in his eyes made her heart feel as if it was doing anatomically impossible things, she went for distraction, too. 'And I can tell you something else. Right now, you need cake.'

He blinked. 'Cake?'

'Let's go into Oxford and I'll buy you afternoon tea. Anywhere you like—I'm assuming you know where they do the best scones in the city?'

'I guess.' He paused. 'You know what would be even better, in May?'

'What?'

'How are you in boats?' he asked.

Where was he going with this? 'Boats?'

'Punting, to be precise.' He gestured outside. 'It's sunny. The river will be gorgeous today.'

'I've never been punting,' she admitted.

'What, when you live in Cambridge?'

She saw in his expression the moment he realised why. 'Your parents were worried about you falling into the river, getting an ear infection and losing the rest of your hearing?'

'Something like that,' she agreed. 'Though they didn't wrap me up in cotton wool to constrain me; they just wanted to keep me safe. Besides, if I fall in and get my hearing aid wet, it'll stop working.' Leaving her with hearing on one side only, which wasn't quite enough to let her follow every nuance of a conversation. She could manage for a couple of days, but it would be a struggle and she'd be bone-deep tired and frustrated at the end of it.

'I promise faithfully,' he said, 'not to let you fall in.'

There was enough of a smile on his face to let her know that they'd pulled back from the danger zone. She took the risk of going a little further and teasing him. 'So as well as being a super-hot racing driver, you're an expert at punting, then?'

'Honey,' he drawled, 'I'm good at everything.'

Their gazes met, and suddenly she couldn't breathe.

He was certainly good at kissing; and she went hot all over at the thought of what it would be like if they took this thing between them any further. What it would be like if they actually made love.

Except… Would she have to tell him about her woeful, embarrassing inexperience? But, if she did, maybe he'd think there was something wrong with her.

Maybe there *was* something wrong with her.

She pushed the thought away. She'd just given him a lesson on avoidance tactics. Going over the top and flirting outrageously was clearly his way of doing that.

'OK. Let me get changed and we'll do the river. And then we're doing cake,' she said.

By the time Angel had changed back into her business suit and he'd changed out of his own racing overalls, Brandon had got himself back under control. He was still shocked that he'd actually confided in her; he never talked about his feelings to anyone, especially when it came to Sam's death. Yet there was something about Angel that made him feel grounded, safe enough to talk about the dark things in his head.

That in itself was worrying. He didn't want to get close to her. This was all meant to be about getting her to sell McKenzie's to him. He was on his home ground; it should be easier to resist his attraction to her here.

Yet it wasn't.

He needed to keep this light and easy. Play on their differences. Bring up the Oxford-Cambridge rivalry, maybe, rather than the Stone-McKenzie one.

'Ready to go?' he asked, giving her his best full-wattage smile.

'Ready,' she confirmed.

'Great.' He drove them into the city and managed to find a parking space. As they passed the Ashmolean Museum, he gave her a sidelong look. 'I should probably point out the Ashmolean. We have rather better museums in Oxford.'

'Than Cambridge, you mean? Nope. Raise you the Fitzwilliam,' she said.

He was relieved that she was playing along with him, so he could push all the emotions back where they belonged—in the locked box around his heart. 'Raise you the Pitt-Rivers,' he said. 'And we have the Bodleian Library—which is one of the oldest libraries in Europe, and the second-biggest in Britain.'

'I'll give you that,' she said. 'But in Cambridge we have one of the four remaining round Templar churches in the country.'

'We have a Saxon tower in St Michael's church,' he said.

'And we have St Bene't, which also has a Saxon tower.' She smiled. 'I think we're going to have to declare a tie on that one.'

'Perhaps.' That smile was irresistible. And he really wanted to hold her hand. What on earth was wrong with him? He wasn't a teenage schoolboy. He didn't do soppy.

But something about Angel made him feel different.

Brandon managed to keep himself under control until they got to Magdalen Bridge, where the punts were all set out waiting for business. He paid for their punt, and then he glanced at Angel's business suit. Her skirt was definitely too narrow to let her clamber into the punt. 'Can you forgive me for doing something a bit troglodytish?'

She looked surprised. 'What?'

'I'm still not with you.'

He gestured to her skirt. 'Short of asking you to hike that up…' And then, before she could protest, he picked her up and climbed into the punt with her.

She felt really, really good in his arms.

But they were in public, so that was enough to stop him giving in to the urge to kiss her until they were both dizzy—which would be a stupid thing to do on a boat in any case, especially as he'd promised to make sure he wouldn't let her fall in.

'Sorry about that,' he fibbed. 'It was just the safest way of getting you into the punt.

Her violet eyes were wide with shock and the expression on her face told him she didn't think he was sorry in the slightest. It was a real effort to hold himself back from stealing a kiss.

'Take a seat, my lady, and I'll punt you down the river.'

'As long as you don't try to sell me down the river,' she said dryly.

'As if I'd even try.' He smiled at her. 'Right. Note that I'm punting from the Oxford end.'

'There's an Oxford end and a Cambridge end of a punt?' she asked.

'There is indeed. Here, we punt from the sloping end. It's also less slippery as well as being traditional.'

'Right.'

She sat on the padded red velvet seat, and he gently steered them out into the middle of the river. 'I feel as if

I ought to be wearing a stripy jersey and singing "*O Sole Mio*".'

'Oxford is hardly Venice,' she teased back.

He liked this light-hearted side of her. 'Ah, but we have a bit of Venice in Oxford, and I don't mean the punting. I'll show you later. All righty, my lady. Your tour of Oxford starts here at Magdalen Bridge.' He pointed up at the golden stone bridge with its gorgeous parapet.

The sunlight sparkled on the river Cherwell; the river looked almost as green as the trees in the summer afternoon light, and the ducks and swans were out in full force, paddling lazily between the punts.

Funny how being on the river made him feel grounded again. He'd spent so much of his earlier life trying to drive as fast as he could and stay ahead of the pack, yet the slow pace of punting and the sound of the water lapping against the banks and the sight of the swans gliding always made him feel better. Right now he really wanted to share that with her. But sharing his favourite places didn't mean he was letting her close—did it?

'And this is Christ Church College Meadows,' he said. He gestured to the golden stone building in the background. 'This is where Lewis Carroll taught when he wrote *Alice in Wonderland*.'

'It's beautiful,' she said. 'I think it'd inspire anyone.'

Even though the conversation between them lapsed, it didn't feel awkward. He liked the fact that Angel didn't need to chatter on and on—something that had grated on him with quite a few past girlfriends.

Not that Angel was his girlfriend, exactly.

He didn't want to let himself think about what she could be to him, and instead concentrated on punting, on the slow steady strokes of the pole that propelled the boat forward past the college buildings, all red roofs and mellow golden stone, and under the little white bridges.

Finally, he glided the punt into a berth at the station.

'You are *not* lifting me out of the boat,' she said.

Because she didn't want to be close to him?

Maybe the question showed on his face, because she said, 'I'm not a helpless little princess.'

No. She was independent, stubborn and bright. And he liked that about her, too.

'Can I at least offer you a hand? Simply because it's tricky for anyone to get out of a punt, and not because I'm trying to make you feel pathetic. I did promise not to let you fall in, and I don't want to break that promise.'

'Hmm,' she said.

And then she hiked her skirt up.

Not too much, but enough to let her climb out of the boat. Though she did at least hold his hand for balance. And somehow he forgot to let her hand go again.

'Cake?' she asked.

'Soon. I want to show you what I meant about Venice, first.' He took her to New College Lane. 'Behold the Bridge of Sighs.'

'Except it's over the street and not over a canal.' She looked at it thoughtfully. 'And it looks more like the Rialto than the Bridge of Sighs.'

He smiled. 'Trust the engineer to notice that. And I suppose you're going to tell me that the one in Cambridge looks more like the one in Venice?'

She grinned. 'No. It's kind of like this one: it's simply the fact that it's a covered bridge. Though at least ours is over the Cam and not over a road.'

'Noted,' he said dryly. 'Score another to Cambridge.'

She smiled back. 'So was the bridge always part of the college?'

'No, it was built in 1913 to join the two parts of Hertford College.' He smiled. 'According to legend, someone did a health survey of the colleges and the students here were the heaviest, so they closed the bridge to make the students take the stairs and get more exercise.'

She laughed. 'You're kidding!'

'Sadly, it's just an urban legend. Apparently you end up taking more stairs if you use the bridge than if you don't, and the bridge has never been closed to students.' He smiled. 'I think it'd be better if they pinched the legend from the proper Bridge of Sighs—that love lasts for ever if you kiss under the bridge at sunset.'

Love lasts for ever if you kiss under the bridge at sunset.

Angel looked at Brandon. She didn't think that he even believed in love, let alone that he thought it could last for ever.

And then she thought about kissing. Remembered what it had felt like when his lips had teased hers, the way he'd sent her pulse thrumming.

She really didn't know what to say. All the words had gone out of her head.

He was still looking at her. And she could see the second his gaze dropped to her mouth. So he was thinking about it, too…

Then he seemed to shake himself. 'Cake. We're supposed to be looking for afternoon tea.'

She seized on the suggestion gratefully. 'Yes. Tea. I take it you know somewhere?'

'Oxford,' he said, 'had the oldest coffee shop in England. Pepys mentioned it in his diary.'

She couldn't quite come up with a Cambridge quote to match that. 'So does it still exist?'

'No,' he admitted. 'But there is another café on the site. And actually I do know somewhere that does good tea.'

The café he took her to turned out to be a stunning building with pillars, lots of gold leaf, chandeliers and potted palms. The waiters were all wearing black suits and white shirts. And the high tea was delightful, a tiered plate with a selection of finger sandwiches, still-warm scones served with clotted cream and strawberry jam, tiny lemon tartlets with a raspberry on top, pistachio macaroons and tiny sticky ginger cakes studded with stem ginger.

'This is perfect,' she said.

He gave her an impish smile. 'Better than Cambridge?'

She rolled her eyes. 'As if I'm ever going to say that.'

'We're on opposite sides in so many ways,' he said.

And yet they were on the same side, too. 'Maybe,' she said, and refilled her cup with Earl Grey tea.

She'd still been thinking about his idea for an updated version of the Mermaid. And she was itching to sketch. 'Can I be rude?' she asked.

'An important phone call you need to make?' he asked wryly.

'No.' She pulled a pad and pencil from her bag. 'Give me five minutes. Drink your tea.'

Brandon rather liked Angel's occasional little flashes of bossiness. And he liked the fact that she'd asked if she could take her attention away from him for a few moments. Too many of his past girlfriends had spent a meal out checking their phones for texts or social media notifications, or taking endless selfies. He'd guess that Angel had never taken a selfie in her life.

It looked as if she was sketching, and her face was really animated as she worked. Clearly she loved what she did. And Brandon wondered when the last time was that he'd felt that kind of passion for something.

Though he knew the answer. It had been before Sam's crash. Brandon had loved driving more than anything else. Racing. Using all his skills to anticipate his competitors' moves and when to make a bid for the front spot. Seeing the chequered flag come down as he went over the line.

He'd lost that along with his brother.

And he didn't know if he'd ever get it back. If anything would ever fill the holes in his life that he didn't usually let himself think about. Angel had suggested focusing on what he loved, but the guilt still got in the way.

Angel finished sketching, then pushed the pad over to him. 'Were you thinking about something like this?'

He stared at the picture. It was only a rough sketch, but it was incredibly close to the picture he'd had in his head when he'd talked to her about the high-end car he wanted to produce.

'I was thinking teal iridescent paint,' she said, 'with chrome accents on the curves here and here.' She pointed out the areas on her sketch. 'Or we could mess about and make it two-tone—say, black and red.'

'And you kept the fins. That's going to affect performance.'

She nodded. 'I guess it depends on the angles. We can tweak the aerodynamics.'

We.

So was she going to work with him? Were they going to turn this whole thing on its head and do something new, instead of concentrating on the old Stone's and McKenzie's firms? Did this mean they'd be partners—and not just in business?

The thought made him feel dizzy.

He hadn't expected this—for them to be this compatible, to see things the same way. It scared him and thrilled him at the same time.

'A rear spoiler would work better,' he said.

'Yes, you're right. Give me a minute.' She took the pad back and did a second sketch.

Brandon couldn't take his eyes off her. Her hands were deft and sure, and he couldn't help wondering what they'd feel like against his skin. And when she was all serious and concentrating like that, she looked stunning. It made him want to lean over the table and kiss her, regardless of who was around them.

This was bad.

Really bad.

He needed to get himself back under control. He didn't *do* relationships. Falling for the CEO of his family's bitter rival would be very stupid indeed.

She pushed the pad back across the table to him. The second sketch was very similar to the first, but this time she'd drawn a spoiler instead of the fins.

'That's brilliant. Can I keep these?' he asked. And then he frowned. 'I mean for *me*. Not because I'm going to run off to another designer and ask them to work on this or anything like that.' But because working closely together, she'd made him remember how much he'd loved cars. How much he still loved them, deep down. And it was the first time he'd felt this kind of lightness of spirit in years.

She smiled. 'Sure you can.'

'Thank you.' He folded the pieces of paper and put them into his wallet.

When they'd finished their tea—which she insisted on buying, and he decided not to argue because he knew how independent she was, plus then he could claim it was his turn to pay for whatever they did next—they walked back to his car. Somehow his fingers ended up tangling with hers, but she didn't pull away and neither did he.

Weird.

He just wasn't the soppy sort.

Yet here he was, walking hand in hand with her through Oxford. He'd taken her punting. She'd bought him afternoon tea. They'd talked about their mythical joint car and come up with a first design tweak to it. And his heart felt lighter than he would've ever thought possible.

Funny how he didn't want today to end.

She just made polite conversation with him on the way back to the factory. He didn't invite her in, after he'd parked next to her car—the last thing he wanted was for Eric to appear and come out with some stupid comment and ruin the mood—but, before she could get out, he said, 'I've really enjoyed today.'

She turned to face him, her violet eyes all huge and beautiful. 'Me, too.'

'Maybe,' he said carefully, 'we could do something at the weekend. If you're not busy.' Which was a bit disingenuous of him, he knew, because she'd more or less admitted to him that she didn't have a social life.

'I'd like that,' she said, rewarding him with that gorgeous shy smile.

'Can I call you?' God, he sounded like a seventeen-year-old. The weird thing was, she made him feel like a seventeen-year-old, ready to conquer the world. When had he last felt like this—as if there was hope and light at the end of the tunnel, instead of a black hole dragging him in?

'Yes.'

He smiled, leaned forward and touched his mouth to hers. Just once, enough to remember the feel of her lips against his but not for long enough to let him lose control. 'Drive safely. Text me when you get home.'

'I will.'

He got out of his car and leaned against it, watching her drive away. Once she was out of sight, he headed for his desk.

Gina smiled at him as he walked back into his office. 'Angel not with you?'

'She's gone home.'

'I see.' Gina paused. 'I liked her.'

Which sounded to Brandon as if Gina had been talking to his mother. 'Uh-huh,' he said, trying to sound casual.

'I mean *really* like her—and I think you do, too.'

He groaned. Yes, she'd definitely been talking to his mother. 'We're not discussing this, Gina.'

'She's nice. Really nice. And I think she understands you a lot better than those clothes horses you normally date.'

She did. Which was one of the things that worried him. He didn't want to get close to her; yet, at the same time, he did. 'This wasn't a date.'

'No?' Gina scoffed.

He smiled. 'This morning was business.'

'But this afternoon was a date?'

'She hadn't been to Oxford before. We did some touristy things. As you'd do with someone you're trying to sort out a business deal with,' he said.

'Hmm,' Gina said.

Busted. But he still wasn't going to admit to it, because he really wasn't sure how he felt. Angel McKenzie was nothing like he'd expected her to be. She made him feel all kinds of things he couldn't quite pin down, and it made him feel ever so slightly out of control.

'It's purely business,' he said again, knowing that he was lying to himself as well as to his PA. 'I'll make the coffee.'

'You do that, sweetie.' Gina wrinkled her nose at him. 'It'd be good to see you happy.'

'No matchmaking.'

''Course not,' she deadpanned.

She'd *definitely* been talking to his mother. 'Coffee,' Brandon said, and fled before Gina could grill him any further.

CHAPTER EIGHT

ON FRIDAY MORNING, Brandon texted Angel.

When are you free for me to Skype you?

She really appreciated the fact that he'd remembered she preferred to speak face to face rather than struggle with the phone.

Lunchtime? she suggested. Around twelve?

OK. Talk to you then.

He was as good as his word. 'Hey. I've found something we can do this weekend.'

'What?'

'It's a surprise.'

She narrowed her eyes at him. 'I'm an engineer. I'm not keen on surprises.'

'It's something you'll definitely like,' he said. 'But it does mean staying away overnight. Is that OK?'

Overnight.

Did that mean he wanted to take things further with her—and this soon?

Her worries must've been obvious, because he said, 'I planned to book us separate rooms.'

'OK,' she said cautiously. 'As long as I pay for my own room.'

'We'll talk about that later,' he said. 'Can I pick you up at nine tomorrow morning?'

Meaning he'd have to leave Oxford at the crack of dawn? It still gave her no clue about where they were going; but she had to admit to herself that she was looking forward to spending time with him. They'd definitely become closer, this last week, and she was starting to feel comfortable with him. 'All right.'

'Good. I'll see you then.' His voice and his eyes were filled with warmth. 'Text me your address so I can put it in the satnav.'

'Will do. What's the dress code?'

'Casual. And do you have good walking shoes?'

'Yes.'

'Excellent. Bring them,' he said. 'I'll see you tomorrow.'

So they were going walking? But where? And wouldn't it make more sense for her to meet him wherever it was, rather than make him drive for two hours to her place first? Surely she was out of his way?

Though Angel was pretty sure that if she asked him straight out, he'd come up with some excuse that told her even less.

On Saturday morning her doorbell rang at nine o'clock precisely.

Brandon was wearing faded jeans, boots, and a white shirt with the sleeves rolled up halfway to his elbow and the neck unbuttoned. He looked utterly gorgeous; but he also seemed to be unaware of it rather than preening like a peacock. A couple of weeks ago, she'd had him pegged as arrogant and vain, but she was learning that he was nothing of the kind. And she really liked the man she was getting to know.

'Hi.' He leaned forward and kissed her on the cheek. 'Ready to go?'

She indicated her small overnight bag, and he grinned. 'That's another good thing about dating an engineer. She packs sensibly.'

She pulled a face at him. 'That's horribly sexist. That, or you've been dating the wrong women.'

'Probably true on both counts,' he said with a smile. 'My car's parked a couple of doors down from you.'

She set the alarm, locked the front door and followed him to what turned out to be a newish and very expensive sports car.

'How many cars do you actually own?' she asked. There was the Mermaid, the car he'd driven to St Albans, and the one he'd driven in Oxford; this made at least the fourth different one.

'I've always liked cars. And I've been lucky enough over time to afford to indulge my whims without making life hard for anyone else. It's an entirely un-guilty pleasure.' He looked totally unabashed. 'Come and see my collection some time.'

'Is that as in "come and see my etchings"?' she asked wryly.

'It wasn't a ruse to get you into bed.' He paused. 'Though now you've made me think about doing precisely that.'

That made her think about it, too, and she went hot all over. She was glad of the excuse to put her bag in the boot of his car to cover her confusion.

Brandon noticed that Angel had gone quiet on him by the time she climbed into the passenger seat, and he wondered if he'd just pushed her too far. He needed to get the easiness back with her.

'You can pick the music, if you like,' he said.

She raised an eyebrow. 'You're telling me you don't already have a driving playlist sorted out?'

'Like the compilations you can buy which have the same songs on, just in a different order? No.' He smiled. 'There is something I like to drive to, but you have to promise to sing it with me.'

She shook her head. 'I'm not a good singer.'

'Neither am I. But we're the only ones who can hear us,' he pointed out, 'so who cares?'

'I guess.'

He put on the track and gave her a sidelong glance; OK, so it was retro, but she had to know it? 'Mr Blue Sky' never failed to put him in a good mood when he was on a long business drive; hopefully it would have the same effect on her.

To his relief, she joined in, albeit a little hesitantly at first. But when he hammed up the falsetto bits of the song, she was smiling—laughing with him rather than at him. And then suddenly the easiness was back between them. They were just a girl and a guy, driving down the motorway for a weekend away, and life felt good. Enough for him to forget that he was supposed to be keeping her at a distance.

When they stopped at the service station for a comfort break, Angel asked, 'Do you want me to drive for a bit?'

'No, it's fine—unless you're tired of being a passenger?'

'I just thought you might want a break, especially as you had to drive for two hours to get to me first.'

He liked the fact that she'd considered that. His previous girlfriends had always taken for granted that he'd do all the driving. Or maybe he'd chosen them partly because he knew they'd take him for granted and wouldn't get close to him, and he'd be able to walk away from them with barely a second thought.

'I know, but I like driving.' Particularly with her, though he wasn't going to spook her—or himself—by saying it. He didn't want her to back away. Or for him to lose that feeling and slide back into the darkness again.

Finally, they turned off the main road onto a series of narrow, winding rural roads which led them through pretty Cumbrian villages.

'This is a really gorgeous part of the world,' she said, 'but where exactly are we going?'

'The satnav claims it's about half a mile further,' he said, and turned into a very long driveway.

At the end was a sprawling ancient farmhouse built of grey stone. 'Here we are,' he said when he'd parked, and climbed out of the car.

'Who lives here?' she asked, joining him.

'Bill Edwards.'

Which left her none the wiser. Why did Brandon want to visit this mysterious Mr Edwards, in the middle of nowhere? And why was he being so secretive about it?

He rang the doorbell, and an elderly man answered, a black Labrador with a grey muzzle at his heels. 'Mr Edwards? Brandon Stone,' he said. 'And this is Angel McKenzie.'

'Good to meet you.' Mr Edwards shook their hands warmly. 'Come in, come in. Martha, we need tea for our guests.' He ushered them into the kitchen and indicated for them to sit down at the scrubbed pine table; his wife greeted them and bustled round the kitchen, preparing tea.

'Is there anything I can do to help?' Angel asked.

'No, love, you sit down and relax,' Martha said with a smile.

The dog sat at Brandon's feet and rested his chin on

Brandon's knee; Brandon absently scratched behind the dog's ears, and Angel found an unexpected lump in her throat. The dog clearly liked him, and didn't they say that animals were good judges of character?

'So you're a relative of Jimmy McKenzie, Miss McKenzie?' Mr Edwards asked.

'His granddaughter,' she confirmed, 'and please call me Angel.'

'Then you can call me Bill,' he said. 'And you work in the family firm?'

She nodded. 'Dad retired a couple of years ago. I took over from him.'

'And you head up Stone's,' Bill said to Brandon.

'I do,' Brandon said.

Bill's weathered face creased with a smile. 'Well, it's a surprise you're even in the same room as each other, let alone driven all the way up here together.'

'We're…' Brandon looked at Angel. 'Friends.'

Their relationship was a good deal more complicated than that, but she wasn't about to contradict him.

'Well. It's fitting that you should come here together.'

Angel was still mystified, until after Bill and Martha had made them drink two cups of tea and eat a slice of the lightest, fluffiest Victoria sponge she'd ever tasted. And then Bill led them outside.

'Here she is,' he said with pride as he ushered them through a door.

Angel blinked as she saw the ancient car sitting in the garage. 'Is that what I think it is?'

'Did Brandon not tell you he was bringing you to see it?' Martha asked.

'No. I wanted it to be a surprise,' Brandon explained.

'I can't quite take this in. That's the first McKenzie-Stone car,' Angel said. 'I've only ever seen photographs of one. I wasn't even sure there were any left in existence.' And to see one in such perfect condition, obviously well loved, was incredible.

'Brandon here's been trying to persuade me to sell it to him for months,' Bill said.

And then she understood. This was Brandon's 'missing' car from his collection. The one he wanted for the museum at Stone's. He'd said that the owner couldn't be persuaded to sell by offering more money; clearly he'd hit on a strategy that he thought might be rather more effective.

Using her as a kind of leverage.

Bitterness filled her mouth, but she forced herself to smile. 'It's lovely to see it, and especially in such amazing condition. So have you had it for very long?'

'It's been in the family since day one,' Bill said. 'My grandfather bought one of the first ones they ever made, and he handed it down to my dad, who handed it down to me.' He looked regretful. 'Me and Martha, we lost our lad when he was tiny, or it would've gone to him.'

'I'm sorry,' Angel said.

'No, lass, don't cry for us. We've had a good life,' Bill said. 'But our nephew, he's not really one for classic cars. He'd rather have the money to use on some newfangled equipment for the farm. And it's time this old girl went somewhere she'll be appreciated.'

'Brandon will look after her properly,' Angel said. Even though she was furious with him for using her to get his own way, she couldn't deny that he'd do right by the car.

'It was a shame they didn't make more,' Bill said. 'But your grandfathers fell out.'

'Yes.' And she and Brandon would be having a big falling-out, once they'd left here, she thought crossly. 'It's a shame that they let love get in the way. I didn't really know my grandparents, but my mum once let it slip that Esther really regretted the rift between Jimmy and Barnaby. I think she wanted to do something to heal it.'

'But I think both our grandfathers were too stubborn to make the first move,' Brandon said.

'Something like that,' Angel agreed. Before today, she'd thought that maybe she and Brandon could change things and heal the rift between their families. But maybe not. She'd believed that he'd wanted to go away for the weekend with her, whereas clearly he'd seen this whole thing as a business opportunity. He'd opened up to her in Oxford, or so she'd thought; but maybe he'd just been playing her all along. What a naive, stupid fool she was. He was a Stone. Ruthless to the bone.

'You came here together to see the car,' Bill said thoughtfully. 'Does this mean there could be a new McKenzie-Stone car in the future?'

The car she'd sketched for Brandon. Their joint idea.

That definitely wasn't going to happen now.

Before she could open her mouth to say no, Brandon said, 'We're talking. Which is more than our families have done for decades.'

'And that's a good start.' Bill held out his hand. 'I'll sell the car to you, Brandon. It's a deal.'

Brandon shook his hand warmly. 'Thank you. I'll take good care of it.'

'I know,' Bill said. 'Because your young lady vouched for you.'

She was absolutely not his young lady. No way was Brandon Stone ever going to kiss her again, let alone anything else. But Angel would prefer to have this particular fight in private.

Once Brandon had wrapped up the terms of the deal—and Angel had insisted on washing up the tea things—they left the farmhouse.

As soon as they were out of sight of the farmhouse, Angel said, 'I don't appreciate being used.'

'Used?'

Was he going to deny what he'd done? Angel felt her temper snap. 'You told me about this car, but you said the owner wouldn't sell to you. Clearly you worked out that family and history mean a lot more to him than money, and that's why you brought me along. As leverage. And I don't appreciate it.'

'Actually, I didn't use you.'

She scoffed. 'Come off it.'

'Bill told me he wouldn't sell the car, and I'd pretty much given up trying to persuade him. But I wanted to see the car for myself anyway, and I thought you might like to see it, too—considering that your grandfather built it with mine.'

Which was true. Part of her had been thrilled to see a piece of their joint family history, something from happier times. But she also knew that Brandon was competitive and he liked to win. He'd use every business advantage he could get. 'So are you saying you *didn't* use me to get him to change his mind?'

'No. If I'd thought that strategy would work, I would've contacted you months ago, when I first started talking to Bill, and I would've discussed it with you first.' His mouth thinned. 'Actually, I'm pretty upset that you think I'd be so underhand. I thought we'd got past our family rift and all the nonsense the press writes about me, and we were actually getting to know each other for who we are, not who we thought each other might be.'

His words made Angel feel guilty, but she still couldn't get rid of the suspicion. Not knowing how to deal with the situation, she lapsed into silence. He was clearly just as angry, because he didn't try to make conversation all the way to Keswick.

But when he parked outside the hotel, he turned to her. 'I really wasn't using you today, Angel. We're in separate rooms, so technically we can ignore each other for the rest of today—but then we're going to have a really horrible drive home tomorrow.' He folded his arms. 'I don't want to fight with you. And I'm sorry for not being honest with you right from the start. You told me you didn't like surprises and I didn't listen to you. I thought I was being so clever. I should've just told you that Bill owned one of the first McKenzie-Stone cars and I wanted to see it, and I wanted to share it with you because I thought you'd like to see it as well.'

His eyes were utterly sincere, and guilt flooded through her. Maybe she'd got it wrong after all. And if he'd told her in advance what they were going to see, she would've been really pleased that he'd asked her to go with him. She took a deep breath. 'Then I'm sorry for jumping to conclusions—and for judging you without listening to what you had to say first.'

'Apology accepted,' he said.

'I accept your apology, too.'

'So we're good?'

'We're good,' she confirmed. 'Though I still kind of want to smack you for making me feel used.'

'It sounds to me as if I'd be taking the smack for someone else,' he said. 'Who hurt you, Angel?'

'Nobody.'

He looked as if he didn't believe her; but how could she explain without telling him the shameful truth about her past? The college students who'd seen her as the ice maiden, a challenge to boast about. She couldn't remember their names or their faces now, but she still remembered the hurt when she'd realised they weren't interested in her: they were only interested in boosting their egos and their reputations by being the one who conquered the girl who said no.

To her relief, he dropped the subject and they booked into the hotel. He'd been true to his word and booked them separate rooms. She'd just finished unpacking when there was a knock at her door. Brandon stood in the corridor. 'I, um, was wondering if you might like to go for a walk. Considering we're about ten minutes away from the Derwent and the weather's good.'

And he had pretty much told her about this bit of the weekend in advance, asking her to bring walking shoes.

Guessing that this was a kind of peace offering, she nodded. 'I'll just change my shoes.'

'Come and get me when you're ready,' he said.

She felt awkward, knocking on his door.

'Have you forgiven me yet?' he asked when he opened the door. 'Because I really didn't do anything wrong.'

'I guess.'

She walked alongside him towards the lake, and eventually his hand brushed against hers. Once, twice. She let her hand brush against his. And then finally he linked her fingers with his. Neither of them said anything, and walking in silence among such beautiful scenery eventually lifted her mood.

'It's lovely out here. I haven't been to the Lakes since I was small.'

'Me, neither,' he said. 'We took a boat out. Not here—I can't quite remember where. I was desperate to help row the boat, but I wasn't strong enough. Then Dad sat me on his knee and suddenly I could move the oar.' He smiled. 'Dad was doing all the work, but he let me think I could do it.'

'You're close to your parents?' she asked.

'Yes. That's why I don't race any more. Dad hid it better than Mum, but I know how much he worried. When he had that heart attack and I thought I was going to lose him as well as Sammy, only a couple of weeks apart...' He shuddered. 'Thankfully he recovered. They're both doing OK now.'

'I'm glad.' She tightened her fingers round his. 'And I meant what I said to Bill Edwards. You'll do right by his car.'

'It'll be in pride of place at the museum,' he said. 'What about you?'

'Me?'

'You're close to your parents?'

She nodded. 'I see them or speak to them most days, though they're on an extended tour of Europe at the moment, seeing all the places they've always wanted to see but didn't have time because Dad was so busy at the factory. Mum sent me a selfie of them at the Colosseum yesterday.'

He smiled. 'My mum hasn't quite got the hang of selfies. And the family dog's not very co-operative when she tries to take his picture.'

She smiled back. 'Bill's dog liked you.'

'I like dogs,' he said. 'I've been thinking about getting one. But I'm away on business a lot, so it wouldn't be fair.'

'I can imagine you punting with a spaniel sitting patiently on the deck.'

'Yeah. I'd enjoy that.'

And all of a sudden she had the weirdest picture in her head. Brandon standing on the platform of a punt, the dog sitting on the deck, and herself on the red velvet seat—accompanied by a little boy who was the spitting image of Brandon and desperate to help his father propel the punt along the river, and a baby cradled on her lap.

Where on earth had that come from?

She'd been so focused on the business that she hadn't really thought about her future relationships. She'd never really been one for fantasising about weddings, even when she was small and playing with her cousins. So why was she thinking about it now? And why Brandon?

It spooked her slightly, but she couldn't make the picture in her head go away.

'Everything OK?' he asked.

'Sure.' She gave him her brightest smile, not wanting to admit to what she'd been thinking about.

They stayed by the lake long enough for dusk to fall, then headed back to the hotel for dinner.

'You know what Bill was saying, about the first new McKenzie-Stone car in decades… We could do that,' he said. 'The one you sketched for me.'

'That was just a sketch,' she said. 'It's very different from a full design spec.'

'I know.' He paused. 'You've already said no to my job offer, so I'm not going to ask you again. But maybe we could do this one thing together. You design it, I make it, and it goes out under our joint name.'

It was so very, very tempting.

But they were going to have to heal the rift between their families first. 'We'll see,' she prevaricated.

'Isn't that what people say when they don't want to come straight out with a no?' he asked wryly.

'It'd be a big project. A couple of years, maybe, from the initial thoughts to final production. I'm not sure either of us could fit it in.'

'We could make the time.'

'Maybe.'

'So what's your big ambition?' he asked.

'For McKenzie's or for me?'

'Both.'

'I guess it's the same thing,' she said. 'I want to design the iconic car for my generation. Granddad made the Mermaid, Dad made the Luna, and I…' She stopped, realising how close she'd come to telling him about the Frost.

'You,' he said, 'will make something amazing, because your ideas are great.'

Should she tell him?

But they were still business rivals. And the Frost was still under wraps. Better to say nothing for now. Though it warmed her that he actually seemed to believe in her.

After dinner, they sat in the hotel's garden and watched the stars come out. As the night air began to cool, she shivered.

'Cold?'

'A bit,' she admitted.

He slid his arm round her shoulders. 'Better?'

'A little.'

'That was a polite fib,' he said. 'Let's go inside.'

But he didn't take his arm away as they walked back into the hotel.

Outside the door to her room, he said, 'Come and sit with me for a while.'

Her mouth went dry.

'Just sit with me,' he said. 'I'm not going to push you into anything you don't want.'

She believed him. The problem was, she was starting to want more. 'OK.'

'Your choice,' he said as he unlocked the door. 'Chair or bed?' He paused. 'Or we could both sit in the chair.'

'Both?'

'Like this.' He scooped her up, sat down and settled her in his lap.

To keep her balance, she slid her arms round his neck.

'You know what you said to me about hating myself being pointless because it won't bring Sam back?'

She winced. 'Sorry. That was a bit harsh.'

'Don't apologise. It was something I needed to hear.' He leaned his forehead against hers. 'It's true about the car, too.'

'The car?' She didn't quite understand.

'It was Sammy's dream to complete the museum collection,' he said. 'So when this opportunity came up… It's why I wanted to buy the car. For Sammy.'

'And it doesn't make any difference?' she asked softly.

'It doesn't make any difference,' he confirmed. 'The hole in the centre of my world's still there.'

She stroked his face. 'I'm sorry. But I bet he's proud of you.'

'What, for haranguing an old man for months?' He lifted one shoulder in a half-shrug.

'If you'd told Bill Edwards why you wanted the car so much, he probably would've sold it to you months ago.'

He frowned. 'Why?'

'Because you weren't doing it for you, you were doing it for Sam. Meaning you're not one of the ruthless Stones.'

'Ruthless?' He stared at her for a moment, then sighed. 'OK. I guess you have a point. After your grandmother broke my grandfather's heart, apparently he was pretty focused on the business.'

'But he must've fallen in love with someone else, or you wouldn't be here,' she pointed out.

'I guess.' He paused. 'I didn't really know Barnaby. He died when I was too young to remember him. But Dad was always pretty focused on the business, too.' He grimaced. 'I know he tried to buy McKenzie's in the last recession.'

'That kind of explains why my dad always muttered about your family being ruthless,' she said thoughtfully.

'He sold his entire private collection of cars to make sure he didn't have to sell McKenzie's.'

'A whole collection at short notice?' Brandon grimaced. 'The sharks would've circled and he would've got less than it was worth.'

'It was enough to keep the bank happy,' she said dryly. 'So is that why you want to buy McKenzie's now? For your dad, or for Sam?'

'Maybe,' Brandon said. 'I don't know if Sam would've wanted to buy you out or not. We never discussed it.' He sighed. 'You're right. Sam was the best of us, but nearly all the Stone men are ruthless. Dad was—until Sammy died. It changed him.'

She could believe that. But Brandon… Brandon was different. 'I'm not so sure that you're ruthless,' she said.

He shook his head. 'I always went out on the track with the aim of being first past the finishing line. There have been times when I could've let someone win a race. When maybe I should've let them win, because I knew they'd been having a hard time; winning a race might've helped them turn things around.'

'And what if they'd found out the truth later—that their own skill and efforts weren't really enough to let them win? It would've punched a hole right through their victory and probably made them feel worse than if they'd come second,' she pointed out. 'Anyway, if you were really ruthless, you would've replaced Gina ages ago with someone younger and with longer legs.'

He scoffed. 'Gina's an excellent secretary. I don't need to replace her.'

'She's a bit more than that,' Angel said. 'She mothers you.'

He raised an eyebrow. 'I can hardly sack my mum's best friend. Particularly as she does a good job.'

'I think you like having her around.'

'Gina's been good to me,' he said softly. 'She's the only one at the factory who believed I could do it when I took over from Dad.'

That truly shocked her. 'Didn't your parents believe in you?'

'Sammy's death broke them.' He looked away. 'I don't think they could believe in anything, right then. So I had to step up to the plate. I couldn't let my family down.'

'Even though Sammy's death broke you, too?' she asked softly.

'I thought working until I was practically comatose from tiredness would get me through it. It kind of did. That and burning the candle the other end and still doing all the racing driver social stuff. But I still don't know how to make the empty spaces go away,' he said, his grey eyes filled with sadness. 'Nothing works.'

She didn't know how to make him feel better, but she had to try. There was only one thing she could think of that might fill the empty spaces.

It was a risk.

A huge risk.

But one she was prepared to take. She leaned forward and kissed him.

His eyes went very dark. 'Angel, my self-control's pretty good, but it's not perfect.'

She felt the colour flood through her cheeks. 'Sorry.'

He stole a kiss. 'Don't apologise.' Then he sighed and traced her lower lip with the pad of his thumb. 'Maybe this is a bad idea. Maybe I should just see you back to your room.'

'Or maybe,' she said, 'this is a good idea.'

His eyes widened. 'Are you suggesting…?'

For a moment, she couldn't breathe. This might be the

most monumentally stupid thing she'd ever done. Or it might be the best idea she'd ever had.

There was only one way to find out.

'Yes. Make love with me, Brandon,' she whispered.

She could feel the tension in his body. 'Are you sure about this?'

Not entirely. But she was tired of being a coward. 'Yes.'

CHAPTER NINE

AFTERWARDS, BRANDON LAY with Angel curled in his arms.

And he was absolutely terrified.

He'd always kept emotional distance between himself and his girlfriends. Always. But he'd let Angel closer than he'd ever let anyone in his life. Told her things he never even discussed with his closest family. He hadn't even sat at Sammy's grave and spilled this kind of stuff, and his brother's grave was the place where he went to spill things. When nobody could hear.

What made him even antsier was that, at the same time, he felt at peace with the world. And it wasn't just the sweet relaxation he usually felt after sex. This was something different. As if something had shifted inside him. As if the empty spaces weren't empty any more.

Was he falling in love with Angel McKenzie?

And what was he going to do about it? Particularly as there was something he and Angel really had to discuss.

OK. Time for a reality check. 'Angel,' he said, stroking her hair. 'We need to talk.'

'Uh-huh.' There was a pause, and then her voice sounded all super-bright. 'Is this where you tell me this was a mistake, it's your fault and not mine, and I need to go back to my own room?'

She hadn't pulled her punches. He dragged in a breath. 'No. Do you really think I'm that cold?'

Her silence confirmed his worst fears.

He sighed. 'The press has a lot to answer for. That's not who I… Well, I admit, I have done that in the past, and it wasn't very gallant of me. But I don't want you to go.'

'So what do you want to talk about?'

'The elephant in the room.'

'What elephant?'

He stole another kiss. 'OK. If you want me to be the one to say it. You just gave me your virginity.'

She blushed. He'd never seen anyone go so red before. 'It's so ridiculous, being a virgin at the age of thirty in this day and age.'

'No, it means…' That it was important to her. And he felt incredibly guilty. How could he explain that without making her feel awkward?

She bit her lip and looked away. 'I'm just not good at relationships. I was too shy to date anyone at school, then somehow everyone at university thought of me as an ice maiden, and I didn't want to be just a challenge that people boasted about conquering.'

'That,' he said, 'shows incredible strength of character. You didn't let anyone push you into doing anything you didn't want to do.'

'So you don't think I'm—well—pathetic? Or there's something wrong with me?'

'What?' He stared at her in utter shock. 'You're kidding. You're not pathetic in the slightest and there's nothing wrong with you.' He dragged in a breath. 'I feel honoured, actually. That you trusted me. And I feel guilty, because if you were saving—'

'—myself for my wedding night?' She cut in. 'I wasn't. And I wasn't using you to get rid of my virginity, either.

I… I could see you were hurting, and I wanted to make you feel better, and…'

'One thing led to another,' he finished.

She lifted her chin. 'I don't regret it, so don't feel guilty.'

'I don't regret it, either.' He stroked her face. 'I talk too much.'

'Agreed. Sometimes it's easier to sweep things under the carpet, but you don't do things the easy way, do you?'

'I probably do. That's why Eric calls me Golden Boy.'

'Eric's bitter,' she said. 'And wasn't King Midas—the original golden boy—lonely, when all he had was gold?'

'You scare me,' he said, 'because you see things that other people miss.'

'Comes of lip-reading,' she said lightly.

'Stay with me tonight,' he said, surprising himself.

'Is this a good idea?'

'Probably not,' he admitted. 'But I don't want you to go.'

'I don't want to go, either,' she said.

'Then let's stop talking and just go to sleep.'

She chuckled.

'What's so funny?' he asked.

'You're the one who said we needed to talk.'

'Sometimes,' he said, 'I'm wrong.'

She laughed. 'I'm glad you can admit that.'

'Me, too.' He kissed her.

He reached over to turn off the bedside light, then moved so that his body was curled round hers and his arm was wrapped round her waist, holding her close against him. Her breathing slowed and she relaxed back against him as she fell asleep, but Brandon stayed awake for longer. This was the first time in years that he'd actually shared a bed with someone and it didn't involve just sex. Why had he asked her to stay? Guilt, because he'd taken her virginity? Or was it that her obvious trust in him had made him relax enough to trust her with himself?

He couldn't quite work out how he felt about Angel McKenzie. What he did know was that she'd changed him. She made him feel as if maybe he had a soft centre after all, instead of a heart of granite wrapped around an empty space. He wasn't sure if that was a good thing or a bad, but for now he'd go with it.

The next morning, Brandon woke first and kissed Angel awake. He was rewarded with confusion in those beautiful violet eyes clearing, and then she gave him a smile of pure unadulterated warmth, as if she was glad to be waking in his arms. Weird that it suddenly made him feel as if he were ten feet tall.

'Good morning,' he said softly.

She stroked his face. 'Good morning.'

'Did you sleep OK?'

'Yes.'

'Good.' He couldn't resist stealing another kiss. 'Do you have to be back home as soon as possible?'

'Do you?'

'No. And as we're in one of the most romantic places in England, I thought it might be nice to go for a walk—oh, and holding my hand is obligatory.'

'Are you always this bossy?' she asked, but her eyes were lit with amusement.

'Pretty much.' He grinned. 'So are you, so this is going to be interesting.'

She bit her lip. 'About last night…'

'I stand by what I said,' he said softly. 'I don't regret a second of it. And I still feel really honoured that you trusted me that much.'

He saw her eyes fill with tears, even though she blinked them away immediately.

'Don't cry,' he said. 'Or was it that bad?'

'No, it was…' She paused, as if not knowing what to say.

'If you tell me I'm like your favourite engine…' he teased.

She laughed. 'Ah, but aren't you meant to do nought to top speed more slowly in this sort of thing?'

He liked the fact that she could laugh at herself, even though he knew she'd felt awkward about her inexperience. He held her close, laughing, and kissed the top of her head. 'Let's have a shower and breakfast, and go for that walk.'

Over breakfast, they pored over his phone and discovered that one of the prettiest sights in the Lakes was only a short drive away. The road, being a narrow single track, was busy and they had to wait at several passing places, but finally they were able to park by Wastwater.

'Oh, now that's definitely worth the wait,' Angel said, gesturing to the way the mountains reflected in the water. 'I can see why it's listed as one of the best views.'

'The deepest lake in England,' he said, referring to a page on his phone. 'And that bit over there is Scafell Pike, England's highest mountain.'

'Don't tell me—you've climbed it?' she asked.

He smiled. 'No. And I don't think we have time to do it today. But maybe we could come back, if you want to climb it?'

'I'm happy just to look at it and admire it,' she said, smiling back.

'OK.' He paused. 'Can we…?' He waved his phone at her.

'Selfie? Sure.'

He took a quick snap of them together. Again, it was

weird: he never did this sort of things with his girlfriends. But with Angel, it felt right.

'Send it to me, please?' she asked.

'Sure.' This was definitely starting to feel official. Even six months ago, that feeling would've sent him running as fast as possible in the opposite direction. But he was actually enjoying this.

He enjoyed the drive back to Cambridge even more, because Angel seemed so much more relaxed with him. This time, he shared the driving with her, and it was so good to talk to her about the car and discuss its pros and cons. Particularly as Angel was talking from an engineer's viewpoint, giving him a completely different perspective.

And he enjoyed the fact that she was comfortable with him looking through the music on her phone and choosing what to play. 'This is really retro stuff,' he said. 'Half of this would go better with the Mermaid.'

'If that's an offer…' she teased.

He grinned. 'Oh, it is. If we pick a time when the weather's good, we can have the roof down and drive along the nearest coast.'

'Oxford's pretty much smack in the middle of the country,' she said. 'And Cambridge is a good ninety minutes from the coast. You'd be looking at Norfolk or Suffolk.'

'Fish and chips, ice cream and candy floss,' he said promptly. 'It's a deal.'

She laughed. 'And a kiss-me-quick hat?'

'I'd prefer you to kiss me slowly,' he said. 'But the coast would be fun.'

'I'd like that,' she said.

'Then it's a date. An open-ended one because it's weather-dependent, but a definite date,' he said. And how weird it felt to be planning things in the future with her. Normally he didn't let people that close. But Angel…

Angel was different. She made him want to do this kind of thing.

When they arrived in Cambridge, she turned to him. 'I would offer to cook you dinner before you go back to Oxford, but, um…'

'You have work to do?'

'It's much more shameful than that,' she said. 'I have an empty fridge. And I'm not much of a cook anyway. I normally get in a stack of ready meals from the supermarket to keep me going during the week, but I forgot to go shopping on Friday night.'

'Well, I'm not leaving you here with an empty fridge,' he said. 'The supermarkets are all closed by now, so either we find a nice little pub somewhere or we get a takeaway.'

'Either's fine.' She paused. 'I've got milk.'

'Milk?' He wasn't quite following her line of thought.

'I normally have a protein shake for breakfast before the gym,' she said. 'But the baker round the corner opens really early in the morning. They do the best croissants in Cambridge.'

He caught his breath. 'Are you asking me to stay for breakfast?'

'Inviting you, yes.' She gave him the shyest, cutest smile. 'If you want to.'

Oh, he wanted to. He smiled. 'Provided you let me do the washing up.'

'I thought you said you had troglodyte tendencies?'

'I'm domesticated. To a point.' Though it spooked him slightly how domesticated he wanted to be with her. He could imagine waking up with her on Sunday mornings, lazing in bed with coffee and the papers and a bacon sandwich.

Her little Victorian terraced house turned out to be totally what he'd expected: neat, with everything in its place. There were family photographs everywhere, and arty black and white prints of close-up details from classic cars. And it felt way more like home than his own, much larger house. Personal. Full of warmth.

Then again, it was his own fault for using an interior designer instead of spending the time to make his house feel like a personal space.

Just as she'd promised, the croissants at breakfast were superb. And leaving her after he'd insisted on doing the washing up after breakfast turned out to be a real wrench. He actually missed her all the way to Oxford, and the only time the ache went was when he threw himself into work.

A few unexpected glitches meant that he didn't have time to meet up with Angel during the week, even if they'd driven to a halfway point. And he was shocked by how much he missed her and wanted to be with her.

Dating her had been supposed to be a way of getting her out of his system and persuading her to sell McKenzie's to him, but it hadn't worked out that way. If anything, he wanted to spend more time with her. The sensible side of him knew that he ought to back off right now, before he got in too deeply.

But then he found himself video-calling her.

'Hey,' she said, and smiled at him.

Oh, man. He'd never understood before when people said that someone made their heart flip. Now he did. Angel's smile did exactly that. 'How are you doing?' he asked.

She laughed. 'Say that for me again, but this time in a Joey Tribbiani voice.'

'*Friends* fan, hmm?'

'Joey's the best. Indulge me.'

He grinned and did what she asked.

'Be still, my beating heart.' She fanned herself.

Brandon almost told her how cute she looked, but stopped himself just in time.

'So how are things?' she asked.

'Wall-to-wall meetings.' Some of them with staff who'd had a spat with Eric and needed their feathers unruffled, which drove him crazy. 'How about you?'

'Similar.'

He wasn't going to tell her he missed her.

He *wasn't.*

'Can I see you at the weekend?' He cringed inwardly as the words came out of his mouth. How needy was that?

But she went pink. 'OK.'

'Come to me?' he suggested. 'If you stay overnight Saturday, I'll cook dinner for you.'

'You cook?' She looked surprised. And then she gave him the cheekiest grin. 'Wait. I forgot. You're good at *everything.*'

The breathy little way she said that sent desire lancing straight through him. 'Nearly,' he said. Right now he didn't seem to be very good at keeping his feelings under control. And his voice had gone all husky. He really hoped she hadn't noticed—or, if she had, that she hadn't guessed why.

'I'll be with you at nine,' she promised. 'Send me your postcode for my satnav.'

'I will.' He stopped himself telling her that he missed her. 'See you on Saturday.'

'How does it go?' She wrinkled her nose at him. 'Ah, yes. *Ciao.*'

No. Just no. He was *not* supposed to find it super-cute that she was teasing him about the ridiculously corny way he'd once said goodbye to her. Or want to drop everything and drive for two hours plus whatever hold-ups he encountered on the motorway just to kiss her goodnight.

'Ciao,' he drawled, and cut the connection.

* * *

On Saturday morning, Angel drove to Oxford, tingling with anticipation. Would Brandon have changed his mind about their relationship by the time she got there? Because she was pretty sure the women he reportedly saw only lasted three dates, and they'd already gone beyond that. Was he even now rehearsing a speech? *It's not you, it's me...*

But all her doubts melted when she parked on the gravel outside his unexpectedly large house and he walked out of the front door to greet her. The warmth of his kiss told her that he hadn't been rehearsing any speeches at all—and that he'd missed her as much as she'd missed him.

Not that she was going to bring that up. Brandon Stone wasn't the kind of man who liked talking about emotions, and she didn't want to make things awkward between them. And she definitely wasn't going to tell him that she was falling for him. She knew it'd make him run a mile.

'Hey.' She stole another kiss. 'Flashy house, Mr Stone. Are you sure you're not a secret rock star?'

He laughed. 'No. You'll probably find the garage more interesting than the house.'

'Garage? That looks more like an aircraft hangar,' she teased.

'Yeah, yeah.' But he grinned and held her close.

'So do I get to see your collection?'

'Later,' he said. 'And I'm not fobbing you off—I'm looking forward to showing you.' He stole another kiss. 'It's your fault you have to wait.'

'How?' she asked.

'Because,' he said, 'you've given me back the joy I used to find in racing cars. I lost it for a while.'

Since his brother's death, she guessed.

'One of the local stately homes is having an open

day—usually they're not open to the public, but today it's a charity thing to show off their garden. And there just so happens to be a vintage car rally in their deer park. I thought you might like to go.'

'Great idea. I take it we're going in the Mermaid?'

'We are. Want to drive?'

'Stupid question,' she said, and kissed him.

Once he'd taken her bag inside and locked up the house, he handed her the car keys. 'I'll direct you,' he said.

Angel thoroughly enjoyed driving the car—and she enjoyed being with Brandon even more. The stately home's garden turned out to be amazing, full of cottage garden plants with butterflies and bees everywhere and a secret garden full of roses. She loved wandering round, hand in hand with Brandon—particularly when he managed to find several hidden alcoves where he could steal a kiss in private.

The vintage car rally was fabulous, too, and they had a wonderful time arguing over the merits of their favourites and trying to convince each other to change their mind.

'You know, the red car on the end there,' Brandon said, 'has been used in a film.'

Cars and films. Angel went cold for a moment. Was this his way of telling her that he knew about Triffid and the Frost? Triffid's PR team had put her in touch with several magazines for features, but they'd all been thoroughly screened and there was an embargo in place. Then again, no matter how careful you were, there were always leaks. News like that would filter through pretty quickly to fellow car manufacturers. Maybe that was how he knew.

But then he turned the conversation to something else, and it didn't feel like quite the right time to tell him about why she didn't need to sell McKenzie's to him.

Back at his house, Brandon proved that his flashy

kitchen wasn't all for show. He produced grilled bream, crushed new potatoes with mint and butter, and steamed asparagus and samphire, all beautifully presented.

'That was utterly gorgeous,' she said when she'd finished. 'If I hadn't been sitting at your kitchen table and seen you cooking this from scratch, I would've guessed that you'd hired a caterer.'

'I did cheat by buying the cheesecake,' he admitted. 'I'm rubbish at puddings.'

'Tsk—and I thought you were good at everything,' she teased.

'Just for that,' he said, 'you can wait for your pudding until you agree that I am.' And he hauled her over his shoulder and carried her off to his bed.

Back in Cambridge, Angel called her parents. 'Hey. So how's Florence?' she asked.

'Wonderful. Is everything OK with you?' Max asked.

'Yes. And you don't need to worry about the business. Everything's fine.'

'Of course it is, with my girl in charge.' She could practically hear the smile in her father's voice. 'But you sound a bit worried.'

'I, um… This might be a bit of a Romeo and Juliet moment.'

'We're in Florence, not Verona,' her father teased.

'I'm, um, seeing someone.' She swallowed hard. 'Brandon Stone.'

'Larry Stone's son?' Max asked, sounding shocked.

'Is it a problem for you, Dad?'

He blew out a breath. 'Actually, love, it is. The Stones are a ruthless bunch. I remember Mum saying once that she chose Dad over Barnaby, because Dad was kind and

Barnaby was driven. Barnaby's sons and his grandsons are chips off the old block—and I don't want you to get hurt.'

'I'm thirty, Dad.'

'I know. But you're my daughter, and I worry about you. If you really have to date the guy, date him. But be careful.' He paused. 'And if he hurts you, he'll have me to deal with.'

'Dad, it's not going to be like that. But thank you for—well, doing what dads do.'

'I meant it,' Max said softly. 'If he hurts you…'

'He won't. He's actually a decent guy.'

'Who's photographed with a different woman on his arm every week.'

'That's the press blowing stuff out of proportion, Dad,' she said softly.

Max sighed. 'All right. You're old enough to know what you're doing. But please be careful,' he said again.

She didn't exactly have her father's blessing, but she didn't quite have his opposition, either, Angel thought. He might have a point about her needing to be careful. She liked spending time with Brandon, but their families were at loggerheads. And Brandon himself had told her that he was about to start developing cars that would be in direct competition with hers. He could afford to drop his prices enough to undercut hers and torpedo her sales.

But she didn't think he'd do that. Brandon had integrity. She'd trusted him with herself, and he hadn't let her down. So could she trust him enough to talk to him about her business—to share the new design with him? It was a risk: it would mean breaking confidentiality, giving him what could be a business advantage. But he wasn't the ruthless, selfish playboy she'd originally thought he was. He had a heart—one that had been broken—and he kept people at a distance to protect himself. Yet he'd trusted her enough to let her close. Maybe she should do the same. She thought about it all week.

And thought about it some more over the next weekend, when Brandon swept her off to the coast in the Mermaid so they could walk hand in hand by the edge of the sea.

The way she felt when she was with him—it was like nothing else she'd ever experienced.

Love?

Maybe. But she'd spent so long struggling on her own, trying to keep everything together and yet unable to talk to her parents about the problems because she was trying to protect them and let them enjoy their retirement. Just for once it would be good to lean on someone, share her worries—and share the joy, too.

He'd said she'd given him back the joy he'd once found in cars. And she'd really value his opinion of the Frost. Maybe it was time to trust him back.

'Can we call in to the factory?' she asked on the way back to her house.

'Sure. Is there something you need to do for work?'

'No. There's something I want to show you.'

He gave her a sidelong look. 'Such as?'

'You'll see when we get there.'

'Should I be worried?'

She smiled. 'No.' But her own fears were back. Was she taking too much of a risk?

As if he guessed that she was warring with herself mentally, he didn't push her to talk further until they got to the factory and she took him into the partitioned-off area.

'This is confidential,' she warned. 'Strictly confidential.'

'Got it. So what did you want to show me?'

'This,' she said, and whisked the tarpaulin off her prototype.

'Oh.' He prowled round it, clearly analysing it and inspecting every little detail. And then he straightened up. 'I'm assuming the design is all yours?'

'And I helped put it together. The engine's all mine,' she said.

'It's *stunning*,' he said. 'May I?' His hand hovered above the bonnet.

She nodded, and he ran his fingers lightly over the paintwork. 'I love the lines of it. And I've never seen a colour like this. Did you use one of your granddad's paint techniques—something from the Mermaid years?'

'No. I wanted the car to be shimmery, like the Mermaid, but I wanted the effect to be otherworldly rather than undersea,' she said. 'It's plain ivory paint.'

'No way is that just ivory,' he said.

'With a little bit of silver pearlescence—I wanted it to be like the moonlight glittering on grass on a winter night.' She paused. 'It's called the McKenzie Frost.'

'And that colour's perfect for the name.' He indicated the door. 'Can I sit in it?'

'Sure.'

He climbed inside, and again there was silence while he looked at the interior.

And then he leaned over and opened the passenger door.

'I want one,' he said simply.

Then she realised how tense her muscles had been while she'd waited for his verdict. 'You like it?'

'More than like it,' he corrected. 'And I want one in my private collection.'

'Technically, it doesn't exist. This is the prototype. It's had a couple of photo shoots, but the world hasn't seen it yet,' she warned.

'Then put me at the head of your pre-order list because I mean it—I really, really want one. And I don't care how much it costs.'

She smiled. 'Are you telling me to overcharge you?'

'No. I'm telling you I want the first production model and I'm prepared to pay a premium for it.'

He was serious. She could see it in his eyes. And it made her heart sing. 'I can't do that, I'm afraid. The first five are already taken.'

'I thought you said you didn't have a pre-order list?'

'I designed this for a specific customer,' she said. 'Triffid Studios.'

'The movie company?'

She nodded. 'It's going to be in the next *Spyline* movie. The deal is they have exclusive use until next summer. But I'll be taking pre-orders when it's announced formally, in about six weeks.'

'I see why you said it's confidential.' He paused. 'And you trust me?'

'Considering our family history, I ought to say no,' she admitted. 'But, yes. I trust you.' The man she'd got to know over the last few weeks was honourable and decent.

'Thank you. I'll respect your confidentiality.' He ran his hands over the steering wheel. 'You know you said you wanted to produce the iconic design of our generation?'

'Uh-huh.'

'I thought it might be the car you started sketching in the tea shop.' *Their* car. 'But you've already done it with this.'

She felt her eyes film with tears. He really thought that highly of her design? 'You're not just flattering me?'

'I'm never more serious than when I'm talking about cars,' he said, and rubbed the steering wheel again. 'I probably shouldn't ask this, and I promise I'm not pressuring you… But I'm dying to know how it handles. Can I drive it?'

'It's a prototype, so it's not perfect,' she warned. 'There are a few things I want to iron out for when it goes into production.'

'Noted, and I'll keep the speed low,' he promised. 'Come with me?'

'Sure. I'll open the doors and you can take it round the track.'

As he'd promised, Brandon drove the Frost carefully, then returned it equally carefully through the hangar doors into its spot in the factory.

'I love the design,' he said. 'But you're right—there are a couple of things that need ironing out, and I think it could be improved from a driving point of view.'

'Tell me.'

He began to list them, and Angel said, 'Hang on a tick.' She grabbed her phone and tapped into the notes section. 'OK. Start again, please.'

He nodded, and went through his thoughts.

'Thank you,' she said when he'd finished. 'I did this as speech to text and it sometimes gets things wrong, so can I send you the text file to review?'

'Of course you can. And if I think of anything else I'll add it to the list.' He raised an eyebrow. 'Our grandfathers would never believe it. A McKenzie listening to a Stone.'

'An engineer listening to a professional driver,' she corrected.

'The same as when you started sketching the car I was talking about and pointed out the aerodynamic issues—that was a driver listening to an engineer.'

'No, it was a Stone listening to a McKenzie,' she teased.

He laughed. 'This is just you and me—and thank you so much for sharing this with me. It's amazing.'

'It's the reason why I don't have to sell the company,' she said. 'I couldn't tell you before. But I'm sorry. McKenzie's really isn't for sale.'

'I understand.' He looked sad. 'And with you putting this in production, you're really not going to have time to do some freelance stuff and work with me on our joint car. That's a pity, because I really would've liked working with you.'

'And I with you,' she said, 'Though I don't think I could work with your uncle.'

'Not many people can,' he said with a grimace, 'but I'm going to have to put up with him until he decides he wants to retire. He's too old to change the way he acts in business, and I'm not going to humiliate him by making him jump before he's pushed. But, just so you know, I wouldn't have let him anywhere near your team if I'd bought you out.'

'I'm glad to hear it,' she said dryly. 'And I'm also glad you don't have to buy me out.'

'The Frost,' he said, 'is beautiful. You're amazing. I'm so proud of you.' His grey eyes were completely sincere, and Angel's heart felt as if it had performed a somersault. 'And I mean it about wanting one when it goes into production properly. I want to be top of your list.'

'You've got it,' she said softly. And she was starting to think that he was top of her list in a lot of other ways, too. If she wasn't careful, she could lose her heart to Brandon Stone.

But would that be such a bad thing?

When Brandon drove back to Oxford on Sunday evening, he made a slight detour via the churchyard in the village. He didn't bother taking flowers, because he knew that between them his mother and Maria always had that covered, but he sat down in front of his brother's grave.

'Hey, Sammy,' he said softly. 'My original Plan A isn't going to work, because McKenzie's isn't for sale. But I think I might just have something even better.' He smiled. 'It's all about a girl. But this one's special. I really like her, Sammy, and I think she might like me back.' In a way he'd never expected, and never experienced before. 'Remember when I used to tease you about being all soppy over Maria? I think I could be like that about Angel McKenzie. No, actually, I think I already might be. Dating her was supposed to get her out of my system, but it's done nothing of the kind. I wanted to charm her into selling to me—but now I just want her to be with me.'

And he could really do with a bit of advice from his brother right now. Not that he'd get it. But he could at least talk to Sam, even if Sam couldn't talk back.

'You're the one person I could talk to about this,' he said. 'I think I might actually be in love. For the first time ever. And it makes me feel as if I don't have a clue what I'm doing. I've always been in control and I've always been able to walk away. But Angel… She's different. I want to be with her. I want to end this stupid feud between our family and hers, and I want a future with her smack in the centre of it.' He gave a wry smile.

'I can't imagine getting married without you as my best man. But until I met Angel I couldn't imagine getting married at all. I haven't asked her. She might even say no. But I think finally I know who I want to be, thanks to her. It's as if I've found my way back out of a black hole. And I'm a better man when I'm with her.' There was just one sticking point. 'Let's just hope we can talk the Montagues and Capulets round.'

CHAPTER TEN

ON FRIDAY AFTERNOON, Brandon arrived to drive Angel to London for the ball. He kept the conversation light, but Angel felt her nervousness growing as they neared the city.

The hotel was seriously posh: it actually had a doorman who wore a top hat and tails. Inside, there was an amazing marble staircase, and all the decor was rich greens and golds.

Parties were the things she hated most. Where people made small talk and she couldn't always pick it up because there was so much background noise and the lighting wasn't good enough to let her lip-read. Conferences, presentations, lectures and interviews were fine. Parties were the seventh circle of hell; if she couldn't fall back on her usual strategy of talking cars, she knew she'd struggle.

Brandon had clearly guessed what was worrying her, because he paused outside the door to her room. 'We don't have to do this, you know,' he said. 'We can skip it and do something else. Go to the theatre. The cinema. Just for a walk along the river. Anything you like.'

'No. You won the bet, and I agreed to go with you. I'm not reneging on that,' she said. 'And people will expect to see you there.'

'I know parties are difficult for you,' he said. 'Look, when you've had enough, let me know and we'll escape.

And I'm staying right by your side tonight—just squeeze my hand or arm twice if you think you've missed something and you need me to rescue you.'

Angel felt close to tears. She really hadn't expected Brandon to be this thoughtful. 'Thanks.'

'Let's get ready,' he said. 'And there's no pressure. Any time you want to leave, we leave.'

'OK.' She took a deep breath. She could be brave about this. She *would* be brave about this.

The room was stunning, with views over the River Thames; she could see the London Eye and the South Bank. Even though the building was very old, the room itself felt completely modern.

She'd just finished changing when he knocked on her door.

His jaw dropped when he saw her. 'Wow. You look stunning.'

Her dress was dark red and A-line, with a skirt that flared out to just below her knees, a sweetheart off-the-shoulder neckline and lacy sleeves that went down to her elbows; she'd teamed it with dark red patent high heels. Angel had spent hours online, trying to find the perfect dress; thankfully, it looked as if it had been worth the effort. 'Thanks. You look pretty amazing, too. The outfit really suited him: a dinner jacket, slim-fitting dark trousers, a crisp white shirt and a black bow tie.

'Sorry—I didn't mean to sound shallow. It's just I've never seen you dressed up like this before.' He smiled. 'I think a lot of people are going to want to dance with you tonight.'

'I hope they're wearing steel-capped shoes, then, or they're going to get bruises.'

He grinned. 'Good.' Then he frowned. 'Hang on, are you telling me you can't dance?'

'I've never really had any cause to,' she admitted.

'All right.' He stood in front of her. 'Let me show you the ballroom hold.' He put her left hand on his right shoulder, and supported her arm with his right arm; then he took her right hand and lifted it up. 'Just follow my lead and it'll be fine.' And, to her surprise, he danced down the corridor with her.

'I feel a bit like Cinderella,' she said.

'My very shy Cinderella.' He stole a kiss. 'Except there aren't going to be any pumpkins at midnight. And you're not going to lose a shoe.'

'I hope not.' She forced herself to smile.

Together they went into the ballroom where the gala dinner was being held. The tables were all laid with snowy white linen and decorated with beautiful arrangements of white flowers; the room itself was incredibly glamorous, with pillars around the edges, floor-to-ceiling windows with heavy velvet drapes, and metalwork chandeliers with delicate glass shades.

And the background noise, particularly when it was amplified by the wooden floor, was horrendous.

'Twice for help,' he said, making sure that she could see his mouth.

Dreading it, she nodded.

Brandon seemed to know just about everyone in the room—well, of course he would, because a lot of them came from the motor racing world. Angel noticed that a lot of the women were staring at them, and a tight knot of nerves formed in her stomach. She wasn't the best at small talk. Hopefully she could get people talking about themselves and it would take the spotlight off her.

She was relieved when Brandon introduced her to a couple of the other drivers, and they started talking about engines and aerodynamics. At least this was a subject she felt comfortable with. And although the other drivers looked surprised at first, they were soon chatting to her as if she was one of them.

Dinner was slightly more difficult, because Angel was placed opposite Brandon rather than next to him. The man sitting on her left had a beard and she really couldn't work out what he was saying, half the time, but she hoped that she was nodding and smiling in all the right places.

Finally it was time for the dancing. Just as Brandon had promised, he stayed with her the whole time, not letting anyone else dance with her. She followed his lead, as he'd directed, and was shocked to find that not only did she feel as if she could dance, she was actually enjoying it. The way he whirled her round the floor made her feel like a princess.

'Midnight,' Brandon said against her ear. 'And not a pumpkin or a glass slipper in sight. Want to stay a bit longer, or do you want to escape?'

'Both,' she admitted. 'I want to dance with you.' And she wanted to be alone with him, too, though it felt a bit pushy to say so.

He laughed. 'One more dance,' he said, and stole a kiss.

And then finally they slipped away together.

'Stay with me tonight?' he asked as they stood outside the doors to their rooms.

How could she resist her very own Prince Charming? She smiled. 'Yes.'

The next morning, Angel woke early. Brandon was sprawled out, still asleep, and she smiled. It was tempting to wake him; but she could really do with a swim and he looked as if he could do with catching up on his sleep.

She managed to climb out of bed without waking him, then scribbled him a quick note and left it on her pillow.

Gone for a swim. See you in the pool or next door.

Then she put on enough clothes to make her decent, tiptoed out of his room, and went next door to her own room to change into her swimming things.

When she dropped her bag on her bed, her phone fell out; she could see that she had several voicemails. She'd kept her phone on silent during the ball and had forgotten to switch the ringer on again afterwards, so she'd clearly missed a call.

Worried that it might be her parents, and something was wrong, she listened to the messages.

But they weren't from her parents.

They were from the legal team at Triffid. Half a dozen of them asking her to call them urgently, and then a longer one which she had to listen to twice before she could make sense of it.

'Miss McKenzie, you should have told us about the takeover. We made the contract with you, not with Stone's. You've also broken the contract terms by breaking the embargo. You've made it clear that the deal's off and we'll have to go with another manufacturer. We may have to look at compensation if it holds up the film.'

Compensation? What? Were they talking about suing her? She stared at her phone in horror. What takeover? And what did they mean about breaking the embargo? Was there something about the Frost in the news?

She flicked into her favourite news site to see if she could find out what had happened and saw the headline straight away: *Racing Champ's Successful Takeover.*

According to the lead paragraph, Brandon Stone was buying McKenzie's. There was a picture of them together from last night, at the ball; she was looking all gooey-eyed at him, and he looked like a predator.

She stared at it, totally shocked. Where had the story come from? The small print talked about 'sources close to the company'; did that mean Brandon himself? Had last night simply been a set-up?

Angel didn't want to believe it. She knew she'd got his motivations completely wrong before, when he'd taken her to Cumbria, and she'd learned from that not to jump to conclusions. Her father had warned her that he was as ruthless as the rest of his family, but the Brandon she'd got to know was one of the good guys. He wouldn't betray her like that.

But the final paragraph was the killer. It talked about the new car. The Frost. It even mentioned the iridescent shimmery ivory paint: a detail that hardly anyone knew. Nobody at McKenzie's would've said a single thing about the Triffid deal: her staff had always been incredibly loyal and they'd worked as hard as she had on the Frost.

She dragged in a breath. The evidence was all in the article. No matter how much she didn't want to believe it, everything pointed to Brandon being the source. And, thanks to his deliberate leak, she'd lost the contract with Triffid. All the work she'd done, the hours she'd put in and the worrying, had been for nothing.

McKenzie's was going to the wall.

He'd ruined her company.

Sick to her stomach, she didn't bother going for a swim. She simply showered, dressed and packed. And then, filled with anger, she went to bang on Brandon's door and confront him.

Brandon woke with a jolt, hearing a banging noise. For a moment, he was disorientated. Where was Angel? She'd fallen asleep in his arms last night. But the bed was empty and the bathroom door was wide open.

Then he realised that someone was still banging on his door. 'Coming, coming,' he mumbled, and grabbed a towel to cover himself.

When he opened the door, Angel stood there, looking ragingly angry. He frowned. 'Angel? What's the matter?'

'What's the matter? You know perfectly well what the matter is.' She thrust her phone at him. 'Look at this. Are you proud of yourself?'

His frown deepened as he saw the headline: *Racing Champ's Successful Takeover.*

'What? I don't understand.'

'Don't play cute with me—it says "sources at the company" told them that Stone's is taking over McKenzie's. They're not going to be stupid enough to print something like this without your agreement, because they know if it's not true they'll end up with a court ordering them to pay damages.' She dragged in a breath. 'And it talks about the Frost. In detail. You're the only one outside McKenzie's and Triffid who knew about it.' Her lip curled. 'You're a player, and I've been incredibly stupid.'

What? But he hadn't talked to the press. At all. He had no idea where this was coming from. 'Angel, I—'

'Save it. I don't want to hear any excuses. I'm making my own way home—and I don't want to see you again. Ever. But I suggest you contact your precious sources at the paper and get this story corrected, or you'll be hearing from my lawyers.' She lifted her chin. 'And if I can't talk Triffid out of dumping the Frost and McKenzie's, you'll be hearing from my lawyers anyway. Because doing something this underhand *has* to be against the law.'

'Angel—' he tried again.

'Goodbye, Brandon,' she said, and walked off.

He grabbed some clothes, but by the time he'd pulled

them on she was nowhere to be seen. It was pointless trying to follow her.

He dragged a hand through his hair and tried to focus. What did he do now?

First things first, he needed to look at the news report properly so he knew exactly what he was working with. And as he worked his way through it, he groaned. She was right. It did claim that the source was someone at Stone's—and she was also right that the paper wouldn't have printed that if it wasn't true. The media had to be careful about defamation law.

But how the hell had the press got the information about the Frost? He hadn't said a thing to anyone except Angel herself.

He pushed away the fact how hurt he was that she thought he could do something like this to her. The emotional stuff could come later. First, he needed to fix this.

Who at Stone's would break a story like this? Who had leaked the news about the Frost?

He had one nasty thought about the person at Stone's—but no, surely…

There was only one way to find out. He rang the newspaper. After being put through to four different people, eventually he got the answer he'd been dreading. Which left him no choice but to act.

And this wasn't something he could do by phone.

He desperately wanted to see Angel and sort things out between them, but he needed to fix things before he talked to her. He showered swiftly, changed, checked out of the hotel without bothering with breakfast and drove back to Oxford.

Finally, he pulled up outside his uncle's house and rang the doorbell.

'Oh. You,' Eric said when he opened the door, not even looking surprised to see Brandon.

'Yes, me. We need to sit down and talk.'

Eric scoffed. 'You're not even going to thank me for doing your job for you?'

'Doing my…?' Brandon looked at him in disbelief. 'You didn't do my job, Eric. What you did was to cause a huge amount of trouble. It was unprofessional, underhand and unacceptable. That's not how we do things at Stone's.'

'Rubbish. You were dragging your feet about the take-over. We all knew what the outcome was going to be, but you weren't man enough to seal the deal. So someone had to give her a push.'

'You didn't give her a push. She wasn't selling.' Much as Brandon wanted to shake his uncle until his teeth rattled, violence wouldn't make anything better. 'How did you get the information about the Frost?'

Eric shrugged. 'If you will leave your PC on with your mail program up, you can expect people to read it.'

Brandon stared at him, hardly able to believe what he was hearing. 'What? You went into my office and snooped?'

'It's something that affected Stone's, and I'm on the management team. I had a right to know.'

So that was what this was about. Brandon gritted his teeth. 'Eric, I know you're angry that I'm in charge, but this has to stop. Now. I don't want you in the factory any more.'

'Are you trying to sack me? You can't,' Eric sneered.

'Actually, as the CEO of Stone's, I could sack you for gross misconduct,' Brandon said. 'I've put up with you sniping at me for years, because you're my uncle and I've been trying to cut you some slack, but this isn't healthy for anyone, And, by telling the press we're going to take over McKenzie's when we're not doing anything of the kind, you've damaged both our companies. She could sue us for misrepresentation—and more, if her business goes under.'

Eric flapped a dismissive hand. 'She's a McKenzie, so who cares if her business goes under?'

'*I* care,' Brandon said.

'Because you've got the hots for her.'

'I'm not discussing my private life. I'm discussing the business.' He raked a hand through his hair. 'Eric, you need to retire.'

'Jump before I'm pushed, you mean?'

'You're not happy in the company.'

'Are you surprised, with you walking in and taking the place I should've had?' he snarled.

'But,' Brandon said, 'I'm making a success of it. If I was making a total mess of things, then you'd have every right to be fed up with me. But I'm not making a mess of things. I've got a vision for our company. And you're working against me rather than with me. It's not helping either of us.'

'But I've worked there all my life.'

'Maybe,' Brandon said, 'it's time for you to find out what actually makes you happy. Even before I took over from Dad, you weren't happy.'

Eric said nothing.

'I don't want to sack you. But surely you can see this isn't working.'

'So you want me to jump before I'm pushed,' Eric said again.

Brandon sighed. 'Eric, I need my team to work with me. You're clearly not prepared to do that. What other option do I have?'

'Let me take over—as I should've done when your father retired,' Eric said, his face suffused with anger and resentment.

'I'm a second son, too,' Brandon said softly. 'If Sam hadn't been killed—'

'If Sam hadn't been forced to race because you'd just had to show off on the ski slopes and broke a rib,' Eric cut in.

'I have to live with that every single day,' Brandon said. 'But, as I was trying to say, if Sam hadn't been killed, I would've been happy to work with him here in whatever capacity he wanted me. Or I might've chosen to go and set up my own business, find my own way. Maybe it would've made you happier if you'd done that.'

Eric said nothing,

'Why do you hate the McKenzies so much?' That was the thing Brandon really couldn't understand.

'Because of Esther,' Eric said, 'and Angel McKenzie is the spit of her grandmother.'

Brandon sighed. 'Two men fell in love with the same woman. She chose one of them. It was seventy years ago. Don't you think it's way past time we moved on from that?'

'Barnaby was my father,' Eric said, 'and I spent my childhood seeing how miserable my mother was because she never matched up to Esther in his eyes. It was why she used to drink. Why she died when I was five.'

Brandon knew his grandmother had died young, but he hadn't realised she'd had a drinking problem that had led to her death. 'That's really sad for both of them,' he said, 'and I'm sorry I never actually knew my grandmother. But don't you think it's Granddad's fault rather than Esther's that Alice drank? Plus my father's five years older than you and he saw it all, too, but he's not bitter towards the McKenzies.' Or was he? Was that why he'd tried to buy McKenzie's in the last recession?

'You'll never understand,' Eric said.

'No, because thankfully my parents were happy together.' Though Brandon could understand now why Eric had never married, with his parents as such an unhappy example. Brandon's father, being slightly older, had maybe seen happier times that had prompted him to get married, but he'd also obviously decided that he didn't want his son's childhood to be as miserable as his own had been. Even though Larry had followed in his father's footsteps as a ruthless workaholic.

'I'm sorry you suffered, Eric, and I'm sorry my grandmother suffered, but it doesn't excuse what you've done to Angel McKenzie. She worked really hard on designing a car that was going to be used in a movie—the car that would make everything all right again at McKenzie's. The car's amazing.'

'So you've actually seen it?'

'Yes. She trusted me enough to let me see the prototype. I let her down because I was stupid enough to think that nobody at Stone's would go and snoop on my computer and then use private emails against someone who's totally blameless. And I hate to think that this family feud is going to fester and ruin things for this generation, too.'

'But they're McK—'

'They're *people*. Like you and me,' Brandon cut in. 'I understand now why you did what you did, but it's *wrong*, Eric. And hurting other people isn't going to change what happened in the past.'

'Nothing's going to change the past.'

'I know. But we can learn from the past and change the future,' Brandon said. 'Which is what I'm going to try to do. And I'd like you to do the right thing and retire right this very second—and get some counselling, which I will pay for personally.'

Eric lifted his chin. 'And if I don't?'

'Then,' Brandon said, 'I'll sack you for gross misconduct. And I'll face up to all the consequences of that, though I'm pretty sure Dad will agree with me. But whether you retire or I have to sack you, I want you to get counselling. You can't keep living with this kind of misery, Eric, and you can't keep making other people's life hell just because you're miserable. It doesn't help you and it doesn't help anyone else.'

'I…' The fight suddenly went out of Eric and his shoulders slumped. 'So you're taking a McKenzie's side against me. So much for blood being thicker than water.'

Brandon's patience was close to snapping, but he thought of Angel. How would she deal with this? Kindly, he'd guess. 'I'm trying to do the right thing,' Brandon said. 'And I really have to ring LA now and grovel my head off to see if I can fix this for Angel and persuade the film company not to cancel the contract. Because she really, really doesn't deserve what you did to her.'

'But I've got stuff at the factory.'

'Then I'll pack it up for you and bring it to you.'

'Scared I'm going to do something like burn the factory down?' Eric sneered.

'I sincerely hope you wouldn't,' Brandon said. 'But, actually, I'm trying to spare you any embarrassment or pain.'

'Bossing me around, like the jumped-up little—'

'Eric, this isn't good for you,' Brandon cut in. 'You need to let it go. And you need help.'

'I don't need anything from you.'

'If that's what you think, fine, but I need something from you before I go. Your keys to the factory.' He held his hand out.

'But—'

'You don't work there any more—you've retired,' Brandon said.

Eric suddenly crumpled. 'What am I going to do with my life now?'

'Make it happier,' Brandon said softly.

Finally, Eric handed over the keys. He looked as if he'd aged two decades in as many minutes. It made Brandon feel guilty, but he knew he was doing the right thing. Something he probably should've done years ago.

'Thank you,' Brandon said. Once he was back in his car, he called his father and filled him in on what had just happened. 'I don't think Eric should be alone right now,' he finished.

'I'll come over and see him. You did the right thing,' Larry Stone said. 'I'm sorry you had to deal with this, Bran. I should've done more when we were kids or realised how unhappy he was.'

'Dad, you were a kid yourself.' He paused. 'Would you have a problem with me seeing Angel McKenzie? After the way your dad was with your mum, I mean?'

'Because of Esther?' Larry paused. 'If you'd asked me that a few years ago, I might've said yes. But losing Sammy taught me a hard lesson. Love's always more important than business. So if that's how you feel about her, follow your heart. Go after her. Don't let business get in the way.'

'Thanks, Dad. I'm glad we're not going to have to do a Romeo and Juliet.' Brandon took a deep breath. 'You'll like her. She's bright and she's sweet. And her designs are amazing.'

'Gina likes her. That's good enough for your mother. And what's good enough for your mother is good enough for me,' Larry said. 'So what are you going to do?'

'Hope that I can fix things—and then that she'll talk to me.'

'Good luck. And we're behind you all the way,' Larry

said. 'I know you've got this, but call me if you need anything.'

'Thanks, Dad.' Brandon appreciated the support.

His next call was to Triffid's legal team. 'My name's Brandon Stone, and we need to talk,' he said.

'We're not looking to do business with you, Mr Stone,' the lawyer said.

'No, but you've been dealing with McKenzie's and you're under the misapprehension that my company's taking hers over. We're not. And Angel had nothing to do with any of those leaks about the Frost. I'm getting a correction printed in the news.'

'What does that have to do with us?' the lawyer asked.

'That car's amazing. It'll be perfect for your film. And you'd be shooting yourself in the foot if you tried to get someone else to design you a car even half as good. Angel McKenzie is the best designer I've ever met, and she's got guts and integrity.'

'That's as may be, Mr Stone.'

'Think of the time and cost implications,' Brandon said. The bottom line was usually the one that worked in business. 'Your PR team could spin this so everyone wins. And I have some ideas that might interest you.'

'Go on,' the lawyer said.

It took another half hour, but finally the lawyer agreed to talk to his people and reinstate the contract.

Which left Brandon one last thing: to face Angel and persuade her to listen to him.

He tried ringing her, but he wasn't surprised that she refused to pick up. He left her a message: 'Angel, we need to talk. I understand why you're angry with me but things really aren't what they seem. I'm coming to find you so we can talk—and I'm not taking no for an answer.'

Where was she likely to be?

His guess was that she'd be at the factory, looking through her books and trying to work out where she could go next—which was just what he'd be doing in her shoes.

Grimly, he headed for the motorway. If he'd got it wrong and she wasn't at the factory, then he'd drive to her house and sit on her doorstep until she came home; and if that meant staying there all night then he'd do it.

Because he wanted a future with Angel.

The only thing that might work was if he opened his heart and told her everything.

And he'd just have to hope that she'd listen.

CHAPTER ELEVEN

WHEN BRANDON PULLED up at the factory, he could see Angel's Luna in the car park. So she was here: now all he had to do was persuade her to talk to him.

He pressed the intercom switch at the barrier to the car park.

'Hello?' a voice crackled.

'Hello—is that Security?' he asked.

'Yes.'

'Great. I've got a meeting with Ms McKenzie. Can you lift the barrier and let me in, please?'

'I'm afraid Ms McKenzie isn't here, Mr Stone.'

Uh-oh. He'd been careful not to mention his name, but Angel's security team knew who he was. So obviously she'd given them a description of him or his car, and told them not to let him in. He sighed. 'I appreciate your loyalty to her. But this is important.'

'I can't let you in, Mr Stone.'

'Have you ever really, really messed up?' he asked. 'Because I have. And I really want to make it right for her.'

The security guy said nothing.

'Please. I'm not going to cause a scene, I promise. I just want to apologise and ask her to let me explain. If she tells me to go, then I'll go without making a fuss,' Brandon said.

'I can't do that, Mr Stone.'

Brandon knew he was going to have to go for broke. 'If you realised that someone was the love of your life, and you only had one chance to tell them or you'd lose them for ever…'

There was silence, and he knew he'd blown it.

'OK. Thanks anyway,' he said. 'I'll have to resort to sitting on her doorstep until she talks to me. Even if it takes me a week.'

'If she tells you to go,' the security guard said, surprising him, 'then you go immediately.'

'Immediately,' Brandon agreed, relief flooding through him. 'Thank you.'

Angel was in her office, looking through some files on her desk, when he rapped on the door.

She looked up. 'I expressly told my security team not to let you in.'

'Don't blame them. It's my fault.'

'What do you want?'

'To talk to you.'

Her lip curled. 'I don't want to talk to you.'

'Angel. Please. Just give me five minutes, and if you still want me to leave after that, I'll go without a fuss.'

'Why should I even give you that?' she asked.

'Because you were right, and I owe it to you to grovel properly. Plus, if I go, you won't ever know the truth.'

She paused for so long he thought she was going to refuse. But then she nodded. 'All right. You've got five minutes.'

'The most important thing you need to know is that I've spoken to Triffid. They know the truth, and your contract's back on.'

'Supposing I don't want to work with them now?'

'That's your decision,' he said. 'But at least they know now the story wasn't true.'

'Why did you lie about it in the first place?'

'I didn't,' he said. 'I know the evidence all looks as if it points to me being the leak, so in your shoes I'd be livid with me too, but it wasn't me. The paper was quite specific: they spoke to a source close to the company. Not the CEO.'

She still didn't look convinced, and he sighed inwardly. How could he make her understand the truth, but without dragging Eric into it?

'The person who talked to the press no longer works for me,' he said carefully. 'And because I'd got to know you and thought about the way you deal with things, I dealt with the situation slightly differently than I would have done if I hadn't met you. I wanted to be fair, not ruthless.' He paused. This was the really sticky bit. But they didn't have a hope in hell of a future if he wasn't completely honest with her now. 'But I did lie to you about something else.'

She frowned. 'What?'

'When I first met you,' he said. 'I tried to play you.'

She went white. 'So you never wanted to date me in the first place. It was all to get me to sell to you.'

'When I met you,' he said, 'I'd lost my way. I felt responsible for Sam's death, and I didn't feel I deserved love. So, yes, I was cynical about it. I was cynical about everything. I dated you as a way to get close to you and charm you into selling the company to me.'

'I think you've said enough,' she said. 'Get out.'

'I haven't had my five minutes.'

'You don't need it.'

'Oh, but I do,' he said. 'Because that was just the starting point, and I've moved further than I ever thought possible. You've changed me, Angel. All the while I thought I was charming you, actually you were the one who charmed me.'

'Me? Her face was filled with disbelief. 'But I don't play with people like that.'

'I know. It's just how you made me feel. I'm a different person when I'm with you. I like who I am when I'm with you. And all the time I kept telling myself I wasn't falling in love with you and I'd get everything under control, I was in total denial. Because I fell in love with you, Angel. You helped me find my way back. You helped me see that Sam's death was an accident—yes, it was my fault that he was racing, but it wasn't my fault that the accident happened.' He paused. 'And Cumbria. When you and I—'

She went bright red. 'Do you have to bring that up?'

'Yes. Because you gave me something really, really precious.'

'My virginity?' She flapped a dismissive hand. 'It's just an embarrassment in today's world.'

'No. It meant something to you. And it means something to me, too. It means you trusted me.'

'While you were lying to me all along.'

'I,' he said, 'am a first-class idiot. I don't know how to make things right between us. I need your help—I need you to show me the way.'

'There isn't a way.'

'You once told me that there's always a way.'

'Not this time.'

He sighed. 'OK. I can't fix it between us, but I can fix the damage done to your company.' He paused. 'If you change your mind about working with Triffid, you've still got financial problems. I've seen your books. So here's my proposal: if you don't go with Triffid, I'll give you the backing you need.'

She shook her head, looking disgusted. 'So you're still trying to buy McKenzie's?'

'No. I'm offering you an interest-free loan,' he said. 'Not from Stone's but from me personally.'

'Why would you do that?'

'Because the Frost is an incredible car that deserves to be out there in the market, and I believe in you.'

Brandon believed in her.

Or so he said.

He'd already lied to her. Multiple times. How did she know he wasn't lying now?

Her suspicion must have shown on her face, because he said, 'There aren't any strings. I'd also like to marry you, but that's a separate issue. Whatever happens between you and me, I'm still backing your business, because I love you and I believe in what you're doing. I don't want McKenzie's to go under. You rescued me from my private hell. Now it's my turn to rescue you.'

She couldn't get her head round this. Someone at his company had done their best to destroy hers—and he was trying to tell her he *loved* her and wanted to marry her?

More like he'd seen her in the same way as her fellow students had seen her at college: a challenge to be conquered. She'd been so flattered that she'd let him charm her into bed. Worse still, she'd instigated it. How he must have laughed at her. Hadn't he just told her that it had been his original plan to charm her into selling McKenzie's to him? Her virginity had been a cushy little bonus.

And now he was trying to make her believe that he loved her.

Of course he didn't.

She'd just been a means to an end. Only she wasn't selling.

'You've had your five minutes,' she said. 'Please go.'

'I'm sorry you've ended up hurt because of something

that Stone's did,' he said. 'Hurting you is the last thing I wanted to do. And I don't know how to make it better. All I know is that I love you, and I don't want our family history getting in the way.'

'It isn't our family history. You *lied* to me, Brandon. You used me.'

He raked a hand through his hair. 'And I apologise for that. I've been lying to myself, too. But I swear I would never intentionally do anything to hurt you. I love you, Angel. I respect you. You know your business inside out, you're a first-class manager and you've kept McKenzie's going for much longer than anyone else I know could've done in your position. You're an amazing designer whose ideas really inspire me. And more importantly you're an amazing woman. The woman I want to spend the rest of my life with.' He dragged in a breath. 'Except I don't know how to convince you that I mean it. How to get your trust back.'

She didn't know how he could convince her, either.

As if her agreement with him showed in her face, he sighed. 'OK. I've had my five minutes. I don't have any flashy gestures or flashy words or flashy *anything* left. I could go and buy the biggest diamond in the world and offer it to you on one bended knee, but it wouldn't even begin to tell you how I feel about you. All I can do is tell you that I love you and I want to fix it. But I can't do it on my own. I need you to meet me halfway, to show me how to bridge this gap between us.'

Angel wasn't sure she knew how to bridge the gap, either. How could she learn to rebuild her trust in him, when he'd admitted that he'd lied right from the start?

'I've done the best I can to fix things. But please think about what I said. And if you want to talk—well, you know where you can find me.' His grey eyes filled with sadness, and he turned on his heel and left.

Angel wasn't sure how long she sat there just staring at the empty doorway and wondering how her life had turned so upside down, but then her video call buzzed.

Triffid's legal team.

She thought about ignoring it; but then again maybe she could salvage something for McKenzie's from the call. Her personal life might be in shreds, but that was no excuse for letting her staff down. With a sigh, she accepted the call.

'Miss McKenzie, I'm glad I caught you. I've been talking to our people since Mr Stone called me this morning, and...'

So Brandon hadn't lied about that. He really had called LA to tell them the story about the merger wasn't true.

'Sorry. Can you run that by me again?' she asked, when it became obvious that the lawyer was waiting for an answer and she'd missed most of what he'd said to her.

When she'd finished the call, she leaned back against her seat. Brandon hadn't just corrected the story, he'd come up with a host of ideas to spin it in McKenzie's favour. He wouldn't have done that if he'd been the person trying to bring McKenzie's down with rumours.

So maybe he'd been telling her the truth.

He'd said some things that had really hurt her. Things that had shown him in a horrible light. But he'd also said that she'd changed him and changed the way he saw things.

Now she'd thought about it, he'd changed her, too. From a quiet, nerdy engineer who was happiest in her overalls and with no social skills into a woman who wore a red dress and danced at a glittering ball. He'd given her confidence in herself.

And maybe he did love her. He'd let her drive the Mermaid; he'd stepped in when her hearing let her down, but without making her feel useless or stupid; he'd thought about her and what she'd like to do on their dates.

Brandon Stone was a decent, thoughtful, caring man who also just happened to be one of the most gorgeous men she'd ever seen. He made her heart beat faster, but it wasn't just because of the way he looked. It was because she liked being with him. She liked who she was when she was with him.

If you want to talk—well, you know where you can find me.

She did indeed.

She locked up the factory, stopped by her security team to thank them, and headed for Oxford.

Brandon was right where she expected to find him: in his aircraft hangar of a garage, dressed in scruffy overalls, polishing chrome on the Mermaid.

'You missed a bit,' she said, pointing to a tiny area on the rear bumper.

'Engineers. So picky,' he said.

'Yeah. We expect the best.'

'Which is no less than you deserve.'

She knew she was going to have to be the one to broach the issue—because she was the one who'd refused to discuss it before. 'I've been thinking.'

'Uh-huh,' he said, as if he was trying really hard to sound careful and neutral and not scare her away.

'Triffid called me. What you did—you didn't have to.'

'I rather think I did,' he said. 'It was Stone's fault that McKenzie's was damaged.'

'Temporarily.'

'My company. My responsibility to fix the damage.'

'But not,' she said, 'your *fault*. That's the second thing you've taken the blame for. Don't let there be a third.'

'Too late. I hurt you. And you can't deny that's my fault, Angel.'

'True,' she said, 'but you were also being honest. If I'd found out in six months' time that you'd only starting dating me to get your hands on McKenzie's, it would've hurt me a lot more. I'm glad you told me now, because it means we're starting with a clean slate. With the truth.'

His eyes brightened with hope. 'So does this mean I get a second chance?'

'There's been bad blood between our families for too long,' she said. 'I know my dad wrote your dad a letter when Sam was killed, but maybe your dad was too upset to reply.'

'I don't think he got the letter. Eric was helping to deal with all the corr—' Brandon stopped and grimaced. 'Eric again.'

'Eric *again*?' she queried.

'I'm guessing he threw the letter away.'

'I gathered that,' she said gently. 'But what I didn't get was the "again" bit—do you mean Eric was the one who talked to the press about the buyout and the Frost?'

'He thought I wasn't doing a good enough job at making you sell McKenzie's to me, so he put the pressure on. He knows now he did the wrong thing.' Brandon sighed. 'And it didn't help that he was so bitter about the past.' He filled her in on what Eric had told him about the family history.

'That's really sad,' Angel said. 'I'm sorry he had to go through that. Though it's not been a total bed of roses for my family either; my dad's older sister died from scarlet fever when he was five, and I'm an IVF baby.'

'I'm sorry, too. I didn't know all of that,' Brandon said.

'Why would you? I'm guessing maybe one or the other wanted to try to mend things at different points along the way, but they were all too stubborn. Maybe your grandmother wanted to come to my aunt's funeral, but thought it would be rubbing it in because she still had two children and Esther and Jimmy didn't. Or maybe she was afraid that if Barnaby tried to comfort Esther, it might end up…' She grimaced. 'Just as I'm guessing that Esther felt bad when Alice died, but maybe she and Jimmy didn't want to hurt Barnaby by rubbing their own happy marriage in his face.'

'They all wasted so much time,' Brandon said.

She sighed. 'The way I see it, life's so short. You just have to muddle through things together.'

'I agree.'

'So what did you do? You said that the person who talked to the press doesn't work for you any more. Don't tell me you sacked your uncle?'

'No. I asked him to retire—though I didn't actually give him a choice,' Brandon admitted.

'Maybe he could—'

'Be redeemed?' He nodded. 'That's why I'm making him have counselling, and I'm taking him to the counsellor myself. He needs to find what he really loves in life. And only then will he be able to be happy.'

'I hope so,' she said.

Brandon looked at her. 'I've found what I really love in life. You. And I admit I had underhand motives when I first met you, but I fell in love with you along the way. Cumbria was real.'

'I know.' She took a deep breath. 'But our families hate each other. My grandfather married the woman your grandfather loved, your dad tried to buy mine out, and…'

'I spoke to my dad,' Brandon said. 'He said that losing Sammy taught him that love's more important than business. He told me if I loved you, to go after you.'

'I spoke to my dad,' Angel said. 'He says if you hurt me, you have him to deal with.'

Brandon grinned. 'Which is exactly what I'd say to our daughter's boyfriend. That's what dads are supposed to do, be all gruff and protective.'

'Maybe we made a tactical error and should've talked to our mums, and got them to talk our dads round,' Angel said.

'Or we face them together and tell them the family feud ends now. They can judge us on our terms. Which is at face value,' Brandon said.

'You know, seventy-odd years ago, we started as the same company. Maybe that's how we should end the feud.'

He blinked, looking surprised. 'Are you offering to sell to me?'

'No. I was thinking more along the lines of a merger,' she said.

'Professional or personal?' he asked.

She spread her hands. 'Do you have a preference?'

'I'm greedy. I'll go for both,' he said. 'I love you, Angel. And I'm sorry things went bad.'

'Me, too. I didn't want to believe you'd betray me like that.'

'Pretty much any jury in the land would've convicted me on that evidence,' he said wryly. 'Including me. I don't blame you.'

'You said I made you see things differently. You make me see things differently, too,' she said. 'I like who I am when I'm with you.'

He coughed. 'You're missing three words, you know. I've said it to you at least three times.'

'True.'

He groaned. 'Do you want me to beg?'

'Depends.' Her heart did a tiny little flip. 'Would that be on one knee?'

'You engineers drive a hard bargain.' He fished a key

ring from his pocket and removed the key. 'Are you quite sure you don't want this to happen in some flashy restaurant overlooking the sea at sunset, with us both dressed up to the nines and vintage champagne on ice?'

'How can that possibly compare with this—the things we both love?' she said, gesturing to the classic cars around them. 'And I don't need vintage champagne. That mug of tea on your workbench looks good enough to me.'

He grinned, and dropped to one knee. 'Angel McKenzie, I love you. I want to design cars with you and have babies with you and be a better man just because you're by my side. Will you marry me?'

'I love you, too, Brandon. And I want to design flashy high-end cars with you, and have babies with you, and be braver than I think I am because you're by my side. Yes,' she said, and he slid the Mermaid's key ring onto her finger.

'This is only temporary, you know,' he warned. 'You get to choose whatever you want as an engagement ring.'

She smiled. 'This would do me.'

'You can't have a key ring as an engagement ring, Angel.' He paused. 'Though you can have it as your engagement present.'

She laughed. 'The perfect present for an engineer—something useful. Thank you.'

'It comes with a key, though,' he said, and pressed the key to the Mermaid into her hand.

Her eyes widened as she realised what he meant. 'You're giving me the Mermaid?'

He shrugged. 'Looks like it.'

'Brandon, you can't—'

He silenced her by standing up and kissing her. 'It's your grandfather's design. I spent months restoring it. And

I think my favourite person in the world should have my favourite car in the world—right along with my heart.'

'I… Thank you. I'm a bit overwhelmed. And I can't afford to give you anything nearly so expensive,' she said ruefully.

'I don't want a present,' he said softly. 'I just want you. Right by my side.'

'You've got it.'

He held her close. 'So we're agreed: it's a merger?'

'McKenzie-Stone,' she agreed.

'Maybe,' he said, 'we should double-barrel our names. *Both* of us.'

She stared at him in surprise. 'You'd change your name for me?'

'If it means I get to marry you, yes. And it'll show that our families are truly one.'

'I like that idea.' She kissed him. 'It's a deal.'

He kissed her back. 'The deal of a lifetime.'

EPILOGUE

'ALL SET?' ASKED Sadie McKenzie. 'Something old?'

'Esther's pearls,' Angel said.

'Something new's your wedding dress. Something borrowed?'

Angel lifted her left arm. 'Lesley lent me Alice's bracelet.'

'That leaves something blue.'

Angel grinned. 'Brandon sent me a package this morning.'

'Right.' Sadie paused. 'I'm going to ask you about this while Lesley's sorting out Jasmine's fairy wings and can't hear me. You're totally sure about this?'

'I am,' Angel said. 'More sure than I've ever been in my life.'

Sadie hugged her. 'He's lovely and he's crazy about you, and that's all that matters.'

'Mum, don't. You'll make me cry and Maria spent ages doing my make-up this morning.'

'I know, love. She's a sweetheart,' Sadie said. 'And I'm glad the rift between the Stones and McKenzies has finally been healed. I know your dad was a bit worried that it was all going to go wrong, but I think he and Larry have surprised themselves by actually liking each other.'

Brandon and Angel's doubts had vanished as soon as

their mothers had started talking. There was only one Stone who hadn't been welcoming. The one who also hadn't responded to the wedding invitation. Angel had talked Gina into giving her Eric's private mobile number and had called him, but when he hadn't picked up she'd left a message that she hoped would make him put aside his anger for one day and come to the wedding.

Between them, the mothers had taken over to organise the wedding. They'd agreed that it wouldn't be tactful for Brandon and Angel to marry in the Cambridge church where her parents and grandparents had been married; instead, they'd chosen a local stately home which had a small and very pretty fourteenth-century church on the estate. And the McKenzies and the Stones were all getting ready at the McKenzie family home.

There was a knock on the door. 'Can I come in?' Lesley Stone asked.

'Of course,' Angel called.

Lesley walked in. 'The bridesmaids and flower girls are all rea— Oh, my. You look beautiful,' she said to Angel.

Angel smiled. 'Thank you. And so do you. So Maria, Gina, Stephie and Jas are all done? We're done, too— aren't we, Mum?'

'Then I think it's time for the girls to have champagne,' Lesley declared, linking arms with both Sadie and Angel.

Downstairs, the bridesmaids, flower girl and matron of honour were waiting; all were wearing simple deep violet dresses with a sweetheart neckline and wide straps, slim-fitting and falling to their ankles. Jasmine was wearing fairy wings and a sparkly tiara, which made Angel smile even more. The perfect outfit for a perfect day.

'Look at you! Turn round, Angel,' Gina directed. 'Brandon isn't going to know what's hit him.'

'You look like a princess,' Jasmine said, her grey eyes wide.

Her dress was ivory, strapless and with a sweetheart neckline. There was lace on the bodice, and then layers of organza falling to her ankles. Her shoes, for once, weren't flat but were strappy high heels to match the bridesmaids' dresses.

'That's because your mummy's very good with make-up,' Angel said.

'No, it's because you're beautiful,' Stephie said. 'Don't argue. You're not allowed to argue with pregnant women.'

'Aren't our girls all gorgeous?' Sadie said to Lesley.

'Aren't they just?' Lesley said. 'And I'm so glad our family's going to be one.'

There was just enough time for one glass of champagne, and the cars were ready to take them to the church.

'You look beautiful,' Max said outside the church. 'And best of all I know Brandon's going to be exactly the kind of husband I want for you—a man who really loves you.'

There was a lump in her throat a mile wide. 'Thanks, Dad. It means a lot, knowing we have your approval.'

'He's a good man. And his family's all right. I think we understand each other, now,' Max said. 'Ready?'

'Ready.'

Angel walked through the doors holding her father's arm. The church was all soaring arches, full of light, and the ancient box pews were crammed full of their family and friends. There were white and lilac and deep purple flowers everywhere and the organist was playing 'Here Comes the Sun'.

Brandon was standing at the top of the aisle next to his father, who was his best man. Larry looked round and saw her, then nudged Brandon and whispered something.

Brandon looked round and his eyes were so full of love; Angel could see him mouth, 'I love you.'

And then she was at the aisle by his side, plighting her troth, repeating the words after the vicar.

Finally, the vicar smiled. 'You may now kiss the bride.'

'About time,' Brandon said with a grin, and gently peeled back her veil before bending her back over his arm and kissing her soundly, to the applause of the congregation.

The signing of the register was a blur, but then they were walking back down the aisle, and the church bells were pealing as they came outside. Everyone was pelting them with white dried delphinium petals and cheering as they walked down the little path to the gate through the wall to the ancient hall next door.

The house itself was a beautiful eighteenth-century mansion with pale gold bricks and white sash windows, a porticoed entrance, a red-tiled roof with dormer windows jutting out, and wisteria on the walls. The photographer took photographs of family groupings by the car, next to the wisteria and on the steps, then finally went up to the parapet on the roof of the house and took photos of the whole group from above.

'The perfect day,' Brandon said.

'Absolutely,' Angel agreed, though she was aware that one person from his family was missing. The one person they hadn't seen at the church.

They lined up with both sets of parents to do the meet-and-greet. Angel was humbled to realise how many people there were to wish them well: family, old friends, staff from both their factories, and some of Brandon's old racing colleagues. Everyone hugged them soundly, all wishing them every happiness for the future.

'I don't think he's coming,' Brandon said softly.

'Trust me, he will,' Angel said. 'I left a message on his voicemail. He'll be here.'

And then, at the end of the line, there he was.

Angel greeted Eric with a hug.

'I'm sorry I didn't make the church,' Eric said. 'And I'm sorry about…'

'It's fine,' Angel said.

'I just wanted to wish you both well for the future.'

'I'm really glad you came,' she said. 'I meant what I said in that message.'

'That it wouldn't be the same without me? Even though I wrecked everything?' He looked shocked.

'It was fixable,' she said, 'and we all wanted you here. All of us. Because you're part of our family.' She paused. 'And you had a point. We're merging the businesses. And I meant what I said about coming back to the factory as a consultant. I've been looking through some of your paperwork and I really like your ideas about new fuels. We want you on our team to build the first McKenzie-Stone car in seventy years.'

Eric blinked away the tears in his eyes. 'If Esther was half the woman you are, I can quite see why my grandfather lost his head over her.' He turned to Brandon. 'Look after her.'

'I'd never make the mistake of wrapping my wife up in cotton wool,' Brandon said with a smile. 'But I'd lay down my life for her. So, yes, I'll look after her.'

'And the same goes for me,' she added.

'You'll be good for each other,' Eric said, and gave them both a hug.

And then he shocked everyone by hugging Angel's parents, who reacted by hugging him back.

'I have a feeling,' Brandon said, 'that everything's going

to be just fine. Come and sit down for our wedding breakfast, Mrs McKenzie-Stone.'

She smiled. 'I'd be delighted, Mr McKenzie-Stone.'

'To us,' he said softly at the table, lifting a glass. 'And our families. Joined at last.'

* * * * *

If you loved this book, don't miss
FALLING FOR THE SECRET MILLIONAIRE
by Kate Hardy.
Available now!

If you enjoyed this feel-good romance, watch out for
HER PREGNANCY BOMBSHELL
by Liz Fielding,
part of the SUMMER AT VILLA ROSA *series.*

MEET THE FORTUNES

Fortune of the Month: Olivia Fortune Robinson

Age: 28

Vital statistics: The smart one and the pretty one. But don't waste your time.

Claim to fame: The last single Fortune Robinson daughter.

Romantic prospects: Her heart is shut up so tight it would take a crowbar to pry it open.

"After everything I've seen in my parents' marriage, I'd have to be crazy to want to get married myself. But I never intended to make my sister Sophie call off her own wedding! If I don't do something fast, she's going to lose Mason. He's one of the good guys. I can't let that happen.

Enter exhibit A: Alejandro Mendoza. Our family has a long-standing tradition of falling for Mendoza men, and Alejandro is the hottest hottie of the bunch. If I can make Sophie believe that I've fallen head over heels for him, her own cold feet will warm up. As for me? Having Alejandro as my make-believe boyfriend is a price I'm more than willing to pay. The trick is remembering it's just pretend..."

* * *

The Fortunes of Texas:

The Secret Fortunes: A new generation
of heroes and heartbreakers!

FORTUNE'S SURPRISE ENGAGEMENT

BY

NANCY ROBARDS THOMPSON

All rights reserved including the right of reproduction in whole or in part in any form. This edition is published by arrangement with Harlequin Books S.A.

This is a work of fiction. Names, characters, places, locations and incidents are purely fictional and bear no relationship to any real life individuals, living or dead, or to any actual places, business establishments, locations, events or incidents. Any resemblance is entirely coincidental.

This book is sold subject to the condition that it shall not, by way of trade or otherwise, be lent, resold, hired out or otherwise circulated without the prior consent of the publisher in any form of binding or cover other than that in which it is published and without a similar condition including this condition being imposed on the subsequent purchaser.

® and ™ are trademarks owned and used by the trademark owner and/or its licensee. Trademarks marked with ® are registered with the United Kingdom Patent Office and/or the Office for Harmonisation in the Internal Market and in other countries.

First Published in Great Britain 2017
By Mills & Boon, an imprint of HarperCollins*Publishers*
1 London Bridge Street, London, SE1 9GF

© 2017 Harlequin Books S.A.

Special thanks and acknowledgement to Nancy Robards Thompson for her contribution to the Fortunes of Texas: The Secret Fortunes continuity.

ISBN: 978-0-263-92295-0

23-0517

Our policy is to use papers that are natural, renewable and recyclable products and made from wood grown in sustainable forests. The logging and manufacturing processes conform to the legal environmental regulations of the country of origin.

Printed and bound in Spain
by CPI, Barcelona

National bestselling author **Nancy Robards Thompson** holds a degree in journalism. She worked as a newspaper reporter until she realized reporting "just the facts" bored her silly. Now that she has much more content to report to her muse, Nancy loves writing women's fiction and romance full-time. Critics have deemed her work "funny, smart and observant." She resides in Florida with her husband and daughter. You can reach her at www.nancyrobardsthompson.com and Facebook.com/nancyrobardsthompsonbooks.

This book is dedicated to Susan Litman
and Marcia Book Adirim, the heart and soul
of the Fortunes. And to Melanie Ashman for
naming the signature drink Olivia served
at Sophie's bachelorette party!

Chapter One

"It's time to break out the Fuzzy Handcuffs, Mike." Olivia Fortune Robinson gave the sexy bartender her most flirtatious smile.

He cocked a brow and grinned. "It's my pleasure to hook you ladies up."

"Excuse me?" Her sister Sophie frowned at him and then her eyes went wide as realization seemed to dawn. "Oh, no." Sophie held up her hands as if to ward off Mike. "Please tell me you are not a stripper." She pinned her panicked gaze on her sister. "Olivia, Dana and I specifically told you we didn't want strippers at our bachelorette party. No offense, Mike. I'm sure you're very good at what you do. You just can't do it here. Not tonight. Not for us."

She looked at her sister-in-law-to-be, Dana Trevino, and the other Fortune Robinson sisters seated on the plush love seats and overstuffed armchairs grouped around a glass cocktail table in a cozy corner of the Driskill Hotel bar.

Sophie's brown eyes were huge and color blazed high on her cheekbones. By contrast, Dana seemed to have gone pale as she perched hesitantly on the edge of her seat, as if weighing whether or not to bolt. Watching the pair of them squirm was worth all the effort Olivia had put into planning this sisters' weekend. Olivia almost hated to burst their horrified balloons.

"Unfortunately, Mike is not a stripper," she said, pausing to let them sit with thoughts of what they would be missing.

Her sister Rachel sighed. "Aw, that's too bad. For one glorious moment, I thought we had our very own Magic Mike."

Zoe, another sister, nodded in agreement.

Mike laughed. "Sorry, ladies. It's true, I'm not a stripper. Although I will be tending to your every need tonight."

The innuendo was thick.

"Does that mean you're a gigolo then?" Rachel asked, her eyes sparkling with mischief.

Mike laughed. "No, not a gigolo, either. I am your personal bartender and I am happy to be at your service."

Sophie's mouth formed a perfect O before her brows knit together. "And exactly what were you planning to do with the fuzzy handcuffs?"

Olivia and Mike exchanged a conspiratorial look.

"Forgive them," she said. "They don't get out much."

"There is nothing to forgive," he said. "Would you like to tell her about the Fuzzy Handcuffs or shall I?"

"Please, do the honors," Olivia said.

"Your sister commissioned me to create a signature cocktail for your bachelorette party." He stopped and looked at Sophie. "I'm guessing you are one of the brides."

"Yes, I'm Sophie."

He took her hand and lifted it to his lips before he asked, "Which one of you is Dana?"

"That would be me." The pretty redhead gave a hesitant wave before she tucked her hands into the fabric of her flowing gypsy skirt. Mike winked at her. Rachel and Zoe promptly introduced themselves, laughing as they made a dramatic show of extending their hands for a kiss. Mike didn't disappoint them.

Mike was a very good sport. As Olivia made a mental note to tell the manager how he'd gone above and beyond, her gaze was snared by a tall, dark, good-looking man walking into the bar. Though she only caught his profile before he turned and sat down with his back to her, he reminded her of someone. Who, she couldn't place, but Olivia hadn't gotten a very good look at him.

"Congratulations, ladies," Mike said. "I'm honored to serve you on your special night. I understand you're staying at the Driskill?"

"We are," Sophie said. "We checked in this afternoon. Olivia has planned a fabulous weekend for us."

"Nothing but the best for my sisters," Olivia said.

"When is the wedding?" he asked.

"Next weekend," Dana said. "Right here in this hotel in the ballroom. But there will be a full week of events leading up to the ceremony. This girls' get-together is a nice way to kick off the festivities."

"Well, don't let me hold up the party," Mike said. "One round of Fuzzy Handcuffs coming right up."

"Fuzzy Handcuffs." Rachel shook her head. "Only you would come up with a name like that, Olivia. Only you."

They all laughed.

"Originally, Mike wanted to call the drink the Bride's First Blush, but that was boring."

"No it's not," Sophie said. "It's pretty."

Olivia resisted the urge to roll her eyes. The name Bride's First Blush was too sweet for such a potent cocktail. The drink itself was perfect. It was festive and fizzy, but it also had just the right amount of something stronger to pack a pop. It needed a name that was just as strong, not one that sounded like a virgin cocktail. Fuzzy Handcuffs was perfect.

Olivia had gone to the ends of the earth to ensure that every single detail of this sisters' weekend was perfect. And of course, it had been perfect so far. She may have been a computer programmer by trade, but if she ever found herself in need of a career change, she did have a knack for event planning.

Sophie and Dana weren't party girls, so they'd

been ecstatic with the plan of a weekend of pampering. After they'd checked into the suite at the Driskill, a limousine had whisked them away to the spa where they'd enjoyed hot stone massages, facials, seaweed wraps, special conditioners that had brought out the shine in their tresses and luxurious aromatherapy soaks in jetted tubs. At noon, they'd taken a break from the pampering to enjoy a light lunch complete with mimosas. Afterward, they'd returned to the spa for mani-pedis before adjourning to the pool to sip fruit-infused reverse-osmosis water while they relaxed and soaked up just enough sun so not to burn, but to give them a healthy glow.

"I wanted my sister and sister-to-be's last weekend of freedom to be something you two will never forget. Since you nixed the strippers, I had to sneak in something edgy somewhere else. Voilà—Fuzzy Handcuffs. At least I didn't call it the Ol' Ball and Chain."

"No, that'll be the name of the drink we serve at your bachelorette party," Zoe quipped.

"Hell Froze Over might be a more apt name for my bridal cocktail, since that's what would happen if I ever got married."

"Don't be so cynical," Zoe said. "You reap what you sow."

"I beg your pardon?" Olivia knew exactly what her sister meant, but she wasn't going to give in that easily. Zoe was the consummate Pollyanna when it came to love and romance—despite every bad example their parents' screwed-up relationship and sham of a marriage had set for them.

"You know exactly what I mean." Zoe sighed and looked at Olivia as if she was hopeless. "You draw to you exactly what you put out into the world."

Olivia blanched, but now wasn't the time to get into a philosophical discussion about the realities of love and happily-ever-after. Besides the fact that this was supposed to be a happy occasion celebrating Sophie and Dana's imminent wedding, her other two sisters were newly married. Zoe was still in the honeymoon phase of her own marriage, having just wed Joaquin Mendoza last year. Rachel was married to Joaquin's brother Matteo.

Wait a minute—

Olivia's gaze found the tall guy at the bar. Was that the other Mendoza? The single one—what was his name?

She turned to her sisters. "See that guy over there? Isn't that your brother-in-law?"

They turned in unison and looked.

"Is that Alejandro?" Rachel said.

"I think it is," Zoe said.

"I didn't realize he was coming to town early," Sophie said. "We should say hi and invite him to join us for a drink." She started across the bar toward him and the next thing they knew, she was walking back arm-in-arm with him.

"Look who I found," Sophie said, triumphantly. "Alejandro, I'm sure you remember my sisters, Olivia,

Rachel and Zoe. And this is Dana, the other bride-to-be."

They exchanged hellos.

"When did you get in?" Rachel asked.

"A couples of hours ago. I came in early to take care of some business before the wedding."

All of the Mendoza men had been blessed by the tall, dark and handsome Latin gene, but Alejandro seemed to have gotten an extra helping of good looks. Olivia wondered how she'd failed to notice that before now. Of course, she'd only seen him on two other occasions: Rachel's and Zoe's weddings. She'd brought dates both times, so she hadn't exactly been looking.

"You came in from Miami, right?" Olivia asked. She did remember that much.

He turned his sultry gaze on her.

"I did."

"I didn't realize you had business ties to Austin," Sophie asked. "What do you do, Alejandro?"

"I'm in the wine business," he said. "I'm a wine sales rep, but I'm in town because I'm in the process of buying a small vineyard about twenty miles west of here."

Zoe's mouth fell open. "Your very own vineyard? That's so cool. Why hasn't Joaquin mentioned it?"

Alejandro shrugged. "Until last week, it was still up in the air, but everything finally fell into place. I'm going to meet with the owners tomorrow and do one last walk-through before we finalize the deal."

"Which winery?" Rachel asked.

"It's called Hummingbird Ridge." He kept stealing glances at Olivia.

"I've never known anyone who's actually owned a winery," Sophie mused. "I'd love to see it. Can you give us a tour?"

Alejandro's brows shot up as he considered the possibility. "I'm sure I can arrange a tasting for you. Is there time this week?"

Everyone looked at Olivia as if she was the keeper of the schedule. There were events and outings scheduled for every day of wedding week—tours of Austin for those from out of town, rounds of golf, tennis matches, couples' massages, luncheons, teas and dinners. But with a guest list close to five hundred people, the only activity they would all be doing as a group was watching the couples exchange their vows and celebrating at the reception afterward.

"How many people could you accommodate?" Olivia asked him.

"I'd say about two dozen," he told her. "Of course, I'll have to check with the winery and see how their availability looks. But this is their slow time of year when they don't get many large groups. It shouldn't be a problem. Maybe you can start organizing on your end and we can touch base and coordinate. Give me your number."

Out of the corner of her eye, Olivia saw Sophie elbow Zoe. The only reason she didn't make a face at them was because she didn't want to draw Alejandro's attention to their antics.

Olivia rattled off her cell number and Alejandro

put it in his phone, calling her to make sure he'd input the right digits. When her phone rang, Olivia entered his name.

"There," she said. "We should be all set."

Mike reappeared with a tray full of hot-pink cocktails. True to the drink's name, a pink-and-black fuzzy handcuff graced the stem of each frosted martini glass. A drink stirrer that seemed to be exploding silver tinsel decorated the top. The tray looked like a mini Fourth of July fireworks display.

As the five women expressed their delight, Mike looked pleased, but Alejandro took a step back.

"Why don't you join us for a drink, Alejandro?" Rachel said.

"Actually, he's welcome to mine," said Dana. "As much as I hate to leave this fabulous soiree, I have to go pick up my maid of honor from the airport. It's a pretty long haul out there. I really shouldn't drink and drive. I'm so eager to hug Monica. It's been ages. And she's bringing my wedding dress. She's letting me borrow an antique dress that belonged to her grandmother. I've seen pictures, but I haven't had a chance to try it on yet. I'm a little anxious about it. That's one of the reasons I need to go. I hope you understand."

Their future sister-in-law's early departure wasn't a surprise. Monica had made her reservations nearly simultaneously with Olivia finalizing the plans for the bachelorette party. While they wanted her to stay, they understood. Monica was like family to Dana, who had lost her parents in an accident when she was twelve and had grown up in foster care. While the guardianship had been adequate, it hadn't been warm enough to warrant keeping in touch or inviting them to the wedding.

The redhead, whose style was more boho-vintage than traditional, would look perfect in an antique gown. She twirled a long strand of copper hair around her index finger and drew in an audible breath.

"Wow. My maid of honor is arriving and I finally get to try on my dress. I guess that means this wedding is really happening." She put a hand on her heart. "I can't believe it's finally here."

The look of love was so evident in Dana's sparkling blue eyes that for the briefest moment, a pang of envy stabbed at Olivia's insides. It was an odd feeling. If given the chance, she wouldn't change places with her sisters. She cherished her independence. Even though the thought of tying herself to one man for the rest of her life made her feel claustrophobic, she was happy for her sisters. It was the happiness that she envied.

"I know." Sophie swooned. Feeling like an outsider, Olivia watched Rachel and Zoe coo right along with Dana and Sophie.

Her little sister, Sophie, and Mason Montgomery had gotten engaged in February, and just last month her brother, Kieran, had asked Dana to be his wife. Her siblings were certainly falling like flies bitten by the love bug. Olivia was the only one who hadn't succumbed. Even so, just because she didn't believe in the institution of marriage, it didn't mean she couldn't be happy for them.

That's precisely why she'd decided to go all out for Sophie and Dana's bachelorette party. Olivia couldn't resist a good party, especially when the guests of honor were women she adored and it gave her a chance to get together with her sisters Zoe and Rachel. Who, other than herself, could she trust to make sure that every detail was perfect?

"I'm so sorry you can't stay," said Sophie. "Why don't you pick up Monica and bring her back here? She could join us for dinner. As far as we're concerned, the more the merrier. Right?"

The sisters nodded. But Dana's left shoulder rose and fell. "As much as I'd love to, I can't. Monica is bound to be exhausted. But we will definitely come for brunch tomorrow, if that's still okay."

"We wouldn't have it any other way," Rachel said. "I'm sure you want a chance to catch up with Monica before everyone gets swept away by the festivities leading up to the wedding. It's going to be a busy week. And I know you want to try on your dress. I wish we could be there for that."

Sophie reached out and squeezed Dana's hand. "Of course, we completely understand. Monica needs to be rested up for the wedding. This really is the calm before the storm hits."

Something that sounded like a cross between a squeak and a squeal escaped from Sophie and she covered her mouth with both hands. She shook her head and wrung her jittery hands, excitement rolling off her in waves. "Oh, my gosh. You're right. It just got officially real. This time next week we will be married and dancing at our wedding reception. Maybe I should make my next Fuzzy Handcuffs a double."

"Good, that means you can have one for me," Dana said. "On that note, I'd better say good-night."

As the four Fortune Robinson sisters took turns hugging Dana, Alejandro, who had been silent since all the wedding talk started, spoke up. "I have some work to catch up on. I, too, will leave you ladies to your festivities."

His gaze caught Olivia's and lingered long enough to cause a slight shift in the room's temperature. It was like wading into a warmer current of water.

"Have fun," he said. "Olivia, I'll be in touch."

In reverent silence, the sisters watched Alejandro walk away.

"Gotta love those Mendoza genes," Rachel said under her breath.

"Oh, yeah. Highly recommended," Zoe said and sipped her drink. "Olivia, I think Alejandro is into you. You should go for him this week. Isn't it a lovely coincidence that he's Joaquin's last single brother and you're my last single sister?"

Sophie squealed. "I think Alejandro would be a perfect match for Olivia."

Olivia could think of many worse things than "going for" Alejandro Mendoza. A wedding fling with a gorgeous Latin man? *Hell, yeah.* It didn't get much better than that. Especially since he lived in Miami and she lived in Austin. That was just enough distance for a no-strings-attached fling.

A slow heat burned deep in her belly. She threw back her drink to cool herself off. The Fuzzy Handcuffs went down way too easily.

Yeah…but, no. Hooking up with Alejandro wasn't a good idea. He was family. Sort of. But not really. There was no blood relation. Her sisters were married to his brothers. That in itself was a problem. If she didn't handle the fling just right, it could get awkward at future family gatherings. And really, when was the last time she'd had a fling? Olivia liked to talk a good game, but she wasn't into casual sex. Anyway—

She plucked another drink from the tray and took a healthy sip.

"This night is not about me," she said. "It's about our sister and her happiness." She raised her glass high before she threw the drink back.

"Hear, hear," said Zoe. "I have an idea. Rather than a traditional toast, I think we should each take turns offering sweet Sophie our best words of sisterly advice for a long and happy marriage."

"Olivia, you go first," Zoe said.

Olivia frowned, already feeling the effects of the alcohol. "Marital advice is not exactly my department."

Zoe batted her words away. "Don't be a killjoy, Liv. You know what I mean. Give her your best sisterly advice."

Run! Run for your life. Get out now while you can still save yourself.

She chuckled at the thought. It was what she wanted to say, but even as tipsy as she was, she had enough good sense to know the reaction that comment would inspire in her sisters. Then she really would be the killjoy that Zoe had accused her of being. That wouldn't do. She'd have to dig deep to come up with something.

Of course, Zoe and Rachel and their husbands could be the poster couples for happy marriage. "You two go first. Come back to me."

As Rachel and Zoe spouted pearls of matrimonial wisdom, Olivia searched her soul to find something to offer—*anything*—that didn't sound jaded or bitter. But her head was spinning. Either she was a lightweight or these Fuzzy Handcuffs really did pack an über-potent punch.

That's when she realized three sets of sisterly eyes were focused on her, waiting expectantly.

"Guys, come on." Was she slurring her words? *Nah*, she was just thirsty. Water, she needed water. She looked over and signaled for Mike to come over. He gave her a thumbs-up, which Olivia took to mean he would be there as soon as he was free. He had a couple of customers at the bar, including Alejandro Mendoza. God, he was one sexy Texan—no, wait, he was from Miami. With a vineyard in Texas. So he was sort of an honorary Texy sexan…uhh, a *sexy Texan*. Whatever. He certainly was the best of both worlds: a head for business and a body for sin.

A body she really wouldn't mind taking for a test drive, she thought as she watched him sitting at the bar sipping his beer and doing something on his phone.

"Olivia!" Zoe demanded. "Earth to Olivia. We're waiting for you."

"Come on, Zo. You know I'm the worst person to ask about this. I don't believe in love."

She tried to wave them away, but realized that gesture probably looked as sloppy as she felt right now.

"How can you not believe in love?" Sophie pressed. Her voice went up an octave at the end of the sentence. "Everyone believes in love. I mean, what kind of a world would this be if people didn't believe in love?"

Rachel, who was still holding her first drink, shot Olivia a look. "You might want to slow down a bit, too. You're starting to be a bit of a buzzkill, Liv."

Oh, first she was a killjoy. Now she was a buzzkill?

"You want a buzzkill? I'll give you a buzzkill. I'm happy for the three of you, that you think you've found your soul mates. How fabulous for you. But just because it works for you, doesn't mean love and marriage are for me."

"It's because you're too guarded," Zoe said. "Of course you're not going to find love with that attitude. You have to open your heart before love can find you."

Rachel and Sophie nodded earnestly.

Olivia snorted. "Please tell me you're not going to start singing 'Kumbaya' in three-part harmony."

She rolled her eyes and when she did, she saw Alejandro looking in her direction. She looked away fast.

"I just don't understand why you feel that way," Sophie said in a small voice.

Olivia should've left it alone. She should've just made up something that sounded warm and fuzzy. Grabbed the first thing off the top of her head, something about love being the merging of two souls and blah, blah, blah, and tossed it at her sisters.

But they kept pressing her about *why.*

Why? Why? Why?

"You want to know *why* I don't believe in love? I'll tell you. Love is a crock. Every single guy I've dated has had some ulterior motive for dating me. They've wanted money or wanted a job or thought our father could make them rich by buying the app they've designed. They didn't want me as much as they wanted a piece of Robinson Enterprises."

"Sounds like you've been dating the wrong guys," Rachel said.

It was probably true, but there was something in Rachel's tone that sounded so judgmental. It was the last straw.

"And that's only half of it." Olivia leaned in and set her empty glass on the cocktail table. "The other reason is our parents. Their marriage is a mess. It's a phony sham of a relationship. I don't know why they stay together, because they hate each other. They are slowly but steadily eating each other alive. Anyone with good sense would take a clue from them and realize all relationships are doomed."

"But they're still together," Sophie said.

Olivia shrugged. "Why *are* they still together?

They don't love each other. Even if they did, what about the general state of society? Fifty percent of all marriages end in divorce and the other fifty percent—like our parents—make each other so miserable that divorce probably seems like a preferable option. And that's why I can see no reason to yearn for a doomed institution. On that note, why don't we go get something to eat?"

Her sisters sat stock still, silently staring at her. Rachel looked irritated. Zoe looked shell-shocked and Sophie looked like she was about to burst into tears.

Uh-oh. Obviously she'd gone too far.

"Look, you asked." She softened her tone. "That's why I didn't want to get into it."

All three were still frozen in their seats. The only thing that moved was the tears meandering down Sophie's cheeks.

Crap.

"Okay. I'm sorry. I understand that y'all are newlyweds—even you, Rach. So your relationships are still shiny and new—"

Now Sophie was shaking her head.

Sometimes it was as if she was the only one in her family who didn't have their head in the clouds. Maybe being the one with a clear head and common sense was her burden. If so, she could deal with it more easily than she could deal with a broken heart. She was a realist when it came to love—it never lasted. Her parents were living proof. Why should she fool herself into believing it would turn out otherwise for herself? Nope. She would save herself the heartache and focus on her career, which was in her control.

"I'm really sorry," Olivia said. "I didn't mean it the way it came out."

"Yes, you did." Sophie's voice broke and she stood up abruptly. "I'm tired and I want to go to bed."

"No, Soph. Come on. We need to get something to eat. I've made us a reservation at the Driskill Grill. I'm sure they can seat us early. Come on—"

"No." Sophie took off.

Her sister had barely cleared the bar when Zoe said, "I'll go check on her."

"I'll come with you," Olivia offered.

"No," Zoe and Rachel said in unison.

"Stay here," Zoe said.

"Bring her back," Olivia said. "It's Saturday night. It's her bachelorette party. We're supposed to have dinner. And then right after dinner, we're supposed to have fun."

"And clearly not a minute sooner," Rachel said under her breath, but Olivia heard her loud and clear.

"That wasn't very nice," she said.

Rachel shrugged. "Look, Olivia, I know you mean well, but why did you do that?"

"What?"

"Your down-with-marriage campaign was harsh. Even you have to admit it wasn't your best moment."

She covered her eyes with both palms. "I know. I already said I'm sorry. These Fuzzy Handcuffs are stronger than I realized. I think I'm a little drunk."

"Ya think?"

As if right on cue, Mike delivered another round of five Fuzzy Handcuffs.

"Who ordered these?" Olivia asked.

"I thought you wanted another round when you signaled me a few minutes ago."

"No, I need water."

"Oh, sorry," he said. "Well, these are on the house. I'll bring you some water."

Rachel stood.

"Where are you going?" Olivia asked.

"I'm going to go check on Sophie and Zoe."

"I'll go with you."

"No, stay here and drink some water."

"Will you please bring them back so we can go to dinner? I think we're all hungry. That's probably why the drinks hit us so hard."

Rachel sighed. "I'll try. I'll text you and let you know what Sophie is up for. Okay?"

As her sister walked away, Olivia sat down on the love seat. She'd already said too much tonight. The best thing she could do was give her sisters some space.

Fifteen minutes later, Rachel texted:

Sophie's asleep. Zoe is on the phone with Joaquin and frankly, I'm exhausted. I think it would be best if we call it a night and start fresh with the brunch tomorrow morning.

I'm sorry I ruined the night. I feel so bad.

Not your fault. I think the reality of the wedding is finally hitting Sophie. She'll be fine tomorrow.

Olivia wasn't mad; she was frustrated. This wasn't the way tonight was supposed to turn out—her sister in tears and the evening going up in flames.

Okay, maybe she was a little bit irritated. Why had they pushed her? Why had she been so weak as to give in? Sophie'd get over it. They'd be fine, but she needed to stay away until they all cooled off.

Olivia texted her again:

I'll be up after I get something to eat. Want me to bring you something?

Thanks, but no. I'm going to talk to Matteo and then I'll call it a night. Are you okay? Do you just want to come up to the suite and order room service?

It dawned on Olivia that her married sisters missed their husbands. Melancholy pushed at Olivia's heart. As she looked up from her phone, thinking about how to answer, she caught Alejandro Mendoza looking at her. This time she didn't look away.

She had plenty of drinks in front of her and a reservation for dinner for four that was about to become dinner for two. Olivia texted: I'm fine.

And she was about to get a whole lot better.

Alejandro couldn't hear what the Fortune Robinson sisters were talking about on the other side of the bar, but one minute they'd been toasting, raising their Fuzzy Handcuffs high, and the next it looked like they were arguing.

He shouldn't have been watching them. They were out for a girls' night, which appeared innocent enough, but what man in his right mind could've kept his eyes off such a collection of beauties? They were like magnets. He couldn't help but steal glances their way. His brothers were lucky men. Sophie would soon be married. What about Olivia? No doubt he'd meet the fortunate dude who'd claimed her heart at the wedding.

They'd seemed oblivious to him even as one by one they'd gotten up and left the party. First, Sophie left looking upset, followed by Zoe looking concerned. And finally Rachel, looking like a mother hen.

Olivia was the only one who remained. She'd been sitting alone for a solid five minutes staring at the tray of drinks the bartender had delivered shortly before the mass exodus. Maybe her sisters were coming back? Maybe she could use some company until they did. Alejandro stood, slid his phone into his shirt pocket and went over to Olivia.

"Is the party over already?" he asked.

She blinked up at him as if he'd startled her out of deep thought—or deep, stubborn brooding, based on her irritated expression. That full bottom lip of hers stuck out a little more than he remembered from when he saw her at his brothers' weddings.

As she gazed up at him, she pulled it between her teeth for a pensive moment before she spoke.

"May I ask you a question, Alejandro?" She slurred her words ever so slightly.

"Sure."

"Do you believe in love?"

"Is that a trick question?" He laughed and cocked his right brow in a way that always seemed to get him out of tight spots and trick questions like this one.

Answering questions about love qualified as a very tight spot, because the last thing he wanted to do right now was get into a debate about affairs of the heart with a woman who'd had too many Fuzzy Handcuffs. In his experience, drunk women pondering love were usually vulnerable women, especially when their sisters were all married or in the process of getting hitched.

"No, it's not a trick question," Olivia said. "In fact, it's a fairly straightforward yes-or-no query. You either believe in love or you don't. So what's it going to be, Alejandro? Yes or no?"

Wow. Olivia Fortune Robinson was a force. An intense force. And he could see that she wasn't going to let him off the hook without a satisfactory answer. The problem was, he didn't want to talk about love.

He'd been a believer once—but that was a long time ago. Another lifetime ago, when things were a lot simpler. So simple, in fact, that he'd never had to ponder love's existence. He'd just had to feel; he'd simply had to *be*.

He hadn't thought about love for a very long time.

It had been even longer since he'd felt any emotion even remotely resembling it. In fact, these days he didn't feel anything. But he definitely didn't want to conjure ghosts from the past, because they haunted him randomly even without an invitation.

"You're not going to answer me, are you?" Olivia said.

He smiled to lighten the mood. "That's some heavy pondering for such a festive occasion. Where did everybody go? And more important, are you going to drink all those Fuzzy Handcuffs all by yourself? Because if your sisters left you to your own devices, what kind of gentleman would I be to let you drink alone?"

She gestured with an unsteady wave of her hand. "Don't worry about me. I'm used to drinking alone." She grimaced. "And even though I might be a little tipsy, I'm not so drunk that I don't realize how pathetic that just sounded. Please, sit down and save me from myself."

"If you insist," he said and lowered himself onto the cowhide-patterned love seat that was set perpendicular to her chair. As he made himself comfortable, she shifted her body so that she was angled in his direction and crossed one long, lean, tanned leg over the other.

Damn.

If he'd been a weaker man he might have reached out and run a hand up the tempting expanse, past where skin disappeared under that sexy little black slip of a thing that was riding a little too high on her toned thighs—not in a trashy way, because there wasn't a trashy thing about her. Olivia Fortune Robinson seemed to have mastered the art of classy-sexy, which was a very beautiful fine line to walk.

And he was also treading a very fine line, because Olivia Fortune Robinson was so very off-limits, since she was practically family.

He lifted a drink off the tray and handed it to her, then he took one for himself and raised it to hers. She looked him square in the eyes as they clinked glasses.

"You know, they say you'll have seven years of bad sex if you don't look the person you're toasting in the eyes as you say cheers," she said.

"I guess that means we'll have good sex," he said, still holding her gaze.

"Will we?" She sipped her drink.

He knew she was baiting him and he also knew she was probably drunker than she realized. The drinks were more powerful than they looked. The kind that went down easily and, before you knew it, knocked you flat on your ass. Probably not so dissimilar from the effect that Olivia Fortune Robinson had on men.

"Are you hungry?" Olivia asked.

"For food? Or did you have something else in mind?"

She tilted her head to the side. "You're a naughty boy, aren't you, Alejandro?"

Her words were unwavering and unabashed.

He shrugged.

"I made a dinner reservation for four at the Driskill Grill," she said. "It seems my sisters can't make it.

The only thing worse than drinking alone is dining alone in a fancy restaurant. What do you say, Alejandro? Will you let me take you to dinner?"

"That depends on what you expect in return," he said. "Are you going to feed me and then try to take advantage of me?"

"Absolutely."

This was fun. Much more fun than poring over facts and figures of the Hummingbird Ridge purchase.

When he was fresh out of college, would he have found bantering with a clever woman preferable to dotting the *i*'s and crossing the *t*'s on the details that would make his hard-won business dream a reality? Then again, he hadn't eaten and he was starving.

"In that case," he said, "how can I refuse?"

He knocked back the last of his drink. It was a lot stronger that it appeared.

"Good," Olivia said, handing him another drink from the tray. "The reservation isn't until eight o'clock. We have time to finish our cocktails."

They clinked glasses, locking gazes again before they sipped and settled into an uncomfortable silence. Alejandro was way too aware of how damn sexy she looked in that black dress, too intent on that full mouth that kept commanding his attention, speaking to the most primal needs in him.

He didn't do well with silence.

"Is this your favorite kind of drink?" he asked.

"Me? No. I'm all about champagne. This drink was made especially for the brides-to-be."

"I don't mean to be nosy, but is everything okay with your sisters?"

She shrugged. "I'm sure they're fine. That reminds me. You didn't answer my question. Do you believe in love? I'm guessing you do. Because what else would possess you to tattoo a woman's name on your arm? Who is Anna?"

Reflexively, his right hand found his left forearm, covered the ornate script.

"Anna was someone who made me know that love is very real. But I also learned that love can be a total SOB, too."

Olivia leaned in. "You said 'was.' So I'm guessing that Anna is no longer in the picture?"

The curtain of dread that always closed around him when he remembered Anna started falling. "No, she is no longer in the picture."

That's all he was going to say. He was opening his mouth to change the subject when Olivia got up from her chair and sat down next to him on the love seat.

"That's what I was hoping you'd say," she slurred. "People accuse me of a lot of things, but no one can ever say I go after another woman's man. You don't have a girlfriend who isn't named Anna, do you, Alejandro?"

He shook his head. His gaze fell to her lips. She was sitting enticingly close to him. Suddenly, the room temperature seemed to spike.

"Good," she slurred again as she slid her arms around his neck. "Because I'm going to kiss you. You don't mind if I kiss you, do you, Alejandro?"

Before the words *hell no* could pass his lips, her lips closed over his and smothered the reply.

At first, the kiss was surprisingly gentle, tentative. She tasted like the cocktails they'd been drinking and fresh summer berries and something else he hadn't realized he'd been craving for a very long time. When she opened her mouth wider, inviting him in, passion took over and the gentle kiss morphed into wild, ravenous need, feeding a hunger that he didn't realize was consuming him. He reveled in it, wallowed in it, until it blocked out everything else.

She moved against him, sliding her hands over his shoulders and down his back.

A rush of hot need surged through him. His hands followed the outline of her curves until he cupped her bottom and pulled her closer. Damn. She felt good. Keeping one hand on her, he found the hem of her dress with his other and dipped his fingertips beneath the silky barrier that stood between them.

When she moaned into their kiss, he wanted to pull her onto his lap.

But she was drunk and they were in the bar of the hotel where her sister was getting married next weekend. He had enough of his wits about him to know that if she wasn't in the shackles of too many Fuzzy Handcuffs, she probably wouldn't be doing this. She'd probably be mortified tomorrow.

"Alejandro, take me to your room." Her words were hot on his neck and his body was saying *Let's go. Now.*

But he couldn't. And not for lack of want or interest. It just wasn't right. Not when she was like this.

He stood up and gently tugged her to her feet.

"What's your room number?"

Chapter Two

"Olivia, wake up."

The soft voice bounced around her dreams, beckoning her to open her eyes. Maybe if she ignored it, it would go away and she could go back to the dream of kissing Alejandro… His hands in her hair, pulling her mouth to his; him slowly but firmly guiding her in a backward walk, until he'd pinned her against the wall… His fingers lacing through hers, then pushing their joined hands out and up over her head so she could feel the length of his body pressed into hers.

It was glorious and she wanted more of him, all of him.

"Olivia. I'm not kidding. Wake up. It's an emergency." Why was Rachel's voice in her dream? She was intruding again. Only this time she was being more insistent and it seemed like she wasn't going away. Olivia tried to force her eyes open…to no avail.

"Olivia." Something was shaking her body in a way that didn't mesh with Alejandro's tender caresses. She managed to force one eye open. She saw Rachel's and Zoe's anxious faces staring down at her as searing pain shot through her head.

She felt as if someone had clocked her.

As she pressed the palms of her hands over her eyes, everything came back to her. She'd been clubbed by one too many Fuzzy Handcuffs. Okay, maybe a few too many. And then there was Alejandro. She'd all but had him for dinner. Kissing him hadn't been simply a dream. It had been very real—

Oh, no.

"Olivia, wake up!" It was Rachel shaking her. "We have a situation."

At the sound of her sister's no-nonsense tone, Olivia removed her palms from her eyes and forced her eyes open. For the love of God, her head was about to split wide open.

"It's Sophie," Zoe said. "She's missing. We can't find her anywhere."

It took a moment for Olivia to piece together last night's events: the drinks, her spilling the beans to her sisters about how she felt about their parents' relationship—or lack thereof—Sophie getting upset and running off.

"What do you mean she's missing?" Olivia asked. "Maybe she went out for coffee?"

Every word was a nail in her brain. Her mouth

was so dry her lips stuck to her gums like they'd been pasted together. She needed water. It probably wouldn't be a good idea to ask them if they could go look for Sophie and bring her back a bottle of ice-cold water.

"Do you think she's in danger?" Olivia asked.

Rachel and Zoe looked at each other.

"No," Rachel said. "Otherwise we would've called the police."

"All of her stuff is gone," Zoe said. "She must have packed up and taken it with her. And I must've been sleeping deeply because I didn't even hear her moving around."

Zoe and Sophie had shared one room in the two-bedroom suite. Olivia and Rachel had shared the other one.

"Personally, I think she's freaked out over what you said last night and has cold feet," Zoe said. "You know, prewedding jitters. I get it. I totally understand. It happened to me. That's why we need to find her and let her know the way she's feeling is perfectly normal and everything will be all right."

"Have you talked to Mason?" Olivia's voice was scratchy. "I'll bet she's with him."

Again, Rachel and Zoe exchanged a look.

"He just called. In fact, his call woke Zoe up," Rachel said. "He was looking for Sophie."

"Did you tell him she's at her bachelorette party and that means no boys? He can live without her for a weekend."

Zoe sighed. "Normally, I would've told him that,

but he said she'd left him a distraught message last night after he'd gone to bed. Apparently she said she needed to talk to him as soon as possible and he should call no matter the hour. Now she's not picking up, and she hasn't returned any of his calls or mine. We're worried about her, Liv."

Olivia regarded her sisters, who were still in their pajamas. "I'm guessing you haven't gone out to see if she's down in the café? She might've just gone out for some breakfast or some fresh air."

Olivia could have used both right about now.

She forced herself into a sitting position, trying to ignore the daggers that stabbed at her brain and filled it with a soup-like fog that refused to let her think straight.

As if reading her mind, Rachel produced a bottle of cold water and a wet washcloth.

"You look like hell," she said. "You're positively green. Drink this and wipe your face with this cool cloth."

Olivia did as she was told. Only then did she realize she was still fully dressed in the outfit she'd worn last night. At least she was dressed. She might have smirked at the thought, if the reaction wouldn't have hurt so badly. Of course she was dressed. She'd only kissed Alejandro. She hadn't slept with him. The memory of him walking her up to the suite and the two of them indulging in a delicious good-night kiss right outside the door flooded back. Her sisters didn't need to know about that. Besides, they had more important things to worry about with Sophie going AWOL.

"What time did you get in last night?" Zoe asked.

Olivia took a long drink from the water bottle. When she was finished, she said, "I don't know. Late. You all jumped ship and left me with a tray full of drinks to polish off. It took a while."

Zoe frowned. "I'm sorry we left. We were concerned about Sophie after your little down-with-love tirade."

Tirade?

It hadn't exactly been a tirade. It'd been honesty.

"Yeah, well, I wish you wouldn't have kept pushing me to offer love and marriage advice. I felt like you backed me into a corner."

The sisters sat in silence for a moment.

"Of course, the drinks didn't help matters," Olivia said. "They sort of greased the hinges on propriety's trapdoor and once the words started spilling out, there was no stopping them. I feel bad that Sophie was so upset. It wasn't what I intended."

The washcloth had warmed up. Olivia held it by the corners and waved it back and forth to cool it off before pressing it pressed to her eyes again.

Visions of kissing Alejandro played out on the screen in her mind's eye. She was so glad her sisters hadn't pressed her about whether or not she'd polished off the remaining drinks alone. The thought of those Fuzzy Handcuffs made her stomach churn, and the thought of trying to explain what happened with Alejandro tied it up in knots.

Olivia looked at her sisters. "Was Sophie here when you went to sleep?"

"She was," said Zoe.

"In fact, I thought she was out like a light when I finally turned in. I tried to talk to her before she went to bed, but she said she was fine and just wanted to go to sleep. So I went in and took a shower and then I was on the phone with Joaquin for a while. When I came out of the bathroom, she was snuggled down under the covers. I thought she was just missing Mason."

"Me, too," said Rachel. "But that's why we're concerned that he can't get in touch with her. Where do you think she would go?"

"So obviously you two haven't even been out of the room," Olivia said.

"No, not yet," Zoe said. "We hated to wake you since you obviously played a little hard last night." She gestured to Olivia's outfit.

"Not really. It's not as if I did the walk of shame this morning."

But she had kissed Alejandro. The thought made her already knotted, churning stomach clench a little bit more. She put her hand on her belly to quell it.

It would've been easy to give in to lust and do a lot more than kiss Alejandro last night, but she hadn't. Actually, she'd tried, but he'd been the gentleman.

Even so, the essence of him clung to her. Like he had gotten into her pores. If she shut her eyes, there was Alejandro invading her thoughts the same way he had invaded her dreams. Her fingers found their way to her lips as she remembered every delicious detail about their kisses.

Olivia had a lot of faults, but getting blackout drunk wasn't one of them. No matter how much she had to drink, she was always in control of herself. Sometimes it made her a little looser. She paused. Maybe *looser* wasn't the best word in this particular situation. The Fuzzy Handcuffs had unshackled her inhibitions. That was a more apt description. The drinks had simply allowed her to experience a pleasure in which she might not have otherwise allowed herself to indulge. Yes. That was what'd happened.

She was more than willing to own her actions.

And in owning them, she had enough good sense to know kissing Alejandro last night was as far as things would go. She'd gotten him out of her system and it wouldn't happen again. Of course not. She would be far too busy focusing on her bridesmaid's duties this wedding week.

As fractured as the night had been with her sisters, it was still a girls' weekend. Never mind how gorgeous Alejandro Mendoza was. She'd resisted him. She hadn't bailed on her sisters to spend the night with him.

Even if her sisters had bailed on her.

With great care, Olivia swung her legs over the side of the bed. She put her feet flat on the floor, hoping that the effort would ground her and help her regain her sense of equilibrium. Instead, the room spun. She hated being hungover, but she'd done this to herself. She had no choice but to power through. Do the crime, do the time.

"You do look like hell," Zoe said.

"I'm fine," Olivia answered, pushing to her feet.

"I'm going to get dressed and head downstairs to look for her," Rachel said. "Will you help me look, Liv? I think Zoe should wait in the room in case she returns."

She considered asking, *What if she doesn't want to be found right now? What if she just needs a little time? I'm the one who has a pounding headache. Why can't I wait in the room?* But she knew this was their way of nudging her to make amends with Sophie. To go look for her and find her so the two of them could talk this out and make up.

Of course, that's what she intended to do. She took a deep breath and tried to shake off the irritation that prickled her. How had this suddenly become her fault?

Olivia knew her sisters meant well. This was simply their sister dynamics in play: Zoe was the hopeful one; Rachel was the strong one; Sophie was the baby; Olivia was the one who fixed problems and rallied everyone to take action.

Often, Rachel and Zoe formulated a plan and Olivia made sure it got done.

Olivia cleared her throat and shook off the cobwebs from last night the best she could. It gave her a little more clarity. She made a mental note to have someone kick her if she ever felt compelled to finish off a tray of drinks. Though it would surely be a while before she imbibed again.

Her sisters were chattering at her. As their words bounced off her ears, she pulled jeans, a black blouse and fresh undergarments out of her suitcase and disappeared into the bathroom.

"I have to take a shower before I do anything," she said.

"We can go down to the lobby together," Rachel said. "I'll talk to the bellhops and ask if she called for a cab or if they remember her taking an Uber. Since we all rode here together, we know she didn't drive away and I doubt she walked. We can split up and have a look around the hotel."

Minutes later, after they'd dressed, Olivia grabbed her cell phone and room key and said to Zoe, "Let us know if you hear from her and we'll do the same."

When they got down to the lobby, Olivia looked around as if she might see Sophie standing there waiting for her. She wasn't there, of course. Next, they pulled up a picture of Sophie that Olivia had taken last night with her cell phone and asked the attendants at the porte cochere if they'd called a cab for her or seen her this morning. They hadn't. Next they decided to split up and each search a different half of the hotel.

Had Sophie really taken her words to heart? Regret churned in Olivia's stomach, adding to last night's bile, making her feel sick again. Only this time it had less to do with the Fuzzy Handcuffs and more to do with her big unfiltered mouth and how it had shoved her sister down this spiral of doubt on the eve of wedding-week festivities.

She had to fix this. She would fix this.

She decided to check the café first since it seemed a likely place to find Sophie.

Olivia pulled open the beveled glass doors of the 1886 Café & Bakery and stepped inside. The place was buzzing with families and couples and individuals sitting at the dark wooden tables and booths enjoying Sunday breakfast. She scanned the room with its white honeycomb tile floor and kelly green accent wall that separated the open kitchen from the dining room, and the flagstone archways that partitioned the dining room into smaller, more intimate sections. She fully expected to see Sophie sitting at one of the tables, noshing on a warm chocolate croissant and a café latte.

The place was crowded so Olivia had to walk around. As she did, she breathed in delicious breakfast aromas. Maybe, she thought, a good breakfast would be the cure for her hangover. Or at least the start. But first—Sophie. She would locate her sister—it couldn't be that difficult, even though she clearly wasn't in the café—and then she would treat herself to something delicious. In fact, it would be a good idea to treat Sophie to breakfast too, so they could talk things out and settle this once and for all.

Speaking of delicious…

As if she'd conjured him, there sat Alejandro Mendoza, at a small table tucked into a corner of the restaurant. He was enjoying a hearty omelet that looked like it could feed three people. As if he sensed her watching him, he looked up from the piece of the Sunday *New York Times* that he had folded neatly into quarters, allowing him to read while he dined. He snared her with his gaze before she could turn away and pretend she hadn't seen him.

That sexy, lopsided smile of his that crinkled his coffee-colored eyes at the corners made her breath catch. Visions of kissing him last night—of how perfectly their mouths and bodies had fit together—flooded back, swamping her senses and throwing off her equilibrium.

Get it together, girl.

"Good morning," she said, trying her best to appear nonchalant, to act as if it hadn't taken every fiber of her willpower to go to bed alone last night rather than give in to the chemistry that pulsed between them. She could still feel his kisses on her lips. Her mouth went dry at the thought and she bit her bottom lip to make the memory go away. As if.

He looked her up and down and smiled as if he approved of what he saw. She was acutely aware of the fact that her face was scrubbed fresh and makeup free. She'd pulled her long dark wet hair into a simple ponytail. She felt exposed and vulnerable, but he didn't seem to be turned off by her appearance. Not that it mattered. In fact, maybe it would be better if he was turned off because she would want nothing to do with someone that shallow. Still, she sensed that Alejandro Mendoza might be something of a player.

Maybe he was playing her right now.

"Good morning," he said as he stood. "You're up early."

"So are you," she returned.

He laughed, a deep sound that resonated in her soul and wove its way through her insides.

"Please sit down and enjoy your breakfast," Olivia said. "I don't want it to get cold."

He waved her off and remained standing.

"I have to drive over to Hummingbird Ridge for a business meeting later this morning," he said. "I wanted to grab a bite before I go. Join me. You know what they say about breakfast. It's the most important meal of the day."

The thought of having breakfast with Alejandro conjured all kinds of other possibilities—of what might have happened after the kiss and before the eggs and bacon if she hadn't said good-night—but Olivia blinked away the naughty thoughts.

"Thanks, but I'm looking for Sophie. You haven't seen her, have you?"

He looked confused. "Not since last night before she left the bar."

"So she hasn't been here this morning?"

"Nope. Please join me until she comes." He pulled out the other chair at the table for two.

Needing an ear, she sat down and he helped her scoot in her seat, and he motioned for the server to bring another cup of coffee.

She appreciated his gentlemanly way. Of course, she was perfectly capable of scooting in her own chair, but she had to admit the gesture was nice. It said a lot about him. She thought that chivalry had become a dying art these days. It was nice to meet someone with such good manners.

She bit her bottom lip again as she weighed how much to tell him. He already knew that Sophie had left last night's party upset and that Olivia's blunt words about love had offended her. They'd kissed and shared that secret. She might as well share this, too.

"I can trust you, right?"

He leaned in and studied her, as if he was trying to figure out what she meant, but he nodded. "Of course."

The server delivered a cup of coffee. After adding cream, she took a sip and felt some of the fog lift from her brain. She leaned in and rested her chin on her left hand, toying with the handle of the mug with her right.

"When my sisters and I woke up this morning, Sophie was gone."

"Gone? As in…?"

"Gone. As in packed up her things and left."

"She's not in any danger, is she?"

"We don't think so. Well, not physical danger, anyway. Maybe in danger of calling off the wedding because of my unfiltered tirade on love. I need to find her and fix this."

Alejandro looked concerned. "Have you called her fiancé?"

"He called us, saying he couldn't get in touch with her. That she'd called him last night while he was sleeping and left a couple of messages, and when he tried to call her this morning he couldn't reach her. She wasn't picking up. I've looked all over the hotel and she's not here. The best I can figure is that she called an Uber and left."

"Where would she go?"

Olivia thought for a moment, changing gears from likely hiding places in the hotel to where Sophie might go outside of the place. She had an idea.

"We know she's not at Mason's. He said he'd call if he heard from her. I can think of a couple of places I'd look to start. She probably went home to her condo."

She shook her head. "I'm going to have a lot of explaining to do when I find her."

"Don't jump to conclusions," Alejandro said. "Maybe it's not as bad as you think."

Olivia shrugged. "My sisters and I think that last night sent her spiraling into a case of prewedding jitters. You know, cold feet."

Alejandro opened his mouth as if to say something, but sighed instead.

"What?" Olivia asked.

"Nothing."

"No, it's something. Tell me, please."

"If she's so easily spooked, maybe she knows something we don't."

"Such as?"

"Maybe she's questioning whether she should get married or not. If so, that's not your fault. In fact, maybe you did her a favor. Maybe what you said made her think. If she's having second thoughts, isn't it better to call off the wedding than to get a divorce?"

"We can't call off the wedding, because it's Dana and Kieran's wedding, too. And if Sophie opts out, it will certainly put a damper on their day."

"So you're saying truth be damned? She should just suck it up for propriety's sake? Because if so, maybe you're not as antiestablishment as you think you are."

She squinted at him. "That is *not* what I'm saying. This has nothing to do with me and everything to do with my sister's happiness."

"But you're making it sound like this is all about you. You must think you have some kind of power over her if you think your feelings about love and marriage can change her mind."

"I'm not saying I changed her mind. I'm saying I've spoiled the mood, cast a black cloud and now she's got cold feet."

Cocking a brow that seemed to say he wasn't convinced, Alejandro sat back and crossed his arms. He looked at her as if the judge and jury resided inside his head and they'd already come to a verdict on the matter. "You're saying all you have to do is talk to her and you can change her mind."

It wasn't a question. It was a statement, and Olivia didn't like the implications. She stood.

"Look, you don't know me or my sister. I don't know why it seemed like a good idea to burden you with the details. So please forget everything I told you. Sophie will be fine. The wedding will be fine. Good luck with your meeting."

As she turned to walk away, something made her

turn back. He watched her as she returned to the table. "I hope it goes without saying, but please don't mention this to anyone. Okay?"

"Of course. And I won't mention the kiss, either."

He had the audacity to wink at her. All cheeky and smug-like. That's what he was—cheeky and smug. And a player who took advantage of drunk women.

Okay, so maybe the kiss wasn't so bad.

Olivia flinched and waved him off. Her stomach remained in knots even as she made her way into the majestic Driskill's lobby, away from Alejandro Mendoza. The guy was a piece of work. A smug, cheeky piece of work who called it as he saw it no matter how awkward it rendered the situation. In fact, he seemed to get some kind of pleasure out of making her uncomfortable.

She'd do her best to steer clear of him for the duration of the wedding.

She hated the disappointment that swirled inside her. Because she wanted another taste of Alejandro's lips—she wanted more than just another taste of his lips, if she was honest. But she also knew that the only thing she should be focusing on this week was making sure she got Sophie to the wedding and down the aisle. The conflict tugged at the outer reaches of her subconscious, and she shoved it out of her mind.

She stared up at the gorgeous stained-glass ceiling, taking a deep breath and trying to ground herself. She took her cell phone out of her pocket and checked the time. It was almost eight thirty. There were no calls from her sisters. Dana and Monica were supposed to join them for brunch at eleven, which gave Olivia two and a half hours to find Sophie and make amends.

She called Sophie's cell again. After one ring, the call went directly to voice mail.

She did not leave a message. Instead, she texted her.

Where are you, Sophie? We're worried about you. I understand why you're upset and I'm sorry. I really am, but please let us know where you are...that you're safe.

Fully expecting the message to sit unanswered, Olivia shoved her phone into the back pocket of her jeans and made her way toward the elevators. As she waited for the doors to open in the lobby, her cell phone dinged.

Olivia's heart leaped when she saw that Sophie had replied.

I'm safe.

With shaking hands, Olivia typed:

Where are you?

She stared at her phone as if she could will her sister to answer. But by the time the elevator arrived, Sophie still hadn't replied.

Olivia tried to pacify herself with the thought that maybe there was no cell service in the elevator hallway. She walked back into the lobby and typed another message.

Thank you for letting us know you're okay. Will you please meet me for a cup of coffee before the brunch so we can talk about this?

There's no need. I'm going to pass on brunch. Please give my regrets to Dana.

She was going to pass on brunch?

What am I supposed to say to Dana?

Tell the truth. Tell her I'm not getting married.

I'm going to call you. Please pick up.

There's nothing to talk about.

Are you kidding me? I worked my butt off to give you and Dana a nice weekend. You can't just opt out without so much as a phone conversation. I don't care if you thought I was a little harsh last night. Sophie, you need to grow up. Your deciding not to get married affects others besides yourself.

Seconds after she sent the message her phone rang. It was Sophie.

"Hi," Olivia said. "Thank you for calling me."

"Say what you need to say." Sophie sounded like she was crying and Olivia's heart broke a little more.

"Sophie, please, you can't take to heart what I said last night." She moved out of the lobby and into the bar area where they were last night, looking for a quiet corner where she could talk to her sister privately. "Please don't let my cynical drunken words cause you to make the worst mistake of your life."

"Those weren't just liquor-inspired words, Liv. It's the truth. Every single word of what you said is true. Are you trying to tell me it's not?"

It was true. Her parents had a terrible marriage. If you could even call it a marriage. They led separate lives because they couldn't stand each other.

"I thought so," Sophie said on a sob when Olivia didn't reply. "Look, I need some time to figure out what I'm going to do. I appreciate all the time and hard work you put into the bachelorette party, but I need some space right now. I hope you understand."

"What do you want me to tell Dana?"

Sophie was inconsolable. It killed Olivia to hear her sister in so much pain. Especially since she was the one who'd caused it.

"Tell her whatever you want, Liv. I have to go."

"No, Sophie. Please tell me where you are—"

But it was too late. Her sister had already disconnected the call.

Olivia stood there trying to get her bearings, trying to figure out how to fix this mess—and quickly. It was best not to push Sophie about the brunch. Olivia kicked herself for scheduling the bachelorette party the weekend before the wedding. She should've done this last month. Sophie wasn't a partier and she was probably exhausted and overwhelmed by all the hoopla leading up to her wedding day. The best thing Olivia could do right now was to show her sister some compassion, give her the space she so clearly needed.

They'd simply tell Dana and Monica that Sophie was under the weather. Given the Fuzzy Handcuffs, that wouldn't be such a stretch.

As Olivia made her way upstairs to tell Zoe and Rachel that she'd talked to Sophie, she saw Mason at the front desk.

She called out to him and steeled herself for a frantic response from the bridegroom, but Mason smiled at her, appearing remarkably calm.

"Hey, Liv. What's the latest?"

Good old Mason, the calm to Sophie's occasional dramatic storm. She said a silent prayer that they would be able to weather this Category Five. How, exactly, did one explain that his fiancée was possibly backing out of the wedding? Then, in a moment of clarity, Olivia realized that even if her careless words had set off Sophie, it was Sophie's responsibility to tell Mason she wanted to call things off, not hers.

Olivia put on her bravest face. "I just got off the phone with Sophie. Have you spoken to her?"

"Not yet." Mason pulled out his cell phone. "I'll text her and tell her I'm talking to you."

Olivia waited and watched as Mason sent a message. Sophie responded immediately but it was a good two minutes before Mason finally looked up and said,

"What we have here is a good old-fashioned case of cold feet. She'll be fine. Just give her a little bit of time."

Mason's calm was rubbing off on Olivia. Still, she made sure she had her filter firmly in place before she spoke. She had learned her lesson after last night. The less said the better.

"I figure until she feels better, we can simply tell people she's got a bug," Mason said, looking so confident. "That's all they need to know."

"Sure," Olivia echoed. "That's all they need to know."

In the meantime, Olivia silently vowed, she would fix this mess.

She uttered a silent prayer that she could pull it off.

Chapter Three

On Monday evening, Alejandro handed the rental car keys to the valet parking attendant outside the Robinson estate and accepted his claim check. He'd been to functions at the sprawling estate when his brothers, Matteo and Joaquin, had married Rachel and Zoe, but the magnitude of its grandeur still rendered him awestruck.

The place made a statement about who Gerald Robinson was and what he stood for: a man who had started with nothing and built himself an empire with his brainchild, Robinson Computers. The man was brilliant. Alejandro might have found him intimidating if he hadn't been so intriguing. As an entrepreneur himself, Alejandro devoured biographies of successful businesspeople. Seeing how someone else created an empire was better than any business course he could take.

He would've been lying if he'd denied wanting all of this for himself. He wanted it so badly he could taste it.

Someday, he thought, as his shoes hit the pavers of the cobblestone path that was lined with tiki torches and directed people to the back of this castle of a house.

"Aloha. Good evening." Two attractive women dressed in loose-fitting Hawaiian-print dresses greeted Alejandro with warm smiles. Both had tucked a white flower into their long, dark hair. The print of their matching dresses reminded him of a shirt he used to wear back in his college days—only it looked much classier on them.

"Welcome to the wedding luau," the one holding a lei said.

She stepped forward and placed it around his neck and her dark hair glistened in the golden tiki-torch light, reminding him of Olivia and the unfortunate way they'd parted. He regretted grilling her the way he had yesterday morning. As soon as she'd walked away, he'd been planning his apology. He'd been out of line debating her sister's obviously fragile state. He knew it, he owned it and he would apologize for it. He didn't want anything to detract from the wedding festivities—certainly not bad blood or resentment stemming from yesterday's disagreement. Or Saturday night's kiss, either.

All day, the two events had played tug-of-war in

his mind. He'd had to hyperfocus during his business meeting at Hummingbird Ridge. It was a rare occasion when he allowed anything to distract him from business. But he hadn't exactly invited Olivia into his brain. She'd barged in unbidden, as strong a presence when she wasn't in the room as when they were standing face-to-face.

As soon as the woman who had presented him with the lei stepped away, her cohort stepped forward and offered him a drink served in a hollowed-out pineapple. The beverage was adorned with exotic flowers, a blue plastic straw and a tiny umbrella.

He took a sip. The rum and tropical fruit juices combined for a delicious drink. The Fortune Robinsons seemed to have cornered the market on signature cocktails. He certainly wasn't complaining since he was on the receiving end of all this libation creativity.

But since signature cocktails and Olivia Fortune Robinson had proven to be a rather explosive combination, he decided he needed to exercise the utmost caution tonight. Then again, given Olivia's demeanor the last time he saw her, he probably didn't have to worry.

The woman who had handed him the drink gestured to her right. "Please follow the torch-lined path around to the tent on the rear lawn and enjoy the festivities."

"Thank you," he said, raising his pineapple in an appreciative toast.

He followed the path and the sound of music. As he rounded the corner and the tent came into view, he took a deep breath and inhaled the sweet scent of gardenias mingling with delicious, smoky BBQ and firewood burning in outdoor fireplaces. A crowd of people mingled on the manicured lawn as a country band played on a stage in front of a parquet dance floor that had been laid out on the grounds.

Alejandro's gaze scanned the crowd for familiar faces. His stomach growled and he realized he hadn't eaten since breakfast. The meeting with the fine folks of Hummingbird Ridge had lasted through the lunch hour. He'd taken some time to drive around the area to get a feel for the town, which was located about a half hour west of Austin. Once he'd returned to the hotel, he'd been tied up on calls with investors, bankers and his partners—his cousins Stefan and Rodrigo Mendoza. Before he knew it, he'd had just enough time to shower, shave and get dressed for tonight.

Skipping lunch was a small price to pay because today he had taken another step toward creating his own empire. The trip out to Hummingbird Ridge had proven that the winery and its acres of thriving vineyards were, indeed, a good investment. The Texas Hill Country was one of the country's upcoming wine destinations.

Alejandro's interest in the wine business had started as a fluke. When he was in college at the University of Florida, he used to come home for the summer. Between his freshman and sophomore years, he'd taken a summer job at a South Beach wine bar to save money for tuition. What he'd thought would be a fleeting means to an end had sparked a passion in him, triggering him to change his major to agricultural operations and eventually get a master's degree in viticulture and enology. Not only had he learned the complexities and distinctions the different grape varietals lent to the bottled end product, he'd become educated on theories such as *terroir*—how the climate and land of an area worked together to make wines unique. He had spent a summer in France interning at a vineyard and another summer at a winery in the Napa Valley. Winemaking fascinated him, but he'd known if he wanted to make enough money to one day buy his own vineyard, he needed to be in sales. After scrimping and saving and working his ass off for a decade, his dream was close to becoming a reality. In fact, it was so close he could almost taste the wine.

Alejandro accepted a bacon-wrapped scallop off an hors d'oeuvre platter passed by a server dressed in Polynesian garb. As he bit into it, he continued to scan the crowd for familiar faces. Hundreds of friends and relatives had started to trickle in for the week of prewedding festivities outlined in the itinerary he'd received when he'd checked in at the Driskill. The information packet had included a schedule of events with dates and times for romantic couples' massages, rounds of golf and dinners. If nothing else, they would be entertained and well fed while they were here.

He hadn't forgotten his promise to check into the logistics of an informal wine tasting at Hummingbird Ridge. Even if the wedding party couldn't fit it into their schedule, which was pretty packed, it would be a great opportunity to spend some time with his father, his brothers and their wives. The Mendozas were a close-knit bunch and he didn't get a chance to see his siblings much now that they were married. His three brothers, Cisco, Matteo, Joaquin, their sister, Gabriella, and their dad, Orlando, had traded in Miami and moved to Texas. If everything panned out with the winery, Alejandro might be following suit, or at the very least visiting more often.

Before Alejandro could locate his family—his brothers and father were there, but his sister, Gabi, and her husband, Jude Fortune Jones, would arrive Saturday morning for the wedding—Kieran Fortune Robinson and Dana joined the band onstage. Kieran accepted the microphone from the guitar player.

"Good evening, everyone," Kieran said. "On behalf of my beautiful fiancée, Dana, my little sister Sophie and her fiancé, Mason, I'd like to welcome you to the start of our wedding week celebration. We are so glad you could join us as we count down the days leading up to the big event. Unfortunately, Sophie is a little under the weather tonight. She stayed home to rest up so that she'll be back to one hundred percent for Saturday."

Alejandro flinched as he recalled Olivia's frantic search for Sophie yesterday morning. Olivia had been so certain that her sister would be fine that Alejandro hadn't even considered the possibility that Sophie might not be here this evening. Was she still having second thoughts about the wedding?

Obviously Kieran and Dana's nuptials were still on. Alejandro watched the couple kiss when the crowd interrupted Kieran's welcoming remarks with chants of "Kiss her! Kiss her! Kiss her!" Kieran grabbed Dana and rocked her back as he planted a smooch on her lips.

The spectacle reminded him of kissing Olivia Saturday night at the Driskill Hotel. He immediately shook away the image, because thoughts like that could only lead to trouble.

Instead, he trained his focus on Kieran and Dana, who looked so happy together. Alejandro understood how they felt; he'd been there before, a long time ago. Were they so caught up in their own happiness they didn't know that Sophie was having second thoughts? Then again, for all he knew, maybe Olivia had found her sister and everything was just fine. Maybe she really was under the weather and the illness was what had driven her away from the Driskill Sunday morning.

Obviously he needed to find a friend here at the party if he'd been reduced to standing here alone pondering situations that had nothing to do with him.

"Please, help yourself to some barbecue and the open bar," Kieran said once he and Dana had come up for air. "In fact, if everyone could grab a drink, I would like to make a toast."

Olivia had groaned when Kieran had dipped Dana back in that shameless public display of affection. She'd groaned and then she'd been ashamed of herself. She'd wished she could take back the ugly sound as she'd glanced around to see if anyone had heard her.

They hadn't.

Of course not. Everyone was too busy *oohing* and *ahhing* over the blithe display of love. Good grief. Her brother had no shame.

As inappropriate as the groan had been, what she'd really wanted to do was shout *Get a room!* She'd been tempted, but she'd never actually do it. The groan had been the slightly less inappropriate compromise. Her attempt at good party manners.

Right.

She wanted to be happy for Kieran and Dana—and she was. Really, she was. But she was so wrecked over Sophie not being here tonight that her guilt was pretty much all-consuming.

She wished she could borrow some confidence from Mason. He loved Sophie so much and he was determined to stand by her while she figured out her heart.

Mason was willing to fight for Sophie's love—even if that fight entailed him attending the barbecue solo and keeping up the cover that Sophie was home sick with the flu and would be good as new by Saturday. His resolute love made Olivia do a mental double take. No one had ever been willing to fight for her like that. Every person she'd ever allowed herself to feel anything substantial for had walked away when the going had gotten tough. Most of the men who had hurt her—two of them in particular—had been more interested in cozying up to her father, who they'd believed could help them get ahead. When that didn't pan out, they'd left. No one had ever fought for her or believed in her the way Mason believed in Sophie. Sophie and Mason had something special and while it didn't alter Olivia's own thoughts on love, she was willing to concede that her little sister might have actually lassoed the unicorn.

Men like Mason were rare, almost mythical, and Olivia wasn't about to let Sophie make the biggest mistake of her life by letting Mason get away.

Even so, with Sophie refusing to attend the party tonight, Olivia was enough of a realist to know that nothing short of a miracle was going to change her sister's mind. Nothing less than Olivia being struck by lightning…or cupid's arrow. But that wasn't going to happen. She needed to come up with another plan.

Olivia racked her brain, but she kept coming back to one thing. Cupid's arrow. She had a feeling that the only way she was going to make amends with Sophie was by convincing her that she believed in love, that somehow, overnight, she'd had a total change of heart. It was crazy, but it might work. What did she have to lose? Olivia had to take action or otherwise risk earning the title of Prewedding Homewrecker—and carrying around the guilt from being responsible for ruining Sophie's life.

But how in the world could she pull it off? How could she make her sister believe she thought true love was possible?

Olivia was in full panic mode as she scanned the

crowd of guests who had gathered for the barbecue, as if the answer lay in the midst of people—both familiar and those she'd never met—who were enjoying the hors d'oeuvres and raising glasses in anticipation of Kieran's toast and in honor of the soon-to-be newlyweds.

Her gaze lit on her sister Rachel, who was talking to her husband, Matteo. Next to them, Zoe was flirting with her husband, Joaquin. There, like a very handsome third wheel, stood Alejandro, bedecked in an orchid lei and holding his pineapple cup.

The last single Mendoza.

Olivia's mind replayed the kiss they'd shared on Saturday night. In an instant her lips tingled as the feel and taste of him came flooding back, as if he'd kissed her only a moment ago.

That kiss... That. Kiss.

Suddenly, she was struck by a bolt of sexy inspiration. The idea was crazy—and a little bit naughty—but it just might work. As long as Alejandro went along with her plan.

Servers appeared with trays of champagne flutes. As Kieran gave the guests a moment to arm themselves with libations, Alejandro sensed someone standing too close behind him, invading his personal space. Before he could turn around a pair of feminine arms encircled his waist and a sultry voice that sounded a lot like Olivia's whispered in his ear.

"I know this sounds crazy, but I need you to kiss

me right here, right now, and make it look real. Please just go along with it and don't ask questions."

Was this some kind of a joke?

"What?"

She didn't answer him. She simply moved around so that she was standing directly in front of him. She took the pineapple drink from his hand and set it on the tray of a passing server then she cupped his face in her hands and laid one on him with the same ferocity she'd shown Saturday night.

As she opened her mouth, inviting him deep inside, he obliged. And the rest of the world—and all the questions that had popped into his head as Olivia had whispered her request—faded away. Alejandro pulled her in flush with his body and did exactly as she had asked. There would be plenty of time for questions later. Right now her wish was his command.

The kiss was a lightning bolt that seared Alejandro to his core. He wasn't sure how long they'd stood there, lip to lip, locked in each other's arms, breathing each other's air, but he was vaguely aware of distant cheering as he and Olivia slowly broke the kiss and separated. People were, in fact, cheering, and it wasn't for Kieran and Dana. Everyone who was standing near them was looking at them.

Everyone except for his brothers. Cisco, Matteo and Joaquin weren't cheering; they were piercing him with looks that screamed *What the hell are you doing?*

What the hell *was* he doing?

That was all it took to sober him up. But then Olivia, who still had her arms draped around his neck, leaned in and whispered, “Thank you. Please just keep up the act. I’ll explain as soon as we’re alone.”

Alejandro understood that her version of being alone probably wouldn’t include more kissing. But that wasn’t the most pressing problem at the moment.

“Quiet down, everyone,” Kieran instructed the buzzing crowd. “Olivia, is there anything you’d like to tell us?”

All eyes turned to Olivia, who still had her arms draped over his shoulders. She just smiled sweetly and made a show of shrugging in a noncommittal way that only fed the fire of speculation.

What *was* she doing? She seemed too smart and sure of herself to be unstable. Olivia clearly knew what she was doing. She was up to something and she was pulling him into it. Yesterday, she was arguing with him and asserting that they needed to act like the kiss had never happened, that everyone would be better off if they kept their distance from each other. Then today she was stealing her brother’s thunder and making a spectacle of kissing him senseless.

“Should we start making plans to accommodate a third bride and groom?” Kieran said into the microphone.

As Olivia turned toward her brother, her arm dropped to Alejandro’s waist and she held on. He followed suit, putting his arm around her.

One of the servers appeared in front of them with a tray of champagne flutes. They both took one.

"This is your night, my dear brother. Yours, Dana's, Sophie's and Mason's," she said. "To you and to your love and happiness."

The crowd cheered again and raised pineapple drinks and champagne flutes in tribute. The collective attention shifted back to Kieran and Dana.

"Thanks, sis," Kieran said. "That was a perfect toast. I couldn't have said it better." He sipped his champagne. "We hope everyone enjoys this magical week with us. Obviously we're off to a great start." He gestured with his head toward Olivia.

Alejandro felt a little uneasy being dragged into the spotlight. He was happy helping Olivia with whatever she was trying to accomplish—especially if it involved kissing her—but he'd prefer to know what he was working toward.

As everyone settled back into their groups and others made their way toward the food, Rachel, Matteo, Joaquin and Zoe cornered them.

"Hello?" Zoe said. "I think the two of you have some explaining to do."

"What do you mean?" Olivia asked. Alejandro both admired and resented her poker face. He wanted an explanation, too.

"Um, this?" Zoe gestured back and forth between Olivia and Alejandro with her manicured fingers. "When did this happen? What exactly is happening? And when were you going to tell us?"

Alejandro gazed down at Olivia. This was all her

show. He smiled the message to her when she glanced up at him, looking every bit like the smitten lover.

Without missing a beat, Olivia said, "Surprise! We just sort of fell into this. Isn't it great?"

As the quartet uttered sounds of confused surprise, Alejandro said, "Yes, we just couldn't resist each other."

Spoken aloud, the sentiment didn't quite sound as convincing as it had in his head.

"Will you excuse us for a minute?" he said before he could say anything else inane. "Olivia and I were getting ready to—"

Getting ready to what?

"We were getting ready to take a tour of the house," Olivia said. "Come on, sweetheart. Let's do that now so we can get back and have dinner."

As Olivia slid her hand into his, Alejandro said, "Excuse us. We'll be right back."

They walked hand in hand in silence, across the lush green lawn to stone steps that led past the pool to a travertine porch. Alejandro looked back at the grounds and the lake that bordered the massive property.

"Is that Lake Austin?" he asked.

"It is," she said as she opened the back door and they stepped inside the house. Alejandro thought they'd be alone once they were inside, but staff milled about everywhere, carrying platters of food and drink and working purposefully. The buzz inside the house, coupled with the sheer grandeur of the place, stunned him into silence.

Alejandro did not speak another word until Olivia had shut them inside a room on the second floor. It was larger than his first apartment.

He blinked as Olivia flicked on a light. The expensive-looking feminine decor registered on him. "Is this your bedroom?"

"It is," she said. "Or it used to be. I have my own place now."

"It's nice that your folks kept it the way you left it. You know, that they didn't turn it into an exercise room or a man cave."

Olivia shrugged. "The house has always had a gym and my father has three man caves. My parents aren't sacrificing anything by keeping my space intact. It's not as if they kept it like this as a shrine to me. It's just not beneficial for them to change it. You know, it was easier to just shut the door. But that's not why I dragged you up here."

She bit her bottom lip again, pulling it into her mouth, a gesture he was beginning to associate with her pensive side.

"Did you bring me in here to make out?" he joked.

"No, I didn't." The sharpness of her tone shouldn't have surprised him, but it did.

He crossed his arms. "Would you care to share why you felt compelled to put on that display out there? You made it look like you couldn't wait to jump my bones."

She looked visibly deflated, but she nodded toward a black chair situated across from a plush sofa and a glass coffee table. The decor looked like it could've been featured in one of those designer house magazines. The sleek, sophisticated, expensive look of it perfectly reflected Olivia's own style.

After they'd seated themselves, she confessed, "I do owe you an explanation and a debt of gratitude. I just don't quite know how to say this. And before I say anything, I need you to swear on your family's life that you can keep a secret. Because if one word of this gets out, it would be very hurtful to certain members of my family."

He made a cross over his heart with his right hand. "I would offer to stick a needle in my eye, but I don't like needles."

She cocked a dark brow. "What? A big, strong, tough guy like you is afraid of needles? I don't believe it."

He wanted to say that needles didn't scare him nearly as much as she did. It was becoming clear that she addled his brain so much that she was able to lord some kind of power over him.

"Look, this has nothing to do with needles," he said. "Why don't you just tell me what's going on? Why did you kiss me like that out there?"

"I did it because I need everyone to believe we're in love—or that I'm in love with you. No, it would be better if they believed that we love each other, you know, mutually."

"But, Olivia, you don't love me. Why do you want everyone to think you do tonight, when yesterday you made it clear that me kissing you again was strictly forbidden? Because it would detract from the wedding, take the focus off the brides and grooms?"

When she didn't answer him, he said, "You're a beautiful woman. You're smart and funny and you're a hell of a good kisser, but I'm starting to think you're off your rocker."

"Oh, well, there you go," Olivia said. "For a second there I was tempted to think you were paying me a compliment. You know, calling me a beautiful woman."

"I was. You are. But I'm a little confused here. I was prepared to make the sacrifice of never kissing you again—for the greater good, for your sister's happiness, but—"

"You wanted to kiss me again, Alejandro?"

"Of course I did."

"Oh. That's good. Then how do you feel about being my pretend lover for the duration of the wedding? You know, my boyfriend—or my intensely romantic date. No, it needs to be more than just a date. I need for Sophie to believe that I've fallen in love with you. I messed up big-time Saturday night. Because of my big mouth, my sister has lost all faith in love. I figure the only way to undo the damage I've caused is by making her believe that I've had a change of heart about love. It's the only way to renew her faith. Would you be willing to do that for me… for my sister?" She suddenly looked very small and fragile, but she looked at him intently. "I promise I will make it worth your while."

Now it was his turn to cock a brow and mess

with her. "And just how would you make it worth my while? Can you please be more specific? I'm talking details. The more vivid the better."

His mouth crooked up on one side and she obviously caught his drift because her cheeks flushed the same color as the hot-pink area rug under their feet.

"Certainly not in the way I think you're implying. You have a dirty mind, Alejandro."

"Hey, I didn't say a word. I was thinking along the lines of dancing and being dinner partners. So the hordes of adoring women will think I'm taken and leave me alone." He was smiling so that she would know he was joking. "That's what I was thinking. However, I am not responsible for whatever that mind of yours conjures up. If you'd like to try out your thoughts and see if it works for you, I'm happy to be at your service."

Her mouth fell open and he could tell she was trying to feign disgust, but the pretense hadn't reached her eyes. "Why are you making this so difficult?"

"Because watching you squirm is so much fun." He held her gaze as he grappled with a peculiar feeling in the pit of his stomach. Something he hadn't felt in ages. Interest and attraction. Maybe this wedding was going to be more interesting than he'd thought. At the very least, it would be fun.

He'd go along as her pretend boyfriend. It wasn't as if he was agreeing to marry her.

He shrugged, to appear not too eager. "I guess I've had worse offers," he said. "I'd be happy to play the role of your lover for the duration of the wedding." But he couldn't resist needling her a bit. "Just how deeply into character would you like to go?"

Chapter Four

"You pride yourself on being the king of the innuendo, don't you?" Olivia said, exercising great restraint to resist adding another layer to his insinuation. The chemistry between them begged her to keep the banter going, to tell him she was all about method acting and she was at his service for any research he needed in order to deliver a convincing performance.

Actually, her body was all in for the research, but her brain knew better. They needed to keep this strictly aboveboard.

"That's the thing about innuendo," he said. "You can interpret it however you choose."

"Okay, since you put it that way, I'd love an Oscar-winning performance, but we need to keep this act strictly PG."

He frowned. "That's disappointing. I was thinking an R-rated production would be so much more convincing."

"Sorry to disappoint you, Romeo, but let's not get carried away. Need I remind you that while this show we're about to put on is a limited engagement, we'll still have to stage a breakup and coexist at future family functions."

He frowned.

"It's not like we'll have to sit across the dinner table from each other every Sunday," he said.

"True."

Maybe this wasn't a good idea. Was it fair to ask a guy she barely knew to pretend to be her lover? To play the part convincingly without giving him all access? For a fleeting moment, she let herself go there. What if for one careless week she allowed herself to go off the rails and immerse herself in the part—onstage and off?

"What are you getting at, Alejandro? Do you expect me to sleep with you?"

After she set the words free, released them from the cage in her mind, the prospect of letting go like that was petrifying. She might not believe in love, but she did believe in feelings. And feelings, when you allowed them to meander unchecked, made you susceptible to hurt.

No. If there was ever a time that she needed to stay completely in control it was now. This was about Sophie. It wasn't about her. It was a means to an end to fix what she had nearly broken.

"You make it sound so romantic," Alejandro said.

When she didn't jab back, he seemed to ease up. "It's clear that's not what you want. So, no, I don't expect you to sleep with me. I would never use sex as a bartering chip. Don't worry, Olivia. You're safe with me."

She should've been relieved, but the most primitive part of her was disappointed that sex was off the table. But she reminded herself that she needed to set the ground rules up front and they needed to stick to them. For their own good. Hadn't the Sophie disaster been enough of a cautionary tale of what happened when she got careless?

"That's good to know," she said. "I'm glad we're on the same page."

He nodded, but things still felt off-kilter. Before they left this room, she needed to make sure everything was as right as it could be.

"Please know that I do appreciate you helping me," she said. "It's good of you, Alejandro. I realize you don't have to do this. I mean, Sophie is my sister. I'm the one who opened my big mouth and set everything spinning out of control."

Olivia clamped her mouth shut. She was talking too much. She always did when she felt out of control. Obviously she needed to admit to herself that Alejandro Mendoza made her feel that way. *Yes, just acknowledge it—look the problem in the eye, stare it down—and move on.*

She locked gazes with him. Looked deep into those brown eyes, straight into the lighter brown and golden flecks that she hadn't noticed before. He was the first one to blink, breaking the trance, but she still didn't feel any more in control than before she'd tried to stare down the dragon. She needed to try another tactic.

"Even though I'm appreciative and I shouldn't question your motives, I'm wondering why you would do this for me."

There. She'd said it. And it needed to be said.

He was frowning at her again. Not an affected frown this time, but a genuine look of consternation. Still, she was glad she'd said it. Knowing what he was expecting in return for helping her might put things on a bit more of a level playing field.

"What's in this for me." It wasn't a question. The way he repeated her words was more like he was turning them around, looking at them from all angles. "What's in this for me. I don't know, Olivia. Should I expect personal gain? Because I wasn't, other than maybe the satisfaction of helping you out."

"Look, Alejandro, I didn't mean that in the way you seem to be taking it. I just wanted to make sure we're both laying all our cards on the table before we go any further."

"Is everything a business venture to you? I get the feeling you're about to whip out a contract for me to sign."

She wished it was that easy. For a terrifying moment, she feared that her plan was a mistake.

She stood. "I'm sorry. Let's just forget about this whole thing and proceed with business as usual between us. It's not you…it was a bad idea."

He reached out and took her hand, tugging her gently to get her to sit back down. And, of course, she did. Because it was clear that her better judgment, which was telling her to run away and save herself, went belly up when Alejandro did so much as breathe near her. With this man she felt totally out of control. And it was petrifying.

"I hate to be the voice of reality, but after that show we put on before the toast, people are going to have questions. And even though I don't know your sister very well, if everything you said is true—and I have no reason to believe it's not—do you think it will restore Sophie's faith if word gets back to her that it's 'business as usual' between us again?"

The guy was more insightful than she'd given him credit for. And he was absolutely right. Sophie would be completely disheartened, and with good reason. There was no backing out now unless she wanted to put the final nail in the coffin on Sophie's desire to marry.

"You're right," she told him. "You're a good man to allow me to drag you into this, Alejandro. I promise I'll make it up to you somehow."

"I'll hold you to that." He reached out and took her hand. Only this time it felt different. Not as dangerous, even though the butterflies in her stomach still flew in formation.

"Shall we go back to the party? I think we have some explaining to do."

He smiled. "Let the show begin."

Olivia should've known she wouldn't be able to fool her sisters. She shouldn't have even tried. But even though they'd gone along with the charade at the party, pretending to be just as surprised and convinced as everyone else by her love affair with Alejandro, Zoe and Rachel had shown up at her condo early the next morning with a box of doughnuts and plenty of questions.

She'd spilled the beans within the first five minutes.

"So we weren't convincing?" Olivia asked as she put the kettle on to boil water for coffee in the French press. "Please, at least tell me we weren't painfully obvious."

"You were absolutely convincing to the untrained eye," Rachel said as she took down coffee mugs from the cabinet above the stove. "You should know better than to try to pull one over on Zoe and me. Why didn't you tell us about the plan from the start?"

Olivia turned toward her sisters and braced the small of her back against the edge of the counter.

"I didn't have a plan per se. In fact, when I saw that Sophie hadn't snapped out of her funk by last night, I was in full panic mode. She missed the brunch and then the dinner where she was supposed to welcome her guests. It was starting to feel like something more than cold feet. I'm afraid if it goes on much longer,

Mason won't be able to keep up her flu cover-up. Either that, or he's going to lose his patience. I mean, how would you all feel if your husbands had ditched the wedding events and told you they weren't sure they wanted to marry you less than a week before the wedding?"

Her sisters nodded in agreement.

"Thank goodness Mason is a very patient man," said Rachel. "So what are you planning to do? Are you counting on word of your affair with Alejandro magically getting back to Sophie? Or do you have a plan?"

Olivia bought herself some time by grinding the coffee beans she had measured out. It only took a few seconds, but by the time she'd finished, both of her sisters were staring at her expectantly, waiting for an answer.

"I definitely want to be proactive," Olivia said. "There's not enough time to leave matters up to chance. However, before I can do anything I need to figure out where she is. I haven't talked to her since Sunday. Have either of you heard from her?"

Olivia already knew the answer to that question. Because of course her sisters would've rushed to her the minute they had learned Sophie's whereabouts. No, this was a code red situation. And they needed to do something to avert a major catastrophe. Since the three of them were together and would soon be fortified by doughnuts, she was confident they'd come up with something.

Zoe cleared her throat as if she had something to

say. That's when it dawned on Olivia that her sister had been uncharacteristically quiet as she and Rachel had been mulling over the situation.

"I know where Sophie is," Zoe said.

The tea kettle whistled as if punctuating Olivia's agitation.

"What? Where is she?" Olivia demanded as she took the kettle off the flame.

Zoe stood there silently, looking away from her sisters.

"You've been standing here all this time harboring this information?" Rachel said. "Are you going to make us pry it out of you, or are you going to tell us?"

Zoe shot daggers at Rachel. "She asked me not to tell."

"Honey, this is not an ordinary situation," Olivia said. "You're not betraying her trust by telling us. In fact, you just might be saving her marriage. Where is she?"

"I still can't believe she's been right here the whole time," Olivia said as she and her sisters climbed the stairs of their childhood home. "She was probably watching the party last night from her window. Alejandro and I were right down the hall from her."

Olivia stopped in her tracks causing Rachel to nearly bump into her. "Oh my gosh. I hope she didn't overhear Alejandro and me talking."

"I don't think so," Zoe whispered. "I spoke to her last night and she didn't say anything. And you know she would've had plenty to say if she'd heard you."

"Good point," Olivia whispered back. "Let's—" She drew a finger over her throat in a gesture that meant *silence* and motioned for them to continue on to Sophie's room.

The three sisters traveled quietly down the long hall. Sophie's room was at the opposite end of the hall from Olivia's. She was grateful because if her sister had overheard the conversation it would have made matters even worse. Now, regardless of how dangerous the Alejandro plan felt, it was her last recourse. It had to work, because she certainly didn't have a plan B.

Nor did she have a plan for approaching her sister, she realized when they finally stood in front of Sophie's bedroom door. Zoe and Rachel looked at Olivia, as if they were waiting for her to do something. So she did what she did best and took charge. She gestured to Zoe, indicating that she should knock on the door and be the one to speak to Sophie first.

At first, Zoe shook her head, but through a series of pantomimes Olivia was able to impart that it was only logical for Zoe to be the one to knock because she was the only one who knew Sophie was here. With a resigned shrug Zoe acquiesced and gave the door a tentative rap.

"Sophie?" she said. "Are you in there? It's me, Zoe. I just wanted to check on you. See how you are."

When she didn't answer, Olivia tried the door. It was locked. Olivia motioned for Zoe to knock again. This time Zoe didn't argue.

"Come on, Soph. Open up. Please? You can't hide

in here forever. Besides, it's getting kind of difficult to explain your absence to the guests. You're gonna have to make up your mind about what you want to do. You owe Mason that much."

Olivia gave Zoe the signal to tone it down a little bit. She appreciated what her sister was trying to do, but she was still holding out hope that the soft touch might work.

As if reading Olivia's mind, Zoe changed her tactic. "Besides, if you don't open the door I'm not going to tell you the gossip. And it's juicy. It involves Alejandro Mendoza. You're definitely going to want to hear this."

Sophie almost caught Olivia giving Zoe the thumbs-up. Because the tidbit about Alejandro seemed to be the magic words that made Sophie open the door for Zoe.

Of course, when she saw Rachel and Olivia standing there too, she tried to shut the door again, but the three of them were quicker than Sophie and managed to muscle their way in before she could lock them out.

Before Sophie could say anything, her sisters grabbed her in a four-way group hug as they cooed their concern and happiness about finally seeing her again.

"We were so worried about you," Rachel said.

"How are you doing?" Olivia asked.

"Have you changed your mind about the wedding?" Zoe asked. "Are you getting married?"

All Sophie could say was "I don't know. I don't know what I believe anymore."

Olivia noticed that Sophie didn't utter one word of protest about Zoe's sharing the secret of her whereabouts. That confirmed what Olivia had suspected—that Sophie had told Zoe because she knew Zoe wouldn't be able to keep the secret.

Zoe was the loose lips, Rachel was the vault and Olivia was the problem solver.

"You said there was gossip?" Sophie asked. "About Alejandro Mendoza?"

Olivia felt relief—her sister seemed to be playing right into their hands. Good thing, too, because Olivia didn't know how they would have steered her in that direction if she hadn't brought it up herself.

Olivia said a silent prayer that Zoe would pick up on her cue and proceed in a way that didn't look staged.

"Oh, that's not important," Olivia feigned. "We are here to talk to you, to see what we can do to make you feel better about everything."

Olivia held her breath.

"The best thing you could do for me right now is to talk about something other than the wedding. Because if you keep badgering me about it, you can't stay." Sophie walked over to the door and put her hand on the knob as if she were demonstrating how she would show them out.

"Then you're saying we can stay if we don't talk about the wedding?" Rachel asked.

Sophie eyed her sisters as if she were weighing the pros and cons.

"Olivia and Alejandro hooked up last night." Zoe

spat the words so perfectly Olivia had to remind herself to look suitably offended. After all, if this had been a true hookup, she wouldn't have wanted anyone—even her sisters—gossiping about it.

The ploy seemed to be working, because Sophie's jaw dropped and her eyes were huge.

"Zoe," Olivia admonished, "you promised you wouldn't say anything."

Rachel rolled her eyes. "Well, you two made such a spectacle of yourselves last night that if Sophie didn't hear it from Zoe she would certainly hear about it from someone else."

Olivia stood there silently, channeling her best humiliated/indignant expression.

"This is nobody's business but mine and Alejandro's," Olivia said. "So just stop, okay?"

"Oh, I don't think so," said Sophie. Her eyes sparkled as she took the bait—hook, line and sinker. She grabbed Olivia's arm and tugged her toward the couch by the window. "You are not leaving until you tell me everything."

She looked at Zoe and Rachel. "This happened last night? At the welcome barbecue? And I missed it?"

Zoe and Rachel nodded, a little too enthusiastically.

"Yep. You missed it," Zoe said. "If you would've been there last night you would've had a front-row seat."

No. If she'd been there last night nothing would've happened. There would've been no need.

Olivia's mind replayed last night's kiss. The details

were so vivid she could virtually feel Alejandro's lips on hers. Never in her life had she been at odds with herself like she was over this. Every womanly cell in her body couldn't wait for her to kiss him again, but every ounce of common sense in her brain reminded her to rein it in. Because if the plan worked like it seemed to be working, she was going to be kissing Alejandro a lot more. It was fine if she enjoyed it. In fact, it was probably for the best if she did since they'd be spending so much time together. However, it was in her own best interest to not get carried away.

"Olivia! Oh, my gosh," Sophie squealed. "He's gorgeous, and I knew he was interested in you because of the way he was looking at you Saturday night. Did I call it or what?" She looked at Zoe and Rachel. "I called it. Didn't I call it?"

Sophie clapped her hands gleefully, looking like she'd just opened the front door and found the prize patrol of a sweepstakes holding a big check made out to her.

"You called it, Soph," Rachel conceded.

Olivia crossed her arms and let her body fall back against the couch with a petulant *harrumph.*

Sophie angled herself toward Olivia. "Tell me everything. Start from the beginning and tell me every juicy detail. Come on, Liv. Spill it."

Olivia looked down and shook her head. "I'm glad you all think this is entertaining, but I don't want to talk about it."

"Wait, what?" Rachel asked. "Alejandro is gorgeous and we would all like to live vicariously through you for just a few minutes. I mean, it was just a hookup. What's the harm in sharing?"

Perfect.

Olivia took a deep breath and bit her bottom lip, doing her best to look sincerely offended.

"I'm not sure it was just a hookup," she said. "So you all just hop off, okay?"

"Are you saying you care about him?" Zoe asked.

Olivia gave a one-shoulder shrug. "Yeah, I think I do."

Sophie was watching, rapt. Olivia decided she needed to kick it up a level.

"I didn't think it was possible. Really, I didn't think it would ever happen to me. I thought I was immune." She placed both of her hands over her heart. "But for the first time in my life, I think I'm in love. Truly, madly, deeply in love." One at a time, she looked each of her sisters in the eye, ending with Sophie. That's when she delivered the knockout punch. "I'm in love with Alejandro Mendoza and he feels the same way."

Sophie sat there looking stunned. When she didn't speak, Olivia feared that she'd been a little too melodramatic. Maybe the *truly, madly, deeply* bit was a little over-the-top. *Ugh*, it probably was. It was the title of her favorite Alan Rickman movie, and the name of that corny Savage Garden song, which had to be one of the sappiest love songs ever. Okay, so she'd secretly loved it ever since the time she and her sisters had gotten up and sang it at karaoke night at Señor Iguana's.

The fib had come to her in a rush, but that might

have been the reason Sophie was just sitting there staring at her. Olivia said a silent prayer hoping she hadn't blown it.

Chapter Five

Alejandro was able to arrange a wine tasting for Wednesday afternoon at Hummingbird Ridge Vineyard. It was short notice, but he was psyched when Olivia was able to herd and organize a group of fourteen who were interested in going. It was his wedding gift to the brides and grooms.

Alejandro had left the outing to the discretion of the wedding party, and the final group ended up being comprised of family—Mendozas and Fortune Robinsons. It was great, in theory. The problem was Olivia's "we're in love" plan seemed to be working, as Sophie seemed to have miraculously recovered from her "flu" and had happily agreed to join them. That meant they had to put on a convincing performance for Sophie's benefit in front of key members of the family—Mason, Dana and Kieran; their fathers, Gerald Robinson and Orlando Mendoza; Orlando's fiancée, Josephine Fortune; and their siblings, Rachel and Matteo; Zoe and Joaquin; and Cisco and his wife Delaney. Rachel and Zoe were in on the ruse, but his brothers and Delaney weren't and they believed they were witnessing a romance unfolding right before their eyes.

As they had waited to board the small chartered bus that would take them to the winery, Dana's friend Monica had flirted with him. But then Olivia had walked up and draped her arms around his neck and greeted him with a kiss that made his eyeballs roll back into his head. After that, Monica had kept her distance.

Normally, he would have been enticed by the challenge of a beautiful woman's reserve—especially one who had shown interest in him. After all, it was the thrill of the chase, and it was one of his favorite games. But not only did Monica virtually disappear, his attention kept drifting back to Olivia, who was seated beside him on the bus.

He admired the way her long dark hair was swept back from her face, accentuating dark, soulful eyes, high cheekbones and full lips that begged him to kiss them again. His eyes followed the graceful slope of her neck to the place where her blouse ended in a vee at her breastbone and just a hint of cleavage winked at him. She looked sleek and polished in her snug-fitting beige pants and black tank.

She leaned in toward him. "Thanks for doing this."

Her voice was quiet and husky and made him think of sex, even though he wasn't sure if she was expressing gratitude for the wine tasting trip or for going along with the ruse to draw her sister out of her pre-wedding funk.

"My pleasure." He watched her intently, realizing that in its own way this game of subterfuge was at once erotic and frustrating as hell. The two of them acted like they couldn't keep their hands off each other, like they were merely tolerating the others until they could finally sneak off to finish what they'd started.

Every single person here, with the exception of Rachel and Zoe, thought Olivia and he were sleeping together. The thought made his groin tighten even though the exact opposite was true. They were like the old back-lot Hollywood sets that looked real from the outside, but behind the scenes it was just prefabricated plywood braces and empty promises.

Even though he really could've used a cooldown, he put his hand on the back of her neck and caressed it. The gesture made her look up at him and when she did, he lowered his mouth to hers and planted a gentle kiss on her lips.

"Get a room, you two." Sophie laughed. Olivia had strategically chosen the seats in front of Sophie and Mason to give her sister a front-row seat for the show.

They ended the kiss and feigned embarrassment as Sophie leaned forward and braced her forearms on the seatback.

"So, my big sister isn't immune to love after all."

Her voice floated between them on a note of wonder. "You know, Alejandro, I called this relationship even before the two of you realized you were perfect for each other."

"Yes, you did, Sophie," Olivia said to her sister. She placed her hand on his leg and traced slow circles and she continued to gaze at Alejandro, as if she was so deeply in love she couldn't bear to look away. "You nailed it. You did."

Alejandro smiled. "What do you mean you called it?"

"That night at the Driskill bar," Sophie explained, "I said to Olivia that the two of you were perfect for each other. Not just because you're the last single Mendoza brother and she's the last single Fortune Robinson sister, but because you're perfect together. You're made for each other."

"We are perfect for each other," Alejandro echoed as he gazed at Olivia.

"Well, it's true," Sophie said. "You are the only person in the world that could make my sister believe in love. You're like King Arthur of Camelot, the only one who could pull Excalibur out of the stone."

He raised an eyebrow at Olivia. Had she really never been in love? What was it that would cause her to take such a hardline stance? What would make her close herself off? Granted, love was a risky endeavor. The heart was uncertain by nature. He'd learned that firsthand after he'd lost Anna.

"See, Olivia? I told you that there was someone for you. I told you that Alejandro was your man."

"Yes, you did, Sophie."

Something flickered in Olivia's gaze. She blinked and looked away. But it felt more like she was pulling away. Maybe she was performing the same reality check Alejandro himself was right now. Despite the hot kissing, tender touching and cozy embracing, it was all for show. Every bit of it. He needed to remind himself of that now and again. Hell, if he knew what was good for him, he would write a stern reminder on a figurative sign and nail it to the forefront of his mind. Because he could already see it would be very tempting to lose himself in this game.

Olivia scooted away from him and turned around in her seat to talk to her sister.

"I'm glad to see you're feeling better." Her voice was low. "You had us all worried for a while."

Alejandro didn't turn around. Instead, he sat facing forward and he caught his father, who was seated at the front of the bus, slanting a glance over his shoulder in Alejandro's direction. When the older man realized Alejandro had caught him looking, he pretended to be shifting so that he could more easily drop his arm around Josephine's shoulder. But Alejandro hadn't missed the curious look in his dad's eyes.

He pondered the vague conundrum of what he was going to say to his father and Josephine once they had a chance to corner him. Orlando was bound to be full of questions, and rightfully so. He was his father, after all. A father who wanted nothing more than for all of his children to be as happy as he was.

There was a long stretch of time after Alejandro's mother, Luz, died when he thought his father might never be happy again. Orlando had been so deeply in love with Luz that Alejandro and his siblings had feared that he might will himself into an early grave. That was so unlike the man who had always been so full of life.

When Luz died five years ago, Orlando had been bereft. Alejandro and his siblings had convinced him that he needed a change of scenery, that he needed to leave a lifetime of memories and the hustle and bustle of Miami for the more laidback pace of Horseback Hollow, Texas. That was when he met Josephine Fortune. Since then, Orlando had been like a new man.

Alejandro hated to lie to his dad. They'd always had a great relationship, but he'd promised Olivia he wouldn't tell anyone what they were up to. They couldn't risk anyone slipping up and tipping off Sophie. The more people who knew about the ruse, the greater the chance of someone spilling the beans.

Orlando was nothing if not understanding. As soon as the week was over and Sophie was happily off on her honeymoon, he would level with his dad. Orlando would understand.

Gerald Robinson, however, might be another matter.

Olivia's father sat in the front seat across the aisle from Orlando and Josephine. He'd arrived only moments before the bus left so Alejandro hadn't had an opportunity to introduce himself again. They'd met at his brothers' weddings, but it had only been in passing.

Alejandro ignored the dread that reminded him that Gerald Robinson would probably wonder about this sudden relationship. Any father with a daughter like Olivia would be protective.

He'd done a fair amount of research on Gerald Robinson the mogul, the genius businessman. The guy was formidable. He had a reputation for ruthlessly eliminating competition and systematically taking down his opponents.

Alejandro blinked away a sudden vision of Gerald enlisting his henchmen to teach him a lesson about messing with his daughter. But then he dismissed the thought because he wasn't messing with Olivia. He was helping her. Actually, he clarified to himself, he was messing around with Olivia to help Sophie.

This could get complicated in ways that he hadn't even thought of before he'd agreed to this farce.

Alejandro's hand instinctively found the tattoo on his forearm. He covered it with his palm, as if touching Anna's name might provide answers. The tattoo was his touchstone, anchoring him in the past and grounding him in the present all at once. It was a reminder that he'd been fortunate enough to know true love once. Not everyone was lucky like that. Olivia didn't even believe in love. He didn't know if it was because she'd been hurt so badly that it had cauterized her heart.

He glanced at her as she and her sister had their heads together, whispering and laughing, making happy sounds that had him convinced that their Saturday-night fight, the one that had nearly turned Sophie into a runaway bride, was not only a thing of the past—it was erased from the annals of their sister history.

The bus rounded the corner, bringing Hummingbird Ridge Vineyard into view with its inviting lodge and its acres of weathered grapevines standing like rows of stooped and gnarled old men waiting for the rapture.

The midday sun beat down, casting a golden light on the scene, making it one of the most beautiful sights Alejandro had ever seen.

The blood rushed in his ears as his pulse picked up at the thought of how hard he'd worked to bring his plans to life. Soon, this would all be his. His kingdom.

"Is that Hummingbird Ridge?" Olivia asked.

He nodded.

"It's beautiful," Olivia said. "It looks like a postcard. Isn't it sad that for as long as I've lived in Austin, I've never been to a Hill Country winery? So this is a real treat for so many reasons."

"Never?" Alejandro asked. "Why not?"

"That's a good question. I have no idea why not and I don't really have any good excuses. I guess I just haven't had time to venture out here. Or, actually, I've been so bogged down by the day-to-day grind that I haven't made time."

He wanted to ask her what she did for fun, if she even had fun. Or was she always all work and no play?

He wanted to tell her that he could help her with that, if she'd let him. After all, he had made an art form out of having fun while working his way to success. But the bus was pulling into the winery's parking lot. He made a mental note—right across the large sign in the forefront of his mind that reminded him their escapades were all for show—to help Olivia learn how to have fun this week. Right now, he had a winery to show off and a captive audience that was eager to learn more.

As the driver parked, Alejandro told her, "I'm going to go inside to make sure everything is ready for us. Will you corral everyone outside until I get back?"

"You bet."

She already had her work face on, ready to take charge. It would be fun to see her spring into action organizing everyone.

"Thanks. Why don't you take them for a walk around the grounds? There's a sculpture garden around the back. I want to make sure everyone gets a chance to enjoy it. I'll come and get you as soon as they're ready for us."

Without even thinking about it, he leaned in and kissed her. It felt natural. Maybe a little too natural. But she kissed him back. When she pulled away, they both seemed to have the same question in their eyes: *Is this okay?* And the same answer: *It's fine.*

He stood and made his way to the front of the bus. Since it was a weekday the staff had agreed to close the tasting room for their private party. A sign was tacked to the large rough-hewn wooden door. It read: "Closed for private party from 1pm-3pm. Please come again." Alejandro reached out and grabbed the brass handle and pulled the door. It creaked open, exposing an airy reception area with high vaulted ceilings with dark beams. A marble-topped tasting bar crowded with wineglasses and corked bottles graced the wall directly across from the front door. In the center of the room, someone had set a wooden trestle table for the tasting. They'd laid it with breads and cheeses and other appetizers to pair with the various wines.

The rusty squeak of the door sounded behind Alejandro and he turned to see Gerald Robinson walk in. The man stopped just inside the threshold, scowled and took his time looking around, taking in everything as if he were judging the place and finding it wanting. Even after his gaze skewered Alejandro, Gerald didn't speak. He stood there silently, challenging him with his blank expression.

There he was—*the* Gerald Robinson. Creator of empires, eviscerator of men who got in his way… And of men who dated his daughter?

Obviously his brothers and Mason had battled the monster and lived to marry his daughters.

When Gerald agreed to join them today, Alejandro had known the mogul was bound to have a conversation with him about what Alejandro was doing with Olivia. What the hell was he supposed to say? Lying to Orlando was one thing—it wasn't really lying because he would confide the truth later—but lying to Gerald by saying he was in love with his daughter was another. It was best to be proactive and take charge of the conversation.

"Mr. Robinson, welcome." Alejandro walked over to Olivia's father and extended his hand. "I'm Alejandro Mendoza. We've met before at Rachel's and Zoe's weddings."

Gerald offered a perfunctory shake, but his grip was firm and commanding. "I know who you are. Olivia tells me you're buying this place?"

"I am."

Again, Gerald's steely gaze pinned him to the spot. Alejandro steeled himself for the inevitable interrogation.

"Nice place," Gerald said. Unsmiling, he broke eye contact and gave the room another once-over. "You're from Miami. I take it you know something about wine."

They weren't questions. They were statements that proved the guy had already done some investigating. Hell, for all Alejandro knew the man might've hired a private detective to perform a full-scale inquiry.

It was fine if he had. Alejandro had nothing to hide. He made his living honestly.

"I know a lot about wine. Are you an oenophile?"

"I have no idea what you're talking about," Robinson said.

"An oenophile is a wine enthusiast," Alejandro explained.

Gerald scowled at him. "Why didn't you say that in the first place?"

It was a fair question. Gerald probably thought he

was being pretentious, showing off. Maybe he was. But that wasn't something he'd admit out loud.

"I don't like wine," Gerald said. "But I read something just the other day about how over the past few decades, Hill Country wineries have been growing steadily and Texas wine production has become a viable player in the industry. Fascinating. The article said that winemakers are forgoing the Napa Valley because it's expensive and exclusive and basically out of their reach."

That was exactly why Alejandro had chosen to buy a place in Texas. When he'd discovered it was a viable option it had almost seemed meant to be, since most of his immediate family had relocated to the Lone Star State. In fact, if he'd believed in fate, he might have thought it'd had a hand in aligning the stars and moon to make this possible. It just seemed to make sense that this was where he would invest the money his mother, Luz, had left him when she passed away.

In typical Luz fashion, she'd made arrangements to take care of her children even after she'd left this earth. She'd taken out a small life insurance policy, leaving equal sums to each of her five kids. She'd left each of them a handwritten note telling them how much she loved them, that it had been a privilege to be their mother and that she hoped the money she was leaving each of them would help make their dreams come true.

Alejandro had invested the gift from his mother and, while it wasn't enough to allow him to buy Hummingbird Ridge free and clear, that investment, along with the money he'd saved, was the seed money he needed to interest his cousins, Rodrigo and Stefan, and a couple of investors who would be silent partners. Together they had the buying power to make the deal. They were almost there. The last hurdle was to clear due diligence and inspections and they'd be home free.

"That's exactly why I chose Texas," Alejandro said. "Most of my family has relocated to Texas. I've had my eye on wineries here. I've made several scouting trips, during which I became friendly with Jack and Margaret Daily—the couple that owns Hummingbird Ridge. They wanted to sell and I wanted to buy. It just seemed like a good fit."

Gerald grunted as he stood there with his arms crossed. Alejandro couldn't tell if he was boring him or if the sound indicated contemplative interest.

"Hummingbird Ridge has been in Margaret's family for several generations," Alejandro explained. "She inherited it and wanted to pass it on to their daughter, but the daughter's not interested. She's a surgeon and doesn't have the time or the inclination to take over the family business. I asked them if they wanted to adopt me, but they said they'd cut me a deal instead," he joked, but Gerald didn't laugh.

"If I would've known it was for sale, I would've bought it."

"Really?" This was unexpected coming from a guy who professed to not like wine. "You're interested in getting involved in the wine industry?"

Gerald shrugged. "To diversify."

"If you find a vineyard and you do decide to invest, make sure you've got a good crew. Even though this is becoming one of the top wine production states, it still has its challenges. It has distinct regions that are different enough to the point of being incompatible in terms of vine selection. Depending on the area, the microclimatic and geographic factors can vary considerably, but that's what I find so appealing about it."

Gerald didn't say anything. Alejandro could tell from the man's body language that it was time to stop talking. So he just stood there. The faint whir of the air conditioner was the only sound in the room.

"Well," Gerald finally said, "thanks for arranging this tasting. And if you hurt my daughter, you'll answer to me and there will be hell to pay."

The older man's forced smile reminded Alejandro of a great white shark as Gerald turned around and let himself out of the tasting room.

"Alejandro, welcome. We're excited that you could be here today."

Alejandro turned to see Margaret stepping out of the office, which was located down a hallway to the right of the wine bar.

"Hi, Margaret. Everything looks great. Thanks for going the extra mile to make today special for my guests."

"My pleasure. Will they be arriving soon?"

"They're already here." He motioned to the door. "They're enjoying the grounds until you're ready for them."

"We're ready when you are," Margaret said. "Shall we invite them in?"

As Alejandro and Margaret set off to find the party, she told him that Jack was sorry to miss him, but he had some business in Dallas he had to take care of.

Alejandro's phone rang, interrupting the conversation. His cousin Stefan's name flashed on the screen. "Excuse me, Margaret. I need to take this call."

"That's fine, honey. I'll find everyone and bring them inside."

"Stefan, my man," Alejandro said. "You must have been picking up the good vibe. I'm standing here in the Hummingbird Ridge tasting room. What's going on?"

Stefan didn't speak right away and for a moment Alejandro thought they'd lost the connection.

"Stef, are you there?"

"I am. I don't have good news. Masterson is pulling out of the Hummingbird Ridge deal."

Alejandro's gut contracted. "Bad joke, bro."

"I wish it was a joke. It's not. We're not going to have the money we need to buy the place. We're going to be short by a third."

Chapter Six

That evening, Alejandro stared straight ahead at the stretch of highway ahead of him as he drove Olivia to the barbecue, which was hosted by Mason's family. Losing the investor was nothing more than a setback.

Still, if he'd had a shred of a hint that the deal wouldn't go through, he wouldn't have brought everyone to the winery. He would've come up with some other way to celebrate the brides and grooms, but he certainly wouldn't have dragged everyone out in the middle of all the wedding festivities had he known that the vineyard might not be his. Or at least he wouldn't have announced that it was his new venture. But after the sting of the setback had subsided a bit, his mind turned to more constructive thoughts: getting replacement funds.

Before they'd boarded the bus to leave for Austin, he'd asked Gerald Robinson if he could meet with him on Monday morning after the wedding because he wanted to present an investment opportunity in Hummingbird Ridge. It was a long shot, but Robinson hadn't cut him off at the knees. Instead, he'd dug around in his wallet and come up with a business card.

"Call my assistant and tell her I told you to set up a meeting." He hadn't asked any questions or expressed any interest; he'd just walked away and gotten on the bus.

Immediately, Alejandro had excused himself and had gone back inside the winery and placed the call. Before the bus had left Hummingbird Ridge, he had an appointment with Robinson on the books at three o'clock Monday afternoon. He'd have to change his flight back to Miami from Monday to Tuesday, but it was a small price to pay for possibly saving the winery purchase.

The biggest problem was whether or not to tell Olivia he was meeting with her father.

He remembered what she'd said about the guys who had used her to get to Gerald. He didn't want her to get the wrong idea, that he was using her. Sure, they weren't dating, but after weighing it, he thought it was best not to involve her so that she wouldn't feel obligated.

He kept hearing her say, *I owe you. I'll make it up to you*, after he'd agreed to help her with her plan to make Sophie think Olivia believed in love.

He didn't want her to feel beholden. Plus, he really didn't want to get into the details of how the deal was hanging by a thread. Not when it came to a business deal of this magnitude. If Gerald said no, that would be the end of it. She'd never know. If he said yes, he would tell Olivia.

"Do you want to talk about whatever is on your mind?" Olivia asked from beside him in his car.

He slanted a glance at her, but returned his focus to the road.

He had worked damn hard to keep his poker face in place. He hadn't wanted to spoil the festivities. Obviously he hadn't been as good at hiding his frustration as he'd intended. "Talk about what?"

"What's had you tied up in knots since the start of the tasting."

"I got a phone call while we were at the vineyard. There's a slight snag with one of the investors. But it's not a problem. Everything will be fine."

Telling her that much made him feel better. Since she'd picked up on his mood, sharing that was more honest than if he'd tried to pretend that nothing was wrong.

He deflected the focus off himself with his next comment. "And speaking of fine, it seems like Sophie and Mason are doing well. It's nice to see that your plan worked. I guess we make a convincing match."

On Friday evening, the wedding rehearsal went off without a hitch and Sophie seemed to be herself again, in full bride-to-be mode. Now she was seated across the rehearsal dinner table from Olivia, laughing and flirting with Mason, stealing kisses and whispering private words in his ear.

Good. The plan had worked out exactly as Olivia had hoped it would. In less than twenty-four hours Sophie and Mason would be on their honeymoon and Olivia would officially be disqualified from receiving the title Prewedding Homewrecker of the Year.

Maybe Sophie had simply experienced a case of cold feet, but Olivia still owned the responsibility of pushing her sister into the desperate weeds of despair after she brought up their parents' dismal excuse of a marriage. Ever since the night of the Fuzzy Handcuffs, Olivia had limited herself to one alcoholic beverage during wedding festivities—at the winery she had only allowed herself a single sip of each wine they had sampled. It was at once her own self-enforced punishment for being so sloppy at the bachelorette weekend and insurance that it wouldn't happen again.

Being one of the few sober people at the parties was a strange experience. But it was necessary. She could enjoy herself without social lubrication, and it was the only way to ensure that her sister actually made it down the aisle, headed in the right direction for the start of the rest of her life.

The private dining room where the rehearsal dinner was taking place was awash in golden candlelight and gorgeous white flowers. The party planner had strung hundreds of tiny golden twinkle lights around the room. She had crafted them into hanging topiaries and stuffed them into glass cylinders that were grouped with dozens of candles and more flowers to create ethereal tablescapes. It was a dinner fit for a princess—two princesses, Sophie and Dana. Olivia almost allowed herself to breathe a silent sigh of relief—almost—but she'd hold off on that until Sophie and Mason had been pronounced man and wife.

Still, she had never seen her little sister look so happy, and she couldn't help but smile along with her. But then she realized that as soon as Sophie and Mason said *I do*, she and Alejandro would part ways.

She slanted a glance at him and remembered the kiss at the luau. How it had started as a means to an end and had turned into something electrifying. His hands on her body. The way her body had responded to his touch, and how neither of them had seemed to want to stop. But they had. And now that it appeared certain that Sophie would make it down the aisle tomorrow evening, Olivia needed to start mentally distancing herself from Alejandro. She was going to miss him and his kiss. Miami was a long way from Austin. Not that either of them wanted to try to keep this chemistry alive long distance. Because chemistry did not a relationship make.

Even so, too bad he didn't live in Austin. If he had, maybe they could see if this chemistry could evolve into something less ethereal. But he didn't live in Austin and that's why it was safe for her to daydream about what-ifs that would never happen.

Although if he did end up buying that vineyard, he would be in Austin now and again. She thought about the way he'd looked when he'd told her about the snag with the investor. It had been obvious that he hadn't wanted to talk about it. That's why she hadn't pressed him further. Since she didn't want to pry, she had no idea where his financing stood. Even though she shouldn't get involved, she had an idea about how she might be able to help him—just in case he needed it. After all, she owed him. If not for him, Sophie might not have gone through with the wedding. Olivia felt like the least she could do was help Alejandro find a replacement investor. Her gaze combed the crowd until it landed on her father.

Yes, she just might be able to secure Alejandro's vineyard purchase. She would talk to her dad after the brides and grooms had each said *I do* and the wedding was over.

In the meantime, she was going to make sure she played her role of Cupid-struck lover to the hilt, to make sure Sophie didn't have any reason to back out at the last moment.

Matteo, Mason and Joaquin were talking about the eighteen holes they'd played that morning. Alejandro had begged off on the round of golf because he'd needed to make some phone calls.

The guys talked about bogeys and birdies and the difficulty of the fifteenth hole, but Olivia wasn't a golfer and the conversation didn't hold her interest. Alejandro seemed to be in his own world, too. She wondered where that world might be and who he might be thinking about.

Olivia leaned over so that her arm rested flush

against Alejandro's. She let her hand fall onto his thigh. Granted, his leg was hidden by the table and no one could see it, but it helped her get into character.

Following suit, Alejandro did the same thing, letting his hand wander over to her thigh. It happened so naturally. His thumb and forefinger toyed with the hem of her dress. The feel of his thumb on her bare leg sent shivers coiling outward from her belly.

In response, she traced tiny circles over his pant leg, on the inside of his thigh, going high, but not *too* high. This was for their own entertainment, of course, but it was just for play. He was teasing her and he was blurring the line between pretend romance and giving in to the attraction that they were both feeling. Last night's kiss had confirmed that. It had been filled with curiosity and longing and pent-up desire.

For a crazy moment she wondered what would happen if they just gave in to their feelings…

She thought it through, making a crazy attempt at justification. By making love with Alejandro, this act they had been putting on for Sophie's benefit wouldn't be a complete farce. It wouldn't be a total lie. Of course they wouldn't be in love as they claimed, but they would be involved. Even if she'd made love with Alejandro, they would still break up right on schedule and move on with their lives.

But in the end, common sense won because the thought of rendering herself so vulnerable to Alejandro, making love to him knowing that they would say goodbye, made her heart ache.

She laced her fingers through his and took his

hand off her leg, putting it on the table, where everyone could see.

This was just another act in the play. A play that was for her sister's benefit.

"May I have your attention, please," said Gerald Robinson. The room quieted down at the sound of her father's commanding voice. "Sophie and Mason, Dana and Kieran, please come up here. Join me. I'd like to say a few words. Even though the Montgomerys are cohosting this evening with me, I hope they won't mind me proposing a toast to the four kids whose lives will change forever tomorrow night."

Olivia flinched, suddenly wishing she could muzzle her father, because he was a man who spoke his mind and she could never be sure exactly what was going through that head of his. She squeezed Alejandro's hand as she watched the foursome join him at the front of the room.

"You okay?" he said, looking at her with eyes so dark and soulful it made Olivia's breath hitch.

"I'm fine. Or at least I hope I will be—or everything will be—" She gave an almost imperceptible nod toward her father and leaned in closer to whisper to Alejandro. He smelled good—like citrus and something grassy and clean. It instantly calmed her nerves. "I hope he doesn't decide to unload his ideas about love and marriage. I did that and we saw where that got us."

Alejandro smiled that lazy, hypnotizing smile of his. For a split second Olivia wanted to lean in and kiss him.

"If he does," Alejandro whispered, "we will just have to put in some overtime."

His gaze dropped to her lips and lingered for a moment before he freed his hand from hers and put his arm around her shoulder, pulling her close in a display so convincing that Olivia wanted to believe it was real.

Good grief. What the hell is wrong with me?

She inhaled, trying to clear her mind, but all she managed to accomplish was filling her senses with the scent of him. She needed to get some air.

Her father was in the middle of giving his toast. He hadn't said anything offensive yet—then again, Olivia had only been listening with half an ear—but there was still time.

She sat forward in her seat. "Will you excuse me for a moment, please?"

As she stood, she caught Zoe's eye.

Out in the hall both Rachel and Zoe fell into step with her as she made her way toward the ladies' bathroom.

The restroom was decorated with dainty pink flowered wallpaper and gold fixtures. It was divided into two sections: a sitting area with a love seat and a vanity where guests could freshen up makeup or wait for friends to finish in the second area, which contained the toilets and lavatories. The two areas were separated by old-fashioned swinging doors.

"What's going on?" Zoe said, once they were inside the restroom.

Olivia considered making a sarcastic quip about

being in here because nature called, but she was tired of pretending. That wasn't why she was here.

"For a moment, I was afraid our father was going to single-handedly undo all the hard work we've accomplished this week bringing Sophie and Mason back together. It's one thing for Sophie to get upset over my indiscretion—that's fixable, as evidenced by the events of this week. But if Dad is in one of his moods and he starts going to town and giving a dissertation on his views of the institution of marriage, I don't know if I'll be able to fix it."

"You can't worry about that," said Rachel. "She seems fine. I really doubt anything could sway her now. She loves Mason. I think if she did have another episode like she had last weekend, maybe it would be a good idea to question whether or not she was ready to get married."

"You're right," Olivia said. "It's just that we've come this far. I don't want anything to go wrong."

"I have something sticky on my fingers," Rachel said. "Come in here so I can wash my hands." She pushed through the double doors into the area with the sinks and stalls. Olivia and Zoe followed her.

"You are still blaming yourself and you need to stop," said Zoe. "You have done everything you can to ensure that Sophie makes it down the aisle. I mean, not many sisters would go to the lengths that you've gone to, pretending to be in love—although getting to cozy up to Alejandro Mendoza isn't really a hardship."

Rachel and Zoe laughed.

"I must admit you two have put on a pretty convincing performance this week," Zoe said. "There were times that even I believed you. I don't think anyone suspects that your relationship is anything but real. Certainly not Sophie. She'll be fine."

Rachel turned off the water and reached for a paper towel just as Sophie pushed through the double doors. Her smile was gone and so was her rosy glow. "So it was all an act? You and Alejandro have only been pretending to be in love with each other?"

Olivia's heart stopped. Rachel and Zoe stood frozen in place with huge eyes and gaping mouths.

"You lied to me." Sophie's voice was laced with hysteria and kept getting higher with each word. "Why would you do something like that, Olivia?"

Alejandro looked up at the feel of someone tapping him on the shoulder.

Rachel leaned down and whispered, "We have a situation. Can you help me, please?"

A feeling of dread spread over him as he glanced around the ballroom and realized that the other three Fortune Robinson sisters weren't in the room. He had no idea what was up. Had Sophie changed her mind again? She had looked perfectly happy a few moments ago when she had joined her father at the front of the room for the toast. Gerald Robinson had seemed uncharacteristically sentimental and Sophie had seemed to bubble over as she leaned in and kissed her father on the cheek. But Alejandro was quickly learning that the Fortune Robinson family was strangely complex. Just when he thought he had them figured out they left him guessing.

He followed Rachel to another room near the one where the rehearsal dinner was taking place and found Sophie reading Olivia the riot act.

"So this was all a horrible trick?" she asked.

"Sophie, I can explain if you'll just let me," Olivia said. She reached out to take hold of Sophie's hand, but Sophie pulled away.

"Don't. Don't touch me."

"Sophie, I did this for you. You were getting ready to make the biggest mistake of your life deciding not to marry Mason, and I felt like I'd caused it. I wanted to fix it. There's no reason for you to be mad—"

"No reason to be mad? You lied to me, Olivia. I suppose this has all been one big joke to you?"

"Calm down, Sophie," Zoe said. "You're acting like she stole your fiancé rather than try to help you make things right."

It seemed like Zoe's words didn't even register with Sophie.

"How many other people are in on this joke?" Sophie demanded. "How many? Tell me."

Olivia seemed to be stalling and stammering as Alejandro approached. She looked at him with desperation in her eyes, but she finally found her voice. "Only Zoe, Rachel and—"

"There you are, *querida*," Alejandro said. "I've been looking all over for you, my love. Is everything okay?"

"You can drop the act, Alejandro," Sophie said. "I know all about your little game and I don't appreciate it one bit."

"Game?" Alejandro asked, lacing his right fingers through Olivia's and putting a protective arm around her shoulder. "I have no idea what you're talking about."

Sophie wasn't buying it. "This." She gestured at Olivia and Alejandro with a dismissive wave of her hand. "This lovey-dovey act. Olivia isn't in love with you. She doesn't even believe in love. She's made that perfectly clear too many times over the years. So just stop. Right now. Okay? This is insulting."

Olivia glanced up at him with a look that suggested she wished she could melt into the ground. He did his best to reassure her with his eyes. *Don't worry. I've got this.*

He dropped his arm from Olivia's shoulder and pulled his fingers from her grasp. "Wow. Did I read this all wrong? I'm so embarrassed. I think we need to talk, because obviously I've gotten the wrong message."

Sophie snorted. "Please don't tell me she used you. She concocted this elaborate scheme and didn't even clue you in? Olivia?"

"No," Alejandro said. "I know it started out as a way to convince you, Sophie, that love was real. Olivia thought that the best way to do that was to make you think she had fallen in love with me. The funny thing is, somewhere along the way in the midst of all this craziness, we really did fall in love. Or at least I did, and I thought she felt the same way."

He turned back to Olivia. "After everything we've shared. I… I just don't know how I could have been so wrong. I know you said you didn't want to tell your sisters about how things have changed between us because you didn't want to upstage the wedding. But all those kisses we shared felt so real. I'm in love with you, Olivia. Maybe we should leave and talk about this privately. I don't want to ruin your sister's night. However, I do need to know right now if this is just a game to you."

He was playing his part so convincingly that he almost believed himself. It wasn't hard. Olivia Fortune Robinson would be a very easy woman to love. But then something flashed in her eyes that made him get ahold of himself and he knew she understood what she needed to do.

"No, it's not a game. I love you, too," she replied.

Sophie exhaled impatiently. Her mouth was tight and her dark eyes glistened with tears. Alejandro half expected her to stomp her foot. But she didn't. She got right to the point.

"Just knock it off, you guys. This really is getting to be insulting. The more you lie the more furious it's making me."

Alejandro waited a beat, giving Olivia the opportunity to come clean. When she didn't, he knew it was up to him to pull out the big guns. So he did the only logical thing he could do: he fell down on one knee and took Olivia's hands in his.

Zoe, Rachel and Sophie gasped in unison.

"If you feel the same way I do," he said, his gaze fixed on Olivia, "if you love me as much as I love you, then, Olivia Fortune Robinson, will you be my wife?"

Chapter Seven

Two hours before the wedding, Olivia watched as the stylist pinned a stunning cathedral-length veil to Sophie's head. The salon was abuzz with late-day clients. Dana, Monica, Rachel and Zoe had already come and gone. Madison, the owner of the salon where Olivia and her sisters had been coming for years, had already worked her magic on the rest of the bridal party. Sophie was the last of the lot since placing her long veil proved a little tricky. Unfortunately, it did nothing to quell her curiosity.

"When is Alejandro getting you a ring?" She turned to look at Olivia. Her expression promised she wasn't going to let this go.

"I need you to sit still and face forward, please," said Madison.

"Sophie, are you five years old?" Olivia asked. "Quit looking at me and do what Madison needs you to do. Come on, the wedding is in two hours and we still need to get to the hotel so we can get dressed."

Olivia had appointed herself Sophie's handmaiden for the day. After everything that had happened, she was doing her best to make sure her sister made it down the aisle on time. In the meantime, she needed to distract Sophie from the details of last night's surprise engagement. *Surprise* being the key word. It was the last thing she had expected from Alejandro, but it had worked like a charm. Sophie's mood had turned on a dime. One minute she had been furious with her for the deception—and frankly, Olivia had been at a loss for what to do—and the next minute she had been crying tears of happiness for her sister whom she thought would never find love.

By the time she and Alejandro had left Sophie, she had seemed convinced. Today, not so much. She hadn't outwardly questioned the sudden proposal, but she was full of questions.

"Well, if you would just answer my question, I wouldn't have to keep moving my head to look at you," Sophie said. "If you would just tell me, I could close my eyes and relax. You don't want to be the cause of the bride's anxiety, do you?"

Olivia walked over and stood in front of Sophie, and leaned her hip on the vanity in front of the chair. "I don't know when he's going to get me a ring, Sophie. His proposal was as much of a surprise for me as it was for you. I—"

"Wait," said Madison, stopping midpin. "You're engaged? When she was talking about a ring, I didn't realize she meant an engagement ring. I didn't know you were even dating anyone, much less engaged. Oh, my gosh! Olivia! That's fabulous news. Congratulations! Have you set a date?"

Olivia cringed inwardly, but she dug deep, determined to keep up the happy, newly engaged charade. Really, all she wanted to do was change the subject. Last night, Sophie had been so upset. Even though Alejandro had shocked her with a fake proposal, in hindsight it really was just about the only thing that would've worked.

Alejandro had indeed saved the night, but it was a temporary fix.

Olivia couldn't help but feel that they had dug themselves in deeper and wonder how she was going to mend things with her sister when she and Alejandro called off the engagement. They had a couple of weeks before they would have to deal with that. It wouldn't be an issue until after everyone got home from their honeymoon. By that time Alejandro would be back in Miami and Olivia would be left with the task of announcing the broken engagement. But that seemed worlds away.

"Madison, today is Sophie and Dana's wedding day," she told the hairdresser. "I don't want to steal their thunder by putting the spotlight on me. So let's focus on them and I will give you all the details the next time I see you. Is that a deal?"

"Of course," Madison said, returning her focus to Sophie's veil.

"Hey," said Sophie. "Dana's gone to the hotel. I'm the only bride here and I say I want to talk about the engagement. Did you really not have any inkling? I mean, I'm so happy for you, but you guys met a week ago." She turned her head slightly to look at Madison. "Well, actually, they didn't just meet. They've seen each other at Zoe's and Rachel's weddings. Alejandro is the brother of their husbands. My sisters have a thing for Mendoza men, I guess. But I digress." She turned back to Olivia. "*Inkling.* Did you really not have an inkling this was going to happen?

"Come on, Soph," Olivia said. "I mean it. I don't want today to be about me. Let's keep the proposal on the down-low for the time being. Okay?"

Sophie shrugged. "I'm almost more excited about this news than I am to walk down the aisle."

"I'm going to pretend you didn't just say that," Olivia said.

Sophie rolled her eyes and turned her head away from her sister. Madison sighed and put both hands on either side of Sophie's face and gently moved the bride back into position.

"If you keep moving your head, I'm going to stick a bobby pin up your nose."

Sophie squinted at Madison. "How could you stick a bobby pin up my nose if I'm looking in the opposite direction?"

Madison cocked a brow. "Obviously you don't understand. If you don't sit still, I'm going to stick a bobby pin up your nose on purpose. To get your attention. I really don't want to do that to you on your wedding day. So, please?"

Sophie looked momentarily stunned, but sat up straight and faced the front, folding her hands primly in her lap. "Okay. I'm sorry."

Olivia chuckled to herself. Madison was one of the few people who could get away with saying something like that without making Sophie mad.

"You know, it might be a good thing that he hasn't gotten the ring yet," said Sophie. "That means you can pick out exactly what you want."

She held up her left hand. The two-carat diamond glistened in the overhead lights. "Mason proposed to me with the ring of my dreams. He knows me. He gets me. I am so lucky."

Sophie paused for a long moment and Olivia thought that they had turned a corner, until her sister said, "But don't worry, you and Alejandro will have the rest of your lives to get to know each other. I mean, on one level, I think you two know each other better than some couples who have been together for decades. That's what love at first sight is—or in your case, second or third sight." She smirked at her own joke, then went on, undeterred. "I think we need to announce your engagement tonight."

Olivia held up her hands. "No. Stop. Look, we have talked about nothing else but Alejandro and me since we've been here. That's precisely why I'm asking you to not say anything about our engagement tonight. No, scratch that. I'm asking you to not even *think* about my engagement tonight. I want you to focus on your own wedding. Soph, this is *your* night. I promise we can make the big announcement after you all return from your honeymoons. And not a minute sooner, okay?"

God help me.

Sophie shrugged. She looked like an angel in her lace veil. Her dark hair was pulled back away from her face, accentuating her exquisite cheekbones. The makeup artist had done a beautiful job creating a smoky eye that brought out the almond shape of Sophie's without looking too heavy. It was sweet and sultry… It was just right.

"When we get home from Tahiti," Sophie said, "Mason and I are going to throw the biggest, splashiest, most spectacular engagement party for you and Alejandro. We're going to invite everybody in Austin and Miami. Because it's a pretty spectacular happening when my sister, who had sworn for as far back as I can remember that she didn't believe in love, finally meets the man who makes a believer out of her. How does that sound?"

Sophie looked Olivia square in the eyes and held her gaze. Olivia did her best not to squirm.

Liar, liar. Pants on fire.

"That sounds—" Olivia's voice broke. She cleared her throat. "That sounds fabulous. But you might want to discuss the rather large guest list with Mason before you commit."

Still holding her sister's gaze, a slow Mona Lisa–like smile bloomed on Sophie's face.

"Mason will be happy to host the engagement party of the century for you and Alejandro. After all you've done for us."

Olivia couldn't breathe.

Oh, no. Oh, boy. Here we go.

She hoped she didn't look as pale as she felt.

"But you know," Sophie said, "it really was just a temporary case of cold feet. I would've married Mason no matter what. Because I love him and I can't imagine my life without him."

To Olivia's great relief, the double wedding went off without a hiccup. Sophie and Mason, Kieran and Dana were joined together as husband and wife in the grand ballroom of the Driskill Hotel, in front of nearly five hundred of their closest friends and family members.

The ballroom was festooned in white flowers—peonies, roses, lilies of the valley, freesias and hydrangeas arranged in tall gold-toned vases. The place looked like a florist's shop had exploded and it was glorious. The guests sat in gilded chairs situated in two sections on either side of an aisle. But tonight there weren't brides' and grooms' sides. The bridal couples had made it clear that everyone was gathered for the sake of love.

The place proved a perfect backdrop for her sister and sister-in-law.

Sophie looked stunning in her satin-and-lace ball gown, with its long train and veil trailing behind her. She looked like royalty.

Dana looked artistic and beautiful in the vintage silk shantung wedding gown that belonged to the grandmother of her maid of honor, Monica. She had graciously lent it to Dana for the special day and it served as both her something old and something borrowed. If Dana had designed a wedding gown for herself, it couldn't have been any more perfect than that one.

Honestly, Dana and Sophie both looked so radiant they could have worn bathrobes and slippers and still looked gorgeous. They were both so full of love as they promised to love, honor and respect their grooms for the rest of their lives.

As Olivia listened to the minister's touching opening words, her gaze picked Alejandro out of the guests. When he caught her looking at him, Olivia couldn't look away. Emotions she'd never experienced before zinged through her—happiness for the two couples pledging their love before God and everyone, wistfulness at the beauty of that love, and maybe even a touch of envy. She may not believe in love, but never in her entire life had she wished she did more than that moment.

Little Rosabelle, Dana and Kieran's adopted daughter, was the one who drew her out of her reverie. Bedecked in her pink princess dress, complete with floral crown, four-year-old Rosie was the flower girl. She did a fabulous job strewing rose petals down the aisle. Her new nanny, Elaine, stood at the side of the dais, smiling encouragingly at the little girl, poised at the ready to gently correct Rosie's course should she veer off track. But the child played her part perfectly, smiling bashfully at the guests seated on her either side. Given that she was so young and it was getting close to her bedtime, Rosie couldn't have done a better job.

At the beginning of the ceremony she stood with the bridal party. It was no surprise when she grew a little restless. Standing next to Olivia, she began to entertain herself by playing with the skirt of Olivia's dress. She grabbed a handful of skirt and pulled it around herself like a cape. It enlisted titters and *awwws* from the audience. The sound made Rosie hide her face and then peek out from the fabric. When she saw everyone looking at her, she stepped around behind Olivia and hid. Olivia placed a reassuring hand on the little girl's blond curls. Actually, she didn't blame her one bit for wanting to hide. She was getting a little weary of these wedding games herself. There were many times this week when she had wanted to hide her face from the world. But her sister was happy and within a matter of minutes she would be married. It was all worth it.

Alejandro was smiling at her again. He looked so handsome in his dark suit and white shirt. It was a different look from the cool Miami casual that he had projected most of the week. The more dressed-up look suited him. He was such a handsome man. All of his brothers were married. Why wasn't he?

Olivia recalled the conversation she and her sisters had last week at the bachelorette party before everything blew up. If she were inclined to be a romantic she might have believed that the reason Alejandro had never married was because he had been waiting for her.

But that was just crazy.

"By the power vested in me," said the officiant, "I now pronounce you husband and wife. Err—husbands and wives?" The man shrugged and looked out at the guests. "Ladies and gentlemen, it is my pleasure to present to you Mr. and Mrs. Mason Montgomery and Mr. and Mrs. Kieran Fortune Robinson."

The guests erupted into boisterous applause as the recessional music sounded, signaling the end of the ceremony. Olivia handed Sophie her bouquet, scooped up Rosie, balancing her on her hip as she waited her turn to walk back down the aisle.

The bridal party exited the room where the ceremony had taken place and waited for the wedding planners to usher everyone out and into the room where they could enjoy cocktails and hors d'oeuvres. Then the bridal party and immediate family returned to the ceremony room for pictures.

They were using the same photographer as they'd used for Rachel's and Zoe's weddings, because she had done a beautiful job. But Olivia didn't remember the photos taking this long.

Joaquin and Matteo Mendoza were in the photographs because they were married to her sisters and therefore full-fledged immediate family. As with Alejandro, they had not been in the bridal party, so at first impulse it seemed strange that they would be in the pictures and Alejandro wouldn't. But it made sense.

I think maybe Alejandro would be a perfect match for Olivia.

She tried to blink away the memory of her sister's words. It was just crazy girl talk.

Isn't it a coincidence that he's the last single Mendoza and you're the last single Fortune Robinson?

Obviously it was time for a reality check. There were good reasons that the two of them were still single. Good sense topped the list.

It had been a long week of wedding festivities and pretending. She was tired and her defenses were down. That always happened when she let herself get worn out. That was the only reason she was thinking these irrational thoughts as she watched her sisters interact with their husbands.

As the photographer arranged them into a grouping for a shot of the entire family Sophie stepped out of place and surveyed the group.

"Where is Alejandro?" she asked. "It's my party and I'll do what I want to," she said with a sassy smile. "And I want Alejandro in the family picture. It's important."

"It's not just your party," Olivia reminded her sister.

"Dana?" Sophie asked. "Do you mind if Alejandro is in the family picture?"

Dana shook her head. "Of course not. It's fine."

"Mason? Kieran?" Sophie said. "Any objections?"

As they indicated their approval, Sophie shot her sister a triumphant look.

Sophie wasn't letting this go. Olivia realized if she put up too much of a fight, things could get ugly. Granted, Sophie and Mason were married. Technically, her job was done. However, if she took this opportunity to announce that there was no engagement or that they had called off the engagement, pretending it was too sudden or logistically difficult, it would cast a dark cloud over the festivities.

This was one of those times when it was best to lose the battle so she could win the war. In that spirit, the best thing she could do was to just go along with it.

"In that case, if nobody objects I will go find Alejandro," Olivia said. "I'll be back as soon as I can."

It wasn't hard to locate him. He was standing with his father and Josephine, sipping a cocktail that looked like scotch and soda. He was holding a flute of champagne in the other hand. As she approached she was about to tease him about being a double-fisted drinker, but he smiled the warmest smile at her and held out the champagne.

"This is for you," he said. "You look like you could use it."

"I look that bad, huh?"

His smile faded. "No, not at all. It was just a figure of speech. You look beautiful."

Olivia felt her face warm at the sincere compliment. She never blushed. It was unfortunate that her body was choosing this moment to start. Then again, her body seemed to have a mind of its own when it came to Alejandro.

Just accept the compliment, she told herself. It was only a compliment. "Thank you. Hello, Orlando. Josephine, you look lovely. I'm so glad you both could be here for the wedding. It means a lot to our family."

They exchanged pleasantries about the ceremony and about how adorable Rosabelle was in her flower girl debut.

"You're so good with children," Josephine said. "Do you have any of your own?"

A hiccup of a laugh bubbled up in Olivia's throat. "Oh, heavens no. I'm not married. Of course, you know that since— I mean, I've never been married."

Her gaze fluttered to Alejandro, and she felt her face heat up again.

"I'm sorry to barge in but, Alejandro, your presence is requested in the photo room."

Photo room? Ugh. Get ahold of yourself.

"I mean, the bridal party would like for you to be in some of the pictures, if you don't mind."

She smiled and tried to look normal, but she felt like one of those grimacing emoticons.

"I don't mind at all," Alejandro said, just as calm and cool as if she had asked him to bring the car around so they could escape this circus.

Now, there was an idea. Maybe they should get in his rental car and just keep driving until they were far away from here. Maybe they could go to Miami. She could stay until both couples were back from their honeymoons, when she could announce that she and

Alejandro were no longer engaged. Then it wouldn't be a bombshell. In fact, Sophie might be so wrapped up in her own marital bliss that she wouldn't want the gray clouds of a broken engagement to shadow her own happiness.

"Where should we go?" Alejandro asked, waiting on her to lead him.

"Miami," Olivia mused aloud. "Let's go to Miami. Right now."

Alejandro shook his head and laughed. "That's one of the things I like the best about her," he said to his father and Josephine. "She has the best sense of humor. She always keeps me laughing and guessing."

The three of them laughed again and Olivia joined in so that they would believe that she really was just making a joke that hinted at her being a weary maid of honor.

If they only knew.

Actually, no. She didn't want them to know the truth. She didn't want anyone else to know about the ticking time bomb that she had created. She simply wanted to pacify her sister until the married couples got into their respective limousines and drove off into the night toward the first days of the rest of their lives.

She took his arm to lead him toward the photo room. After they had said their goodbyes to Josephine and Orlando and were out of earshot, Alejandro asked, "Why do they want me in the photos?"

Olivia slanted him a look that suggested he should know why. "Because, darling, you are my fiancé. Remember?"

"Right." He ran a palm over his eyes and raked his fingers through his hair, a tic that Olivia was beginning to associate with him being stressed. "Did Sophie tell everyone?"

Olivia shook her head. "No, but she is definitely testing me. I can't tell if she's on to us or if she's just excited because she thinks I've finally come over to the dark side."

"The dark side? Is that what you think of marriage?"

Maybe she was being overly sensitive, but there seemed to be a bit of rebuke in his tone.

"Don't you?" she answered. "I mean, you're not married and how old are you?"

"I'm thirty-four. And no, I don't necessarily think of marriage as the dark side."

"Then why aren't you married?" She instantly regretted asking the question that had been lurking in the back of her mind since she realized he was the last single Mendoza. "Or do weddings make you sentimental?"

He shot her a look. "I was actually engaged once."

The revelation hit Olivia like a sucker punch. "Really? What happened? I mean, if you don't mind me asking. I really thought you and I were similar in our thoughts about marriage."

One side of his mouth quirked up. "That's what happens when you assume."

She made a show of flinching. She remembered the old saying—*when you assume you make an ass out of u and me.* She arched a brow as she asked, "Are you calling me an ass, Alejandro?"

"Don't be ridiculous." The way he looked at her had her blushing, and inwardly going to pieces. It should be illegal for a man to look at a woman like he looked at her, making her feel things she shouldn't be feeling in this elaborate charade that they had orchestrated. Especially when he was set to leave in a couple of days.

"Again, when you assume, you run the risk of jumping to wrong conclusions," he said as he reached for the door to the ballroom where the ceremony had taken place. "Here we are, my most cherished fiancée." His dark eyes danced with mischief. "Let's give the bride the show she's expecting."

They were already inside the ballroom when Olivia realized how neatly Alejandro had evaded her question. He'd been engaged. Who was the woman he had loved enough to want to spend the rest of his life with—or at least want that for a brief period of time? What had happened to break up the engagement?

Now wasn't the time, but she fully intended to find out.

Alejandro's participation in the photos hadn't taken long. Sophie had only wanted him in one shot: the family photo. He had stood on the end and quietly joked with Olivia that they could cut him out of the picture if they wanted to. He probably should've found a way to gracefully bow out of the photo session. She could've told them she couldn't find him.

But it was done now. He was officially part of the family photo.

He got the distinct feeling that Sophie might've been calling their bluff by including him in the family shot. If she was, then she knew she was taking a chance. Maybe she'd had the photographer snap a few shots without him after he'd left.

This wasn't the first time he'd wondered if he'd pushed the envelope too far when he had proposed to Olivia in front of Sophie and her sisters. But seeing Olivia in distress had made him desperate to fix the situation. He'd just wanted to see her smile again. Of course, he wanted Sophie to be okay, too, but for a crazed moment, when he'd seen Olivia in such turmoil, he'd known he had to make things right. His knee-jerk reaction had been a proposal.

There was no getting around it now. The fake-proposal die was cast.

Before he returned to Miami, he would help Olivia clean up any family repercussions the "breakup" might cause. It was important they left family relations as good as possible. Olivia had already said she would be the heavy and take responsibility for the breakup. She'd claim they'd gotten swept away by the romance of the double wedding, but with distance and a fresh perspective, she realized she wasn't ready for a lifetime commitment.

Alejandro was prepared for the breakup. What he hadn't thought through was that he would have to delay his meeting to present the investment proposal to Gerald Robinson until after they called off the engagement. He didn't want it to appear that he was using Olivia for his own personal gain.

He'd debated whether or not to tell Olivia about his plan to ask her father to invest in Hummingbird Ridge. He'd ultimately come to the conclusion that it was best not to involve her. It was a long shot that he would buy in anyway.

If Robinson said no, Alejandro was perfectly prepared to leave it at that—no hard feelings. He didn't want Olivia to feel as if she needed to plead his case because she owed him.

Most people wouldn't feel the need to get involved on someone's behalf, but Olivia was different. Once she invested in someone, she was all in. Making sure her sister made it down the aisle was a case in point. She'd said more than once that she would make it up to him for helping her. A sixth sense told him that if she knew about the investor dropping out, she'd make it her mission to make that right. He couldn't take that chance. He'd fight his own fight.

If Gerald wasn't interested, he'd return to Miami and continue the frantic search for replacement funding. He could only hope that the Dailys wouldn't find another buyer before that. They had been so kind to refund his deposit, though they had every right to keep the money as stated in the contract. But Jack Daily had said he couldn't take the money in good conscience. That was one of the things that Alejandro loved about that winery in particular. It came from good stock, and he wasn't simply talking about the vines. He was talking about the family who had invested generations of blood, sweat and tears to make it what it was today.

They were good people and if he was given the chance, he wanted to carry on that legacy.

However, the way they'd left things was that if a viable buyer materialized before Alejandro could come up with the money, they would have to take the offer.

The Dailys were ready for the next phase in their life. They deserved the chance to write this next chapter. He hoped he would be able to write his own next chapter at Hummingbird Ridge. It would put him a hell of a lot closer to Austin than Miami. It would be easier to see Olivia if she was into seeing him. Maybe then he'd be able to figure out what had made her so down on marriage and romance.

The band leader called the crowd to order, putting an end to Alejandro's reverie. The man's deep baritone voice introduced the bridal party. As Olivia walked in, Alejandro watched her scan the crowd and find him.

He'd never met anyone who could flirt with her eyes the way Olivia did. She had great eyes. He felt mesmerized as she stood with the other bridesmaids and groomsmen until the brides and grooms had entered the room, acknowledged their guests and took to the parquet floor for their first dance.

She looked confident and happy—not a bit worried—as she closed the distance between them. If she wasn't worried, he wouldn't worry. At that moment, he decided he was going to forget all the challenges he was facing with the vineyard and the charade and just enjoy himself tonight. It was one of the easiest decisions he'd made in ages.

Olivia couldn't remember when she'd had so much fun at a wedding. It wasn't usually her preferred way to spend a Saturday night. But Alejandro knew how to show a girl a good time. The ballroom was awash in gold and white and there were so many flowers and tiny golden twinkling lights it seemed like their very own secret garden right in the middle of the busy city.

Sophie and Dana opted not to torture the bridal party by confining everyone to a head table. Instead, the two newly married couples dined together and the rest of the bridal party was dispersed among the guests. It was no surprise that they had seated Olivia and Alejandro together. If they hadn't, Olivia had been prepared to do some place card swapping—all for the sake of keeping up their charade, of course.

After dinner—a salad of warm goat cheese with gold and red baby beets; a surf and turf of filet mignon and sea bass served with truffle mushroom risotto—the dance floor heated up.

Alejandro was a good dancer. Olivia had no idea why she thought he might be reserved, but he wasn't at all. They danced to every song and by the time the band slowed things down with a ballad, it seemed perfectly natural when Alejandro, her fake fiancé, pulled her into his arms and held her close.

In the past, Olivia had always had a problem with slow dancing because most of the men she'd danced with had accused her of trying to lead. They would tell her to relax, to feel and respond to the subtle messages they sent with their bodies. Obviously either they were much too subtle—subtext: not man enough—with their bodily messages or she simply wasn't picking up their vibe.

Tonight, as she and Alejandro swayed to the music, was the first time she understood what it meant to let the man lead. Or maybe it was the first time she'd wanted to let someone else lead.

For the duration of the song, Olivia let herself imagine what it would be like if this pretend relationship was real. What would it be like to really be engaged to Alejandro Mendoza? She let herself go there, envisioning everything from what dress she would wear at their wedding—a mermaid-style gown that had caught her eye when she'd gone with Sophie for her final fitting—to what would happen on their honeymoon.

Ooooh, the honeymoon.

The thought made her breath catch. She closed her eyes as tiny points of warmth radiated out from her belly, making her lean into Alejandro and snuggle into his shoulder as they danced.

By the time the song ended, Olivia felt a little off-kilter. The two of them stepped apart, allowing a respectable amount of space between them. Sophie's voice broke the spell.

"I hope you all are having fun," she said. She was holding the lead singer's microphone with one hand. She had a champagne flute in the other. "Before the night gets away from me, I wanted to take this opportunity to give a shout-out to my sister, Olivia."

Olivia's heart leaped.

Oh, no. Please tell me she's not going to do what I think she's going to do.

Olivia grabbed Alejandro's arm to steady herself. He covered her hand with his left hand. She didn't dare look at him because she was trying to catch Sophie's eye to silently beg her not to do what it was becoming more and more apparent that she was about to do. But Sophie skillfully looked everywhere but at Olivia.

"My sister Olivia is my rock," Sophie said. "She's always thinking of and doing things for others. So often, she sacrifices her own needs for those she loves, and she doesn't get the credit she deserves. Olivia and Alejandro, I'm sorry for doubting you two. They know what I mean by that, so I won't bore you with the details. But I will say this—and my sister asked me not to say anything about this because she didn't want to steal my and Dana's thunder—because I just can't resist. Olivia and Alejandro have some great news."

She lifted her champagne flute and smiled broadly. "Everyone, please raise your glasses to the most recent Fortune Robinson bride-to-be and Mendoza groom-to-be. Olivia and Alejandro are engaged to be married."

Chapter Eight

After the wedding, as soon as the brides and grooms were off in a send-off shower of sweet-smelling lavender buds, Alejandro drove Olivia home to her condo in the Barton Hills neighborhood of Austin.

All she wanted was to get out of her bridesmaid dress and the pinching heels, take her hair down and get away from the flood of congratulations that had washed in after Sophie's little announcement.

They were both exhausted and contemplative, so they were mostly quiet in the car. They didn't talk about a plan, but Olivia knew they needed to before Alejandro left her place tonight.

As she changed into her heather gray yoga pants and a soft white T-shirt, she came up with a plan and was ready to present a strong case when she walked back into the living room. Alejandro was on the same page because he took the words right out of her mouth when he asked, "What are we going to do now?"

"First, I'm going to open a bottle of wine," she said. "That's what I'm going to do right now."

"Sounds good to me. Do you think that we're okay sticking to the original plan?"

She stopped on her way into the kitchen and looked back at him. "You mean breaking up tomorrow?"

He shrugged.

"I was hoping we could stay in character at least until after Sophie and Mason were home from their honeymoon and settled into married life. Does that work for you?"

"When will they be back?"

"They're only going away for a week. Mason has some business he needs to take care of. Then I think they're planning a longer trip in the fall."

He seemed to mull things over for a moment. "Yeah, I think I can make that work. I have some Hummingbird Ridge business, but nothing I can't tend to while I'm here."

"Great! A week should be long enough for the wedding sparkle to wear off and for us to realize we were swept away by the romance. Then we can 'take a break.'" She bracketed the words with air quotes. "I'm happy to be the heavy. I'll tell everyone I felt like things were just moving too fast. I'll confess that I got caught up in the romance of the wedding and while I think the world of you, I need time to think things over. My family won't be surprised, believe me. In fact, I'll bet they're already placing wagers on how long it will take me to call off the engagement."

Alejandro frowned at her. "I thought maybe your cynicism about love was all an act, but you've almost convinced me that you're really not a believer."

He was quiet for a moment, as if he was giving her the chance to tell him he was wrong, that it really was an act. When she didn't say anything, he asked, "What happened to sour you on love?"

Biting her lip, she looked away, toward the kitchen. Why did he care? She could read all sorts of things into that, but she wasn't going to.

"How about that glass of wine?" she asked, trying to buy herself a little more time. "After the day I've had, I'm going to need a glass of wine or two if we're going to have this conversation."

"Sure, thanks. That sounds good."

"Is red okay? I have white, but it's not cold."

"Red is perfect. May I help?"

She opened the cabinet and took down the wineglasses, hoping by avoiding the question he would get the hint that she didn't want to talk about it. "I'm good. I've got this."

The phrase was a pep talk for herself. Even though she didn't really want to talk about it, maybe she owed him a little insight about her parents' dynamics. After all, two Mendozas were part of the family and they were bound to pick up on the tension, if her sisters hadn't already filled them in. Alejandro had been so good to help her, and he did care enough to ask. He didn't strike her as the type who would dig just to be nosy. But why was he asking? What did that mean? She supposed it was possible for a man to care about a woman in a purely platonic way, although she had never had any successful relationships of that nature with men. And truth be told, if circumstances were different—if they weren't practically family—maybe she would want more than something platonic with Alejandro. But if it got messy… No, she'd better leave well enough alone.

"When are Dana and Kieran back?"

"They are going to be gone longer. They're heading to Paris for ten days," she said. "Did you meet Elaine Wagner tonight—the new nanny they'd hired to care for Rosabelle? She was the kid-wrangler tonight. She has a son who's just about Rosie's age. She's going to look after Rosie and her dog Sammy. You know that Dana and Kieran adopted Rosie after her father died, right?" She didn't wait for Alejandro's response before she continued.

"Having Elaine come on board has given Kieran and Dana enough peace of mind to know that they can get away for a while. After all they've been through—and with this whirlwind wedding—they deserve some time away."

She looked across the open-concept kitchen and saw Alejandro watching her intently. Since talking about Dana and Kieran had seemed to divert the conversation from her folks, she decided to continue.

"When they get back they're going to live at Dana's house. They want to get a new place together, but with the wedding put on the fast track and the honeymoon trip to Paris they haven't had a spare minute to begin the search. But Dana's house has a nice big yard for Rosabelle and Sammy to play in. Really, there's no need to rush the process. Everything will happen in good time."

She paused to pull the lever of the corkscrew and yank the cork out of the bottle. She knew she was rambling, but it seemed to have worked.

She set aside the cork from the wine, a Cabernet Sauvignon from the Columbia Valley, which *Wine Spectator* had scored a ninety-six. She wasn't a wine connoisseur, but she knew what she liked and she hoped this would be suitable for Alejandro. She poured the wine, secured both glasses between the fingers of her left hand, grabbed the bottle with her right and joined Alejandro in the living room. He was sitting on the couch, with one arm stretched out along the back. He looked so at home, like he belonged there.

As she set the wine bottle down on the coffee table, she realized she was nervous. Even so, she took a seat next to him on the couch rather than choosing the gray toile-print wingback chair. It reminded her of that first night in the Driskill bar when she'd moved from the chair to sit next to him. She hadn't been so drunk that she didn't remember it had felt so natural to sit next to him and just lean in and start kissing him. Of course, they'd kissed many times since. She wondered what he would do if she leaned in and kissed him right now.

She was tempted, but she didn't do it. Instead, she handed him a wineglass.

As had become their custom, they purposefully locked gazes before clinking their glasses. She thought about making another joke about good sex, but she just couldn't summon words that wouldn't sound rehashed or recycled, like ground they had already covered. Was that because she knew they were coming up on the final act of this performance?

With Sophie married and away on her honeymoon, did they really need to stay together? Wouldn't it be easier to end it now? Sophie was a big girl, and if Olivia was perfectly honest with herself she knew that Sophie had gone through with her marriage of her own volition. Olivia and Alejandro dating or not dating, being engaged or not, would not make one bit of difference in her sister's relationship.

If she knew what was best for both Alejandro and herself, she should tell him right now that it would be better for him to leave as planned. Funny though, she really wasn't ready for this to end. She'd gotten used to him being around. Even if it was a farce, she had gotten used to being part of a couple with him.

Alejandro and Olivia.

Olivia and Alejandro.

She liked the sound of that.

She traced the rim of her wineglass with her finger. Even after only a week it sounded natural to link their names. Would they remain friends and keep in touch after he went back to Miami? Would he make a point of ringing her up when he came to Texas on vineyard business? She hoped so. In fact, she wanted that very much.

She looked at him, mustering the will to tell him he was free to go if he needed to, but instead, what came out was "If we're going to make this engagement look convincing, don't you think you should check out of the Driskill and move in here with me?"

He looked surprised, as if he hadn't considered the possibility, and she braced herself for him to be the voice of reason, to not only decline but say everything she had been thinking only moments ago. That it was time to break up. Time to come clean. Time to move on.

"Are you sure?" he asked.

"Since short-term rentals are hard to come by and hotels are uncomfortable and expensive, you can move into one of the spare bedrooms in my condo," she said.

"Short-term rental?" His brows knit together. "I thought we were only talking about a week."

"Yes, well, I was just thinking that you might not want to pay for a hotel. Unless you want to, of course."

She cringed inwardly. This wasn't going the way she'd hoped. Maybe she should just make it easy on both of them and cut him loose.

"No. I see what you're saying and I appreciate it," he said. "I just don't want to impose. It's not easy having someone in your space, even for a week."

True. But it was definitely easier to host a guest

when you wanted the person there. And she didn't mind Alejandro being in her space.

"It'll be fine. And it'll appear more convincing if we're living together. It's the least I can do after all you've done to help me."

"It wasn't such a hardship," he said. For a moment, something shifted between them. She swore he was going to lean in and kiss her. But then she glanced down at her wineglass and when she looked back up the spell was broken.

"I will have to cook dinner for you while I'm here," he said. "It'll give me the chance to show off my culinary chops. I'm happy to say I know my way around the kitchen."

"Did you learn to cook so you could get the girls?"

He laughed. "Of course. Works every time."

She loved the way his eyes came to life when they bantered. Kissing him felt almost as natural as verbally sparring with him.

"How about this?" he said. "I'll earn my keep by cooking for you."

"Works for me. I've been told I have many talents, but domestic pursuits are not among them." She chuckled.

"Hey, my birthday is next week," she said. "Why don't you cook dinner for me then? Otherwise, my parents might insist on celebrating with us."

"Do you think so? I got the distinct feeling that your parents were avoiding me tonight after Sophie's announcement. I'd mentally prepared myself for what I would say to them, but it was probably for the best that they focused on your sister's and brother's wedding. If your dad is one of those old-fashioned types that gets offended if a guy doesn't ask for his daughter's hand, I didn't want to face the wrath of Gerald Robinson. That would've definitely been a party foul."

"You don't have anything to worry about. My father isn't really the traditional type when it comes to love and marriage. In fact, if you asked his permission to marry me, he would probably think you were up to something. Or at the very least sucking up."

"Have they said anything to you?" he asked.

"My mother cornered me earlier tonight. She said she was happy for us and she wants to get to know you better. She and my father want to take us out for dinner. Which means *she* wants to go out to dinner and my father probably knows nothing about it. She was trying to get us to come over tomorrow night, but I told her that we were both busy. I'll keep putting her off as long as I can. Especially for my birthday."

He picked up the bottle and refilled her wineglass. "What day is your birthday?"

"It's next Saturday."

"Maybe you should celebrate with them. When I was growing up, birthdays were always a big deal in our house. My mother would have a cake for us and we got to pick whatever we wanted for dinner."

Olivia shifted, and pulled one foot up and balanced it on her knee. She began to massage her foot. When she noticed him watching her hands, she said,

"Sorry, my feet hurt after standing in those heels all night."

"Here," he said, "put your feet in my lap. I give a mean foot massage."

She looked a little taken aback. For a moment he thought she was going to refuse, but she swung her legs up onto the couch and stretched out so that her feet were in his lap.

He used his thumb to draw small, firm circles on the ball of her foot.

She tilted her head back and moaned. It made him think of the night in the Driskill bar when she kissed him. He had a nearly overwhelming urge to lean over and see if her lips tasted as sweet as they had that night. But it probably wouldn't be a good move since he was going to be moving in with her and they needed to keep things cool just a little longer.

"That feels so good," she said. "Are you close to your parents? It sounds as if they made a big deal over making you feel special on your birthday."

"I'm close to my dad. My mom passed away about five years ago."

"I'm sorry."

He shrugged. "Thanks. My mom was a wonderful woman. We all took her loss pretty hard. But it's good to see my dad happy again with Josephine. There was a time when it seemed like he would never be the same again. I know you and your sisters are close but are you close to your folks? You seem like you're avoiding the question."

"Maybe I am." She sat up and pulled her knees into her chest, hugging them and still managing to hold her wineglass. "My sisters and I are solid, but my parents? They sort of live in their own worlds. Separate worlds. I guess I might as well tell you because you're bound to hear about it anyway. This reporter, Ariana Lamonte, has been doing a big exposé on my family. My dad mostly. Last year, evidence surfaced that he is actually part of the Fortune family."

Alejandro nodded. "The Fortunes are a big Texas family. Seems like everybody's related to them in one way or another—or at least most people have a close degree of separation. My brother Cisco is married to Delaney Fortune."

Olivia shrugged. "This is still new for me. I'm still trying to digest it, because the implications are pretty damning. Not only does it mean that my father has been lying to us about his identity for as long as my brothers and sisters and I have been alive, but we are also coping with the fact that my father seems to have other children who keep popping up. Illegitimate ones."

She closed her eyes and rested her forehead on her knees. A moment later, she looked up at him.

"I probably shouldn't be telling you all this, but for some crazy reason I feel like I can trust you."

He reached out and put a hand on her arm. "You can trust me, Olivia. It sounds like you've been through a lot of change this year."

She nodded. "Not just this year. The truth has

been a long time coming. I've always known that my parents didn't have a great relationship. I just didn't know why. But now that all of my father's illegitimate children keep crawling out of the woodwork, it's just hard for me to be around my parents. Their relationship is such a farce. I have no idea why they stay together because it's all a lie. So you can see going to dinner with them for my birthday would be the ultimate torture. Will you please be my knight in shining armor and save me from that?"

He brushed back a strand of hair that had fallen into her face. He had heard rumblings about Gerald Robinson's Fortune connection, but nobody seemed to know the true story. He hadn't heard about illegitimate children. No wonder Olivia was freaked out about love and relationships.

"I wouldn't want to do anything else," he said. "You know, love is a tricky thing. My parents showed me the best example of true love and commitment. It was real and perfect. Not only did I see it in my parents' relationship when my mother was alive, I've experienced that deep kind of true love myself. Yet I'm even screwed up when it comes to love. That's because when you fall in love, you're so vulnerable. You open yourself up and you expose yourself to the worst pain—"

The words got lost in his throat. Olivia put her hand on his. He looked at her sitting next to him on the couch in her yoga pants and fitted T-shirt and somehow the possibility of falling in love didn't seem so out of reach anymore.

"Sounds like you're speaking from experience," she said. "How did Anna break your heart?"

It had been years since he'd talked about this, but he heard himself speaking before he could stop himself.

"Anna Molino was my high school sweetheart. We would be married right now if fate hadn't been cruel. Anna died in a car accident when we were just twenty years old."

"Oh, Alejandro, I'm sorry."

Maybe it was all the pent-up emotion that he had been harboring for years; maybe it was because he was actually starting to feel something for this beautiful woman. Whatever the reason, he reached out and ran his thumb along her jawline, moved his hand around so it cupped the back of her neck and lowered his mouth to hers.

When their lips met, he lost all sense of time and space. All he knew was things hadn't felt this right in ages.

"Do you want to stay here tonight?" Olivia whispered. "We can go to the Driskill and get your things tomorrow." Her expression was so earnest, he almost said yes, but if he stayed he wasn't sure what might happen. He needed some space to think about what he was getting into by moving in with her—even if it was only for a week. He needed to figure out if he could handle it.

"In the guest room," she amended as if she was reading his thoughts. "Because we probably shouldn't be kissing like that unless we mean it."

"You're right," he said. "I'm sorry. I shouldn't have done that."

"Don't be sorry," she said. "I'm not. But we probably should save the action for our adoring public."

He stood.

"On that note, I should get back to the hotel tonight."

Chapter Nine

Alejandro checked out of the hotel and was at Olivia's condo by eleven o'clock on Sunday morning. After the kiss last night, she wasn't sure what to expect today. Olivia had even prepared herself for the possibility of Alejandro deciding to stay at the hotel rather than with her.

They were both a little shy this morning as she showed him to the spare bedroom down the hall.

"Here's the closet where you can hang your clothes. I put some extra hangers in there for you. There's a dresser if you need some drawers. I'm sorry this room doesn't have an en suite, but the bathroom is right across the hall. Here, let me show you."

She knew she was talking too much, rambling away like a Realtor showing a house rather than someone welcoming a houseguest. But he wasn't just a houseguest. The thought that she and Alejandro would be sleeping under the same roof made the muscles in her stomach knot a little too tight.

He smiled at her. "This is perfect. Thank you for letting me stay here."

"It's for a good cause. I'll leave you alone while you get settled in. Please let me know if you need anything else to be comfortable. I put fresh towels in the bathroom and—"

"I can unpack later," he said. "What I'd really like to do right now is go get something to eat. Are you hungry?"

She hadn't really thought about it until he'd asked, because she'd been so anxious about whether or not he would end up bailing on her. She put a hand on her stomach and realized that she was famished.

"I am hungry," she said. "Did you have someplace in mind? I would offer to whip us up something but I don't have any food in the house. And that's probably a good thing because I'm not much of a cook."

He laughed. "I was serious last night when I said I was happy to serve as the chef while I'm staying here with you. I might even teach you some of my secrets."

She would love to learn Alejandro Mendoza's secrets, and not just those that pertained to the kitchen. And just like that, all of the potential awkwardness she feared would be spawned from last night's kiss melted away like ice cream on a hot Austin day.

"I'll hold you to that," she said. "Maybe you can give me a cooking lesson tomorrow? But in the meantime why don't we go to the South Congress Café? They have carrot cake French toast that is to die for."

Olivia's condo was just a short walk to the restaurant. It was a beautiful, sunny day, cool enough to make it pleasurable to be outdoors, but warm enough that the walk had Olivia working up a thirst even in the light sundress and sandals she wore.

Alejandro looked crisp and cool in his khaki shorts and ivory linen shirt.

When they arrived at the restaurant they found there was a short wait for a table. This was one of her favorite places to eat and Olivia was happy to see it doing such brisk business.

Even though she'd been there more times than she could count, the place looked both familiar and brand-new as she tried to see the exposed-brick walls and blond-wood-beamed ceilings through Alejandro's eyes.

Once they were seated, Alejandro asked her, "Do you have to do anything constructive today? If not, do you want to order Bloody Marys? One of those would really hit the spot right now."

"I scheduled myself to do absolutely nothing today but recover from the wedding," Olivia said. "A Bloody Mary sounds good, but I think champagne is what I need."

They ordered the drinks along with water and coffee, but asked the server to come back for their food order.

It was nice to be out like this with Alejandro. The pressure of the wedding was off her shoulders, and there was nobody around that they needed to impress. The entire day was theirs. It dawned on Olivia that this was the first time they had been together without any expectations weighing them down.

"I'm guessing that your day is clear since you're drinking?"

He gave a one-shoulder shrug. "For the most part. I have some calls to make later this afternoon. I need to get in touch with my cousin Stefan. He and his brother Rodrigo are my business partners. Since I was basically out of pocket yesterday, I need to go over some things with them."

"Do they live in Miami?" she asked.

"They do."

"Will they be relocating to Austin once you take over Hummingbird Ridge?" That was a clever way of asking whether he'd found a new investor without appearing too nosy.

He shook his head. "Right now, I'm the one who will be in Texas. I know the Dailys so it stands to reason that I would be the one stationed here. Basically Stef and Rod are silent partners. Although I imagine they will want to take a much more hands-on approach once the wine starts flowing."

Well, that sounded encouraging.

"Who wouldn't?" Olivia said. "In fact, if you're ever in need of a taster, I'd be happy to volunteer. It's a tough job, but I am willing to step up and sacrifice myself."

He laughed. "That's magnanimous of you. Not many would sacrifice themselves like that."

Their server reappeared and they ordered—the French toast for Olivia, and the goat cheese and bacon omelet for Alejandro.

"How long have you lived in Austin?" he asked once the server had refilled their water glasses and left to turn in their order.

"All my life. I was born and raised here. I've done a fair share of traveling—you know, study abroad semesters and a postgraduation backpacking trip through Europe. But I keep coming back to Austin. It's home. My life is here. It's where my heart lives. Are you sad to leave Miami?"

"I don't know that I will completely leave. It's hard to say where I'll be after everything is settled with the winery."

Oh.

Disappointment tugged at her insides. She hadn't realized it, but she had been hoping he would say he was eager to call Austin home. It was a crazy thought, though. He was so Miami sophisticated, so big-city, he probably wouldn't be happy here long-term. For all its quirks and artistic originality, Austin had a different vibe from Miami.

"So Miami is home?"

He shrugged. "For now. But less so than it has been. My uncles and cousins still live there, but my father and my immediate family are all in Texas now. As I told you, we're a pretty tight-knit bunch."

"That's nice. Maybe you should think about joining them and making the move. Austin has a lot to offer thanks to the university, and the town has a pretty progressive music scene. Have you ever been to the South by Southwest festival? It's a fabulous film and music festival."

"I know what it is. Or maybe I should say I've heard of it, but I've never been. I'll have to catch it sometime."

"It's always in March. So you just missed it by a couple of months. But there's always next year."

He raised his glass to her. "Here's to next year."

They spent the next ten minutes or so asking personal questions, in a verbal dance of getting to know each other: colleges, careers and craziest things they'd ever done. When their food finally arrived, they ate in the companionable silence that came from good chemistry, each digesting the fresh information they had gleaned—until a familiar voice pulled Olivia out of her reverie.

"Olivia? I thought that was you."

She turned to see Pamela Davis, an accountant at Robinson Tech.

"Hi, Pam. Happy Sunday."

Pamela looked expectantly at Alejandro, obviously waiting for Olivia to introduce her. She was opening her mouth to do just that when the older woman beat her to the punch.

"And this must be your fiancé." Alejandro was a good sport as the woman introduced herself and fawned all over him.

"I was so excited for you when Sophie announced the big news. I had no idea that you were even seeing somebody." Pamela reached out and grabbed Olivia's left hand. "Where's the ring?"

Olivia shot Alejandro a glance. She should have anticipated this. She should simply go to the mall and buy a suitably impressive, but budget-friendly, cubic zirconia because this would surely not be the last time this happened. But then again, if they were going to call off the engagement by this time next week, a ring might complicate matters.

"I wanted to take her to pick out the ring of her dreams," Alejandro said. "We've been so busy with Sophie's wedding that we haven't had a chance to do that yet." He turned to Olivia. "*Querida*, would you like to do that as soon as we finish here?"

"That sounds lovely." For Pamela's benefit, they made googly eyes at each other.

The older woman put her hand over her heart. "Be still, my heart. There's nothing like young love. It makes an old woman like me feel like a kid again. Alejandro, it was so nice to meet you. You take good care of our girl. She's a keeper. And I'm sure you are too if she chose you. I'm going to leave you lovebirds so that you can finish your breakfast and go get that ring. I'll come by your office first thing tomorrow and get a good look at it."

As soon as Pamela cleared the doors of the restaurant, Olivia turned back to Alejandro. "What kind of a fiancé are you to not give me a ring?"

He laughed.

"*Querida*, you heard what I told the lady. We are going right now to pick out the ring of your dreams."

When the dishes were cleared and the server presented the check, Olivia tried to reach for it, but Alejandro was faster. "This is on me."

"Don't be ridiculous," she said. "Please let me split it with you. You need to save your money for that ring."

"Yeah, I'll do that, but this is my treat." He smiled at her. It was a knowing look that made her feel like he could see right through to her soul.

"You can't stand not being in control, can you?" he said.

What was she supposed to say to that? Of course, the answer was yes, but she wouldn't acknowledge it, nor would she admit how she was feeling—as if she and Alejandro had just had their first date.

As they made their way back to her condo, arms bumping and hands brushing occasionally as one or the other slightly leaned into the other's space, they passed a block of storefronts. Olivia paused to linger at the windows. She wasn't in any hurry to get home. Out here they were a man and a woman spending time together, getting to know each other. Once they got back to the condo, he would make his phone calls and she would prepare to return to work tomorrow after being off this week for the wedding. And they would be swept back into their separate lives—separate lives lived under the same roof for the next week. At least she had him to herself right now.

One of the storefronts was an art gallery. They slowed down so she could look at the display cases housing original, handmade jewelry. Earrings and necklaces of hammered silver and burnished metals shared space with ornately rendered rings boasting gemstones of all colors. Olivia caught a glimmer of an exquisite fire opal ring set in an ornately carved rose gold band.

"That's gorgeous," she said, pointing to the ring. "I've always wanted something like that. I'll have to come back and try it on. I'm guessing that you're not a shopper. Am I right?"

"I'm guessing you've got me pegged. But if you want to try it on, you might as well since we're here."

She shook her head. "I don't want to subject you to that torture, because once I start in a shop like that I can't promise how long I'll linger."

She flashed him a flirtatious smile as she started walking away from the shop. "But since we're getting married, maybe that could be my engagement ring."

"Ariana Lamonte of *Weird Life Magazine* is here to see you," Judy Vinson, Olivia's administrative assistant, said over the phone. "I know she doesn't have an appointment, but she asked me to see if you could give her a few moments of your time. She said she's been trying to get in touch with you for more than a month."

"Ugh," Olivia groaned into the phone.

No! Not Ariana Lamonte. The woman was the last person Olivia wanted to see today. It was her first day back and all day she'd felt as if she had been stuck in first gear when she needed to be in fourth to make serious progress toward catching up. Work did not stop even when the boss's daughter got married.

Olivia had already fended off Pamela Davis who, as promised, had appeared in her doorway first thing that morning expecting to see the ring. Olivia was surprised the woman hadn't brought her jeweler's loupe. She stopped her sarcastic thoughts. She was just being defensive because she felt bad for having to tell yet another white lie—this one about the ring being sized.

Lies begat lies. She should be used to that by now. But it didn't mean she had to like it.

Now she had to contend with Ariana Lamonte. The woman was relentless. She had been dogging Olivia for over a month now, trying to pin her down for a meeting. Until now, Olivia had been able to avoid her. Ariana was writing a series of articles about the Fortune family, more specifically about her father's children. She'd been interviewing both the legitimate and illegitimate children of Gerald Fortune Robinson. It was juicy news that Austin's resident genius had sown his seeds far and wide.

"Olivia?" Judy said. "Are you there?"

Olivia sighed loudly. "I'm here, Judy. Look, I can't deal with Ariana Lamonte today. I am drowning in work. Can you get rid of her, please?"

"I'm sorry. Ordinarily, I would have already done that," Judy said, her voice low, "because I know how you feel about her. But I think you might want to talk to her today. She says she has some news that you need to know."

Oh, for God's sake.

Olivia leaned her head back on her chair. If she sent the reporter away, she would only come back. She might as well deal with her once and for all and make the problem go away today.

"Okay, Judy, tell her I'll be with her in a few minutes. I'm going to take a walk with her outside the building. She makes me nervous being in here. Please make sure she stays put. Don't let her wander around. She has a knack for finding the exact place she shouldn't be."

"I hear you," Judy said. "No worries. I have it all under control."

"Thanks, Judy."

Olivia took a moment to smooth her long dark hair—she was wearing it down today. Thank goodness she had taken the extra time to flatiron it smooth. She retouched her powder and reapplied her crimson lipstick. Finally, she stood and smoothed the wrinkles out of her black pencil skirt and white silk button-down blouse.

If the truth be told, she had put in the extra effort for Alejandro's benefit. Why else would she have subjected her feet to the black stilettos she'd chosen if not to show him her professional side. When she'd walked into the kitchen this morning he'd given her a cup of coffee and a look that said he approved, one hundred percent.

Actually, as painful as the heels could be, they made her feel pulled together and in command. They made her feel badass. So, with that in mind, there couldn't be a better day for Ariana to ambush her.

As Olivia walked down the hall toward the reception area, she chuckled to herself because she really was feeling pretty badass today. That meant the notorious Ms. Lamonte, who thought she could stage this surprise attack, would soon be discovering that the joke was on her.

When Olivia walked into the reception area, she saw a woman who looked to be in her mid to late twenties. She had a curvy figure, long brown hair and dark eyes. Her outfit was boho-artistic. Probably chosen to present an image of creative free spirit meets investigative reporter. She had pretty skin and her makeup accentuated her features but wasn't heavy-handed. She wasn't at all what Olivia had expected. Then again, Olivia didn't know what she had expected when it came to Ariana Lamonte.

But here they were, face-to-face.

Olivia stuck out her hand, immediately taking charge of the situation. "Ms. Lamonte, I am Olivia Fortune Robinson. How can I help you?"

The reporter stood. She was probably close to Olivia's height, but the high-heeled boots she wore made her seem much taller.

"Thanks so much for seeing me. I don't make a habit of showing up unannounced, but I've called several times to set an appointment to no avail. So here I am. I had a feeling this would work."

Ariana tilted her chin up a notch and smiled.

"Yes. I can only give you five minutes because

I'm very busy. I'm in the process of digging myself out after being out of the office all week last week."

Ariana's eyes flashed. "Yes, I know. For your brother's and sister's weddings. I hear the ceremony and reception were absolutely beautiful. And I understand congratulations are in order for you, too. You're engaged! Even though it does seem rather sudden, all of Austin is abuzz with the excitement of the happy news."

It had been less than forty-eight hours since Sophie had opened her big mouth at the wedding and spilled the news. How could "all of Austin" already be abuzz?

"Is that so? You must have some very good inside sources because we haven't announced that news yet. Who told you?"

Ariana widened her eyes and smiled an innocent smile. "Oh, Olivia, surely you know a good reporter never reveals her sources. But I can say this—everyone is very complimentary about your fiancé. I hope I will have the honor of meeting him sometime soon?"

Yeah, not on your life.

"Yes, well, what can I do for you today?"

Ariana hitched her leather handbag up onto her shoulder. "As you know, I have been writing a series called 'Becoming a Fortune.' I was hoping you would allow me to interview you for the next installment."

"Why don't we take a walk, Ariana." Olivia didn't wait for the reporter to weigh in. She simply started walking. "We can talk while we walk."

Olivia cast a glance over her shoulder and saw Ariana stepping double time in those high-heeled boots to catch up. When she did, she fished in her shoulder bag and pulled out a small notebook and pencil.

"What can you tell me about your fiancé?"

Olivia frowned. "He's a very private person, Ariana. I'd rather not talk about him in his absence." They exited the front door of the office building and started walking down the path. "What other questions do you have? If that's it, I really do need to get back to work. I hope you understand."

"Of course. Well, I wanted to ask if you know anything about your father's life before he moved to Austin. I have uncovered some evidence that he may have been married before. Can you tell me anything about that?"

Olivia felt the edges of her peripheral vision go fuzzy for a split second. What? Oh, the fun never ended. Was her mother now going to have to deal with a harem of Gerald Robinson's ex-wives in addition to the flock of illegitimate children? If so, maybe the wives—or *wife*, singular, as Ariana had said—would legitimize some of her father's newfound offspring.

"Ariana, I have no idea what you're talking about. All I know is that my father has been married to my mother for many years. If he had been married to someone else before her I can hardly see how that matters or is any of your business, frankly." She turned on her heels. "I need to get back to work now. For the record, I'd rather not be interviewed. Please don't contact me anymore."

Chapter Ten

Alejandro knew there were many different facets to Olivia, but he'd never seen her quite as overwrought as she was when she got home from work on Monday evening.

"I don't know who Ariana Lamonte thinks she is, but she basically ambushed me at work."

Alejandro poured her a glass of Saint-émilion Grand Cru from the bottle he had opened an hour earlier so that it could breathe for a while.

"Thank you." She took a sip and continued. "Wouldn't you put two and two together and figure out that if somebody didn't return your calls it was a hint that they didn't want to talk to you?"

"I know you mentioned her the other night, but who is this woman?"

"She's a features writer for *Weird Life Magazine*. It's an Austin-based magazine. She's been doing a series of articles called 'Becoming a Fortune.' She is completely obsessed with the Fortunes and all my father's illegitimate offspring."

"Why did she want to interview you?"

"She's been profiling my siblings and basically anyone who has a connection to the Fortunes. I can't believe how many people have cooperated and spoken to her. I don't understand why. It really weirds me out to think that she's putting my father's indiscretions out there for all the world to see."

Olivia sipped her wine. "This is good."

"I thought you might like it. It's one of my favorites. But did you talk to her?"

Alejandro motioned toward the living room. Olivia followed him into the room and they sat on the couch with their wine.

"I tried. Really, I did. But when she started asking about our engagement, that was the beginning of the end. She knows about us, Alejandro, and Sophie spilled the beans less than forty-eight hours ago. She's that obsessed with us."

"How do you think she found out?"

Olivia shrugged, then sipped her wine. "There were a lot of people at the wedding. It could've been anyone really. For all we know, she might be paying someone close to us for information."

"What did you tell her?"

"I shut her down. Changed the subject. And she tried to follow up with the most ridiculous assertion that not only had my dad fathering children with women other than my mother, which we do know is true, but she says she has uncovered evidence that my father was married before he was married to my mother. That was the last straw. I asked her to leave."

"How did she take it?"

"In all fairness, she was actually civil about it. She told me if I didn't want to be interviewed, I didn't have to do it. That's how we left it."

"I'm glad she was decent enough to realize she couldn't force you into something you didn't want to do. Do you think she'll leave you alone?"

"I do. Or at least, I'm hopeful. I think she knows better than to show up at my office again."

"I hope so."

Olivia shook her head and stared off into space for a moment. "Every day it's something new. Some new revelation or surprise about my parents that jumps out and hits me between the eyes. That's why it's easiest to not believe in anything that has to do with love and relationships," she said. "Because just when you think you have a handle on it, that you know what's what, a new piece of evidence surfaces that proves that everything you thought was real and good was all a big lie." She turned to him. "Do you know what it's like to live a charade?"

His right brow shot up. "I'm in the middle of living one right now," he said. "I don't mean to make light of your family situation."

She reached out and touched his hand. "I know you don't. The funny thing is, our relationship feels more real and substantive than anything that my parents have lived for decades."

Her expression softened. And she looked like she had surprised herself by saying it.

"That might've sounded awkward or inappropriate," she said. "I don't mean to put any pressure on you. It's just that you and I are more open and honest with each other than my parents have ever been."

She shook her head and waved her hand as if she were clearing her words from the air.

He wanted to reach out and hold those hands, but he stopped himself. "We are open with each other, Olivia. If I lived in Austin, I think I might want to see if things could work out between us—"

"I was hoping you were still considering moving to Austin. Or at least that Hummingbird Ridge would keep you here for a while, while you look for a new investor."

He silently muttered an explicative. He couldn't tell her that he'd planned to talk to her father about investing, but today he had called Gerald Robinson's assistant and canceled the meeting that was supposed to take place at three o'clock because he didn't want to solicit an investment while he was masquerading as his daughter's fiancé. He didn't want her to feel pressured into intervening or going to bat for him, and he didn't want to seem like one of the many guys who'd used her just to get to her father. But he was going to have to tell her *something* now. "I didn't want to mention this until after the wedding, but that slight snag with the winery purchase is turning out to be more challenging than I first thought."

"What's happened?"

He shook his head, trying to decide how much to tell her. "It's complicated, but it's nothing we can't work out. It's not over yet. I just need some time to reconfigure the timeline. But on a much better note, I have a surprise for you. How about something to brighten your day?"

She narrowed her eyes. "Sounds good to me. What did you have in mind?"

"I got you something. Actually, it's a birthday present, but I'm no good at holding on to gifts. Especially for the better part of a week. It's burning a hole in my pocket. May I give it to you now?"

A smile spread over Olivia's face and some of the stress from the day seemed to melt away. He got up and walked to the kitchen island and came back with a small square red velvet box. Balancing it on his right hand, he offered it to her.

"What is this?" she asked.

"Open it and see."

She held the box for a moment, glancing up at him with a skeptical look on her face. Finally, she opened it.

It was the fire opal ring she had fallen in love with at the shop in downtown Austin yesterday. The sight of it took her breath away.

"Alejandro, what is this?"

He slanted her a glance. "The ring you liked? It is the right one, isn't it?"

"Of course it's the right one." She slid it onto her finger and admired it for a moment before she got up and threw her arms around him. "Why did you do this?"

"It's for your birthday. I guess I should've sung 'Happy Birthday' to you, but I'm sure you would've asked me to stop."

"You shouldn't have done this. It's too much. I know how much it cost."

He shrugged. "Nothing is too good for my fake fiancée. Now when they ask you to see the ring you can show them."

"If I was engaged, this is exactly the ring I would choose."

Olivia framed Alejandro's face with her hands and before she could overthink it, she kissed him.

It was supposed to be a quick thank-you kiss. A peck on the lips to show him her appreciation, but somewhere between *quick* and *kiss*, it turned into something more.

Kissing him had become so natural these days. But this was different. It began leisurely, slowly, starting with a brush of lips and a hint of tongue. But at the contact, reason flew out the window.

When she slid her arms around his neck and opened her mouth, inviting him in, he turned her so that he could deepen the kiss. Deeply, fervently. Desperately.

Olivia fisted her hands in his shirt and pulled him closer.

Her entire body sang. Every sense was heightened as his touch awakened the sensual side of her that had been sleeping for far too long.

She heard the ragged edge of his breathing just beneath the blood rushing in her ears. She felt the heat of his hands on her back. He smelled like heaven: a heady mix of soap and cologne with subtle grassy notes mixed with something leathery and masculine. Yet despite the intoxicating way he smelled, it was the way he tasted—of red wine and something that was uniquely him—that nearly made her drunk with pleasure. The two combined were a heady, seductive mix that teased her senses and made her feel hot and sexy and just a little bit reckless.

Here in his arms, she didn't feel like she had to have control. She wanted to melt into him, let him take charge for a while.

As he tasted and teased, the last bit of reason she possessed took flight. It felt too good to touch him, kiss him. It had been far too long since a man's touch had made her blood churn and her body long to be fully taken.

Was this really about to happen? Was she about to make love to Alejandro? Finally. After pretending to be lovers, they were about to stop lying to themselves. After nights spent dreaming about him, about this, it was about to happen. She wanted it to happen.

Judging by the way he shifted and groaned, he wanted it just as much as she did. His kisses made her body hum, her heart sing. It had been so long since she'd been with anyone and even longer since she had let herself trust anyone the way she trusted Alejandro. She took in a deep breath and squeezed her eyes shut, fighting the wave of feelings swelling inside her, threatening to break.

He untucked her blouse from her pencil skirt and slipped one hand beneath the fabric, the warmth of his hand teasing her bare skin, his fingertips gently caressing her before he grasped the hem of her blouse and pulled it up over her head. She wriggled out of it, helping him by straightening her arms and ducking her head so they wouldn't have to worry about undoing buttons. Next she shed her bra and unzipped her skirt. He pushed her skirt down, taking her panties with it.

Clothing was a barrier and she wanted nothing between them. The realization that they were about to be naked sent a shiver of longing coursing through her.

Sure, they had kissed and touched each other and made everyone around them believe that they were lovers, but this was a new level of intimacy. Skin on skin. This time it was just for them.

But that wasn't going to happen if he remained fully clothed. She tugged his shirt over his head, and let it fall to the floor. Sliding her hands over his bare back, she relished the feel of his muscles beneath her fingertips before going for the button on his pants.

"Alejandro Mendoza, we should've done this a

long time ago," she said, moving her hands down his back and cupping his backside.

"Might've been overkill if it had been a way to prove to Sophie you really do believe in love."

"Seeing is believing."

"I'll say," he conceded.

A half smile curved Olivia's lips. "I had no idea what I was missing." Especially now that she had him completely naked.

He leaned back, his eyes intent on her. "Damn." His voice was hoarse in his throat.

"I'm guessing it's a good thing that I've reduced you to one-syllable words?" she said.

He didn't answer; he simply leaned in and pressed a kiss to the sensitive spot behind her ear, his breath hot and delicious on her neck. Anticipation knotted in her stomach as he walked her backward down the hall toward her bedroom.

Once there, he moved his hand down her hip to her thigh. She parted her legs, and he nestled himself against her.

He kissed her again, moving his hands along the curves of her body. Reaching between her legs, his fingertips traced her sensitive skin, dangerously close to her center, where she was aching for his touch.

Olivia feared she might spontaneously combust or possibly melt into a puddle of her own need right at his feet. And when he finally moved his hand, sliding his finger over her center, she heard a low sound rumbling and realized it was coming from her.

After that, she lost all ability to think lucidly. The

only thing she was aware of was the way Alejandro was teasing the entrance to her body with his fingertip before sliding it deep inside her. Her head lolled back. He increased the rhythm and everything went hot and bright like a sparkler on the Fourth of July. She was electric, sizzling like a live wire or a rocket ship launched into space. And when she finally landed, Alejandro was right there with her, kissing her lips. She could feel the hardness of him pressing against her. He was ready for her.

And she was ready for him. She wanted him so badly she felt she would burst into flames.

He eased her down onto the bed. Everything that was dark about his eyes grew even darker.

"Do you have a condom?" he said.

"Me? No, I don't have any." There had been no need. Until now. Oh, for God's sake, why hadn't they thought about this before now? Why? Because they had sworn this wasn't going to happen. A hiccup of laughter nearly escaped her lips. Just making that promise should have been her first clue that she needed to have some on hand. She supposed she should've been relieved that he hadn't come prepared because that would've meant he'd been planning this seduction. But, good grief, if they had come this far and had to stop for lack of protection, she just might actually die.

"I may have one in my shaving kit. If I do, I don't know how old it is, though."

"Not much action lately, huh?"

He groaned and kissed her. "I'm not quite sure

how you want me to answer that. Still, it's worth a look. I'll be right back."

She watched him walk across the room naked and fine. Funny, she thought, you can tell yourself you're immune, you can tell yourself you don't want something or you shouldn't have something, when all the while the *don'ts* and *shouldn'ts* are a colossal lie. Seeing him like this, she knew she had been lying to herself since the night she saw him in the Driskill Hotel bar.

She wanted him. And on some very basic level, she'd known they were going to end up like this—whether she'd wanted to admit it to herself or not.

Olivia turned over onto her side and drew in a deep, measured breath, trying to calm her shallow breathing and slow her thudding heart.

This is happening. This is really happening.

And she couldn't believe how right it felt. It was probably going to make things harder when he went back to Miami; she was well aware of that. But she had known it would be difficult from that first moment, after that first kiss, when they'd started down this thrilling, rocky road. But the thing was, even after that first kiss, things had never been awkward. Even the public displays of intimacy they'd put on for Sophie's benefit hadn't been awkward. In fact, the lack of awkwardness had blurred the line between fantasy and reality that should've been so distinct. She could only hope this wasn't a mistake, that after all was said and done, making love to Alejandro wouldn't be the straw that brought everything crashing down.

He returned a moment later, holding a small square packet.

"Victory is ours," he said. "And it is still well within its shelf life. I am happy we can give it a decent burial."

Olivia propped herself up on her elbow and laughed at the double meaning. "I never dreamed a rubber could make me so happy."

"You obviously need to expand your horizons, *querida*."

She loved how he called her that. The endearment warmed her from the inside out. As if she could be any hotter right now.

"What I meant was, it would've been a real mood killer if you would've had to have gotten dressed and gone to the drugstore."

He ripped open the foil packet.

"No worries. This time. We might want to keep that in mind for the future, though."

The future.

The thought caused Olivia's heartbeat to kick up again. Would there be a next time? She hoped so. But why was she thinking about next time before *this time* had even happened. And it was about to happen.

It had been a long time since she'd been intimate with a man, but he was worth the wait.

She watched, mesmerized, as Alejandro positioned the condom over himself and rolled it down his hard length. Arousal ripped through her, knocking the breath right out of her lungs. But that was nothing compared to when Alejandro slid into bed next to her and, with one swift motion, had her lying flat on her back.

Alejandro kissed her senseless. It was as if his next breath depended on it. Need had her fisting her fingers in the hair at the nape of his neck until he grabbed ahold of her wrists and lifted her arms over her head. He deepened the kiss and positioned himself between her thighs, his hard manhood bumping against the private entrance to her body. And suddenly she needed him inside her.

His gaze locked on hers, he thrust gently to fill her. She raised her hips to take him all the way in. His breath escaped in a rush, and he held absolutely still for a moment, as if he were afraid to break the fragile moment of their joining. Looking into his eyes, Olivia reveled in the sensation, in the wonder of this man inside her.

"You feel even better than I imagined," he whispered, his voice sounding hoarse and raspy.

His eyes were the darkest shade of brown she'd ever seen. As he moved inside her, she couldn't take her eyes off him. He pulled back slightly just before thrusting deeper, closing those dark eyes, getting lost in the rhythm of their love.

The driving need that led to her release grew with every pump and thrust. She held on to him, watching him, his expression, his eyes squeezed shut, his jaw clenched tight.

This was Alejandro. Gorgeous, sexy Alejandro. And he was lost in her.

She looked away, unable to deal with the intensity as he pushed into her one last time and she caught a glimpse of his tattoo. That tattoo. Another woman's name branded on his arm. She turned her face away so she wouldn't have to see it, wouldn't have to think about him in love with someone else.

She refocused on the passion, on how right they felt together, on the feel of him moving inside her, and the next moment pleasure exploded within her, and she felt as if the clouds had parted on a gray day and she was looking directly into the sun.

His eyes closed and his neck tendons strained as the orgasm shook his body. She slid her hands along the rock-hard muscles of his arms to end up with her fingers curled into his hair. He swayed above her for a moment before she pulled him down on top of her. He bowed his head and rested his forehead on hers, kissing her again as if drawing a sustaining life's breath from the final moments of their coupling.

He rolled off her onto his back and she curled herself into his body, amazed by the heat radiating from his skin.

He covered his eyes with his palms. Then, keeping his elbows crooked, he slid his hands beneath his head. She wasn't sure if this was the right thing to do. Her instincts were telling her to hold on to him, snuggle into him, because that's what lovers did after making love. But he wasn't making any effort to hold her. As right and intuitive as the lovemaking had been, this part felt awkward.

The last thing she wanted was for her vulnerability to morph into neediness. Because that was so not who she was. She had never been a clinging vine. And she didn't want to start now.

But, dammit, she felt clingy.

She didn't want to have feelings for him. He made her want things that didn't make sense. Things that she didn't even believe in. He was part of the extended family. She had even hoped after their short-term engagement that they could be friends.

Family and friendship. Those things were far too valuable to mess up. Why was she just considering that now?

She supposed that somewhere deep in her psyche she thought making love to him would exorcise whatever demon had possessed her when she met him. While it had been mind-blowing, it hadn't satisfied that craving. No, she still wanted more. She needed more. She wondered if rather than satisfying the beast, she had simply awakened it.

She lay there lost in thought, heart thundering as she tried to sort out her emotions.

"You okay?" he asked.

She nodded, but he didn't say more. They just lay next to each other, until she couldn't stand the silence anymore. She turned over onto her side, facing him. She stared at him through the golden early-evening light, filtering in through the bedroom's plantation shutters.

Olivia studied his profile as he lay there with his arm raised over his head, his tattoo in full view. She reached out and touched it. She hadn't pushed him to talk about it the other night because it'd felt too personal, as if she were crossing the line. But here they were in the most emotionally vulnerable space. It felt like nothing should be off-limits.

"Tell me about Anna."

He was silent for a long time, and for a moment she thought he wasn't going to answer her.

But she wanted to know. She needed to know. So she decided to prod him.

"You loved her." The words escaped before she could stop herself and she felt awkward after saying them, because obviously he had loved Anna and he didn't love her.

"I did. I still do. I have to be honest with you, I always will."

Olivia felt small, and irrationally jealous of the dead woman.

"We met in our freshman year of high school in English class. Anna was new to the school. She'd just moved to Miami from Venezuela. We were reading *Romeo and Juliet* aloud in class. She read Juliette's part and I read Romeo's. It was love at first sight. I was so taken by her grace and beauty, I wanted to marry her when we turned eighteen. I'd even saved my money and bought her an engagement ring. But Anna's father asked us to wait to get married until after we'd graduated from college. We weren't happy about it, but we honored his wishes. It was important to Anna. But we still got engaged. We ended up going to different universities—she was at Florida State in Tallahassee and I was at the University of Florida in Gainesville. We alternated weekend visits, taking turns making the drive to see each other. Sophomore year, she was killed instantly when a semitruck driver fell asleep at the wheel and hit her car.

"I have always felt responsible for her death. If only I had insisted she leave Sunday afternoon when it was still light outside rather than staying one more night with me and leaving before sunrise the next morning to make it back for an early class."

She heard the pain in his voice, but it was her pain she felt when he said the next words.

"I guess I've always believed each person was only granted one true love in a lifetime. I always believed Anna was mine."

He lowered his arm, held it in front of him, tracing the intricate lines etched into his skin.

"I got her name tattooed on my arm so that I would always remember that once life wasn't hard and happiness wasn't impossible."

She wanted to ask, *What do you think now? Do you think you could be happy with me?* But she couldn't force the words out of her throat.

Chapter Eleven

The following Saturday was Olivia's birthday. Alejandro had planned a perfect birthday celebration for her—a feast featuring filet mignon and butter-poached lobster, and of course it would be accompanied by continuously flowing champagne since it seemed to be Olivia's favorite. And flowers. Lots of flowers. The condo looked like he had robbed a florist. Even though he had given Olivia her birthday present, the fire opal ring, earlier that week, he'd sent her out to the spa to be pampered so that she could relax and he could prepare for their romantic evening in.

During the day, while she was at work, Alejandro had been spending time at Hummingbird Ridge, proceeding as if the deal was still on track despite the fact that they'd suspended the closing indefinitely—or at least until he could secure another source of funding. It was difficult knowing he had a potentially untapped investor in Gerald. But he had to bide his time.

He could not give the impression that he had proposed to Olivia to get the inside track on securing the deal. His conscience simply wouldn't let him do that. He had to wait until after Olivia broke up with him. If she was the one to walk away, Gerald would know that he hadn't broken Olivia's heart, and Olivia would know that he hadn't been like every other guy who had seen an opportunity and used her to further his ambitions. His new plan was to talk to Gerald first and see whether he was interested. If Gerald decided to invest in Hummingbird Ridge, Alejandro would talk to Olivia and explain why he had done things the way he had done them. She would be off the hook and wouldn't feel beholden to him for helping her with the Sophie debacle.

Technically they wouldn't be together, wouldn't be dating or engaged or be lovers— Okay, so they were lovers. That was the one part of the equation that was real. Maybe he should've exercised some restraint and waited until all the pretense was over, all the business deals were closed, and then they could've entered into a relationship of their own volition, but it was pretty clear he had no restraint when it came to Olivia.

Once everything was settled and Hummingbird Ridge was his, Alejandro would move to Austin and he had every intention of starting over and dating

Olivia the right way, treating her the way she deserved to be treated.

He had just taken a pound of butter out of the refrigerator to make a compound butter for the fresh French bread he had purchased when he heard someone entering the condo.

"Hello?" he said.

"Hey, it's me." Olivia was home about an hour earlier than he was expecting her and judging by her expression something wasn't right.

"What's wrong?" He walked over and kissed her.

"I hope dinner can keep."

"Why?"

"Sophie and Mason decided to come back from their honeymoon a day early because of bad weather," she said. "There's this tradition in our family, that we have a big dinner to welcome the newlyweds home their first night back from their honeymoon. That means we are cordially invited to my parents' at six o'clock this evening. Attendance will be taken."

Alejandro raked his hand through his hair. "How can they expect us? Can't you tell them we already have plans? It's your birthday."

"Coming home from your honeymoon trumps a birthday, I'm afraid," she replied. "Besides, when my mother called, she said we would be celebrating my birthday tonight along with Sophie and Mason's return. So she gets her way after all. Should've known. She always does."

Alejandro frowned. "But how can they pull together a dinner party on such short notice?"

"The plans have been in place since before the wedding. The menu was planned, the flowers, the decorations, the tablescapes, the guest list. Even though it was planned for tomorrow night. Oh, I guess I forgot to tell you about that, didn't I? Sorry. If it makes you feel any better, there will be another dinner when Dana and Mason get back next week. Just be glad you won't have to attend that one."

What she didn't say was: *You won't have to attend because by that point we will be broken up.*

The unspoken words hung between them.

He thought he saw regret and sadness in her eyes, but maybe he was just projecting his own feelings onto her. The plan was to break up after Sophie and Mason returned. He needed that to happen so he could execute the next phase of his plan. However, Olivia told him about the dinner tradition. Probably because she had no idea that he was trying to avoid her father. The two of them had bonded over a joke of avoiding her parents for a completely different reason than the one that had him steering clear of Gerald. It appeared that he would have no choice but to go tonight. Unless—

"We haven't really talked about the logistics of our breakup," he said. "Maybe it would facilitate matters if I didn't go tonight."

He knew it was a bad idea before Olivia started shaking her head. That's when he realized how weary she looked.

"I know it's a lot to ask, and I've already asked way too much of you." She looked too vulnerable and tired. "Can you just hang in there one more night? If I go without you, the attention will be focused on where you are and why we aren't together. Not only will it detract from Sophie and Mason's homecoming, but..."

She stared at her hands for a moment. When she looked up at him again, that's when he noticed that she had tears glistening in her eyes.

"It's my birthday, Alejandro. It's bad enough that I won't get to celebrate the way I want to, but I really don't want to break up on my birthday."

They were supposed to start the evening in the living room with drinks and hors d'oeuvres and a toast to the newlyweds and Olivia.

She had asked her mother if they could just focus on Sophie and Mason tonight. After all, her birthday happened once a year; her little sister only returned from her honeymoon once in her lifetime. But when Charlotte Robinson had a plan, no one changed her mind. That stubborn streak was probably what had kept her married to Gerald all these years. She lived in one of the largest homes in Austin; she had money and a lofty position in Texas high society. Those things mattered to Charlotte. Olivia supposed that was why she stayed with her husband despite the humiliation of everyone knowing that he had not only cheated on her repeatedly, but had flesh and blood souvenirs from those dalliances. Souvenirs who shared his DNA.

Compared to that, a birthday party was inconsequential. Still, Charlotte wasn't about to change the plans and forget tonight was Olivia's birthday. It didn't matter what Olivia wanted as long as Charlotte could put on airs and pretend like everything was fine.

Olivia led Alejandro down the polished wooden hallway to the first door on the left—the living room—and they joined a handful of family members who were already there. Sophie and Mason had arrived and were sipping champagne and happily mingling with the others.

Olivia wished she and Alejandro could stay in the background, that they could be flies on the wall and observe the festivities from a safe distance, because talk was bound to meander to the engagement. Olivia's thumb found the back of the fire opal ring Alejandro had given her for her birthday. The makeshift engagement ring burned her finger. As much as she loved it she wanted to take it off and stuff it in her purse. She loved that ring, but with everyone oohing and ahhing over the gorgeous stone, she wondered if she would be able to look at it the same way after Alejandro returned to Miami and she resumed her life. Funny, she used to feel she had a full life, a fulfilling life—no one to answer to, no one to consider, no one to make her realize she really did lead a small and lonely existence that consisted of getting up in the morning alone, working sixteen-hour days, coming home and falling into bed alone, only to get up in the morning and do it all over again. She was twenty-eight years old and this was all she had to show for herself. She balled her hand into a fist so she couldn't see the ring.

A server stopped in front of her and Alejandro with a tray of champagne. He grabbed two flutes and handed her one. The two of them locked gazes before they toasted each other. She wondered if he was thinking the same thing that she was thinking—that yes, the sex had been great. Mind-blowing, in fact.

In that instant, he slipped his arm around her, falling so naturally into the part he had been playing so well, and she knew she didn't want it to end. She didn't want to tell everyone the engagement was off, that they had broken up. She encircled his waist with a possessive arm. Because somewhere along the line Alejandro Mendoza had proven to her that there were decent men left in the world. Men who were trustworthy. Men who didn't use you for your father's wealth and your family's social standing. In fact, this man had selflessly helped her and wanted absolutely nothing in return.

And now he was about to walk out of her life.

They were too good together for her to let him go without knowing exactly what he meant to her, what she felt for him. She had to have faith that he was starting to feel the same way. Because how in the world could two people be so good together and not want to last?

It would be her birthday present to herself. Tonight, after they got home, she would tell him exactly how she felt.

She smiled at him and he leaned down and kissed

her. It was just a quick, whisper-soft kiss, but it filled her heart and nourished her entire being.

"Olivia!" Sophie said, coming up to them and huddling in close so that no one else could hear. "Look at you two. If this is still an act for my benefit, I do beg you to stop. I mean, I appreciate all the trouble you went to, but look at you two." She turned to Mason. "Honey, besides us, have you ever seen two people who are more perfect for each other?" She turned back and whispered to Alejandro, "Please tell me the two of you have figured that out."

Sophie and her exuberance. You had to hand it to her. Only, Olivia wished that all this enthusiasm was coming after she'd had a chance to talk to Alejandro, because she wasn't quite sure what to say. Of course, the plan was to keep up the ruse through tonight. Alejandro had been so gracious about not spoiling her birthday by staging the breakup tonight. So all she had to do was tell Sophie of course they were in love, just like they always had been, and always would be.

Until the breakup.

All she had to do was open her mouth and say it—except for the part about the breakup. That would come soon enough. Unless it didn't. But pretending tonight made Olivia fear that it might jinx everything.

They were here, together. The less said the better.

Before she could say anything, Sophie took Olivia's left hand and lifted it up. She gasped at the fire opal. "This is new. This is beautiful. Is this the engagement ring? Because if it is, I am starting to believe that this game you've been playing might in fact be real. Please tell me it's real and you two really are in love."

Before she could answer, her parents joined them. They were making the rounds greeting their guests, pretending to be the perfect host and hostess. Olivia wanted to roll her eyes and say to her sister, *If you want an act, talk to the two of them. They are insufferable.*

"Hello, Alejandro, I'm Charlotte, Olivia's mother. I'm sorry we haven't had the opportunity to formally meet before now." Charlotte extended her hand as if she expected Alejandro to kiss it. He did, and somehow he made it look so incredibly natural and genuine.

"It's nice to meet you, Mrs. Robinson. Thank you for allowing me to join in the celebration tonight."

"You're family, Alejandro. Of course you would be included this evening. I'm sure very soon we will be planning a similar party for you and Olivia."

Gerald had been talking to Mason while Charlotte had been addressing Alejandro. As if perfectly choreographed, they switched. Olivia's stomach knotted as Gerald zeroed in on Alejandro.

But she was confused when her father said, "He does exist. I was beginning to think that you were a figment of my imagination since Olivia doesn't make a habit of bringing many men home. Or, after you canceled our meeting, I thought maybe the Hummingbird Ridge deal had completely fallen through and you had left town."

"Meeting?" Olivia said. "What were you two meeting about?"

"Alejandro here has a business proposal for me. I did some investigating and I learned that a large portion of his financing for Hummingbird Ridge fell through. I'm guessing he wants me to plug the gap. I was interested." He turned to Alejandro. "But I must admit I'm a little skeptical since you haven't shown very good follow-through."

Olivia's blood ran cold. She looked at Alejandro. "Are you going to ask my father to invest in your business?"

Alejandro looked panicked, but when he nodded the edges of Olivia's vision turned red.

"I'm getting ready to leave on a business trip day after tomorrow," Gerald said to him. "If you're serious about this you need to get in before I go. Otherwise I think the window of opportunity is closed. The only reason I'm giving you a second chance is because of Olivia. If she loves you, that has to speak to your character. And if you marry her you'll need to be able to support her in the manner in which she is accustomed."

So Alejandro Mendoza was no better than any of the others. Oh, wait, yes he was. He was much smoother. He had actually convinced her that she could trust him.

"Excuse me," she said, fighting back hot, angry tears. "I need to leave. I'm not feeling well."

Alejandro excused himself and went after Olivia. Sophie came after her, too, but Alejandro said, "If you don't mind, I'd like to talk to her privately."

"Is she okay?" Sophie asked. "I don't understand what just happened."

Alejandro didn't try to explain. "Liv, please wait, please," he said, and went after her. Sophie must've stayed back, because he was alone as he stepped out the front door and made his way to the driveway where he caught up with her. "Will you please let me explain? Because I can explain."

"I'm sure you can," she said. "The only problem is I don't want to hear it. However, I do need you to take me home. Or if you'd rather, I can call for an Uber. But you will need to come and get your things tonight so you might as well drive me. Unless you'd like to go in and see how much money you can get out of my father."

That hurt. But he knew from her point of view she thought he deserved it.

"Get in the car and I'll explain."

Miraculously, she complied. Once they were inside he said, "It's true, I did ask your father for a meeting to discuss investing in Hummingbird Ridge. But I asked him before you and I got serious. That day at the winery when we were there for the tasting, I got a call from my cousin telling me that one of the key investors had pulled out of the deal. Minutes earlier, I'd been talking to Gerald and he had been saying that he was intrigued by the Texas wine industry and had been looking into investing. After I got the call—actually, before we left Hummingbird Ridge—I asked him if I could meet with him to discuss possible investment opportunities. I scheduled an appointment for Monday. This past Monday. At three o'clock. But after things took a turn and everyone thought we were engaged, I canceled the meeting with him. I canceled because I didn't want to go into that meeting under false pretenses."

"But you're still going to meet with him. You made love to me knowing full well you have a plan. Otherwise you would've told me about it. Why didn't you tell me, Alejandro?"

She sat there with her arms crossed, walls up, glaring at him, a mixture of hurt and rage contorting her tearstained face.

"I didn't tell you because I didn't want you to feel like you had to intervene, or feel like I was using you. Because I wasn't, Olivia. I didn't want you to know anything about it until it was a done deal. I didn't want you to think my business deal with your father had any bearing on us or that I expected anything from you."

She shook her head. "But don't you see it has everything to do with us? You kept it a secret. You went behind my back and didn't tell me—"

Her voice broke. He reached out to touch her and she shook him off.

"Liv, please."

"Alejandro, we were going to break up after Sophie and Mason got back anyway. This is as good a time as any to end it. Please take me home and we can both get on with our lives."

Chapter Twelve

"Olivia, open up. I know you're in there."

Sophie's voice sounded between the bouts of intermittent knocking.

"Olivia, if you don't open the door I'm going to call the police to do a safety check," she continued. No, wait, that sounded like Rachel.

"Don't test us, because we mean it." And there was Zoe.

All three of her sisters were standing outside her condo door. Experience reminded her that they were absolutely serious about calling the police. They would do it. This wasn't a mere battle of wills. It was three Fortune Robinson sisters against one. There was no winning that battle.

Olivia dragged her yoga pant-clad self off the

couch, raked a hand through her tangled hair and opened the door.

"Why aren't you three at work?"

They glanced at each other. "Because it's Sunday?" Zoe offered.

Was it only Sunday? Yikes. Time really did stand still when you had a broken heart. Since Alejandro had left, she had been dozing on and off, in and out of a fitful, tearful, nightmare-laden sleep. She'd confined herself to the couch, because she couldn't make herself sleep in the bed that she and Alejandro had shared the previous week, the bed in which they had made love. The bed in which she had given herself to him body and soul.

She was such an idiot.

How had she allowed herself to fall for him? To be so taken in, so gullible, so ready to believe that he was different from any of the other jerks who had used her.

She looked at her sisters, all three of them happily married to good, decent men. Sure, they'd had their own challenges when it came to finding true love, but never like she'd had.

What was wrong with her?

A saying came to mind. *If every guy in the whole world uses you, maybe it's not every guy in the whole world who has a problem.*

It went something like that, some permutation of that. But it didn't matter if she'd mentally quoted it exactly. She got the gist.

Apparently not every guy in the whole world was

a scumbag since her sisters were all happily married. So that meant something was wrong with her that she kept attracting the users.

Zoe held up the doughnut box and smiled. "We brought you something. They're birthday doughnuts, since you didn't get cake yesterday."

"I'll make coffee," Rachel offered.

"I'll help Olivia wash her face," Sophie said.

Like a child, Olivia allowed her sister to shepherd her into the bathroom. Olivia caught a glimpse of herself in the mirror and winced. She looked like hell. She hadn't bothered to take off her makeup after Alejandro left. Her tears had washed away most of it, but there were still vague brown and black streaks where her mascara had meandered down her cheeks, mixing with her foundation and bronzer.

Sophie opened the bathroom linen closet and took out a washcloth. She wet it and gently blotted Olivia's face.

"Rough night?" she asked.

Olivia shrugged, not quite sure what to say. Because really what could she say? Sophie would probably think this was what she deserved. Maybe her sisters were right. Maybe her bad attitude was what drew the negative to her. Maybe because she expected all men to be the same, the ones she met were exactly that.

But she had let herself believe that Alejandro was different.

Dear God, what a mistake that had turned out to be.

"Where's your ring?" Sophie asked.

Olivia tamped down the irritation that sprang to life at Sophie's question.

Have you not been paying attention? The words strained and pawed at the tip of her tongue, but somehow, in the haze of her grief, she knew better than to unleash them.

"I gave it back to Alejandro. I don't need it anymore."

Actually, what she had done was return it to the little red box it'd come in and slide it into his briefcase when he had been in the guest room packing. She knew he would've never accepted it if she had handed it to him. But she couldn't keep it when all it would do was serve as a reminder of how he had broken her heart.

"You know, in Texas some courts have said that the woman is allowed to keep the ring if the guy breaks off the engagement."

Olivia frowned and blinked up at Sophie. "And why do you know this?"

"Who knows? I heard it somewhere and my brain has a knack for hanging on to useless information. I probably retained it for the same reason I can still sing every single word of *Sesame Street*'s 'Rubber Duckie' song. Want me to sing it for you? Would that make you happy?"

Olivia held up her hand. "That's okay. Really."

But the joke made Olivia smile. Her sisters. What would she do without them? Especially sweet Sophie, who should be spending this Sunday with her new husband, not helping her spinster sister nurse her broken heart. The warmth she felt at the gesture began to sting her eyes and soon the tears had started again.

God, she hated feeling out of control like this.

Sophie grabbed her into a hug. "Oh, Liv, I'm so sorry you're hurting. You really do love him, don't you?"

Adding to the out-of-control feeling, she realized she was nodding her head when she should've been shaking it and convincing herself that she didn't love him.

"I know your relationship started off as a ruse to get me back in the wedding, but from the minute I saw the two of you together I was holding out for you. I knew this was real even if you all didn't know it."

She wanted to tell Sophie to stop. It was over. She'd loved and lost and now her heart was broken and she didn't want to talk about it anymore. Rehashing everything was only making it worse. Salt in the wound. Insult to injury.

"Olivia, if you love him, why are you sitting here? Why are you letting him get away? I don't even understand what happened last night."

The two of them sat down on the edge of the jetted tub. Olivia found her voice and gave Sophie the lowdown.

Sophie listened without saying a word until Olivia had talked herself out. When she was quiet, Sophie said, "Okay, let me get this straight. You're upset with him about a winery deal that he already had going before he met you. The one that would keep him here in Austin. And you're upset because he intended to ask our father to buy in to save the deal, but he put off asking him because he didn't want to approach dad under false pretenses and he didn't want to involve you because he didn't want you to feel obligated to help him after you had roped him into this wedding farce he gained absolutely nothing from. Hmm... Let's think about that for a minute."

Sophie let the words hang in the air.

"I don't know, Liv. I'm not quite seeing the same picture of a liar and a scoundrel and a cheat that you seem to think he is. Am I missing something?"

"Yeah, I'm not seeing it, either," Rachel said. Olivia looked up to see Rachel and Zoe standing in the bathroom doorway. "I think you're in love and you're scared. I think you're projecting your fears onto him so that the relationship will end and you'll be exactly where you thought you would be."

Olivia sucked in a quick breath.

"Well, congratulations," said Zoe. "You did it. You wanted him to leave. And he did. Happy now?"

"Zoe, *shush*," said Rachel.

"No, she's right," said Olivia. "She's absolutely one-hundred-percent right. I've been so busy wallowing in my misery over being left, over thinking any man who is interested in me is a scoundrel who wants something. But that's not Alejandro. I may have lost the best thing that's ever happened to me, because I'm an idiot."

"No, you're not an idiot," said Sophie. "You are a smart, wonderful, generous person with a huge heart.

You will go to the ends of the earth for those you love. You proved that in what you did for me. Now be kind to yourself and go after him. Go get your man."

"I will," Olivia said. "I mean, I would, but I don't know where he is."

"He didn't tell you where he was going?" Rachel asked.

"He had to sleep somewhere last night. Obviously he didn't go to his brothers, because you would know if he had. He didn't stay with Cisco and Delaney. Maybe he went back to the Driskill?"

"Let me get my cell phone and I'll look up the number and we can call and see if he's registered there," said Zoe. "Rachel, you call Cisco and ask if he's there."

"Or we could just call his cell phone," Sophie said.

Of course. Why hadn't she thought of that? It was the only logical thing to do, but her brain had been so addled she hadn't even considered the obvious.

Olivia got her phone and called Alejandro's number. When it started ringing, they heard a strange ringing sound coming from the spare bedroom. The four of them went to investigate and finally found Alejandro's cell phone underneath the foot of the bed. It must've fallen out of his pocket as he was packing.

Olivia sighed. "Well, now I have a valid reason to see him again."

"Olivia, your feelings for him are a valid reason to see him again," said Zoe. "You need to think positively. As positively about the outcome of things for yourself as you do for those you love. Because you are worth it. You deserve the same kind of love that you bestow upon other people."

After her sisters left, Olivia sat in the silent living room for a long time thinking. Rachel had called her husband, Matteo, and had gotten the phone numbers of Rodrigo and Stefan, Alejandro's cousins and business partners.

Now Olivia placed a call to Stefan.

"Hi, Stefan, this is Olivia Fortune Robinson. I'm a friend of Alejandro's. He was staying with me in Austin while he was here for the wedding."

"Hey, Olivia, I know who you are. Alejandro had a lot of nice things to say about you."

Her heart clenched. He had nice things to say about her, but she'd thought the worst of him. Well, he probably wasn't thinking nice things about her now. With just cause.

"He left Austin yesterday and I'm not sure where he went, but he left his cell phone here and I'd like to get in touch with him to let him know I have it. Is he back in Miami, by any chance?"

"No, he's still in Texas. He went to see his dad in Horseback Hollow. If you want, you can probably get in touch with him through Orlando."

Stefan gave Olivia the telephone number.

"Stefan, can you tell me a little bit about Hummingbird Ridge? As an investment...and what you're looking for in an investor. I know that one of your investors pulled out. Can you give me a ballpark dollar amount? I may know someone who is looking for an investment opportunity."

It was a whim, and she knew a whim could be dangerous because, as a general rule, spontaneity had always gotten her in trouble. But then again so had planning everything out to the last painstaking detail. So she took a deep breath and threw caution to the wind.

He filled her in on the details.

"Thanks so much, Stefan. I'll get back with you. Or Alejandro when I see him."

"Hey, no problem. It's nice to talk to the woman who has stolen my cousin's heart."

Alejandro had confided his feelings in Stefan?

The thought renewed her hope.

She called Alejandro's phone. She knew he wouldn't pick up, but that was beside the point. She wanted to hear his voice. That's all she meant to do—call, listen to his voice on his voice mail greeting and hang up. Instead, she ended up leaving him a message, even though she knew he wouldn't get it until she gave him back his phone.

"Alejandro, it's Olivia. I'm sorry. What I hate most about this fight is that I might've ruined something that could've been so good. I hope that we can talk about this. Will you give me that chance? Because if I don't get the chance to tell you I love you, I know I'll regret it for the rest of my life. I love you."

He might not want to hear from her. He might want her to mail the phone to him since he would probably be back in Miami soon. But she had to tell him how she felt.

Since Rachel lived in Horseback Hollow, and Stefan said Alejandro was there… If he was still going to be there tomorrow when her sister went home, maybe Rachel could take the phone to him. Or maybe Olivia could go with her and deliver it herself.

One way or another he had to hear her message.

Alejandro should've trusted his instincts. If he hadn't gone to the party, Gerald wouldn't have had the opportunity to dump on them like that in front of Olivia. But who was he kidding? If he hadn't gone to the party, Olivia would've gone by herself and her father probably would've sent a message home through her about what a flake he was for canceling the meetings and avoiding him.

In hindsight, he should have been upfront with Olivia. He could've told her he didn't want her to get involved in his offer to her father. If only he could go back and do it over again. But he couldn't. He had to deal with the way things were. He needed to focus on finding another investor for Hummingbird Ridge.

On his way out of Austin to Horseback Hollow he had stopped by the winery. Jack and Margaret Daily had agreed to give Alejandro first right of refusal if another buyer came along. That motivated him to quit moping and get the job done.

In the meantime, it was good to be sitting at the Hollows Cantina in Horseback Hollow having a beer with his father before returning to Miami.

"I'm sorry the engagement is off," Orlando said.

Alejandro waited for his father to add that everything had happened too fast and they'd probably gotten caught up in the moment, but he didn't. They sat in companionable silence not needing to talk, just happy to be in each other's company.

Alejandro had already decided that he wouldn't tell his father that everything started off as a farce, a ruse to get Sophie down the aisle, and somehow it had turned into something real. That, for the first time since Anna, he had been able to feel again.

"You love her," Orlando said as if reading his mind.

"Yep."

"Then what are you doing here when you should be there telling her that?"

By the time Olivia talked to Orlando, Alejandro had already left Horseback Hollow.

Her heart sank. Orlando hadn't been very forthcoming with information about Alejandro's whereabouts. She couldn't blame him; after all, he was protecting his son. However, he had promised to relay the message to Alejandro that she had called and she had his phone.

It should've been enough, leaving messages with both Stefan and Orlando, but Olivia spent a restless Sunday night tossing and turning and coming up with a crazy plan. By six o'clock Monday morning she was at Austin–Bergstrom International Airport, boarding a flight to Miami.

Rachel was the only person she told of her plan. Olivia knew it was a crazy thing to do, but she had never been the type to sit around and wait for things to happen. In fact, when it came to love she had proactively prevented anything from happening. Not this time. When she went to bed tonight, she would know that she had done everything possible to save the best thing that had ever happened to her.

When she landed in Miami armed with Alejandro's address, she got a cab to his house. The only problem was Alejandro wasn't there. He wasn't at his office, either. That's where she met Stefan and Rodrigo in person. They told her he was still in Texas.

"But Orlando said he left," she told them.

His cousins seemed truly baffled. Or maybe they were just good actors covering for him—after all, his acting ability might run in the family. Maybe he didn't want to see her and his family was running interference.

She tried to leave his cell phone with them, but they refused. "I know he has a meeting at Hummingbird Ridge at the end of the week," Stefan said. "I think you would be better off taking the phone back with you. He can pick it up from you when he's there. If he needs a cell in the meantime, he can get one of those disposable phones."

"If he does, would you please let me know the number?"

She sounded desperate, even to her own ears. Well, she was desperate.

Maybe Alejandro was right. Maybe true love only came around once in a lifetime. He'd had his with Anna. Olivia had found hers—as short-lived as it had been—with him.

Olivia and her bruised heart returned to Miami International Airport. Disappointment was her only companion. Instead of leaving with the fulfillment—or at least the closure—she was certain she'd find when she saw Alejandro and he realized the great lengths that she would go to for him, she left feeling uncertain and small.

By the time she landed in Austin, it was nearly seven thirty in the evening. She was tired and she should be hungry, but she wasn't. All she wanted to do was go home and put on her jammies and pull the covers over her head.

She was intently digging in her purse for her car keys as she exited the airport and she wasn't really watching what she was doing.

"Excuse me, miss. Do you need a ride?"

In the split second before she could fully register who was speaking, the deep, masculine voice still sounded hauntingly familiar. She flinched and looked up, her heart nearly jumping out of her chest as her eyes focused on Alejandro. He was standing there holding a sign that said Fortune Robinson.

Instinct took over. She dropped her purse and ran into his waiting arms. He greeted her with the deepest, most possessive kiss and for a moment the entire world faded away. If she'd fallen asleep on the flight home, if she was dreaming this, she never wanted to wake up.

When they finally came up for air, he cupped her face with his hands. "I got your message."

"Which one? I left messages with both your dad

and Stefan, who is very nice, by the way. I met him in Miami."

Alejandro smiled. "I heard. I can't believe you went all the way to Miami. And I wasn't talking about either of those messages. I got the one that you left on my cell phone."

"How could you hear that message? I have your phone."

That reminded her that her purse and its contents were on the ground. When she stooped down to pick it up and gather her belongings, Alejandro bent down and helped her.

"Here it is, right here." She handed him his phone.

"I have a computer program that allows me to check my messages remotely. When I heard your voice and what you had to say, I knew I had to come to you right away. Olivia, I love you. How could we just walk away from each other?"

All she could do was shrug and shake her head.

"Let's never do that again. I almost grabbed a flight to see if I could meet you in Miami. But with the way we've been narrowly missing each other, I figured it would be best to be right here when you got home. Rachel gave me your flight information."

She hugged him again. "Alejandro, I'm so sorry for everything. I hope you can forgive me for pushing you away."

"Let me think about that for a moment." He turned over the sign and held it up. The other side read, "Olivia, will you marry me…for real?"

Her heart felt as if it would burst out of her chest. "You know how much I love champagne?"

"Yes," he said, his eyes locked with hers.

"You know I love it more than anything. But I love you more. I would give up champagne forever to have you."

"There's no need for you to give it up. Especially now."

"Why is that? Is it because you heard that there's another investor interested in joining you in the Hummingbird Ridge venture?"

His eyes flashed and she waited for him to ask if it was her father, but he didn't. So she offered the information. "It's me. I want to invest in you and Hummingbird Ridge and make it possible for you to be in Austin permanently."

"I would be here with or without Hummingbird Ridge. We will definitely talk about that later. But I want you to know I want to be with you, wherever you are. Obviously it isn't a good time to give up champagne. Because we'll need it to toast both of our partnerships—business and personal," he said. "But first, this time, I need to do this right, *querida*."

He pulled a familiar small red box out of his pocket and opened it. It was the fire opal ring she had put back in his briefcase.

He fell to one knee. "Olivia Fortune Robinson, will you do me the great honor of being my wife?"

"Yes! This time, I am not letting you get away."

As he slid the fire opal ring on her finger, a crowd of people broke into a rousing round of cheers and applause. It was her family—her sisters and brothers and their spouses. And his family—Orlando and Josephine and his sister and brothers. They were all there to see him propose.

He pulled her into his warm embrace, into that spot in his arms where she fit so perfectly. For the first time in her life, Olivia Fortune Robinson knew with her whole heart that love was real.

* * * * *

Don't miss the next installment
of the Cherish Edition continuity

THE FORTUNES OF TEXAS:
THE SECRET FORTUNES

Quirky—but determined—blogger Ariana Lamonte has spent months tracking down Fortunes near and far. But when she crosses paths with rough and ready cowboy Jayden Fortune from tiny Paseo, Texas, will she discover a new branch of the family tree—as well as love, small-town style?

Don't miss
WILD WEST FORTUNE
by
NEW YORK TIMES *bestselling author*
Allison Leigh

On sale June 2017, wherever
Mills & Boon books
and ebooks are sold.

MILLS & BOON®

Cherish™

EXPERIENCE THE ULTIMATE RUSH OF FALLING IN LOVE

A sneak peek at next month's titles...

In stores from 18th May 2017:

- **Behind the Billionaire's Guarded Heart** – Leah Ashton *and* **Wild West Fortune** – Allison Leigh
- **Her Pregnancy Bombshell** – Liz Fielding *and* **A Conard County Homecoming** – Rachel Lee

In stores from 1st June 2017:

- **A Marriage Worth Saving** – Therese Beharrie *and* **Honeymoon Mountain Bride** – Leanne Banks
- **Married for His Secret Heir** – Jennifer Faye *and* **Falling for the Right Brother** – Kerri Carpenter

Just can't wait?
Buy our books online before they hit the shops!
www.millsandboon.co.uk

Also available as eBooks.

MILLS & BOON®

EXCLUSIVE EXTRACT

Miranda Marlowe has just discovered she's pregnant with her boss's baby...

Read on for a sneak preview of HER PREGNANCY BOMBSHELL

Tomorrow she would go down to the beach, feel the sand beneath her feet, let the cold water of the Mediterranean run over her toes. Then, like an old lady, she would go and lie up to her neck in a rock pool heated by the hot spring and let its warmth melt away the confused mix of feelings; the desperate hope that she would turn around, Cleve would be there and, somehow, everything would be back to normal.

It wasn't going to happen and she wasn't going to burden Cleve with this.

She'd known what she was doing when she'd chosen to see him through a crisis in the only way she knew how.

She'd seen him at his weakest, broken, weeping for all that he'd lost, and she'd left before he woke so that he wouldn't have to face her. Struggle to find something to talk about over breakfast.

She'd known that there was only ever going to be one end to the night they'd spent together. One of them would have to walk away and it couldn't be Cleve.

Four weeks ago she was an experienced pilot working

for Goldfinch Air Services, a rapidly expanding air charter and freight company. She could have called any number of contacts and walked into another job.

Three weeks and six days ago she'd spent a night with the boss and she was about to become a cliché. Pregnant, single and grounded.

She'd told the border official that she was running away and she was, but not from a future in which there would be two of them. The baby she was carrying was a gift. She was running away from telling Cleve that she was pregnant.

She needed to sort out exactly what she was going to do before, have a plan firmly in place, everything settled, so that when she told him the news he understood that she expected nothing. That he need do nothing…

Don't miss
HER PREGNANCY BOMBSHELL
by Liz Fielding

Available June 2017
www.millsandboon.co.uk

Copyright ©2017 Liz Fielding

Join Britain's BIGGEST Romance Book Club

- **EXCLUSIVE offers every month**
- **FREE delivery direc to your door**
- **NEVER MISS a title**
- **EARN Bonus Book points**

Call Customer Services

0844 844 1358*

or visit

millsandboon.co.uk/subscriptior

*** This call will cost you 7 pence per minute plus your phone company's price per minute access charge.**

MILLS & BOON®

are delighted to support World Book Night

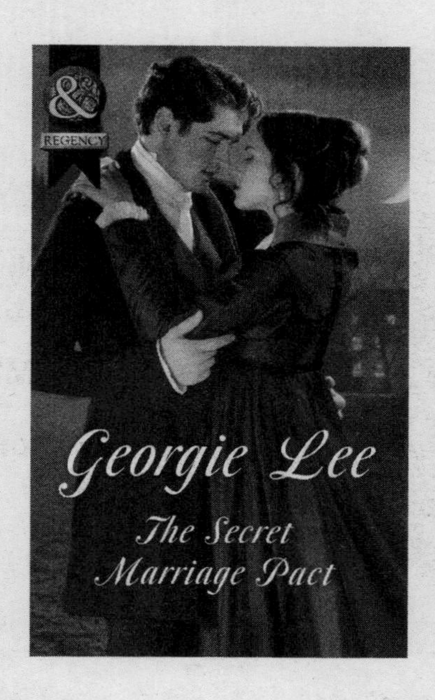

World Book Night is run by The Reading Agency and is a national celebration of reading and books which takes place on 23 April every year. To find out more visit worldbooknight.org.

THE READING AGENCY

www.millsandboon.co.uk

30517_2